A COAT OF VARNISH

A COAT
OF
VARNISH

❧ *C. P. SNOW* ☙

NEW YORK

CHARLES SCRIBNER'S SONS

Copyright © 1979 C. P. Snow

Library of Congress Cataloging in Publication Data
Snow, Charles Percy, Baron Snow, 1905–
  A coat of varnish.

  I. Title.
PZ3.S6737Cm 1979 [PR6037.N58] 823'.9'12 79-16221
ISBN 0-684-16315-2

A COAT OF VARNISH

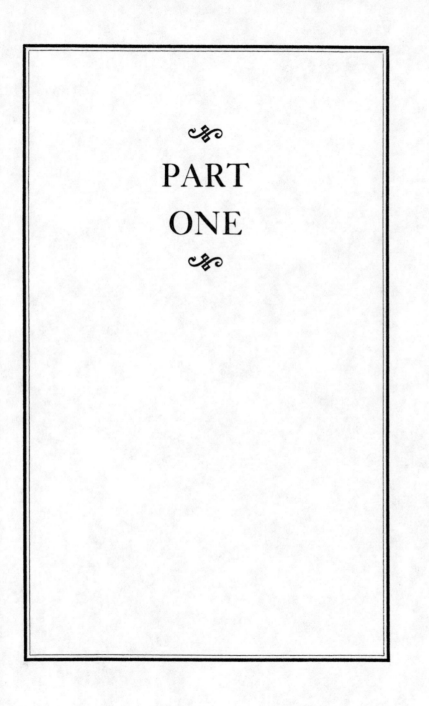

PART ONE

❧ 1 ❧

About half past eight on a July evening, Humphrey Leigh was walking along the side of the Square. It was very hot for London and hot enough for most other places. It had been so for weeks past. This was the summer of 1976, and that day the temperature hadn't dipped below eighty, and stayed there still. Through the trees in the Square garden, the houses opposite gleamed in the light, an hour to go before sunset, the clear white stucco fronts as unbroken and unyielding as the heat.

Humphrey Leigh was walking slowly. As a rule, his pace was light-footed but not smoothly coordinated. He remained an active man, although he had retired from his official job the year before. There was nothing conspicuous about him. He was tallish, five feet eleven or so, not one to pick out in a crowd. His face was seamed, lines from nostrils to mouth and a single line across his forehead, but that made him seem observant or amused rather than grave. Most people meeting him would have guessed him to be years younger than he was.

A young man and woman were coming toward him and called out that they would be seeing Humphrey later that night. He was not walking slowly because of the temperature. He had put on a tropical suit, and that was enough concession to discomfort. He was walking slowly because he didn't want to arrive at his destination. He was having to pay a duty call on an old lady in distress. That would have been bad enough, even if there had been anything to say. There wasn't. She had telephoned him at dinner time, telling him that she had been at the hospital for hours that day. They had finished their tests: she would know the verdict, as she called it, within a week or two; she couldn't tell precisely when.

She was being stoical, but she asked him to call in for a few minutes, begging for company, which he couldn't remember her doing before. She was as proud as a woman could be, or at least as any woman he had known. Not that he was a close friend. He was not sure that he even liked her. She was more than twenty years older than he was: from all he had heard, she might have been easier to love than to like. Still, she was a relation, if a remote one, and he had known her on and off since he was a boy. If one had known anyone for long enough, one often felt that one liked them more than one truly did.

On his way to her house, he didn't make that reflection, though in better spirits he might have done. He was just thinking that there was no conceivable comfort to give. The date was Tuesday, July 6, 1976. That particular day had no significance in anything that was to follow, but there came to be some significance, which strangers didn't completely understand, in the actual neighborhood. The square in which Humphrey Leigh was walking was called Aylestone Square. It lay between Chester Square and Eaton Square. All were part of the district known as Belgravia. At this time, Belgravia remained the most homogeneous residential district in any capital city in the world, and in a quiet and seemly fashion the most soothing to the eye—in the center of a capital city, that is. Belgravia was not a suburb. It had its frontiers, Knightsbridge to the north, Ebury Street about two miles away to the south. Buckingham Palace was just outside its eastern edge, Sloane Square and Chelsea a mile and a half to the west. Westminster and Whitehall were quite near. Within this area were something like three thousand houses and apartments and a population of something over twelve thousand residents.

It had been built, as a piece of hard-boiled speculation, largely in the generation between 1820 and 1850. The Grosvenor family owned great stretches of these parts of London, and they discovered a remarkable property developer by name of Thomas Cubitt, who was later approved of by the prince consort, a fine judge of talent. More than any single man, Cubitt was responsible for the Belgravia as Humphrey Leigh knew it. When Cubitt started, the

4

land didn't look overpromising. It consisted of dank water meadows and equally dank kitchen gardens ("I refuse to live in a swamp," said Lady Holland in her old age, offered one of the new houses in Belgrave Square). If one looks now at some of the ragged countryside on the way to Heathrow, one can get an impression of what Cubitt had to work on. But, as with Venice, building on swamps seemed to lead to pleasing aesthetic results.

Cubitt and his associates were very fortunate. They were, of course, out to make money. They were building mainly, though not entirely, for the well-to-do. In Belgrave Square they put up mansions for the aristocracy; in Eaton Square, land being very short, the mansions were joined together in terraces, connected by party walls. In exile after 1848, Prince Metternich lived in a terraced house: but it was one of those terraced houses (known, by what seemed a somewhat discouraging use of nineteenth-century naval terminology, as second-raters) for the upper classes. There were some streets of quite small terraced houses for artisans and clerks, by the 1970s lived in by persons more privileged than their original occupants. Streets of shops filled up—the streets discreetly renamed by Cubitt. Elizabeth Street, a hundred years later the main shopping quarter of half Belgravia, started life as Eliza Street, disreputable, tarts earning a few pence from the river traffic. Mews for the horses, quarters and cottages for the grooms. It was a mistake to think that the Belgravia of the 1870s was quieter than that of this story. Horses were clattering and clopping all day and a good deal of the night, and the streets were thick with smell.

There was no reason to think that Cubitt, or anyone else, was self-conscious about the architecture. Belgrave Square was an elegant piece of urban composition and looked, as it did a century later, as if it came from one architect's mind. It didn't. It was the work of at least four. For posterity, here was one of the major pieces of Cubitt's luck. He and his other builders were all working in a decent unfussy domestic idiom. It wore well. It ought to have looked monotonous. Thousands of houses, none of them much decorated, nearly all shining white up to the second story.

In Aylestone Square, in this respect like the whole of the district, permutations had been played with the simplest of means. The building style had been prescribed from the beginning; so had the height, four stories plus basement for the tallest; so had the frontage, except for the corner houses; so had the colors, where there was an unspectacular choice between stucco over brick or stone. Plain enough: but people could do their best with unspectacular choices. They could play with the harmony of repetitiveness. Which they had done.

On his way toward number seventy-two, the house he had to visit, similar to his own and on the same side, Humphrey Leigh hadn't noticed any of the minuscule variations in the house fronts. That was natural enough. No incumbent was ever likely to. He took it all for granted. Occasionally, when he had nothing on his mind, he might have thought that this was an enclave, a comfortable and restful enclave to live in and, of course, a privileged one. He probably wouldn't have recognized that he was glad he could still live there.

While he hadn't noticed any of the architectural details along the Square, he had, brooding the minutes away, absently noticed something else. In two of the houses young men and girls, who looked like students, were climbing down the area steps to the basement. It was long odds that those basements had been sublet. Once, they had all been servants' quarters and kitchens. But by this time, domestic service in London was difficult to get. Some people in the Square were rich enough to buy anything. Usually they acquired Filipino or Spanish couples to live in. A very few were lucky, like Humphrey Leigh himself. He had a housekeeper who had once looked after his mother and needed a home. Many made do on daily help, and some on none at all. Even Lady Ashbrook, the old lady who had called for Leigh's company, had nothing but a Portuguese "daily woman," as they called her, five mornings a week.

As in most of Belgravia, Lady Ashbrook's house had a narrow front, but it was bigger than it looked. Apart from the basement, it had ten rooms, which was about standard for the neighborhood. Lady Ashbrook was well over eighty. Others wondered how she managed. Of course she could afford, the gossips said, to spend any amount of money on herself. The gossips had been busy on Lady Ashbrook for a lifetime. She was one of those few—and this was more true as she became older—who seemed grander the more she was talked about. It was generally thought that she was living so simply just to lavish gifts on relatives and charities.

Domestic service unobtainable, it wasn't surprising that those basements were being sublet, residents turning an honest penny when they could. It was not, however, quite such an honest penny. It was certainly a breach of contract. Humphrey Leigh might not know many of his neighbors, but he had a good idea of their terms of tenure and the value of their property. All those houses had been acquired by leasehold. In his own case, though he had been brought up within the tantalizing sight of money, he had never had much. After the war, he had married his second wife, who had died two years before these events of July 1976. They had nothing to live on except his salary. But if one had been brought up within the sight of money, as he was the first to point out, a little sometimes came one's way. A little did, by way of a legacy. With it, and with a mortgage, they bought a forty-year lease of the house in Aylestone Square. It cost them £15,000. Humphrey Leigh later reflected that it was the only successful financial transaction of his life. Twenty years later, it would have cost five times as much.

Coming near to number seventy-two, Humphrey quickened his pace, as though he were at last impelled to get the visit over. When he had rung the bell, sound tinkling distantly back in the house, there was what seemed a long wait. Then slow footsteps, a woman's steps on stone. The door opened. He didn't see much, for the hall was in shadow, but he heard a familiar voice.

"Oh, Humphrey," Lady Ashbrook was saying, "it is nice of you to come."

That voice hadn't changed much with the years. It was at the same time deep and half-strangulated. Humphrey had heard that peculiar tone in the past from other upper-class women, but by now it had gone out of fashion, and none of the young produced such a sound at all.

Humphrey heard himself being bluffer and heartier than he liked, because he wasn't much at ease.

"You haven't got Maria [the Portuguese help] here, then? You know, you ought to have someone with you."

"Why should I?" she said.

Humphrey was repeating himself, but she just said, "Come upstairs."

In those houses, most people lived as their predecessors had done, a dining room on the ground floor, drawing room on the floor above. Humphrey followed Lady Ashbrook up a flight of stairs, passed a bathroom on the half landing, six more stairs, along a corridor. She did it slowly and paused once, but her back was straight as a guardsman's. The drawing room stretched through the depth of the house, the front windows looking over the Square, the back windows over strips of garden. Each house in the Square and nearly all in the entire district had, this being England, a kind of token garden behind it.

Originally that room would have been divided into two with folding doors between. Now it was nearly fifty feet long but still looked cluttered. On other visits there, Humphrey, less preoccupied, had thought that she had accumulated the debris of a lifetime. Tables, whatnots, tallboys, writing desks, some old, some looking like last year's presents: even a prie-dieu, though she attended the most evangelical of the Anglican churches nearby. A box of tools, among which a hammer head protruded, lay in what had once been a fireplace, witnessing that she did her own repairs.

There was no sign of what her visual taste was, if she had any. True, there were two fine pictures, a Boudin and a Vlaminck, badly hung and too near to other, meaningless landscapes. One academic painting of her second husband, Ashbrook, who, according to some worshiping gossip, had been the great love of her life, from whose death—collapsing over his desk in Whitehall, the perfect way for a minister to die, said somewhat less worshiping commentators—she was reported not to have recovered. No picture of her first husband, who had been a marquess and much more of a grandee. A painting by Sargent of herself at the age of about twenty, just at the time of that first marriage, a flattering romantic picture of a young woman strong-willed, elegant, beautiful, certain of happiness.

Sixty years after, in her drawing room with Humphrey that evening, it would have needed imagination, maybe romantic imagination, to feel that her face could have been as soft and tender-smiling as in the painting. There her arms were shown as slender but rounded. Now the bones were left. But in the painting the neat skull-like Hamitic head foretold the head of today, sculptured under the parted hair. The eyes, set deep in the skull, burning brown, hadn't changed, though they stared more now that the flesh had shrunk away. Occasionally, Lady Ashbrook had been known to harangue pretty women who were sad that age was gaining on them, pretty women half a century younger than herself. She did so by a vigorous exhortation: Once a beauty, always a beauty. It was to be inferred, so the cooler of her listeners had reported, that she was speaking from direct experience of her own. Had she ever been a beauty? Not according to the standards of the 1970s, they thought, and some said not at all. But she had had the confidence of one, and that was nine points of the game.

"Help yourself to a drink," she said to Humphrey after she had sat down. "You know what you like."

Humphrey did help himself, and to a distinctly stiff drink. He didn't trust all the myths about Lady Ashbrook, certainly not about her reasons for existing so frugally. Humphrey, who had observed her for a long time, believed that she was, to say the least, somewhat parsimonious. He didn't expect to be asked to have another drink that night.

She was sitting, still straight-backed, in an armchair that rested on the carpet in front of the extinct fireplace. He returned to another chair opposite hers and started on what he had come determined to say.

"You oughtn't to live here alone. You know that, Madge. You must have someone here."

Madge was the most incongruous of names for her, but for mythmakers she had glorified it.

"Why?"

"You oughtn't to be by yourself."

"It makes no odds." Voice ungiving.

"I wish you'd listen to sense." It was useless, he knew, to force or bully her, as others must have found, and so he became easier, not so overhearty. He asked if there was anything he could do.

"Nothing at all." Again she said brusquely, it had been nice of him to come, but she said it as though she felt weak for having asked him.

"How are you feeling?"

"It's a tiring business, having those wretched tests." Suddenly, turning the subject, she went on, "How are you, my dear?"

"Oh, I'm all right." He couldn't let her divert him. He said, "Of course there can't be any news."

"Didn't I tell you there couldn't?" she had rasped out in anger.

9

"They said they'd have some next week. I suppose they'll report to my doctor; that's the way they do it. You know Ralph Perryman. They'll tell him. He's a good little man."

This Dr. Perryman had other patients in the vicinity and was an acquaintance of Humphrey's. In any normal sense, he was by no means little, but Lady Ashbrook tended to use the term about anyone she employed.

At a loss, Humphrey was asking about the hospital, but she gave a sarcastic smile.

"Look, my dear," she said, "this is all boring. It's boring for you. It's quite as boring for me. There's nothing to say. When there's nothing to say, it's better to say nothing. Let us talk of something else."

Humphrey distrusted some of the myths that had grown round Madge Ashbrook but was sometimes surprised at the myths that didn't grow. He couldn't remember any of her admirers saying that she was a woman of absolute courage, yet that myth would have been true. Flawless courage, stark as she was showing now. Courage of any kind, including brute physical courage. In the war, as a middle-aged woman driving a car through bombings, she had been glacially brave, and made her soldier companions ashamed. The trouble was, it was a courage so stark that it wasn't comforting for anyone like Humphrey, knowing what she was going through.

So they talked of something else. At the best of times her conversation wasn't the most illuminating that Humphrey listened to, and that evening, though it might be gallant, it didn't illuminate him at all. She had, as usual, only two subjects. On both her opinion was simple, acerb, and positive. One subject was the Labour Government and the state of the nation. On that, there was just one thing that puzzled her. Of course the country was being ruined. Were the people doing it Communists, crooks, or fools? She was inclined to think that there was a Marxist conspiracy, possibly abetted by crooks. Her second subject was their common acquaintances, in particular the young women they both knew. It was some time since she had had much of a social life, but she kept a scathing eye on the people round about, particularly the young women. On this pet topic Humphrey had known her to be bleakly funny, but now she was trying too hard. She was not fond of women and thought they were overestimated.

10

"That Kate Lefroy," she said dismissively. "She tries to *do good*. In that hospital of hers. I suppose she tries to do good to her ridiculous husband. Doing good!"

Madge Ashbrook was interested in people's goings on but not overconcerned about their feelings. Kate Lefroy, who lived in a house on the other side of the Square, was a woman for whom Humphrey had affection and in his imagination occasionally something more. It was not the morals of those she called young women (they weren't so young as all that) that she reprobated. With Humphrey, who knew something of her own history, she would have had too much sarcasm for that. No, where she found them deplorable was in their *lack of style*.

"Style! It's all gone," she said. "It won't come back."

Lady Ashbrook made one exception. She had noticed someone who had a little style. She had also noticed the young man who seemed attached.

"Now he's *brilliant*," said the old lady. "It's to be hoped nothing comes of it. He mustn't throw himself away."

Sometimes, in Lady Ashbrook's inspection of the human scene, it seemed that almost any woman, even one with a trace of style, was bad for almost any man.

There was a special and aggravated case, about which her voice became even deeper and more dismissive. Her grandson Loseby had somehow picked up a girl—she pronounced that word *gairl* in the old-fashioned way—who lived in Eaton Square. Contempt growling out, she went on saying that this gairl was totally unsuitable. Loseby was a nice boy, she told Humphrey.

Loseby was neither a surname nor a Christian name. It was a courtesy title. Her own son was now the marquess, and this was one of the titles in the family. Regressing to another old fashion, she continually addressed her grandson by it in company, as though the period were the 1890s, when she was born.

"Totally unsuitable. Does anyone know who she is?" In fact, Lady Ashbrook knew well enough. The girl's father lived in luxury in Eaton Square. He was rich. That might have passed, but he was a Labour Member of Parliament, which made it doubly bad. He was being tipped for office, which was worse. The scandal sheets were also tipping him as a candidate for financial shenanigans, which was worst of all.

"Nothing but a tuppenny ha'penny crook," said Lady Ashbrook on no evidence at all, and not reflecting that, if he were a crook, it certainly wasn't for tuppenny ha'penny.

"The gairl's not bad to look at," she said. "Good enough for a bit of slap and tickle, that's all."

After that peculiar denunciation, and almost without a pause, Madge Ashbrook stared across at Humphrey and said, "Do you know—" She had a hesitation that was not quite the usual hiatus in her throat and then went on, "Do you know, I've always been frightened of *this*."

She hadn't abdicated her authority, but Humphrey understood. It was as near a confidence as she could reach. She hadn't abdicated her authority, but the certainty was gone. She wasn't talking of her grandson's affairs. She had broken the charade. She was talking of her own body. "This" was cancer. Gallant as she was, she couldn't speak the word.

"I know," said Humphrey and added lamely, "It may not be true."

"It may not. What do you think?"

He shook his head. "It's no use giving false comfort. I've no idea. It's dreadful, but all you can do is wait. You said they'll tell you next week, didn't you?"

"I don't want to hear."

She stiffened herself and broke out in a harsh impatient tone, "This is boring. I told you it was boring." Tight with angry scorn, she returned to the qualities, or lack of them, of Loseby's girl.

Soon Humphrey felt that he had done his duty and could decently leave. No expression of hope, or even good wishes, would please her, but he said that he would see her soon.

Out in the Square, the night was still hot, but the air was free. He felt a kind of cowardly relief and shame to be in the free air, out of the sight of fear and courage.

❧ 2 ❧

On his way home, Humphrey could smell flowers from the window boxes, tobacco plants, sweet peas, stocks, a refreshment on other summer nights and on this one too.

He had not been sitting long in his drawing room when the bell rang and, just like the old lady an hour before, he had to go downstairs and along a hall. The couple he had greeted in passing earlier were waiting outside the door. He took them through a back room down rickety steps into his patio garden.

This was the pair of whom Lady Ashbrook, departing from her general form, had approved. The man was in his late twenties, the woman a couple of years older. They were both tall, and he was as stringy as a distance runner. In the garden, her face was obscured in the half light; his was long, intelligent, high-cheekboned, with a mouth ready to smile. His name was Paul Mason, and hers Celia Hawthorne. They were polite and at the same time easy-mannered, calling Humphrey by his Christian name as though he were their own age. Paul insisted on going up to the kitchen to fetch the tray of drinks. "You two wouldn't be as safe on those stairs. They must be a rather useful hazard sometimes, mustn't they, Humphrey?"

Humphrey grinned. Recently he had become used to Paul's kind of conversation and thought he caught glimpses of what went on beneath. Celia he had met only casually, and, while Paul had left them, Humphrey was observing her. She was pretty, in an unsensational fashion, so far as he could make out in the twilit garden—

good skin, clear eyes. When he asked her a question, there was a pause before she replied, but then the answer was fluent enough. Her voice was high, light, sometimes as though absent from the scene. But once, after another of his questions, entirely innocent, she gave a surprisingly, disconcertingly, full-throated laugh.

She was wearing a simple white summer dress. Humphrey found it increasingly mysterious that Lady Ashbrook should have decided, with the force of law, that she had style. Often Lady Ashbrook's verdicts depended on class, but there could not be anything in that. Celia wasn't anything like elevated enough to qualify on that platform. Humphrey remembered Paul saying that she was the daughter of a canon, ordinary professional middle class, less privileged than Paul himself, whose father was an abnormally successful, and an abnormally flamboyant, barrister.

When Paul returned and put the tray on the iron table around which they were sitting, he poured their drinks, gin for Celia, whiskey for Humphrey and himself. The garden was quiet; at last the long summer light was fading. Over the roofs to the east, in the direction of Westminster and the river, the moon had risen, clear silver in the unrefracting air. Roses gleamed ghost white at the end of the garden. That wasn't far away from them, for the garden was very small, about fifteen yards by five. Since the ground had been methodically rationed, that was precisely the same as the size of the gardens visible from Lady Ashbrook's back windows. But, for them all, the gardens were an amenity, and they felt secure from the clutter and the hubbub when they could take refuge there. Humphrey, not a gardener, had been heard to remark that it was fortunate roses grew anywhere and bloomed several times a year.

That night, however, he had dropped out of the conversation, having swallowed one drink and asked Paul for another. The other two were talking cheerfully, but Paul looked at Humphrey as he sat silent. After a while, Paul asked quietly, "Anything happened?"

"I was going to see old Lady Ashbrook when I met you."

"How is she? Is there anything the matter?"

"I think she might say that." With Paul, Humphrey couldn't avoid dropping into the same kind of subsarcasm: but the young man was too perceptive to brush off, and it was a relief to explain.

"God almighty." Paul's expression had gone dark. "Is there anything we can do?"

"What do you mean?"

"Would it be any good to see her?"

"Whatever can be any good?" Humphrey added, "You might try."

"Of course," said Celia in her light, detached voice, "she's over eighty. It's a good age."

"Born in 1894." Paul had a computerlike memory.

"She must have come out before the first war," Celia went on reflecting.

"Do you think that's any consolation to her now?"

Celia's responses were too cool for Humphrey, and his tone was roughening.

Celia seemed to be speaking to herself, "It wouldn't be a nice way to die."

Paul began to talk of the old lady. Finding neutral ground, he said, "She is rather a period figure."

"I suppose she is to you." Humphrey gave a half smile.

"Come on. She must have been talked about as long as you can remember."

Once more Humphrey echoed the young man's tone. "I'll give you that. One sometimes heard the name."

"Were there many men?" By now, Celia had ceased to be remote.

"What have you heard?"

"Well, she can't help being a bit of history, can she?"

"History can get things wrong, you know."

"But there were some men?"

"Of course."

"You're not on duty now, don't mind us," Paul said, looking at him with affection. "You've given that up, remember?"

"Yes, please," said Celia, also with affection.

"If you don't take this for gospel—" Humphrey told them. "I don't know all that much, anyway not for sure. I do know that she skipped from her first husband—bolted, she called it—after she had been married a couple of years. She had the one son. She was only a girl then. But she told me herself she was old enough to know better than marry Max. She hated him. Max was a stinker, she said. Madge has sometimes a simple eloquence of her own."

A little earlier, Celia had been indulging in her full uninhibited sensual laugh.

"What about the son?" Paul said.

"She hated him too. And has gone on doing so. That being her only child."

"It sounds like the sort of thing that happens in dynasties. Too ferocious for the likes of us." Paul bent toward Celia and then apologized for breaking into the story.

"That's all I've ever had from Madge herself. It's on record she married again pretty soon after Max divorced her. She married Ashbrook. Everyone has always said that that was an idyllic marriage. One of the wonderful marriages of the twenties. Made for each other, everyone said. She was heartbroken when he dropped dead, they said. I may be too suspicious, but I have my doubts. I do know one other certain thing. Just by chance. With the perfect marriage now in the public view, she had an affair, quite a long one, with Hal Hillmorton. Well hidden, like most of that old operator's goings on. You couldn't have known him. He died not so long ago. He'd have amused you, though. He'd have liked you," he said to Celia, paying her a compliment, but one, he thought, that might have been true.

They had become comfortable in the dusk, with stories of Lady Ashbrook in her prime. The shades of mortal illness had receded. Emotions were not continuous, even for Humphrey and Paul, in whom they persevered more than was common.

What about Madge after her second husband's death? Oh, there had been other lovers, up to old age. At least Humphrey had heard legends, not just of minor affairs, but of two or three, each of which different authorities, confident and contradictory, claimed to be the great love of her life. A phrase, Humphrey said, that had been used of Madge Ashbrook quite often during her career, but that wouldn't be used of anyone nowadays.

Something like confidences of their own—no, not confidences, but something like the first desire for them—was emerging in the dark. Paul hadn't been married, but Celia had and in law still was.

"He left me. A couple of years ago," she said.

"Did you arrange that between you?" Humphrey asked.

"No, he left me," she said, in a clear, firm tone. "I didn't skip like Lady Ashbrook. It might have been better for my morale if I had." She added, "By the by, he wasn't a stinker. Unless I was too."

Humphrey told her that his first marriage had been a disaster.

Children? Two, by his second wife. Son a doctor in a mission hospital, daughter doing social work.

Had she had children, he asked Celia. One, a son, she said. In fact, she must drive home to him soon. He was six years old, but she had someone reliable looking after him.

Humphrey stood at his front door and watched them walking toward Paul's house, hand in hand, as he had seen them earlier that evening. Beneath the high lamp, they had a long and practiced kiss, and she drove off. Until he had heard more of the circumstances, Humphrey had assumed that she would be spending the night with Paul. But he guessed, with some confidence, that they had been to bed before they called on him. They had the sheen of recently satisfied sex. He would also have guessed, with slightly less confidence, that this relationship had started in bed, without much in the way of acquaintanceship or anything like old-fashioned courting, and that now they were having to make discoveries and learn about each other. He had an idea that their wills had begun to cross.

Humphrey would have liked Paul to come back. It would have been pleasant to go on talking. As it was, Humphrey went down to the garden again. The truth was—he didn't pretend to himself, though it was mildly dislikable—that he was feeling some envy for Paul. Not because of Celia. Not at all. He wasn't envious either, or not much, of Paul's youth. It was agreeable that those two took care not to make him feel old: but, if they had been less considerate, he still wouldn't have done so.

In the living existent moments, people of sixty felt exactly as those two felt, thirty years younger by chronological time. By a conscious effort of mind, Humphrey knew that he wasn't likely to live, by chronological time, more than another twenty years at most. But that was curiously unreal. So far as he had observed in others of his own age, it was—if they were in good health—the same with all of them. It was one of the respects in which existence was merciful. Everyone, including the young, lived with the certain prospect of death, and no one believed it.

For an instant Humphrey thought of Lady Ashbrook. That might have been so with her a few months before. And, moment by moment, even now?

Humphrey was thinking, not with much connection or with any

purpose, about himself. If he had been asked to explain what he envied about Paul, he would have been at something of a loss. Not his intelligence. Lady Ashbrook had pronounced that he was brilliant, using another of her period words, one Humphrey recalled hearing from talent-spotting ladies around smart dinner tables years before. Paul himself wouldn't have accepted the praise. Oh yes, he had had an impeccable academic record; he had been what they now called a "flyer." That wasn't difficult, if one had a decent intellectual machine and worked. Yes, he was a pretty good economist, knew more about international affairs than some, and was worth his money to his employers at the merchant bank.

The curious thing was, Humphrey recalled, that Paul was genuinely modest. Much more so than nearly all the successful people Humphrey had come across, and it might be a disadvantage. Humphrey had never heard him bluff, and in the future that might be a disadvantage too. Humphrey suspected, however, that in his secret heart, Paul did believe that he had a quality that others didn't have. Humphrey believed something similar about him, though they might not have agreed on which quality they meant.

Humphrey believed that the young man had passion. Underneath the precise and balanced mind, the ironic humor, the kindness when he was not himself involved, there was something urgent and untamed. He would try to do difficult things. He would play for high stakes, probably creditable ones, not just money or commonplace credit. He might fail, and it was likely in the world of his time that he would fail. But the passion would drive him. Such a passion was very rare so far as Humphrey's experience went.

It was why Humphrey was interested, and why he couldn't help being envious. For he had had nothing of the kind himself, as little as most men. Sitting in the garden, flickers of the past, hopes or expectations of the future (the secret planner, secretly but burrowingly at work, didn't die at Humphrey's age or any other), drifting now and then into consciousness, he wasn't constructing his own biography. No one could do so. When someone tried, as Humphrey had seen often enough, it was to pick and choose, justify or excuse oneself, sometimes to take too much blame, never to tell the cool and random truth.

In fact, as could be seen from his relationship with Lady Ashbrook, Humphrey had been born not too far from her world. They were second cousins. His family was impoverished upper class, and he was a younger son. He had had the education that they took for granted, and had, without distinction, done pretty well. Unlike Lady Ashbrook speaking of Paul, no one had called him brilliant, but he was thought to be bright. It might have been a misfortune, as he fancied later, but he had had a trickle of private means, which, at twenty-one when he came down from Cambridge, brought him about £250 a year. In the thirties, he could travel on that. He made his way around Europe, picked up languages, for which he had some natural gift, was racked by love for a woman who didn't love him, and by desperate persistence married her.

It had always been a singularly anonymous life, he was fond of saying, explaining how ordinary it had all been, more totally modest than Paul, yet it wasn't totally modest to exaggerate as he did any dim aspect of a life's dimness. During the war, he parted from his wife, neither resisting. He had soldiered in a good regiment, into which, as he predictably pointed out, he wouldn't have entered except through his connections. He wasn't a good officer— this was his own account—nor a specially bad one. Then he had been seconded to military intelligence, where his languages came in useful. He also thought, having his own subliminal vanity, that, though all men were fools who thought they knew much about people, he was a shade less of a fool than some.

That job led to another. When the war ended, he wanted to marry again. His vestigial income had been lost. He had to earn some money. He was sent for, in circumstances of farcical mystery, and asked if he would like to join the security service. Again he was fond of pointing out that this was entirely owing to his connections. More or less derelict, but entirely respectable, upper class. Nothing against him. No obvious sexual velleities (though Humphrey later liked to tell self-righteous persons that out of comparison the most valuable master of any kind of British intelligence, and one as trustworthy as Winston Churchill, had had a tragic obsession for small boys). Humphrey's was the exact specification for someone likely to keep secrets and not betray his country. The curious thing was, Humphrey was also fond of pointing out, that on the whole it worked.

Not many people knew the history of the security service: not many possibly could. Humphrey, for a project of his own, still had access to personal files. There had been fewer defections than from any corresponding service he had knowledge of and much less internal corruption.

Anyway, he hadn't dithered long before taking the offer. For him it didn't present ethical problems. So far as he was political at all, he was vaguely liberal. But that didn't prevent him from thinking that society had a right to look after itself. Any spirited society did that: and if it didn't, it would not be spirited for long. Further, and not unimportant, both he and his future wife wanted a job for him. Here it was.

So, for nearly thirty years, that was what he had been doing. It meant that he had become more anonymous than ever. People wondered how he earned his living. Some guessed. Some, like Lady Ashbrook, with friends in government, actually knew. Lady Ashbrook had never asked him a direct question. She was utterly shameless about probing into love affairs, sex affairs, money affairs, but for his kind of occupation she had a mixture of patriotic and superstitious regard. Anything like military intelligence was sacred, and so was this. Even now, though he told her that he spent most of his time writing, she did not ask him what it was, expecting that that was a state secret. Actually it was nothing more sacrosanct than a study of a pre-1914 predecessor of his, who like Humphrey himself had not reached quite the top of the service but had been an unobtrusive presence. Probably the Cabinet Office would not allow Humphrey to publish the work, since procedures even as far back as the century before were still only mentioned in private, as though they were remarkably prurient anecdotes that the public was not adult enough to hear. So Humphrey's book was likely to exist only in manuscript, which, he said to intimates, would be a suitably anonymous finish to an anonymous career.

If he had had Paul's temperament, he wouldn't have lived, with some approach to satisfaction, certainly to serenity, that anonymous career. It was over now, and perversely, like one repining for a prison or tormented love, he sometimes missed it There wasn't even the duty mode to look forward to next day. That night in the garden he would have liked to have something to look forward to tomorrow. But, though he might not have admitted them, hopes and imaginings were keeping him unresigned. If there had been anyone intimate enough to question him, he would have had to confess that he hadn't handed in his ticket.

❧ 3 ❧

For years past, Lady Ashbrook had walked in the Square garden in the afternoon. She was not willing to break this habit, and on the Wednesday, the day after she had talked to Humphrey, she was to be seen, upright, stalking slowly on the path between the trees. Over her head she held a parasol but soon lowered it, not sustaining the effort. The sky was cloudless, the sun burned down, the heat did not waver.

There was no one else in the garden. It was usually empty, for it was private and only the householders had keys. The Square was as quiet as a deserted village. Cars were parked in front of some of the houses, but they too were still, and cars were quieter than horses or children, once part of the population. No children now. Families were not brought up here, and a good many of the women in the Square went to work. This meant that no one would call on Lady Ashbrook between breakfast time and evening, though Paul and Celia had already done so that morning, and so had Kate Lefroy, who had heard the news from Humphrey.

Humphrey, one of the few people there at leisure in the afternoon, from his drawing room window watched Lady Ashbrook promenade and reluctantly felt obliged to join her. She did not keep him long. She was polite in a stately fashion, discussing the weather and the flowers in the garden beds. He wasn't welcome, because he had listened to a confidence she had not wished to make. She was distant from him because, just for that short while, she had given herself away.

21

Pretty stark, Humphrey thought as he went away. Courage came with different faces. He had known soldiers as brave as she was, who insisted on embarrassing one in precisely the opposite fashion, by confessions of exaggerated timidity.

Lady Ashbrook had been sitting down when he spoke to her. She had done enough to maintain her afternoon ritual and soon returned home. It was about an hour afterward that Humphrey noticed her doctor walking down the Square, away from the direction of Lady Ashbrook's house. Humphrey went downstairs and intercepted him.

This was Ralph Perryman, Lady Ashbrook's "little man." As Humphrey had reflected the previous evening, he wasn't little in any but a Lady Ashbrook sense. He was appreciably taller and larger than Humphrey himself. He was a good-looking man, or at least a striking-looking one, with very light blue eyes, transparent, such as one saw in Scandinavia. They were quite unshadowed, as though unprotected, in deep orbits. Humphrey had heard the doctor well spoken of professionally, and he had something of a private practice in the district. Humphrey hadn't often met him but had sometimes wanted to know him better.

"Can you spare a minute?" Humphrey asked.

Perryman seemed simultaneously overwilling and overelusive. No, he hadn't any patients to see just then. No, but he had a long night's work ahead. Yes, he had been visiting the old lady, as he referred to Lady Ashbrook, using the phrase as a kind of nickname.

"Tell me what you can."

"You know, there isn't much to tell, colonel."

Humphrey had not been a regular soldier, but colonel was a rank that had stuck to him. To use it or let others do so was not in his style. He stopped it at once, but affably, since he wanted Perryman at ease. He suggested sitting in the Square garden and led the way.

"What do you think of her?" Humphrey asked and, as he was speaking, realized that he had been too direct. As with others used to concealment, he got rid of it when he could. Then he sometimes sounded obtuse and blunt, which he was far from being. This man didn't like it and had shied away.

"Oh, I've treated her for quite a long time, you know."

"Yes, I did know. She's often talked about you." Humphrey had become emollient. "I'm by way of being a connection, but I don't suppose she's mentioned me."

The doctor gave a superior smile. "Oh, I've had to ask for names to get in touch with. In case of emergencies. I always take these precautions with elderly patients. Just professional caution, of course."

"Of course. Look, doctor, I'd be the last man to want you to do anything unprofessional. If you can't answer, let it go. But it would ease my mind a little. Can you give me an idea of what her chances are?"

The transparent eyes were gazing into the middle distance, not focused on Humphrey.

"I can't give you much of an idea. No one knows. No one can possibly know until they have seen the plates."

"It really is as unpredictable as that?"

"Sometimes one has an intuition. But you could have an intuition yourself."

"Would it be the same as yours?" Humphrey wasn't getting far with this fencing.

"That would depend on whether either of us looked on the bright side, wouldn't it? I don't know whether you're an optimist or not."

Humphrey said, casting around for another lead, "She has come through a good deal in her time. I don't know whether that's here or there."

"I agree with you entirely, Mr. Leigh. She has a very strong will, of course she has." Dr. Perryman was now speaking with animation; he could escape the topic of Lady Ashbrook now. "The trouble is, we know very little of how the mind affects the body. We know shamefully little. I've often wished I could do some work on it. But it's difficult. We really don't know where to draw the line between the mind and the body, that is, if there is a line at all." Eager, fluent, enthusiastic, Perryman expanded on the mind-body relation. He was intelligent; he had read and thought. In another place and time Humphrey would have been interested: but just then it was a distraction. It was not what he had come for.

At the end Humphrey said, "Well, if the worst comes to the worst—"

"Yes."

Humphrey found himself half echoing what Celia had said the night before: "If it does happen, then it would be an unpleasant way to die."

"There are a great many unpleasant ways to die, Mr. Leigh," said Dr. Perryman.

"I've seen some, but I hope I don't finish up this way. I must say, I should expect my doctor to ease me out."

"Should you now?" Perryman gazed straight at him. After a pause Perryman went on, "You're not the first patient who has said that, you know."

"And I take it you're not the first doctor who's listened."

Perryman didn't reply. It had been a curious interview, and back in his drawing room Humphrey was sure that he had handled it badly. The man was sensitive, not to say prickly: it should have been easier to soothe him. He must have his own foresight: or had he heard the first words from the hospital?

Humphrey was restless. There was a telephone call from a friend of Lady Ashbrook and another from Kate Lefroy. News about Lady Ashbrook, and impatience at the absence of news, was going around among her acquaintances. In spite of her pride, she seemed to have been quite unreserved in telling about her tests and the verdict she was waiting for.

In some of those who knew about her, there was concern. But there was also excitement. Calamities to others raised the emotional temperature, and people, including kind and honest people like Kate and young Paul, found that fact of life difficult to accept with candor. Candor was somewhat lacking those blazing summer days among Lady Ashbrook's circle, though excitement wasn't. Humphrey was a man of fair detachment. He was capable of saying that the disasters of others, unless they belonged to one with animal ties, bedmates or children, were singularly easy to endure: but even Humphrey didn't like thinking that to himself.

Kate Lefroy had asked Humphrey if he would go across to her house. He was glad to be asked. He was fond of Kate. There it was easy to be candid. If she had been free, he would have wanted her: as it was, he hoped that with patience he could get her free.

When, on the other side of the Square, he arrived in her front room (here the original division had been preserved, and there were two smallish sitting rooms with sliding doors between), he was confronted by another disaster that was arousing excitement among their friends, with a similar absence of candor. This was not a disaster to Kate, who looked well but relieved to receive some support. She had, it was obvious, been trying to comfort a girl sitting beside her on the sofa. This was the girl whom Lady Ashbrook had described so scornfully as totally unsuitable for her grandson, though perhaps adequate for a bit of slap and tickle. This evening she did not look adequate even for that. Lady Ashbrook had conceded that she possessed some elements of prettiness, but her face was dense and dark with crying, and Humphrey, who scarcely knew her, that evening would have thought her plain. She was the daughter of Tom Thirkill, the M.P. and entrepreneur. So far as Humphrey could make out, this was part of the misery. For that week *Private Eye*, the modish journal of the day, had produced another of its half-muted attacks. That had been followed by a respectable daily saying there was a rumor that opposition members were calling for an inquiry into one of Thirkill's enterprises. There hadn't, as it had happened, been much in the way of other news, except for the slide on the stock exchange and in the value of the pound. Tom Thirkill's affairs thus became the object of some journalists' attention, along with the heat wave.

The girl, whose name was Susan, was expressing loyalty to her father. Still half crying, underlids puffed out as though they had been injected, she swore that her father was honest.

"Of course, he's a businessman," she told them. "His sort of business doesn't always look straightforward if you don't understand it. But, you must believe it, he's kept to the rules. He's kept to the rules. He's much too clever not to. And, you've got to remember, money matters to him, of course it does, but his political career comes a long way first. He'd never take the slightest risk with that."

Kate had told Humphrey before that the girl was no fool. That was just about the correct line for her to take, he thought. Whether she was right or wrong, he had no conception and no way of making one. He could see that, unfortunately, Kate did have a conception, and a powerfully negative one. Kate would look after anyone in trouble: she was fond of this girl and felt responsibility for her, since she worked in Kate's office at the hospital. Not that the girl had the faintest practical need to work. Her father lavished money on her, cars, horses, anything she asked for or didn't ask for. Yet, in the modern fashion, she needed to have this job: at which, Kate told Humphrey, she perversely didn't show maximum concentration or energy. In any case, Kate had to protect her. She was doing so not effusively but with a kind of astringent warmth.

It was clear to Humphrey that Kate had the lowest opinion of the girl's father and that she accepted all that his enemies were saying. To Susan, she showed a little temper and impatience spontaneous enough, like a slap in the face to rouse one who wouldn't fight, but that helped conceal what her judgment really was. Well, Humphrey thought, she was perceptive, she was often in the Thirkill home, she knew the man. She might well be right. On the other hand, Humphrey had to remind himself that Kate, so willing to devote herself to anyone who needed it, and despised by Lady Ashbrook in consequence, was not impartial about political personages. Kate could be funny, sharp tempered, warm natured, but in politics she made Lady Ashbrook look wishy-washy by comparison, a lukewarm sitter on the fence.

Kate didn't even pretend to sit on fences. To her it would seem in the nature of things that Tom Thirkill was corrupt. For sheer unqualified Toryism you had to go to women of her class, Humphrey thought. Kate came from a military family, a line of officers in a county regiment, not a smart one. She had their virtues and just occasionally, in the midst of her worldly sense, their beliefs. She couldn't understand why Humphrey should be sceptical and uncommitted. He found it endearing that for once her charity deserted her. She found him endearing but didn't budge.

Susan broke out with another grief, or maybe the same one in another shape. Lady Ashbrook's grandson was coming home for a few days' leave. He would hear this new mutter, menace, against her father. Was it going to spoil things between them?

"It mustn't," said Kate.

"Will he hold it against me?"

"Not if he's any good." Kate's tone was hard and tough.

"I don't know what he'll think," cried Susan.

"I'd have thought he'll take it pretty lightly." Humphrey dared not overdo it, but he had to help Kate out. "He knows about the press. After all, he's lived in this world."

"Not in daddy's world." Another of Susan's flashes of realism.

She wanted to talk about the young man, and that enlivened her. Perhaps it was giving the comfort within a love affair when just talking of the loved one seems for mirage moments to make all well.

26

Kate hadn't really had the chance to speak much to Mister, had she? Mister was much more unusual than he seemed. He was artistic, but he kept it dark. He wasn't sure that he ought to stay in the army. Perhaps he was wasted. She didn't want to see him getting bored. He did get bored easily. That was a weakness, and she had to watch it.

Mister was a curious name to hear a girl utter so possessively. It was what his family called him, except for his grandmother with her trenchant Loseby. As a nickname it seemed inexplicable to nearly everyone, except to a very few familiar with certain tribal customs: to them it conveyed two messages, which told that he had once had an elder brother now dead and, second, where Mister had been to school. No one around would have picked up the messages, except Humphrey, who was bred to those customs and, surprisingly, a close friend of his living nearby, an American psychologist of scholarly perseverance and a sardonic fascination with the relics of aristocracy.

With Susan temporarily in better heart, once or twice giving secretive smiles, Kate took charge, ordered her to wash her face and make up again, and then go home. Had she anything to put her to sleep? She kissed Kate, thanked her, managed a challenging smile as she said good night.

"Poor girl," said Kate as they heard the downstairs door bang.

"Poor girl indeed."

"What do you think of the boyfriend?"

"He's very amiable. Also fairly lightweight."

"He's had too much love. He's had too much love from her."

"Of course. She's doing it all wrong."

The two of them were speaking the same personal language, as though they were more intimate than in fact they were.

"You realize that she's been sleeping with him for a couple of years?"

"It seemed a fair guess," said Humphrey.

"You realize that she has slept with quite a few men and it has always gone wrong in the end?"

"That I shouldn't have guessed," he said. "I might have thought she longed for it and was sad at what she was missing."

Kate grinned. "It surprised me a bit," she said. "But whatever she's missed, it isn't that."

The room in which they were sitting was like Kate herself, well groomed, tidy, roses on one table, sweet peas on another. She did her own gardening, her own housework, as well as being the second in command of administration at a large hospital. She wasn't tall, she wasn't heavy, but had strong shoulders, strong hips, firm flesh on shoulders and thighs. It was a physique made to wear, made to work. It was also a physique that had a special attraction for Humphrey. He was one of those men to whom some physical disparities were in themselves attractive. He liked, more than liked, the contrast between the strong active body and the face above. The face might have belonged to a different woman. It was fine and delicate. She hadn't Celia's small-featured prettiness: her forehead was broad, eyebrows arched, eyes piercing gray, nose aquiline, narrow, long. It was a face that could look high spirited and younger than she was (she had just turned forty), but it also told those who studied faces that she lived in touch with her own experience.

"I suppose you've no news of Lady A., you can't have?" he asked.

"You can't have either, can you?"

He told her that he had had a talk with the doctor, irksome, inconclusive.

"I rather like him. You don't."

"I don't react as strongly as you do," Humphrey said, "either way."

She smiled and said that she would telephone Lady Ashbrook that evening. "It's not exactly a treat, talking to her," she remarked. "All she wants is to get me off the line."

"Don't bother about ringing her," he said. "You do enough for duty. Much more than enough."

"Oh, one can't leave her alone. You can imagine what it must be like." She gave a rueful, diffident grimace. "Of course, she hasn't any use for me."

Humphrey knew that Kate was painfully honest when others didn't like her. She even seemed to expect it unless proved otherwise. He said that Lady A. had about as little affection to spare as anyone on earth, but that didn't encourage Kate. So he left it and asked, "How is Monty today?" Monty was her husband.

"He's resting," she replied without expression.

Monty was fifteen years older than she was, and they had been married for nearly as long. Humphrey, not pretending to himself that he was disinterested, had tried to find out about the marriage. She was as loyal as Susan to her father, but Humphrey had discovered something, though not all, from other sources. It seemed to have been a curious history. At the time that Kate first met him, Monty appeared to have had a high reputation as a philosopher; to be precise, as a researcher in mathematical logic. What he did, or was trying to do, was entirely incomprehensible to Humphrey and must have been so to Kate. So far as Humphrey could understand from academic friends, Monty had an ambition to lay down the foundations of mathematics from the inside, proving them to be a man-made construction. It was a megalomaniac ambition, said one of the academics. There had never been anything in it; the man was wasting his time. But Kate had been ready to adore genius; Monty had the aura of a genius and was ready to be adored.

It seemed strange to Humphrey that Kate's shrewdness and insight hadn't saved her. Maybe he didn't realize, or didn't want to, that she also had a longing to worship—when she was a young woman, possibly even now. Humphrey did realize that there must have been physical charm for her too. With a marmoreal head, abstracted, stately in his movements, Monty was still an impressive-looking man.

Kate had duly married and cherished her genius. He had retired from his academic post in order to have all his time to think. They had probably (Humphrey's information wasn't certain about this) bought this house together. Since then she had brought into it the money they lived on. There was her salary from the hospital. With her excess energy, she taught courses in personnel management at a technical college not far away. Even so, their income was low by the standards of the Square, and she had to eke it out. Fortunately, Monty believed that living meagerly would prolong his life. He had taken excessive care about his health. When she had told Humphrey that he was resting, that was the most frequent answer she gave to inquiries about Monty. So far as Humphrey's academic friends recalled, Monty hadn't published any kind of paper for years.

"Couldn't you do with a rest yourself?" Humphrey asked, though he had to do it carefully, tentatively.

"No chance of that."

"Aren't you rather tired?"

"Not too tired to give you a drink."

Unlike Lady Ashbrook, Kate enjoyed being hospitable, though how she afforded the liquor she was ready to pour out Humphrey couldn't begin to imagine. She gave him a considerable whiskey and took one herself. They were able to forget about others outside that room, and there was happiness quivering in the air. There was also strain, a not unpleasurable but pervasive strain. They had not exchanged a word of love, not ever, nor of desire, scarcely even of affection. If either had given an indication of wishing to go to bed, it would have happened. Humphrey knew it: so, he was sure, did she.

He didn't move and tried to keep his voice quite steady. He wanted more. Whether she did, there he couldn't trust his own hopes. He hadn't defined how much she was bound to her husband. She certainly took her duty seriously, but she might feel more than duty. If so, Humphrey would do better to withdraw at once. A light-come, light-go affair would be a relief for a while but no good to either of them.

Yet they were happy. Just before the crystals of recognition were beginning to form, it was good to sit there, the sun streaming in, a hot and sharp-edged beam falling across her lap. It was she who had to answer to herself—to conscience, if that was dividing her, or to something deeper than that. For him there was no struggle. So the initiative had to come from her. Through that glowing evening she didn't take it, and in time Humphrey went away.

4

It's impossible to enter into an extreme situation," Alec Luria said to Humphrey, "unless you're in it yourself. Or have been in it not too long ago."

It was the Friday afternoon of that same week, and they were walking in the constant sunshine around the Square garden. Lady Ashbrook, not departing from her timetable, could be seen sitting on a bench. They had been talking of her, but it was that sight that was the trigger for Luria's remark. Humphrey waved, Luria swept off his panama hat with an unhurrying bow. Lady Ashbrook inclined her parasol, a minimal gesture, in their direction.

Even if Humphrey's own company had been welcome, about which from day to day he wasn't certain, he wouldn't have taken Luria along to meet her. She had conceived one of her harsh dislikes for him. It had made no impact, Humphrey telling her that this was the most distinguished man around that summer. Humphrey had introduced them: she had demonstrated her own kind of politeness, which was not polite, and said later to Humphrey that she didn't wish to make new acquaintances. That was all.

"You can't enter into an extreme situation," Luria went on brooding. "No one has much capacity for feeling. It could be something we're all losing. There are times when that frightens me. I'd choose for us to feel bad feeling rather than not feel at all. I'd choose for us to be cruel with feeling rather than to be cruel without. The evidence is that that's how the maximum horrors have been done."

Luria had a knack of making a scrap of conversation sound like a prophecy. Once or twice in the future, Humphrey was to recall this one. Perhaps it was that his manner was solemn, his voice an octave deeper than an English voice, his face set and patriarchal with mournful Jewish eyes. In fact, he was not much more solemn, mournful, or portentous than young Paul, but he must have seemed patriarchal since he was a boy. At this time he was well under fifty, but at sight everyone thought him much older. Humphrey had first come across him on a professional trip to America years before, and they were closer friends than is common for men to become in middle age. Humphrey had a respect for him, which wasn't an uncommon response to Luria: Luria, to Humphrey's surprise, returned the respect, which, underneath the elaborate courtesy, was an uncommon response from Alec Luria to anybody.

Luria's career had been a pattern carried to the extreme. Father and mother born in Galicia, Alec, eldest son, born in Brooklyn; extreme poverty, father a repairer of shoes and at night a Talmudic scholar; son intelligent, all sacrifices made for him, character and gifts fusing without effort, the highest academic successes. He had become a psychiatrist, but then the power that made him a father figure also made him change his profession. The concepts of psychiatry weren't right: he had to make psychology respectable—to a mind as honest as his own. Thus he had turned from psychiatrist to psychologist, and a dissident one. His reputation was massive enough to get him, very young, a major professorship. He was, also when very young, a major pundit, but lonely in the purity and justice of his mind. Just and pure as his mind was—and this gave Humphrey considerable spectator's pleasure—he was not, however, without a taste for the frailties of this world. He had married twice, both wives gentiles, both rich. He accumulated money. He was fond of luxury. Not many academics, however punditlike, would have thought it appropriate for a summer vacation to rent a duplex apartment in Eaton Square. He had much more tenderness than Humphrey for the charms of the beau monde.

He was an inquiring and, underneath, a pessimistic man. He

took a gloomy view of human possibilities. In practical terms he was worried about his own country and about England, of which he was sentimentally fond. He made plenty of judgments, most of them glum. His scoring rate was reasonably high, but it was not unknown for him to make mistakes. That seemed to give him as much gratification as when he was proved right, and he broke into an extraordinary honking, grating laugh.

In spite of Luria's dark realism, or maybe because of it, Humphrey was glad to have him near at hand those torrid weeks. Humphrey looked forward to their regular meeting each Saturday night. It was a pity that Lady Ashbrook had taken against him. He would have gained Proustian joy from that encounter with the past. And, patriarchal as he sounded, seemed, and often was, he was vulnerable enough to be hurt by what appeared a snub: which was exactly what it was.

Next afternoon, Saturday, July 10, Humphrey, walking alone outside the gardens, had, when he waved and smiled toward Lady Ashbrook, quite a different reception. Her grandson was standing beside the bench. Humphrey had already heard from Kate that he had arrived and that Susan had met him. At the sight of Humphrey, he came soft footed, moving like a games player, across the turf.

"Come along," he said, face open and joyous, as though this was a specially good day. "Your presence is required."

He was a good-looking young man in a way that foreigners thought characteristically English, though in England it was distinctly rare. He had fine brilliant fair hair, though the kind of hair that at twenty-nine—he was an exact contemporary of Paul Mason—was already thinning. His eyes were handsome, very large, not washed-out blue but pigmented. His skin was fresh, healthily pale. People were known to say that he had everything. As Kate remarked, he had had too much love. Certainly he had been much pursued, by men as well as women. He took it all with good nature and presumably with pleasure. He enjoyed looking after others and took trouble over small things. As they walked toward his grandmother, he talked about her.

"She's bearing up extraordinarily well," he said.

"What do you think of her morale?"

"What do you?" Loseby was quick to hear what wasn't said.

"Most of us wouldn't have so much control. But how much is she paying for it?"

"There's an old German military saying." Loseby was talking quietly. "It doesn't matter what your morale is. What does matter is how you behave."

Loseby was a soldier, a captain in the Rifles, which was the family regiment. He was at that time serving in Germany on a special assignment; maybe he had picked up that tough formula there.

"I suppose you came over specially?" Humphrey was also talking quietly as they approached the bench.

"I had to see her, hadn't I?"

Then, coming up to Lady Ashbrook, his expression became unclouded, radiant, his voice buoyant. He announced, "Captured him. Here he is."

"Oh, Humphrey. It's very nice of you to come," said Lady Ashbrook, exactly in the tone of Tuesday evening.

"It must be much nicer to have Loseby here," said Humphrey.

"I'm quite glad of any reasonably civilized company." She gave a sarcastic smile, but the tone was loving. Then, not to be too affectionate, she broke off, "Tell me, am I wrong, or is it really rather excessively hot?"

"Grandmama! That is putting it mildly. I think I ought to take you in—"

"Don't you mean take yourself in, my dear boy? No, I think we can endure it a little longer. I don't have too much sun, you know."

The words were casual. She might have been implying that she wouldn't have much more sun. Loseby's words were as casual as hers.

"Do have a heart, grandmama. I'm not thinking of you, just me. I'm not as tough as you are, after all."

In fact, on his forehead and cheeks the fine Nordic skin was burning. He was wearing only a shirt and linen trousers, and some girl—would it be Susan?—would have to treat him with ointment that night.

"Soon. We'll go in soon, dear boy." Lady Ashbrook wouldn't give him his own way. She was behaving like a spoiled and willful beauty. Between the two of them, the old lady used to being wooed and the indulged young man, there was the air, Humphrey

34

was noticing, of something remarkably like a flirtation. Loseby was better at handling her than anyone whom Humphrey had seen. It emerged in the conversation that he had brought her flowers and a case of champagne. Tomorrow he would arrange a bridge party for the early evening. Humphrey was invited. The champagne would come in useful. Meanwhile, she was to drink half a bottle without fail before she went to bed tonight.

Loseby gave out affection as naturally as a sunny child. It was genuine affection, Humphrey didn't doubt. With his grandmother, was it also love? There could be an element of cupboard love, of course. He was the only relative she cared for. Where else should her money go? It could be that he was making sure. Easy-natured men were often better than the calculating at looking after themselves. And yet, it was very difficult to act love as well as he did.

One thing he wouldn't do. She wanted him to sit with her that night until she went to bed.

"I'll stay with you till seven. Then I really am obliged to go."

"Too early."

"I'm so sorry, grandmama dear. I'd get out of it if I could."

"Do so. You have some talent for excuses. You always have had."

Loseby gave his radiant, shameless smile. "Not this time, I'm afraid. It's a date. Fixed up weeks ago."

"I suppose it's an assignation," she said.

"You can suppose most things, can't you?" he replied. "By the by, did you really talk about assignations in your wicked days?"

"We didn't talk as much as your friends do," said Lady Ashbrook. "We should have thought it took the edge off things."

"Oh, we talk about going to bed. Loudly. No secrets. But if anyone thinks about getting married, it has to be whispered. That really is rather shameful. So it's a dead secret."

"Are you thinking of it?" She sounded accusing, apprehensive, maybe jealous.

"Dear grandmama, I'll tell you if I ever do."

The exchanges went on. Under all his willingness to please, he was as stubborn as she was, and she couldn't tease, persuade, force, cajole him into staying with her throughout the evening. There was one device she didn't use, which Humphrey guessed might have worked. That was the blackmail of pity. She didn't for an instant deploy that. She didn't so much as hint that, in her state, she wanted someone loving near her.

Later in the afternoon, Humphrey made his way to the habitual Saturday rendezvous with Alec Luria. Their meeting place was a public house that the inhabitants of this part of Belgravia referred to as their local. There was nothing special about the pub, which was situated in the street running from the end of Eaton Square toward Buckingham Palace Road. Luria liked it and was fond of explaining how good the English were at making themselves comfortable: there was no equivalent to such a pub in any other country he had lived in. There was a large, sedate saloon with three cozy alcoves, leather-covered chairs and benches, unexacting and quiet. That evening at six o'clock there were about twenty people scattered about the saloon, most of them residents from close by who had called in for a drink before dinner.

It was a peaceful time. Humphrey and Luria settled themselves in the far corner, legs stretched under the table in front of them, on the table pints of beer. Luria, though he had a taste for English pubs, had no such taste for English beer: but this was part of the ritual and he endured it.

They were having a conversation with voices subdued but actually animated. Humphrey wanted to get some hard information about Tom Thirkill. This was part of Kate's concern for the Thirkill daughter that had become a link between Kate and Humphrey—the kind of link they could enjoy while staying mute about themselves. So Humphrey had involved Luria, who had more acquaintances in London than most Englishmen and who also wasn't an innocent in financial dealings, as Humphrey was. Luria had dutifully made inquiries, which he didn't pretend not to revel in. He was explaining, and he was one of the best of expositors. His view was that all such buying and selling of companies and playing the exchanges had its shaded or devious side. Granted that Thirkill had certainly done nothing criminal and probably nothing improper. He might have been a trifle indiscreet, particularly as the English had become prudish about anyone making money. Unless they made it themselves, through wins on the pools or bets or strikes, said Luria, with melancholy sardonic eyes. Thirkill had clearly attracted much political enmity, both from the Tories —natural enough—and from his own left wing—natural enough

36

again. Further, he seemed to have attracted an unusual amount of personal enmity. "Well, you know him, don't you?"

"Only slightly," said Humphrey.

"You ought to have some insights there, though." Luria appeared to regard the problem with a kind of resigned satisfaction.

People of good judgment did tend to suspect the man, Humphrey remarked. He didn't mention the name of Kate. Luria was a friend and to be trusted: but Humphrey would speak to no one until the chances were better than they appeared now. He was a superstitious man.

Thirkill was a good, safe, friendly topic. They were both relaxed. Luria courteously refused another drink, but Humphrey bought himself a second pint of bitter. Then they were disturbed.

There was a commotion, a hubbub mixed with chanting from outside the street door, diametrically opposite to their own corner. A crowd surged into the room. More yells, more chanting, so much that Humphrey was confused. The room pullulated with the crowd and the noise. It was hard, in the din, to see individual faces. Perhaps there were thirty or forty in the crowd, some still jamming the far door. All young, so far as he could make out as he tried to clear his eyes. One or two looked in their twenties. Others very young—sixteen? seventeen? Beards, profuse hair, a few girls hanging on to shoulders. Chant reiterated, unlike human speech. Humphrey couldn't make it out.

Then he had it. It was like the mindless chanting of a football crowd. This was midsummer. They presumably had come from Victoria tube station half a mile away. Some were wearing sweaters with legends, *We are the Champs.* This was a mob from one of the limited-over cricket matches, started and finished in one day. A lot of them were angry drunk. Glasses were swept from the bar. A couple rushed behind, screamed at the barman, punched him in the face, grabbed bottles of whiskey, and knocked off the necks. Others snatched glasses from the tables, swore at anyone around, and sank the drinks. One elderly man was resisting. Raucous cries—"get lost," "stuff it," "do him." His hat was on the bench beside him. One of the slightly older men seized that, put it on, and pranced around. The elderly man was standing now. He was knocked back into his seat and beer poured over his head and shoulders.

37

Other customers were sitting stupefied, quiescent, immobilized. It was as if they didn't notice what was going on.

At last Humphrey collected himself enough to call to the barman. "Gerald Road, quick." That meant get the local police station. The mob wouldn't know that, but they were inflamed by any signs of interference, even of life. The barman, face bleeding, slipped away. Raging, half a dozen youths were milling around Humphrey's table. Both he and Alec Luria were able-bodied men, but it was no use trying to fight at those odds. Humphrey had handled troops in his time, but nothing like this. He tried to recapture his army tone. "Get away. You're all in trouble. Sit down."

Shouts of hate: "Do him!" "We'll do you."

Luria, like Humphrey, was by this time standing up.

"You're doing yourselves no good," he said in a strong bass voice. "I advise you to quieten down."

"Fucking sheeny." That was a cockney accent. Most of the others were north country, but the gang had picked up some camp followers.

Humphrey was shouting to the room for help, but none came. Then there was a susurration near the door. "Fucking pigs." Two policemen in shirt-sleeves came in. That wasn't a result of the barman's call. It was later known that a passerby had seen the mob screeching and surging down the street and had warned a police car.

Some youths were escaping, but hate was still active. The policemen were attacked. A big lad was threatening one of them with a broken bottle. More police cars were arriving. Now the crowd was melting. Kicking over tables, smashing glasses, putting feet through glass panels, they pelted out into the decorous streets. Police cars followed them. It wasn't often, Humphrey remarked as they returned to quietness at their table, that police cars conducted a chase around Eaton Square.

"I was shaken," said Alec Luria.

"Not to be expected in this part of London." Humphrey was beckoning the barman to clean up the table. His glass had been broken, and he was asking for another drink.

"I think we might go."

"No, not yet," Humphrey said, as though this were an occasion for maximum phlegm. "Not to be expected after a game of cricket.

I'm inclined to doubt whether anything like that has happened around here before."

"I found it very frightening." As wasn't common in talks between those two, Luria was being more direct than his friend.

"So did I." Humphrey had seen that Luria wasn't a coward: it was better to talk in the same tone.

"We mustn't fool ourselves." Luria was brooding.

Humphrey said: "The curious thing was, it was so paralyzing. At least for me. More so than going into action. In the military you had an idea what you were supposed to do."

"One of the frightening things," Luria went on brooding, "was that no one stirred—all these men sitting around the room. That is frightening. There was a gang at home, up on Riverside Drive, decent locality, carving a girl up on the sidewalk—and solid citizens looking on from windows. Not doing a thing. Too much like what went on here. I keep telling you, people have damn well ceased to feel."

"They don't want to get mixed up. They're afraid," said Humphrey.

"When people are afraid, they cease to feel, don't they? Isn't that true in war?"

Luria, in spite of his venerable appearance, was too young to have been a soldier in the Hitler war. He thought that that was a grave deficiency for a psychologist: but then, he tended to think the same of any human activity he hadn't performed. Humphrey was accustomed to tell him that almost any human activity, when you were actually at work inside it, inspired less emotion than an outsider could imagine.

"It wasn't pretty tonight." Luria was in earnest. At times he could sound pontifical, but now he didn't. "You must have thought about it often—to be sure you have—I have—there isn't much between us and this sort of mess." He was gazing around as though the mob was still there. "We go on fooling ourselves, that's what I meant a few minutes ago. Especially if we live in a nice, pretty cushioned world. Civilization is hideously fragile. You know that. There's not much between us and the horrors underneath. Just about a coat of varnish, wouldn't you say?"

Humphrey merely nodded.

"And the same applies to you and me. And the rest of us.

39

There's not much between us and our beastly selves. Human beings aren't nice, are they?"

Humphrey nodded again. It had been, by the standards of the time, just a trivial incident they had been caught in, but Luria's phrase somehow passed around among their circle and became part catch phrase, part a kind of jargon joke, the kind of joke they used when they wanted to deny that they were being serious.

They had now stayed in the pub long enough for the sake of normality. They walked along to Eaton Square on the way to Luria's apartment. Also for the sake of normality, Luria gave Humphrey more instructions about the financial structure of Tom Thirkill's operations.

❧ 5 ❧

Loseby had amiable intentions and social skill, but it had been a mistake to provide company for his grandmother on that Sunday evening. They were meeting in the garden down below her house. A table was prepared for bridge, and around it sat Paul Mason, Humphrey, Loseby, and Lady Ashbrook herself. Bottles of champagne stood on another table close by. Humphrey heard Paul call Loseby Lancelot, which seemed another piece of incongruous nomenclature—though they had been at school together, and this actually was one of Loseby's Christian names.

The men were doing their best to talk as though this were an agreeable summer occasion no different from others, but Lady Ashbrook, despite her self-discipline, was on the edge of losing even her formal manners. As for any attempt at displaying pleasure, she did not seem to have the desire or even the energy to try. She had attended church that morning, just as she had all her life. Humphrey had often wondered, and in her garden was doing so again, whether she really had religious faith. It might have been convenient in a life as talked about as hers to show herself punctilious in at least one kind of piety. He had never heard her make a speculative remark. He would have liked to know whether she had prayed that morning, praying for good news in the coming week, for release from danger, as children pray when they are waiting for examination results. But unbelievers sometimes prayed like that. Humphrey recalled, with a blink of shame, that he had done so himself.

There were intermittences of anxiety as there were of hope. Perhaps that afternoon she had no relief from the thought of the coming week. Or perhaps she had some from letting herself get out of temper about the bridge. Herself, she was a very good player. She was partnered by her grandson, who was a very bad one. Paul was passable, but not what she would have expected from anyone of his talents. Humphrey was bad. Not so long before, when she wasn't under strain, she had been heard to remark that the difference between Loseby and Humphrey was that Loseby thought for hours before playing the wrong card, whereas Humphrey did so quickly.

Loseby was playing the wrong card often that long, hot afternoon.

"Really, my dear boy," she began to utter, more than once. She was losing money. Not much, for the stakes were low, but she was losing money. After the end of the second rubber she said again, "Really, my dear boy." That was all she said. It was the signal for the guests to leave.

Loseby was the best of social lubricants, but he couldn't reduce the level of angst in that garden. He tried producing a mildly scabrous discovery that he had just made. As Paul was saying good-bye, Loseby was reminding them of what they all knew, that in this garden and the one next door there was a small back door that led into the adjacent mews. From there it was only a few yards to Eccleston Street.

"Convenient for sinful purposes. For which there were rather good examples round here."

Face shining with shameless delight in other's frailties and his own, he asked whether any of them had heard of fifty-five Eaton Terrace, less than half a mile away. That had a garden and a private door into a mews, precisely like this. One could get out through the mews into Chester Row and so unobtrusively home. In the 1890s and later, number fifty-five had been the most elevated brothel in London, organized by the Prince of Wales's confidants and financed from the royal purse. Presumably, eminent gentlemen walked home or had their carriages waiting at a discreet distance.

"Had you heard about that, grandmama?"

For a moment, Lady Ashbrook melted into an astringent smile.

"Rather before my time, you know. Do you really think I'm a hundred?"

After the bridge party, Humphrey had nothing to fill the day until eight o'clock. He had arranged, as part of Kate's secret services to her protégée Susan, to take Tom Thirkill out to dinner. Though the two of them had met several times, with Thirkill making demonstrations of cordiality, it had been the professional cordiality of a politician. When Humphrey had sent a note around to Eaton Square, he hadn't received an acceptance for three days. Humphrey understood well enough. Persons living in the public scene might be cordial to anonymous neighbors but didn't encourage them. For a man like Thirkill, engagements were for a purpose. Humphrey had no doubt that Thirkill had been making inquiries about him—quite easy if one had access to ministers—and was deciding whether the man was any use to him, or alternatively might be a nuisance if he were turned down.

It had been something of an effort to find a place in London to have dinner on a Sunday night. By himself Humphrey lived simply, except for a taste in wine. His old housekeeper gave him the meals he had been content with as a young bachelor, and alone that night it would have been a cutlet and cheese. If he were going to get anything like confidence from Tom Thirkill, that didn't seem adequate, and Humphrey booked a table at the Berkeley. The random thought occurred to him, entertaining rich men was always expensive, the more so the richer they became: one somehow performed as though they were entertaining you.

Prompt on the stroke of eight, Thirkill's car drew up outside the house. Thirkill stepped out, limber and vigorous, giving an impression that he could dismiss trouble because he was happy in his own health. He was personable in an actor's fashion, not uncommon in politicians, strong facial lines, jaw a shade underhanging. "Good evening to you." His voice resounded. "Where are we going?"

Humphrey told him, was instructed not to trouble about his own car; Thirkill would do the transport.

"This is very civil of you, I must say," Thirkill remarked as he drove through the quiet and empty streets.

"I've always wanted the chance to talk with you," Humphrey replied.

"So have I, so have I." It wasn't the first time that either of them

43

had had that particular exchange, though with different partners.

The Berkeley dining room was cool after the air outside, not crowded, conversation subdued. As they sat at their table, Thirkill having refused any drink but tomato juice, Humphrey said, "Rather different from last night."

"What are you getting at?"

"I was in the pub. Didn't you see in the papers?"

There had been captions, *Vandals in Belgravia.* Unfair to Vandals, Humphrey commented, but Thirkill wasn't interested in references to fifth-century history.

"Oh, that," he said.

"It wasn't pretty."

"I think you must accept"—Thirkill could, without effort, suddenly speak with force and did so now—"that when people get better off, they are going to behave worse. That is, by our standards."

"By any standards, I would have thought."

"Could be. Respect has gone out of the window. But you must accept, the respect isn't going to come back when people are better off. We may not like it, but there you are. And I'm sure you wouldn't think so, but that is no reason under heaven for not making people better off."

It didn't take him long to order his meal. Humphrey had made a misjudgment. Thirkill was less self-indulgent than he was himself. Soup and a cutlet would have been more than enough for him. Further, he drank very little. One glass of wine, perhaps. Humphrey would have to finish the bottle without further help.

At the same time that Thirkill was abstemious about food, he wasn't so about giving disquisitions. He had the gift of making commonplace statements about himself as though he were baring his soul. He had been born just fifty years before, he said. In Birmingham. That didn't get the worst of the Depression, but it was bad enough. You wouldn't see what you saw last night. There was more respect. Better behavior, if people our age have any right to judge. "But I tell you, Humphrey [he was already using Christian names], I wouldn't have that world back in place of what we have now." He had been a young accountant in Birmingham, without a penny—that was at the end of the forties. Then there was the first sign of a breakthrough. That was when he had begun to make his money and had realized that it was his duty, in the long run, to go into politics. *Duty*, said Thirkill, so that his listener couldn't miss the word.

The thick eyebrows, mobile mouth, confronted Humphrey across the table. From most politicians, this would have been a conventional apologia. He wasn't showing any originality of view, but Humphrey, more than he had bargained for, was being bombarded by an originality of temperament. One mightn't like Thirkill, or want to do business with him, but it was hard to think that he was negligible. He began a similar bombardment about the future.

"What is going to happen to us?" he challenged Humphrey.

"What do you mean?"

"I mean this country, this year."

"I can't pretend to be bubbling with optimism."

That year, and for years past, none of Humphrey's friends in private had been bubbling with optimism about the state of the nation or its economy, or, deeper down, about the state of the Western world.

"There I must take issue with you. We [he meant the Government, and his own Labour Party] can get the finances into shape. We shall. With a bit of luck and good management and the right men in the right places, we ought to get things straight."

Once again, those remarks could have come from any conventional politician, especially one with ambitions, seeing clearly the necessity for getting one right man into one right place. Politicians had to be optimistic: otherwise they wouldn't be politicians. In parliamentary societies like this one, the future was as close as their own hopes, and world concern was a very long way distant. They had to live in the present. Thinking ten years ahead, even five, was for spectators, not for them.

Here in the restaurant, Thirkill was uplifted by the prospect before him, speaking like any other professional politician but with a temperament that Humphrey hadn't often met before. "Oh yes," he said, "we shall manage it. The finances will look brighter next year. Our lot can do it. The others can't. It'll come out all right in the wash. No one really wants the other lot. Not the fellows who understand finance. Not industry. Not the City. I give you my solemn word."

Soon Thirkill had other reflections. "I don't mind telling you,

Humphrey, I happen to have about the tenth safest seat in the country. My father was a parliamentary agent; he never earned more than £300 a year in his life, but he taught me most of what I know about politics. Politics is about bread and butter, he used to tell me when I was a boy. So I waited until I could get a seat like mine. Some of the lefty boys in the party don't like me having it at all, at all. They'd like to get me. Let them try."

Suddenly, as between one moment and another, in the midst of the confident, confidential, authoritative voice, had come a tone quite different, so different that for a moment Humphrey might have been listening to another man.

"I suppose you've heard all about these libels that are going around? You know they keep on printing libels about me?"

"Yes, I did know something."

"They come," said Thirkill, "from some of those boys in the party. I can't prove it, but I know it. They get a little cash selling gossip around Fleet Street. Some of them don't even get cash; they just think it's useful to be in with the journalists. I dare say that you're not entirely surprised."

"It's fairly common knowledge."

"I dare say you wouldn't be entirely surprised about who these lefty boys are."

Humphrey was accustomed to persons trying to make him indiscreet about his old profession. He just said, "Of course, you must know them personally yourself."

Thirkill didn't press further, too full of his complaints and intentions.

"I can't get my hands on them," he said in the curious grinding tone that had, minutes before, taken Humphrey by surprise. "By God, I should like to. They're doing their worst for all of us. By God, they're doing their worst for me. But I can get my hands on these journalists they've fed. And their wretched rags and everyone connected with them. I've been waiting. It was good to wait until they had overplayed their hands. I don't mind telling you, it took some patience to wait, when you saw what people were thinking. And what your family was going through. But it was worth it. No one had the score right except my lawyers and me. A handful of writs went out on Friday night. They're going to pay. I'm not a vindictive man, Humphrey and I wouldn't say it in any vindictive spirit. But these fellows have been trying to ruin me, and I don't care if I see them starving in the streets."

"What are the chances? What do the lawyers say?"

"What do you take me for?"

To an extent, this conversation was what Humphrey had been in search of. But he realized that, except for this news about the writs, which in any case would be public within hours, he had learned almost nothing. Thirkill gave the impression of entering into intimacy. He seemed to be making confessions and then made none, except what one could infer. This continued when Thirkill went on, using all his emotional power, which was considerable, to demand sympathy and help. He wanted sympathy and help in what others thought of his financial dealings. It was hard, he said, for an honest man to be written off by people who didn't understand the first thing about finance. It had come easy to him since he was very young. It was a flair, he said, to be able to think about money. Playing the exchanges was like playing poker. You had to guess how other people would play, mainly people not too bright at any other game. It was no use if you let yourself be too far-sighted: money wasn't made that way.

None of this contradicted Luria's view of how Thirkill had performed. Whether it was true, Humphrey hadn't the insight or knowledge to form any opinion at all. The most he could do was ask again whether Thirkill was totally confident about the legal cases. Thirkill said, "They won't even fight them. They'll never come to court."

Some mud always sticks, he broke out, demanding sympathy again. But in responsible circles his name would be as good as it ever was.

By this time Humphrey, though he couldn't be sure of the factual truths (all evening had kept recurring a gibe of a fellow member of the Commons, if Tom Thirkill tells you the time, it's just as well to check it by your own watch), had one or two definite impressions.

This man's confidence didn't go deep. He was borne up by something like physical hopefulness. Whether he was certain that he would be vindicated, or whether he should be, Humphrey couldn't penetrate. But Humphrey was sure that, long before this trouble, all his life, Thirkill had never had the underlying confidence of less aggressive characters such as Luria or young Paul Mason. And, though it didn't occur to Humphrey, he might have added himself. Thirkill, though, had reserves and compensations none of them possessed, great attacking force, and a savage will. Whether his will was stronger than other men's, that needed testing; but it was constantly in operation, and listening, one couldn't escape the pressure of his will.

The strongest impression of all was that Tom Thirkill had a touch, probably more than a touch, of paranoia. It was that that made his tone begin to grind. He felt surrounded by enemies. He was asking for help. Like a good many people who felt persecuted, he might have something to feel persecuted about. It wasn't an uncommon blend, the naive demands for support and protection and the ferocious, intense, attacking venom. It was a blend, Humphrey had sometimes thought, that had much appeal for decent good-natured persons, particularly among the young. Not so much as you grew older. You discovered that such natures took but never gave. But Humphrey could understand that Thirkill had a following in the center of his own party, moderate sensible men who wanted to protect him and who at the same time succumbed to something stronger than charm. Such men gave him hero worship. They were his power base in politics, as a parliamentarian could have told Humphrey before now.

In that tête-à-tête, meal finished, Thirkill hadn't given up the initiative. As they rose, he rapped out a question as though at random, "You're a friend of Mrs. Lefroy's, so I'm told?"

Humphrey answered with a neutral yes. As they got into the car outside, Thirkill persisted, "You're a close friend of Kate Lefroy's, I hear? You know that my daughter works for her."

Humphrey again said yes, he did know that.

Driving up Sloane Street, Thirkill went on, "My daughter is having dinner with that Lord Loseby tonight. What does Kate think of him?"

Humphrey was ready to evade this cross-examination.

"Do you think she's seen much of him? I should rather doubt it."

"Kate's a shrewd woman, isn't she?"

Humphrey didn't reply. Thirkill said, "You'd better stop by at my place. I expect you can use another drink, can't you?"

It was early, and now that he was prepared, Humphrey was curious to see where Thirkill was leading. Yes, he would enjoy a nightcap.

There were no more questions until they were sitting in Thirkill's drawing room. It was one of the high and handsome Eaton Square reception rooms made for nineteenth-century soirées, and it was handsomely furnished. Either Tom Thirkill or his wife (who was living in their country house, so Humphrey had picked up) had taste, a taste not frightened nor overmodest. On the walls hung a Matthew Smith, a Samuel Palmer, a Sickert, a picture that looked like a bright and glorious pastiche of Veronese, and (what surprised Humphrey most) a de Kooning.

Before Humphrey was given a drink, Thirkill had left the room and was away some minutes. When he came back, he said, "The girl's not in yet." Then he went to a cupboard, masked in the paneling, and told Humphrey to come and choose for himself. Thirkill didn't drink, but his acquaintances did, and they were duly provided for.

Each of them in deep chairs, Thirkill leaned forward in his demanding posture and said, "You haven't told me yet what Kate Lefroy thinks of that young man."

"You mean Loseby?"

"Who do you think I mean?"

"I don't see how she can have much idea, you know. She certainly hasn't said much to me. Of course, I don't see her all that often."

"Don't you?" That was attacking, edged with meaning.

"She's very busy. You realize that, don't you? Your daughter must have told you."

Thirkill had free energy to spare on suspicions over Humphrey and Kate. Maybe Susan had them too. Humphrey was ready to be noncommittal until Thirkill got tired. But Thirkill had a greater imperative.

"I want to hear about the young man Loseby. Is he any good?"

"He's very engaging."

"Is he any good for my daughter?"

"How can anyone judge that?"

"Is he a playboy?" The tone was grinding.

49

"You ought to ask his friends. He's extremely pleasant to meet. If you ask me, though, possibly yes."

"Susan has made mistakes before. She's only twenty-three, but she's made mistakes. I'm not going to have another. If this fellow lets her down, then he'll have to reckon with me. I want to see her married. That'll calm her down. She's a good girl. Does Kate say she's a good girl?"

"Of course, Kate is very fond of her."

Thirkill didn't give up. "That family of Loseby's is no good. No earthly good. All they have is an estate they can't keep up. No money. Grandmother was a society tart. Father useless. Useless drunk. Living in a tax haven in Morocco. Why he wants a tax haven God only knows. There can't be anything in the way of tax to pay. This boy is fooling around in the army. Precious lot of use that is. The best he can hope for is to make colonel. If he's lucky."

Then he made another appeal for sympathy. "I wouldn't mind so much about that. Money's no problem for a daughter of mine. All I want to be sure of is that he'd be good to her." After a pause, he added, "Mind you, it mightn't be any good for me."

"Whatever do you mean?"

"Haven't you thought what some of my precious colleagues would say, if my daughter married into that crowd?"

Humphrey permitted himself a breath of realism. If Tom Thirkill, living in state in Eaton Square, thought he could ingratiate himself with the militant left, he had temporarily lost his political senses. Further, Humphrey still hadn't seen a case, even in the England of the 1970s, where a connection with the aristocracy, however down at heel, hadn't done a public figure more good than harm.

For once, Thirkill had the grace to laugh. It was a gritty laugh, but it broke out. Humphrey was thinking, the man wasn't often simple, but now he was. He was nothing but an anxious father. He wanted to see his daughter married. In secret, he might like to see her married to a future marquess, but above all he wanted to see her safe. As the minutes passed, he was violently hoping to see her come in happy and tell him that she was engaged. The minutes passed. The man was anxious, and when he pressed Humphrey to stay, he felt compelled to. He took another drink. They had been sitting there, making spasmodic talk, the attacking force gone out of Thirkill, for an hour and a half—it was getting on for midnight—when the outer door of the apartment banged to. Thirkill's face opened with expectation, anxiety, hope. More minutes passed. Then there was the sound of another door shutting. Thirkill sat in silence. Finally he said, "She must have gone to bed."

6

The following evening, Monday, Humphrey sat in the Square garden, watching for Kate to come home from her hospital. When she had parked her car and he had stopped her, she was already frowning. He gave her an account of what had happened the night before, and the frown deepened, a furrow where there was already a line becoming permanent in the high forehead. "Susan hasn't spoken a word all day," she said.

"I was afraid of that."

"The man's a shit." Kate was in a bitter temper. He was used to her in her lively spirit, not often like this. She was angry with herself because she hadn't been immune to Loseby's blandishments. She was angry with Susan because there was someone she was fond of and couldn't help. She was angry with Humphrey because he brought, or crystallized, bad news.

"Thank you for trying," she said, but Humphrey, feeling ill treated, thought that one day he might remind her that thanks like that were more efforts of politeness than demonstrations of gratitude.

She didn't want to listen to anything more about the Thirkills. "I must rush," she said and forced a smile better shaped but less attractive than her habitual cheerful, disrespectful, ugly grin.

The heat remained constant. People used to complaining about changes in the weather were now complaining because it didn't change. It was Monday, July 12, and at eleven o'clock, when Humphrey went for a saunter around the Square, though the night was getting dark it was still so hot that the air seemed palpable against his cheeks. Lights were shining in the windows. In some, standard lamps were visible and pictures along the walls. Humphrey didn't know the owners and from the pavement couldn't identify the paintings: one or two were interesting but didn't compare with Tom Thirkill's.

Humphrey wasn't giving more than a random thought to the previous night, or to Susan. After all, he barely knew the girl. He was irked—more than he admitted, he was hurt—that Kate had been so brusque and shown him no affection. So far as he had sympathy to spare, it was, perversely, for Tom Thirkill. Not Tom Thirkill as an operator—Humphrey had seen enough of operators for one lifetime and was tired of them—but Tom Thirkill as a father, worrying about his daughter, that was nearer the bone. Humphrey too had worried, still worried, about his children and had been disappointed. For a singular reason. They had both elected to lead sacrificial lives.

Neither was married. His daughter, now in her mid-twenties, was ill paid, hard worked, as an assistant in a slum settlement in Liverpool. She had broken altogether with the circle in which Humphrey had been born. She had adopted a working-class accent, or, not having a good ear, her bad imitation of one. She wrote affectionate letters to Humphrey but wouldn't meet his friends. She might have had lovers; Humphrey wasn't sure. There he could feel with Thirkill. As for the son, he had qualified, with difficulty, as a doctor and then taken a job in a Catholic hospital in South Africa, in the Transkei bush, for which he had to pretend to be a Catholic, not telling the truth. That might be noble, but it seemed to Humphrey quixotry gone mad. The young man wasn't bright, wasn't amusing, but Humphrey loved him. Fatherhood, as the Japanese used to say, was a darkness of the heart.

As Humphrey turned at the end of the Square, he saw light in one of Lady Ashbrook's windows, on the floor above her drawing room. That jolted him from his brooding about his children. The light must come from her bedroom—is she lying awake? The results of her tests could come any day now. How was she getting through the nights?

He had thought all that before; there was nothing fresh to think, it soon passed out of mind.

53

In fact, at that moment Lady Ashbrook was sitting up in bed, attempting to read a detective story. She had never read much, and detective stories were all she could think of reading now. But none of them had captured her attention, and, with the foreboding that news from the hospital was only days, or maybe hours, away, with this one she could not remember the page she had just looked at. She had taken two sleeping pills, Seconals, but sleep would not come. Why did one want to sleep so much? It would have seemed more sensible to hold on to the conscious minutes, and yet, if death was certain next day, perhaps one would still want to sleep. She did not preserve to herself the stark front that she showed to others. She was craving that time would stand still. Like someone waiting for a letter by tomorrow's post, a letter bringing black news that she already knew, she craved that tomorrow wouldn't come. While time didn't move on, she was safe.

If anyone had come into the room, she would have admitted nothing. She had taken care of her going-to-bed appearance after dinner, with the discipline of a lifetime, and if any visitors had called, she would have greeted them in the armor of her caustic style.

She certainly would not have admitted the answer to Humphrey's speculation about the Sunday morning. Had she prayed for herself in church? She wouldn't have admitted even the question to herself, let alone the answer. But yes, she had prayed. She had prayed as she knelt stiff backed before the service. She had prayed again that Monday night, though she hadn't knelt at the bedside. The prayers were simple but had an anxious concentration on exact detail, as though God were likely to misunderstand or cheat. *Let me hear good news this week. I mean, let me hear that I am healthy and that there is nothing malignant, that is, no sign of a malignant growth.*

There was another woman lying sleepless in bed that night. It was Susan, the girl to whom Humphrey hadn't given much thought in that evening stroll. To him, and to most of those who met her, it might have been a surprise to realize the state in which she was seething. She seemed too gentle, inoffensive, almost mouselike—intelligent, so Kate said, but lazy. Some of that was true, but she was lying in a passion of sorrow and even more of violent disappointment and rage. As Humphrey and Kate had inferred,

Loseby, amiably and sweetly, had evaded her on Sunday night; he couldn't make promises, except of course that he would see her soon: his compassionate leave was over, and he would be obliged to fly back to Germany next day.

Susan longed for him, for his body. She existed to be married to him. He was slipping away. She wanted to see him dead. She had thrashed around for any surcease. She got to the point of calling his regiment's number in Germany and then slammed the telephone down. She wanted to go into the streets and offer herself to the first man she saw. Anyone would do who would be kind to her, that friendly American professor, Paul Mason, anyone. She trusted no one. She didn't trust Loseby; no one could. She didn't trust her father. She was loyal about him with others. She would go on being loyal, but she didn't trust him. After Loseby, she trusted no one. She had never trusted Loseby. Perhaps she had never trusted her father. In secret perhaps she believed that her father was a crook. In her rage that night, she was certain of it. She wanted them all dead. She would have welcomed death herself. She couldn't keep still in bed. She kicked, fidgeted, turned. No kind of sex would help for more than moments. Into the scented bedroom air, she howled. She thought about accidents, air crashes, bombs. They talked about nuclear war. She imagined that it might come, annihilating all of them, most of all herself, her shame, grief, passion, humiliation, longing. She wanted the end of it all.

7

About ten in the morning on Thursday, July 15, the telephone rang in Humphrey's sitting room. He had been sitting by the windows reading a newspaper, and it took him a dozen steps to get across the long room. He heard his own name, in a strained, jerky voice that he didn't recognize. Then, "This is Doctor Perryman speaking."

"Well?"

"I have Lady Ashbrook's permission to tell you." Tone still strained.

Humphrey was ready for fatality. "Go on."

"She's in the clear. They can't find anything. No sign at all."

"Good God Almighty." On the instant, Humphrey was astonished, nothing but astonished. "Wonderful," he said. Simple visceral relief was taking over. "I must say I'm surprised. Are you surprised?"

"You can never tell," came the doctor's voice, flat, noncommittal. He sounded as though he was sternly keeping any excitement down—but Humphrey would have liked to see his face.

Humphrey congratulated him. Perryman said that he had done nothing. Humphrey asked how she was. She was alone, so far as Perryman knew, and obviously there was no reason why Humphrey shouldn't pay a call.

It was some time before Humphrey set out along the Square. First he telephoned Kate at her hospital. No, she hadn't heard, but her response was more immediate than his own had been.

"Heavens, I am so glad. What a bit of news." When Kate was happy, Humphrey thought, she was happy from the soles of her feet to the top of her head. Maybe when she was unhappy, the same. She said that she would send some flowers at once and told him that he must take flowers himself. When she was happy, he also thought, she took charge. He duly went into Elizabeth Street, bought a large assembly of peonies and lupins, and carried them on his way to Lady Ashbrook's.

This time the door was opened by Maria, the daily woman. She was small, sturdy, bright-eyed, smiling. She tried to speak English but had very little. She radiated pleasure. Humphrey talked to her slowly in Portuguese. This wasn't one of his languages, but his Portuguese was better than her English. Yes, the lady was well. Nothing bad. Nothing to trouble her. All anxiety had gone away, dismissed. It was a beautiful day, like the sun outside. Maria would be more than unusually eloquent, he was sure, if there weren't a linguistic barrier. One might have thought that Lady Ashbrook wasn't easy to work for, but Maria seemed to like her.

In the drawing room, Lady Ashbrook was sitting bolt upright in her usual chair.

"Oh, Humphrey," she said. "You shouldn't have taken the trouble to come." He went and kissed her cheek.

"Do you really think I would keep away? We don't get anything like this every day, now do we?"

"I suppose that's fair enough," she said, control complete, giving no indication of joy. She was regarding the mass of lupins.

"Thank you very much, my dear. You had better tell Maria to look after them. I've had quite a few flowers already." She spoke as though flowers were the least likely objects to be sent to her and as though she had no conceivable affection for them.

"Do sit down, Humphrey. Forgive me for not getting up. To tell you the truth, I've found all this—just a trifle wearing."

"Most people would have found it worse than that."

"Would they?" she said. She showed a flicker of cool, remote interest. "I take it, it's rather too early for you to have a drink?"

That, Humphrey decided, was a question requiring the answer yes. With the same coolness the old lady asked him for one favor. She wasn't much good at managing calls to the Continent. Could she trouble him to get the news to Loseby? "I think he might be a little gratified, perhaps." Had Humphrey seen Paul and Celia recently? They must have been in touch with someone. "If you ask Maria, you'll find that they have sent me some more of those flowers." She uttered the word as though it were in italics. "Very kind of them, I must say, very well meant."

There was a pause. She appeared to be musing. She gave a hard smile, sarcastic but confiding.

"Humphrey," she said, "I suppose this is rather a turn up for the book."

That struck him as a peculiar remark, coming from her—or in the circumstances coming from anyone else. It was as near an expression of emotion as she could make: somehow it conveyed emotion, both the fatigue of extreme, almost apathetic relief, and also so much joy that she wanted to pretend it didn't exist, to go on propitiating all the fates. Recovering herself from this display, she commanded, "Tell everyone that I won't have any fuss. They can get back to normal as far as I am concerned."

Her way of getting back to normal was to talk with approval of Loseby's visit.

"He's a good boy," she said. "He's not as soft as he looks." She looked with bleak interrogation at Humphrey. "Don't you agree that he's a good boy?"

"He's very good fun," said Humphrey.

"More than that. He's got his head screwed on."

"I dare say that's true."

"Of course it's true. He knows a few things. He knows when a passade has to end."

That was a word from her youth, already out of use when Humphrey was a boy.

"He is *traveled*," she went on. "He gave me a hint, all very discreet. He sent that little Thirkill girl about her business."

At which Lady Ashbrook remembered that she had asked Humphrey to get a message through to Loseby. "Perhaps you wouldn't mind doing it at once? There's no reason to keep the boy in suspense. If he is in suspense, that is."

"He's very fond of you," said Humphrey.

"That would be most unusual in my family," she replied, emitting a harsh but not unappealing laugh. Then she had another thought. Would Humphrey mind making just one other telephone call? She would like to see her solicitor. She felt that it would be a suitable time to make a new will.

"My family might be interested if they knew that I was doing that," she remarked. "Not that there's much money to be interested in, my dear. When I go, everyone will be astonished at how little I cut up for." She laughed again.

"Are you telling the truth?"

"What do you think, my dear?"

At this piece of mystification, she seemed obscurely triumphant.

Some of her acquaintances did "get back to normal" without effort. It was just the end of a minor excitement. There was a certain letdown, a drop in the emotional temperature, and they went back to more direct concerns, how much the stock market and the pound were falling, how good it was to feel excited by a man again, or whether there was a chance of more briefs next session. With a group of them, however, it was no use Lady Ashbrook saying that she wouldn't have any fuss. They were determined that she should have it, whether she wanted it or not: and they didn't trust instructions of that kind, in which they were right.

They made their plans later that day in Paul Mason's house. Meanwhile, Lady Ashbrook had gone through the routine from which, in the days of anxiety, she had not once departed. She performed her afternoon promenade in the garden, waving her parasol at Humphrey, on his afternoon walk to buy a paper, and to other passersby. She walked for a somewhat longer time and sat for a somewhat shorter than on recent afternoons, and held her parasol more firmly above her head. Otherwise, the routine was unchanged: though in the early evening her solicitor appeared, duly summoned by Humphrey.

It was half past six, Kate back from her hospital, Paul from his office, Celia from her young son, when the meeting took place in Paul's sitting room. This, as in Kate's house, was in the old-fashioned manner partitioned off from another room, which he used as a study. The sitting room had a bareness austere and masculine, or perhaps more exactly the bareness of a man with no instinct and no special desire for comfort. There was an expensive-looking writing desk, which some woman might have coerced him into buying. Humphrey, who had joined the other three in that room, was curious about a number of pictures in a manner vaguely neoexpressionist. Whoever painted them might be an amateur but had talent. He asked Paul who it was. Celia. Humphrey gazed at Celia and said that he hoped she would go on painting.

"Why not?" she said, undisturbed. Then she inquired in the same equable tone, "Do you know about pictures?"

Humphrey said, "I've looked at a good few in my time."

That was an understatement, and Kate's eyes flashed at him with confidential gibing. Just once, she had told him that he slipped into anonymity as if it were an overcoat. Humphrey didn't mind. He wouldn't try to change his style, and, as soon as they all talked of Lady Ashbrook, he was infected, and warmed, by the feeling in the room. They were healthy people, and, apart from himself, they were young and active with the pride of life. Healthy people took a usual pleasure in others getting better. Often they had to accept the sight of the sick, but they felt part of the trade union of humans when one recovered. It was a bit of a triumph when someone came out of death's shadow. Humphrey didn't pretend that people, healthy or not, were afflicted by the news of another's death, but sometimes they did get a modest, comradely pleasure at the news that someone was going to survive. That was not all, however, in Paul's sitting room that evening. Their pleasure wasn't only comradely and modest, but as though the old lady were very close to them, like a relative whom they had loved in childhood.

Strange, Humphrey was thinking. They had more affection, as well as regard, for the old lady than he had. Perhaps not so strange. Often it was the cold and ungiving who attracted most loyalty. There was a certain kind of chill, such as Lady Ashbrook possessed, that somehow others revered, were afraid of, and that against any reasonable judgment made them put the owner on a pedestal. So far as moral worth meant anything, in Humphrey's view Kate here had a hundred times more of it than Lady Ashbrook: but he was sure that, if Kate were in extremity, she wouldn't receive a fraction of the devotion that that self-bound old woman was getting now. It was an absurd disposition of providence, but then providence had a knack of being absurd. And Kate was as joyous and enthusiastic about their plans that night as anyone present, and the most spontaneous.

What should they do? Lady Ashbrook was too old to stand much of a celebration. She wasn't strong enough to be taken out. Anyway, Humphrey said that he was certain she wouldn't play. A few people to meet her?

"Not like that bridge party on Sunday," Kate said. "Awful, so I hear." She was smiling at Humphrey, the only source from whom she could have heard.

"That wasn't exactly well timed," Paul added. "Lancelot Loseby seemed to think that no one had any nerves."

"He had reasons of his own." Celia spoke in her cool gnomic fashion and as one totally unmoved by Loseby's arts.

Nerves were stable now. There was no more need for touching wood, they all agreed. She might be pleased to see that others were pleased. Where should it happen? Her own house? No, that wouldn't wash, she wouldn't do it.

"I can lay it on," Kate said with hesitation. "Would that be too far for her?"

No, she walked to the end of the garden most days, that was opposite Kate's house—or someone could drive her around.

"Of course," said Kate without any hesitation this time, but giving the clue to her first, "I'm not her favorite woman."

"I don't think that would trouble her." Humphrey felt that they were all overconcerned with Lady Ashbrook's sensibilities. "She's never had any manners. Not manners of the heart, I mean. You might have noticed that."

"She seems to have put up with me." Celia said it without vanity, with mild surprise. "I never have been able to see why."

Humphrey said to Kate, "It would mean extra work for you. You've got enough."

"Nonsense. I can manage this on my head."

There was some argument, but both this house of Paul's and also Humphrey's were only equipped as bachelor rooms, and Celia's was too far away.

"It'll cost something. You mustn't spend a penny." Humphrey was, for once, giving an instruction to Kate.

"Oh, I can manage all right."

This she was not allowed to do. Paul said that he would pay. They knew he had more disposable money than anyone there, a large salary from his bank, private means.

When should it be? After the weekend? Early next week, perhaps Monday. Who should be asked? Kate was firm, positive, cheerful.

Diffidence all gone. They mustn't overwhelm the old lady: themselves, other acquaintances whom she appeared to tolerate. Also the doctor who had been involved. None of the grand relics of the twenties who lived in the neighborhood—over whom, however, Lady Ashbrook, expecting them to be disappointed that she was still extant, might, so Humphrey thought, have liked to gloat. Then Kate said, "I shall ask Susan Thirkill. And her beastly father."

"Susan?" Humphrey was taken aback. "I shouldn't have thought—"

He couldn't repeat what he had heard that morning, but both Paul and Celia had a shrewd notion of how Loseby had behaved. They all felt that Kate was being callous, but she stuck to it.

"It might do her good," she said.

"I'm not sure that life is a moral gymnasium." Humphrey was cross with her.

"No, she has to face things. You never know what will turn up."

She seemed to be less practical than usual, moved either by a forlorn hope or intention. Then she said that she would invite Alec Luria.

"Lady A. detests him," Paul protested.

"Never mind, it might do her good." She gave Humphrey a defiant grin. "He'd enjoy it, and he'd add a bit of distinction. Also, I like him, and I'm not going to keep him out. Lady A. shouldn't have her own way all the time. She'll have to get used to ours."

With that vigorous statement, Kate closed the discussion. Actually, they were all in spirits both serene and high. It was a little piece of domestic arrangement, prosaic, nothing in it, but they were in tune with each other, warmed by something like a group emotion, as they might have felt working at a purpose more significant than this.

8

Lady Ashbrook was on her best behavior in the Lefroys' house on the Monday evening. Escorted by Paul, she had insisted on going there on foot, walking slowly but erect across the top of the Square and then down the length of the far side. Although there was no shade, she did not put up her parasol but held it in a white-gloved hand as though she were at a garden party; ignoring sunshine, like other material things; telling Paul, in a tone less caustic than he had heard, that they must arrive at 6:25 P.M. precisely. "If they're giving a reception in one's honor, one has to be five minutes early." She went on, "Very obliging of them, I must say. I suppose I am the guest of honor. Though it does seem slightly ridiculous. Just for surviving, I believe. But I'm not the only survivor in the world, don't you agree?"

When they reached the house, Monty Lefroy, not Kate, was waiting at the door. He greeted her in state.

"I am very glad to have you in my house, Lady Ashbrook," he said with a grandiloquent gesture, arms open wide. He had presence, as statuesque as Alec Luria's, though most would have considered with less reason. He stood as though certain of being recognized.

"It is extremely kind of you to ask me, Mr. Lefroy." Surprisingly urbane, thought Paul, having previously listened to her opinion of Monty.

They guarded her on her way upstairs, though she would take

63

no help. Kate had pulled the sliding doors aside so that there was a drawing room as long as Lady Ashbrook's own.

"How are you, Mrs. Lefroy?" Lady Ashbrook nodded to Kate. "I was telling your husband that you are extremely kind."

Kate gave an unconfident smile but said that, before others came, she wanted to get Lady Ashbrook into a chair at the far end. Outside that window loomed an ash tree in the Lefroy patio. "Cooler there." Kate was more than usually brisk, being more than usually diffident. "They'll all want to gather round."

"How kind. How kind." Lady Ashbrook's voice descended to its lowest register.

Lady Ashbrook was already installed before Humphrey entered the room. He was followed by young men and women, some of whom he didn't know. Kate and Paul had recognized that Lady Ashbrook, so far as she liked company, liked that of the young. One or two were distant relatives, collected by Paul; one or two were friends of distant relatives. Celia came in and was at once welcomed.

"Celia. My dear," cried the old lady resonantly and presented her cheek.

Alec Luria was not welcomed so fervently. "Professor Luria, isn't it?" Susan Thirkill, shy and sullen, didn't go near the focal chair. Humphrey noticed, to his surprise, that she looked less ravaged than when he had seen her in that house before. When she talked, though she wasn't smiling, to one of the young men, Humphrey recognized for the first time what a pretty girl she was. Tom Thirkill had led his daughter in, and detached observers had the pleasure of watching him and Monty Lefroy compete for the monopoly of Lady Ashbrook. Neither succeeded. She caught the eyes of Humphrey and Paul, requiring them to flank her.

Tom Thirkill was soon a center of attraction on his own. In spite, or because, of what they had read about him, the young clustered around. He looked entirely relaxed, far more glittering than when alone with any single person. Yes, Humphrey admitted, the man had film-star qualities.

Paul had ordered plenty of liquor, but, for a London party, not much was being drunk. By sheer chance, most of the guests were relatively abstemious, Monty safeguarding his valuable health, Luria out of lifelong custom, the young because of a change of habit—all making Humphrey appear as though he were sousing. Still, the party was going well and, as it happened, was one that a good many of those present came to remember.

Lady Ashbrook wasn't put out of humor by the presence of those she disapproved of, or despised—the Thirkills, that Jewish character whom everyone listened to. She had been brushing off such as those all her life. What she didn't like was the spectacle of her own contemporaries, ladies who had been sought after in her own youth. They were reminders of mortality. There was no such spectacle to affront her. No dinosaurs, Kate and Paul had agreed, and there were none that evening. In private, Paul had allowed himself to say that one dinosaur was quite enough.

So, Tom Thirkill surrounded by the admiring or the inquisitive, or both, Luria having an earnest discussion with Monty Lefroy, Lady Ashbrook cheerful with her male companions—the level of contentment was high. It was a rare event, so far as Humphrey could recall, but Lady Ashbrook was even heard to reminisce, which, the past being the past, was not one of her indulgences. She was reminiscing about Edwardian house parties. "I keep noticing," she said to Paul, "that you and your friends always call people by their Christian name."

"Usually," Paul replied.

"Almost from the word *go*."

"Almost before it."

"It wasn't so when I was a girl, you know," she said. "It can't have been so in your time, Humphrey."

"It was just coming in."

"There was nothing to be said for those horrible weekends in country houses. They were the most boring form of entertainment anyone ever had. If you came down to breakfast, you saw extraordinarily boring young men—I may be imagining it, but they seemed to have collars up to their chins, saying to each other 'Goin' for a grind, Postlethwaite?' 'Not a bad idea, Cuthbertson.' And they'd never call each other anything else as long as they lived."

Lady Ashbrook had given a spirited imitation of a version of an upper-class English which some thought she still spoke. In fact, she didn't drop her final *g*s: the only relic of that odd usage was that she wouldn't pronounce the *g* in *strength*. Paul was thinking something different. If she was so observant of the customs around her,

65

she shouldn't have called Kate, whom she knew well, Mrs. Lefroy. But Lady Ashbrook, though she had the formal manners that made her take care to arrive in time, could never, as Humphrey had told them, have had any trace of the manners of the heart.

Lady Ashbrook was happy. So were most of those present. It wasn't like that star-crossed Sunday. The real reason was simple. For all but one or two who had their own anxieties, there was, when they looked at the old lady, stately in her chair, no suspense because she had none herself.

Although it was so hot, everyone, about as thoughtfully as so many bees, had swarmed into the inner half of the room within a couple of yards of Tom Thirkill's and Lady Ashbrook's chairs. There the temperature had mounted; so had the vocal buzz. In the melee Celia was able to talk quietly to Humphrey without dislodging him from his post beside the old lady.

"This is rather a good occasion," she said.

"I am glad we did it," Humphrey replied.

Monty Lefroy, now circulating with patronizing grandeur, as befitted one who took it for granted that he would be deferred to, had overheard them. In his fine, resonant, modulated voice, he told them, "How right you are. I'm *very glad* we did it. I'm very glad we *did* it."

"It's entirely Kate's doing," said Celia in her most remote manner, no more impressed by consciousness of importance than she was by cultivated charm.

"She's a wonderful woman." Monty, unperturbed, spoke as though he were giving Kate a blessing. "She's been a great help to me, an enormous help."

"Oh, yes?" Celia's voice came from a greater distance still.

"You're preaching to the converted, dear girl," said Monty, blessing Kate again. "I don't know what I should have done without her." He turned toward Humphrey and another subject. "I have been talking to your friend Luria. He's a very intelligent man. I was impressing on him that to solve any of the difficult problems you have to be able to think of nothing else, literally nothing else, for forty minutes a day. It doesn't sound very much, I said, but very very few people in intellectual history have ever been able to do it. It's extremely tiring. I find that it gets more tiring still as one gets older. It makes one sleep. I sleep night and day. *Night and day.*"

66

"Have you solved your problem?" Celia's question was uninflected, not innocent.

"We shall see. We shall see. I expect to begin my book soon."

"How long will it take you to write?" Another uninflected question.

"Some years. One can't rush these things. It will be quite a short book. Two hundred pages, perhaps. Less if possible. The shorter the better. I want to say everything I've thought out."

Once more with the air of benediction he passed on. Humphrey had taken no part in the conversation. Celia was regarding him, he noticed, with something like pity. What she said might have been irrelevant, a casual thought. It was a simple inquiry.

"What do you want to happen?" She watched him with clear eyes, her expression composed and friendly.

"What do you mean, happen?"

"I mean it's not enough for you, just sitting on the sidelines, is it?"

It could have seemed impertinent, from someone not much older than his own daughter. He didn't feel it so. He believed that she knew the answer. She couldn't expect him to give it now. Even if they had been alone, he would have been too secretive or too suspicious to be honest. So he said, "Oh, I take short views. The old Sydney Smith prescriptions for keeping up your spirits. At lunchtime don't think further than dinner. That way, one gets along."

"That won't satisfy you forever, will it? It won't satisfy me—"

Now he could evade talking about himself.

"What do you want to happen, then?"

"I rather wish I knew." She gazed at him totally frankly, uncushioned, demanding nothing. "No, I'm not unhappy. I'm not a depressive. If Paul has a bit of that, I haven't. Perhaps I might stir myself more if I were. I think I should like to paint a few good pictures, but no, I'm not obsessed enough about that."

"You'll get married again, won't you?"

"I'm not sure, you know. I'm not obsessed enough even about that." She said it with a curiously girlish smile. She was echoing herself, jeering at herself. "I wasn't particularly successful at it last time, was I? And I'm not everyone's cup of tea."

"Come off it. Paul would marry you tomorrow."

"He would. If he thought I wanted it. Or needed it. Paul is a dutiful man. But I'm not sure I shouldn't do him harm."

"You love him, don't you?" Humphrey found himself talking as easily as if he and Celia had once been married.

"Oh, yes, I love him very much. Much more than he loves me. But I'm not sure I could live the life his wife would have to. Whatever he says, he's made for the big game. He may even think he can get out of it, but I'm positive he won't. I couldn't cope with the kind of life he's walking into. I should curl up inside. It's all right being a girl friend. But before long he'll want a hostess. I shouldn't be any use at that. It would frighten me off."

"You're too hard on yourself."

"I don't think so."

"I would have thought it was something he had to decide."

She wasn't asking for reassurance, and he didn't offer any more. She seemed utterly self-sufficient.

More noise around them. Lady Ashbrook was wearing her haughtiest smile, possibly after some remark of extreme wickedness, and was being cheered on by those around her. Celia looked straight at Humphrey and repeated, not with irony, quite simply, "This is rather a good occasion, isn't it?"

An hour or so later, Humphrey was walking across to his house with Alec Luria beside him. Talking to Celia, Humphrey had firmly produced the stoical instruction, take short views: but to himself he didn't seem specially apt at obeying it. Luria was saying he had heard Monty Lefroy called a recluse, but he hadn't looked like that in the party they had just left. It had been interesting to see him walking about his own drawing room, preening himself.

Taking short views didn't soothe Humphrey. When he had watched that sight without such detached interest it had filled him with wishes, or even scenarios, for the future.

"Preening himself. A bit of *folie de grandeur*. The way he throws his head back—you've seen that before, in cases of folie, haven't you?"

"I dare say," Humphrey muttered.

"To be sure," Luria went on reflecting, "he's not a nobody. I reckon that there was something in him once. They must have thought he had great promise. Not so pleasant, when people tell you you have wonderful promise and then wait for something to happen. It was an occupational hazard among classmates of mine. Another of the Jewish fatalities. Of course, he's not Jewish, at least

I shouldn't think so, but I could have shown you a few like him in the Village when they all still lived there."

"I dare say."

"Women used to fall for them. It's not so surprising after all that Kate fell for him."

"I dare say." Humphrey suddenly came out of his reverie and spoke brusquely. "She might have found someone better. That would have been more tolerable."

Luria, who had been casting around with a fishing line, wanted to speak directly to his friend. But he gazed at the profile alongside, closed and obstinate, and was certain that this wasn't the right time.

One person who was able to take short views, and was actively doing so, was Tom Thirkill. That was a help, perhaps a necessity, in the political life. Writs had duly been issued and gossip was muffled. *Private Eye* had been daring enough to publish another attack. That had evoked a second writ. Thirkill's lawyers said that it would double the damages. Thirkill might lack ultimate confidence, he might feel persecuted, but feeling persecuted made the adrenalin flow, and he became more active than ever. "The Lord," he said to colleagues, "hath delivered them—." There was a major satisfaction in seeing enemies walk into a trap.

He had made a speech in the Commons on the Thursday before Kate's party, the day of Lady Ashbrook's reprieve: it was on the currency market where he was in technical terms a master. He had received more admiration than ever before in Parliament, except from his own left wing. This was like an actor's triumph. Nothing existed but the speech, the applause, the press next day. It was easy, it was first nature, for Tom Thirkill to take short views.

His engagement book was dark with entries, and that also kept the adrenalin flowing. It did, however, mean that he had to look three weeks ahead before he could discharge an obligation. Thirkill had an obsession that he wouldn't accept hospitality without returning it. He owed Humphrey Leigh a meal: Humphrey was no use to him, but the debt had to be paid. The same with Kate: she had to be paid off.

Thirkill consulted his chief political adviser, his only intimate. This was Mrs. Armstrong, Stella Armstrong. The name was beginning to be known in inner circles in Westminster. She was a woman of Kate's age. She was the one human being with whom Tom Thirkill had no gritty residue of suspicion. With her he became something like ingenuous or naive. For some time in the Commons, there had been gossip about what their relations really were.

Yes, said Stella Armstrong, if he wouldn't be happy unless he had wiped Humphrey and Kate off his obligations, he had better do so. What about turning the meal to some use? Lady Ashbrook—he had met her now—would she come? Most of his colleagues were remarkably snobbish; they would like to meet one of the last grandes dames. Further, you never knew what might happen about Susan. She talked as though Susan were her own daughter. He might get snubbed by the old lady, and snubs added to persecution: but she assumed that he would take worse snubs in the chase for anything that Susan wanted.

His expression clouded; his voice had gone gravel-rough. "I don't know about that old woman," he said. Then he put on his firm fighting smile. Still, he might as well impress useful people. Every little helped. You never knew, the jobs might be going around soon.

It would have to be a luncheon, Stella decided. She had heard that the old lady never went out to dinner. Luncheon at Eaton Square wouldn't be physically difficult for her, if she chose to come at all. The first day Thirkill was free was Friday, July 30; the House wasn't likely to be sitting. So invitations went out, and they waited, with a certain tension, for Lady Ashbrook's response. Stella Armstrong thought that he was tense with waiting, but that she was used to.

❧ 9 ❧

When Humphrey woke on Monday morning, a week after Kate's party, a line of sunlight was bright between the curtains, and a breath of air freshened the room. It was half past seven, and outside, the Square was as usual very quiet. He didn't need to hurry himself into consciousness. He could draw out the minutes, during which the only sound was a car starting some distance away. Then there was another sound, something unexpected in the middle of the great town, horses' hooves slowly, precisely, walking.

Humphrey was used to this. It was soothing; it brought back vague memories of childhood. Actually, it was nothing more of an invocation than a couple of police horses being trained in London streets, of which those in that neighborhood were the least frightening. He couldn't hear much else from three floors up—perhaps the faintest patter of footsteps, the postman, a boy delivering morning papers.

Humphrey was still half dozing. On a waft of morning air, the smell, just perceptible, of geraniums. The weekend had passed without incident: his ritual drink with Alec Luria on Saturday evening, the pub as sedate as it had ever been, on Sunday a lunch with old acquaintances out at Richmond. That was all. He had never been fond of the social life, now less than ever. He had nothing to do on the coming day.

As he lay dozing, there was a tap, a couple of impatient taps, on

71

the bedroom door. The door opened—"Mr. Humphrey! Mr. Humphrey!"

His housekeeper, Mrs. Burbridge, was standing beside the bed. She was a woman in her early seventies, blooming, healthy, as a rule unfussed. But she was not unfussed that morning.

"I'm sorry, Mr. Humphrey. It's the foreign girl, Lady Ashbrook's daily. I can't make her out much. She's asking for you. I'm afraid something's happened to her ladyship."

"What has happened?" Humphrey had come full awake.

"I'm afraid she's dead."

Mrs. Burbridge couldn't tell him more. She found Maria incomprehensible, except that she was asking for Humphrey and seemed to want him to return with her to Lady Ashbrook's house. Humphrey said that he would soon be ready and shortly followed Mrs. Burbridge downstairs.

Maria was standing in the hall, Mrs. Burbridge with an arm around her shoulders. Maria was a sturdy young woman not given to excitement. She wasn't crying, but her face opened when she saw him, and she broke into a stream of her own language. It is horrible, he thought she was saying, and then lost the rest. He had to tell her to speak slowly: he didn't really understand Portuguese, but he would have to try.

"She has been killed," said Maria and crossed herself. Those words were clear, but Humphrey couldn't believe it. A stroke he had been expecting, any sort of sudden death. Not this.

He questioned Maria incredulously. How did she know the old lady had been killed? Was she certain? "You will see," Maria replied phlegmatically. "It is horrible. Her head. Her head."

By this time, Humphrey had to believe. Suddenly, as with other violent happenings, it became certain, almost banal, like a piece of news, obviously true, that he had heard a long time before.

When did Maria discover this? Humphrey looked at his watch: it was nearly eight o'clock. Maria had gone into the drawing room to do the morning cleaning. There she was. You will see, Maria told Humphrey again. She had tried to telephone the police. She had got through to the station but wasn't sure that she had made them understand. Her English was so bad, she apologized. So she had come to Humphrey. She apologized again for giving so much trouble, but she had to find someone to talk to.

She had good nerves, Humphrey thought. Within minutes, after they had walked up the Square, they entered Lady Ashbrook's drawing room. Outside the house, the young woman had touched his sleeve and said that he must be prepared. It was a bad spectacle.

Inside the room, obliterating all else, was a smell that one didn't forget. It wasn't strong. It was sweet and light. If it had been another smell, or rather a smell from another cause, it would not have been dominant, maybe scarcely noticeable. If it had been from another cause, it might not even have been nauseous. There were pleasant smells, just as sweet, just as corrupt.

Affected by the smell, his first sight of the room was blurred. There was a curtain drawn back, the light was bright, but for an instant his eyes were jarred. Chairs were overturned, drawers gaping, lamps, trays, littered on the floor. It deadened him as though he were walking into a party with the noise full on. With peripheral vision he half realized that some pictures had been torn down. Not the Boudin, not the Vlaminck. Then, or really in the same eye flash, he saw Lady Ashbrook, and the confusion of the senses cleared away. As he looked, the smell became stronger. She was lying in front of her chair, which had been tipped onto its side. Her skirt had run up over the knees, bony knees above the thin fragile legs. Her head was raised higher than her shoulders by some support underneath invisible to Humphrey. There was darkened blood on the carpet. Not much more than if glasses of wine had been spilled. He didn't realize until later, but there were flecks of blood elsewhere, on furniture and up the wall behind her—pear-shaped drops of blood. There were also scraps of white. He realized none of that, for he was looking only at her head. He could look at nothing else. Her face was turned toward him and the door. The eyes were glaring open, the mouth wide open too. That was not what transfixed him. In a wound on her temple, there was a stirring. Maybe a maggot there already. That didn't hold his gaze. Along the top of the head, running over hair and forehead, projecting inches outward, was a shaft. It wasn't quite symmetrical above the forehead but inclined slightly to her right side and tilted a few degrees downward. It might have been a new and novel form of hat; no, more hypnotizing, a new-grown physiognomic feature.

By his side, Maria crossed herself once more. It was not until later in the morning, after the doctors had arrived, that Humphrey understood that he had been looking at the handle of the hammer, which Lady Ashbrook, for do-it-yourself purposes, kept in the tool box near to hand. The hammer head had gone through the skull into the brain. Upward from the handle, there stood the hammer claw.

Humphrey didn't move. At last he said to Maria, "Well." He spoke in English and brought out the most inadequate of all-purpose English words. "Well, there's nothing we can do. I'd better use the telephone."

In all the havoc, the telephone hadn't been interfered with, nor Lady Ashbrook's card of friends' numbers, nor her engagement book, open for that month. Absently Humphrey noticed in the space for July 30—Thirkill, 36 Eaton Square, 1:00 P.M. She had accepted that invitation.

The number of the police station wasn't on the card, but Humphrey remembered it. He spoke to the man on duty.

"This is Humphrey Leigh. I've been in the station before. I am ringing from seventy-two Aylestone Square. Lady Ashbrook's house. She's been killed. Yes, murdered. Would you report it at once? Yes, she's quite dead. I guess she's been dead a day or so."

When did Humphrey hear? A few minutes ago, said Humphrey, patiently, used to official inquiries. He had been a friend of the old lady's, and her daily woman had called him. Is the daily woman a foreigner? Yes, Humphrey answered, and there was a sound of discovery at the other end. There had been a call at 7:46; Humphrey was told, they couldn't catch the address. There was a radio car out making inquiries.

"Tell him where it is." Humphrey was brisk. Any action was better than none. "I shall be here. And send another of your chaps around. This has to be cleared up—"

"I get you, sir." That was a reply to authority: Humphrey, without thought, had dropped into a former tone of voice. "This is trouble, all right. An officer will be with you in five minutes."

Meanwhile, Humphrey was trying to reach Dr. Perryman. There would be a police doctor around soon enough, no doubt, but she might as well have her own. Perryman was visiting a patient, but his secretary promised to use his beeper and pass the message on. "Make sure he's told he can't help. She's dead. But when he has time, I think he will want to see her."

Inside the five minutes, a policeman arrived. Humphrey met him outside the drawing room. He was a tall young man, comely, physically confident. He introduced himself as Detective Sergeant and a surname Humphrey didn't catch. The policeman told Maria, who had been standing on the stairs with Humphrey, that he would need to question her. Then he and Humphrey entered the shambles of a room. At first glance, he had let out a curse, but when Humphrey said, "There she is," and looked toward the body, the young man became silent and stayed so. He stayed silent for so long that Humphrey started to speak but then cut off. The man was retching.

Humphrey himself had felt qualms at the sight of that wooden growth. He was quick nerved about emotional things, not especially squeamish about physical ones, and he had seen a good many bodies torn to pieces in war. Worse than seeing fragments of limbs and flesh, he had seen someone known to him cut in two, head and torso one way, the rest another. Like other men of his age, he had become hardened. Yet he had had to detach himself, become clinically cool, at the sight of the old lady's head. This young man must have seen corpses, certainly suicides, casualties in accidents, maybe a murder victim, but now he couldn't take it. He was gulping.

Humphrey said, "Come outside."

As they reached the corridor, the detective sergeant was forcing himself back on duty. Humphrey asked his name again, again lost it, and in the multitude of policemen's names soon to come never learned it. It could have been Robinson. His voice sounded like a man choking, but he gave his orders, "Nothing must be touched in there."

"Quite," said Humphrey.

"Have either of you touched anything up to now?" Humphrey translated to Maria, and she gave vigorous shakes of her head. She had confronted the sight in that room—the bad spectacle, as she kept calling it—with stronger intestines than the policeman's, Humphrey thought, stronger than his own.

Humphrey said that he had touched nothing except the telephone.

75

"Really, you shouldn't have used that." The young man was recovering himself. "Anyway, that's done. Nothing else? I'll have a man stationed outside until we've done all our stuff."

"Her doctor will probably be coming," Humphrey said.

"He'll have to keep his hands off too. I don't mind him having a look from the door."

A constable had just come up the stairs, the man dispatched when Maria's call had mystified the police station. The detective sergeant told him sharply to station himself just inside the drawing-room door, do nothing for the present, permit no one except the police surgeon and senior detective officers to touch or move any object in the room.

"There's a body there. She's not a nice sight, I may as well tell you," said the sergeant, in an offhand, experienced fashion, giving an excellent impersonation of a case-hardened detective who took such things without a blench.

He was getting to work. He asked Maria where there was another telephone and told the police station on Gerald Road that the detective chief inspector had to be informed. And the police surgeon as soon as the chief inspector approved. He'll want to have a look himself first, the sergeant said, becoming even more knowledgeable. Bodies don't run away. The doctor can wait half an hour. While waiting, the sergeant proceeded to score up some credit for himself. There were others taking notes, but he felt he ought to have his own on the record. He was an arrogant young man, but Humphrey rather liked him.

Humphrey had to translate for Maria. He learned little that he didn't already know, except that her husband was a waiter in a Fulham Road cafe. She had arrived that morning at her usual time, about 7:40. She had put a kettle on for coffee and then gone upstairs. She had noticed the drawing-room door was open. Then she had seen what they had all seen. She had noticed one other thing when she went down again in search of Humphrey. The door of the garden room (that is, the room giving on to the stairs that led down into the garden) was also wide open.

"That will do nicely for the present. I don't require either of you anymore, thank you. The chief inspector will want to talk to you. Thank you again." The sergeant was enjoying his last minutes in charge. He was also polite, in his offhand fashion.

76

"Oh, I didn't ask you. The next of kin ought to be informed. Can you tell me who they are?"

"She has a son, Lord Pevensey. When I last heard about him, he was living in Morocco." Humphrey had met Lord Pevensey only once in his life.

"In touch?"

"He's not been here lately, I think." Humphrey went on, "She really was in touch with her grandson. He's posted in Germany. He was visiting her a fortnight ago." If it would help, Humphrey offered to ring up the divisional headquarters and get in touch with Loseby.

By this time, half a dozen policemen were in the house, two of them in plain clothes. The local detective chief inspector heard about Humphrey's account and the possible exits and entries through the garden. He made telephone calls, had a conversation with Humphrey, made notes, and told him with affable respect that there would be time for a formal statement later. It was all quick and practiced. A police surgeon arrived, certified death, made his statement, and left, while Dr. Perryman joined Humphrey in the hall. Perryman was not allowed to go into the drawing room but, as the young policeman conceded, could watch from outside.

"This is a bad business," Perryman said to Humphrey in a reflective manner, his fine eyes not focused on the body or anything inside the room.

More policemen were arriving. "I can't do anything useful here," Perryman said to Humphrey, and they went downstairs.

"Of course," Perryman observed, as though talking to himself, "she would have died soon anyway."

"She was healthy, wasn't she?"

"She was eighty-two. She might have lived a few more years. She might have died this summer."

"Anyway," said Humphrey, "this was an ugly way to die." That was the second time a remark of Celia's left its echo.

"It may have been more merciful than the way she was frightened of," Perryman said. "They don't know how she died, do they? If that head wound killed her, she would have felt almost nothing. Not more than bumping her head against a wall. Then—no pain, just out. Some people die very easy."

"I hope she didn't know who killed her."

"What difference would that make?"

"It wouldn't be good to die in fear."

"It would soon be over. And that's the end." Dr. Perryman said it as though he were talking to a patient. "Perhaps we make too much of death after all. Our ancestors lived with it more sensibly than we do, I often think. They didn't try to pretend it doesn't happen."

All that was true. Perryman wasn't a stereotyped man, his thoughts were his own, but Humphrey had had enough of them that morning. Just as he had had enough of a piece of deviousness when he got on the telephone to Loseby's headquarters. He was answered by a girl, presumably a WAAF, cool and friendly.

"No, sir. Captain Lord Loseby isn't here at the moment. He is in England on compassionate leave."

Humphrey said surely he had returned from compassionate leave two weeks before.

"That is so, sir, but I believe he was summoned back because of his grandmother's condition last Thursday."

Humphrey had spoken to the old lady on Saturday afternoon. She was in caustic spirits, walking strongly in the Square garden. She would have been surprised to learn that Loseby had been recalled to London on her account.

"I can give you the London address we have for him, sir."

The London address was 72, Aylestone Square, London, S.W. 1.

What was Loseby playing at, one of his women? Humphrey didn't doubt that he was capable of any kind of acting. But this could be embarrassing. There were going to be police inquiries. Humphrey, like most others that day, assumed that this was a burglar's killing, but the routine would check the movements of any connection of the old lady, certainly her grandson. The police would discover this story. Humphrey wasn't certain whether it would be wiser to tell them first.

He felt worn down, not so much by the shock of that morning as by the gritty reticences around him. He hadn't heard a straightforward utterance since he set foot in the ravished drawing room. But he did hear one about half past one, when Kate, skin flushed, eyes lit up, came, almost at a run, into his dining room where he was eating bread and cheese.

"I heard it on the one o'clock news," she said. "I suppose it's true?"

"Yes, it's true enough."

"She's been killed?"

"Murdered." Kate might have been in tears or in one of her tempers. She broke out, "It's so bloody unfair. After being told that there was nothing wrong with her. Good news. And she only had ten days to enjoy it."

It was curiously childish. He had never heard her so naive, but he felt better for hearing it and very fond of her.

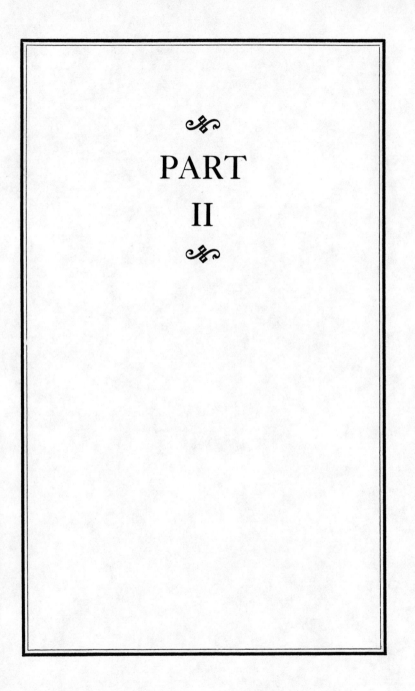

PART
II

❧ 10 ❧

A few minutes after Humphrey left the house, Detective Chief Superintendent Frank Briers entered. He asked a couple of quiet questions of the policeman on duty outside, gave a couple of quiet instructions. Any other entrances? There is another policeman outside the garden door? The same instructions were to be passed on to him. No one was to be allowed inside except his own officers and the technical people. Then Briers looked at the lock on the front door, said it must be changed, and went upstairs. He was followed by a young detective inspector, Shingler, who had been sitting beside him in the police car. Shingler had already been allotted to the chief Scenes of Crime job.

Briers himself was still under forty. He was restlessly springy on his feet, exuding force and energy, of middle height, built like a professional soccer player, light above the waist, muscular thighs. His face was neat featured, not specially distinguished unless his eyes were caught. They weren't the eyes others expected in a detective, not sharp and concentrated. For that the spectator would have done better to take a look, under the general air of composure, at Humphrey Leigh. Briers's eyes were brilliant enough, deep-colored, a startling blue. They were the kind of eyes, set under fine brow ridges, that innocent persons expected to see in artists or musicians and seldom did.

It was an accident that he had been given this new assignment. After the first survey the local police station wasted no time. The murder of Lady Ashbrook was bound to make the news. They tried to summon the chief detective of the division. He was out on another case. In minutes, the station made an appeal to Scotland Yard. Briers was by chance unoccupied, the appropriate rank, with a reputation already made, tipped to go higher. By 9:20 a good deal was already in train. He had sent off two men with whom he had worked before to get an office organized at the police station. Photographers and laboratory technicians were due to arrive. Briers's favorite pathologist should be at the house before long.

Briers went alone into Lady Ashbrook's drawing room. "Give me ten minutes," he had said softly to Shingler. He stayed still, a yard or so from the body. His senses were alive. He was getting impressions as Humphrey had done not two hours before. Some of Briers's impressions were similar to Humphrey's but imbued with more purpose and concentration: it wasn't the first time he had been inside a ransacked room. Some of his thoughts were different from Humphrey's. A suspicion hadn't crystallized but was somewhere, as it were, in solution, at the back of his mind.

He remained still, except for the direction of his glance, which traveled from the body around the room. He was long sighted, and the detail of the spilled-out objects thirty feet away he could make out as though it were bold print.

He didn't take a note. Note taking on the spot didn't suit him. It seemed to shut out impressions that were lurking on the edge of observation. Perhaps that was a minor vanity, for he had faith in his memory. Although he carried a recording machine in his pocket, he rarely used it. He preferred to give reminders to Shingler, who could feed them into his own machine.

After some more solitary moments, he called to Shingler: "Ready now?" Shingler came in with a photographic officer. The camera clicked. Lady Ashbrook was photographed more often and from more angles than ever in the past, even when as a young society beauty she had been caught by journalists after a supper party with the Prince of Wales. The body finished with, Briers told Shingler what shots he wanted around the room. The visual scouring clicked on.

Shortly after 9:50, the constable on duty outside let another man into the room. He was carrying a bag; his face was flushed. His first act was to take off his jacket and throw it back to the constable. "Too hot for this lark," he said in a euphonious tenor. "Sorry I'm late, Frank."

"You always are."

In fact, he had come with maximum celerity. This was Owen Morgan, Professor of Forensic Science, who with the curious Anglo-Saxon lack of inventiveness about nicknames was known as Taffy. He was heavyset, fair, round faced. He and Briers had worked together often. They had respect for each other and a kind of protective friendship. Each thought the other a master of his trade. They found it necessary to express this by outbursts of sparring, or what used to be called ribbing. This didn't seem particularly appropriate for either of them.

"I suppose everyone's made a mess of things already," Morgan said as a thoughtful preliminary. He wasn't referring to the casualty or the litter on the floor.

"Oh yes, our prints and traces—they're all over the place." Briers was responding in kind.

"Actually, professor," said Shingler in a placatory manner and a south-of-the-river accent, "nothing's been touched. It's all yours."

"That's something, I suppose," Morgan said, as though displeased. He hadn't met Shingler before, and Briers introduced them. Morgan said, "Well, let's have a look."

He put on a pair of near-transparent gloves, trod with elephantine delicacy over particles on the floor, and began to touch the body. Out of proportion to his bulky chest and stomach, his hands were small, delicate, quick moving, adept. He pulled up an eyelid, glanced at the scalp wounds, sniffed like one who had just opened a good bottle. He twitched an arm, which was limp, all stiffness departed. He turned back the collar of the dress and exposed a bruise on the upper arm. Carefully he passed his fingers around the neck. He grunted and said, "Nothing much in it for me." He was turning back to Briers. "It's going to be your problem, not mine. Unless you know already."

Briers shook his head. "Tell us. What do you get paid for?"

"My God," Morgan broke out, "why aren't you coppers given a course in medicine? If you were capable of taking it in. Have you looked at her face, man? Couldn't you see the spots? And on the eyelids? It's too bloody clear. Nothing in it for me."

85

"Come off it. You mean she was strangled—?"

"What else? Very easy with a woman that age. There was a bit of a struggle. One or two bruises. Not much good struggling at that age. I shall want photographs of the bruises, of course. Before I cut her up."

"So shall we," said Briers. "What about her head being bashed in?"

"Done after death."

"How long after?"

"Difficult to say. Not much blood. Very soon after."

"Might have been in a frenzy. We've seen that before, haven't we?"

"We have."

They were both used to actions after a killing. More often than not, they would have said, they were not nice for the public to know.

"She passed water, of course," Morgan commented. The others hadn't seen him make an examination, but his nose was acute. "No defecation, I think. Her bowels can't have been loose."

"Any semen?"

"That I can't tell you till I get her to the hospital." They were used to such consequences too. They dropped into the formal text-book words. That made it that much more abstract, more hygienic.

Briers asked more questions, Shingler, anxious not to be left out, putting in his own. Had the body been moved after the murder and the blows on the head? Morgan thought not. The blood on the floor and the urine staining didn't look as if it had. "You mean," said Shingler, "he just killed her, stove her head in afterward, and left her."

"That seems to be the form."

"Time of the murder—any idea?" Briers asked.

"That'll have to wait till the hospital as well. Temperature won't tell us anything after this time. Maggots may. The larvae boys are beginning to be useful—you've seen what they can do. There must be plenty of infestation. The maggots have come along damn quickly in this weather. You can see them. My guess is that she's been dead about thirty-six hours, plus or minus three or four. Saturday night, that would take you back to. But we might get a bit

86

nearer than that. Look, have you finished here? It's time we got down to some serious work."

Briers required some more specimens, from the floor and the walls around the body, and called in a laboratory man. Then the body was lifted onto a stretcher and carried down to the pavement. A few people were watching, for news had filtered around the Square and farther off. A miniature convoy, three vehicles, moved off: ambulance in the lead, Briers's police car, Morgan's private one.

The convoy got through with police speed. Soon they were moving along a wide East End street—low buildings, humble paint-peeling shops, Jewish names, shields of David. Shingler, sitting beside Briers in the back seat, tried to talk. Briers did not respond. He had enough thoughts to occupy him.

❦ 11 ❧

The main hospital building was late nineteenth century, solid and dark, but that they were not entering. Morgan's domain was down a side street, small houses run together, a postwar assembly, including a couple of prefabs. There was a large bright-painted notice, as outside a pub or a trend-seeking church, that read: "Department of Forensic Science and Morbid Anatomy." Morgan's domain might be ramshackle, but he was proud of it.

When the others had gotten out of their car, he said to Briers, "No reason to hang about, is there?"

In fact, none of them gave the appearance of hurrying. Haste was a beginner's fault. Briers and Morgan kept to a tempo without spurts or stops. One of Morgan's staff met them: he was carrying two notes addressed to D. C. S. Briers. Briers skimmed through them, passed them to Shingler. They were briefs from the Yard, with bits of information about Lady Ashbrook. All formal—age, marriages, names of relatives.

They followed Morgan into the mortuary. Under the strip lighting, there was one large room with stone slab tables, white, anonymous; another smaller room with a single table—shining under the daylight lamp. In the smaller room, the mortuary superintendent, introduced as Agnew, was waiting, already wearing a laboratory coat, olive colored, not white. In an alcove, Morgan and the policemen put on similar coats. There were masks hanging up in that robing room, but Morgan did not take one nor invite the others to.

88

He had a reputation for haranguing his pupils, telling them that smell was too important to play tricks with.

When they returned to the mortuary, they could still, from the small room that Morgan kept for dissections, look out to the big classroom. They clustered around the single slab. There were present Morgan himself, one other medical man, the superintendent, a technical assistant, Briers, Shingler, and the photographer. To begin with, the body had been propped up in a chair standing by the dissecting table. It was exactly as it had been in the drawing room, clothed, untouched.

"Right?" Morgan said.

"Right." Briers nodded.

"From the head down. Hair off later, of course."

The camera clicked, in front of the head, at the side, from on top.

"Pictures of those wounds," Briers asked, mechanically.

"I want swabs. Get them to the larvae boys straight away," Morgan said to Agnew. "Tell them it's priority." Swabs of the nose and mouth. From both there had been a discharge of both blood and mucus, and maggots had been moving. "Also for the larvae boys."

More camera clicks.

"Now get the clothes off. We want to know if anything was put on after she was killed. Go slow."

That was Morgan speaking. Briers added, "Photographs at all stages." Carefully, with clinical caution, the hammer was eased out of the head. Photograph of the crevices. Then Agnew and his assistant stripped off the clothing. It was easy. In the heat, she had been wearing little. The dress came off, Morgan interrupting here to have an inspection of the bruises on her neck and upper arms. "Not much force," he muttered to Briers. Throughout, Shingler was whispering into his recorder.

Under the dress, a silk slip. "No stains visible," said Agnew. "You'll test it," Morgan replied. A light bra, a very light girdle.

"She didn't need that," Morgan muttered. "How old was she?" Briers told him.

Another mutter. "Christ Almighty, she kept her figure."

The body did not seem so thin as in her clothes, except for the legs below the knees.

"Who was she, by the way?" Morgan, sotto voce, to Briers. Again Briers told him.

For the first time, Morgan exclaimed out loud.

"My God," he said. "One of the Big People." He had assumed a Welsh lilt, absent from his normal speech. This was some obscure joke, lost to all present but himself.

Stockings off. Silk knickers. "Test those. You'll find urine. I want to know if there's anything else."

The instructions were unnecessary. Agnew was as experienced as Morgan himself.

"That's that," Morgan said. "Get her ready, will you? Ten minutes do you?"

"Just about." Agnew was unfussed. "We'll go outside, then." Morgan took them into the open. "You're allowed a cigarette now," he said to Briers.

As Morgan knew, Briers was an addictive smoker, deprived for hours that morning. He promptly took out a packet. Both he and Morgan were unusually quiet, and it was Shingler, alert, slick as his own shining chestnut hair, who made conversation. He was alert and observant and had to be listened to.

"We'll give them a quarter of an hour," said Morgan, as though he were waiting for unpunctual guests. Then, not delaying for quite as long, they went back to the mortuary.

The body lay stretched out flat on the table. Hair cut from head and body. The head looked much smaller without its hair. The body looked clean, thin but not skeletal, young. Morgan had already said that she was abnormally well preserved. But he, who had dealt with so many bodies, had already noted what amorists had discovered long ago, that, though faces usually aged, bodies often didn't. To some, that had been an agreeable discovery.

"Right," Morgan said. He was spreading his nostrils, as he was to do several times during the next half hour. There was, as in the drawing room, a tinge of the sweet smell of corruption. Nothing else yet, though. Except for another tinge, which he wished wasn't present, the smell of formaldehyde from a previous operation.

Without the policemen realizing, Agnew was already taking off the skull cap. He brought out the brain and handed it, as though it was the most natural of gifts, to Morgan. Morgan studied it for seconds and said, "Two knocks. The second would have killed her. If she hadn't been dead already."

At that point Morgan took over. There was nothing against the cut from throat to pubis for this dissection, and he made it. He often had a taste for the great V cut, Briers was thinking as he watched. Morgan extracted lungs and heart. "Not an indication. Nothing wrong. She was stronger than most of us," he said with a touch of envy. Organs deposited in the sink in a neat row. Liver, kidneys. The stomach bag he held on to longer.

"We'd better have this gone over. We may as well know what she ate at her last meal." He was fingering one of the passages. "She may have had some trouble here. Nothing pathological, I think. Wear and tear. It could have been inconvenient."

The body lay on the table, a cavity, nothing else. The organs were on display. Only the doctors, and perhaps Agnew, could have distinguished them from their own organs if they had been on exhibition too. Or have distinguished them from the offal in an old-fashioned butcher's shop.

"That's as much as we can do for now." Morgan left them all standing, went out, came back with clean white hands. He spoke to Briers, "Let's go along and have a talk." He said to Shingler, "Will you come too?" He asked the question as though he would have preferred Shingler to decline, but that was unlikely.

"Going along" meant a progress across alleyways, up stairs and down corridors, as though in an imperfectly adapted hotel, to Morgan's office. A cluttered room, with photographs of track teams, of medical groups, and, apparently somewhat out of place, of sets of teeth. These were actually mementos of a case reported in Famous British Trials, in which Morgan had given decisive evidence. "Having a talk," in that subdued mortuary language, meant, first and foremost, having a drink. As soon as they reached the room, Morgan was feeling for a whiskey bottle behind his desk. He poured Briers a stiff drink, took a stiffer one himself. Shingler took a drink, diluted it, sipped at it. The others were downing theirs.

Sometimes they talked, patting references across like so many ping-pong balls, as though they were careless. They talked like professionals, as though they were machines. The fact was, they were relieved to be finished with the postmortem. Yes, Morgan had done many. Yes, he liked using his skill and showing it. Yes, Briers loved his job and snatched at the help that the pathologist could give him. But there were parts of the job, and this was one, that were still a submerged strain. He and Morgan were both hearty, natural men, and sometimes they showed it. It broke out in their overdone mateyness. Most of their time they lived close to death. But they didn't like death. As he had his packet of cigarettes in front of him, Briers was more at ease. No one enjoyed a postmortem; no one except the indifferent, perhaps. Norman Shingler here seemed totally unaffected. He was learning from postmortems, intent, preoccupied, just preoccupied with learning his job.

Briers lit another cigarette and they spoke as colleagues, work in front of them, coping with the case.

"Some of it's straightforward," Morgan said. "Cause of death. No doubt in hell what that was. Why her skull was smashed later, you'll have to find out. I can't be any good to you there. Time of death? We're getting a bit closer. You'll be lucky if anything more positive crops up. Unless one of your coppers comes up with an eyewitness. But then I shouldn't believe him after all I've been through with you. Anyway, you've heard the score."

Since they came into the room, there had been two telephone calls. One was from the entomologists. Morgan roared out what he was hearing. "First-generation larvae, second-generation larvae. Of course." Some argument over the phone. Morgan spoke back into the room. "Actually, it's pretty near what I guessed. Assuming her window was open, temperature not lower than twenty-five centigrade—I told them what the conditions were, the bloody fools—earliest time for infestation would be seven P.M. on Saturday night, latest time eleven P.M. That will have to be good enough."

"Head wounds postdate the murder," Briers said. "So time of murder had to be earlier. Not much."

"Very little. So it's Saturday evening to night, not late night," Morgan said.

"Fair enough," said Briers.

The second report over the telephone was shorter and simple. Morgan was surprised—no trace of semen. He had found nothing by sight and touch, but nevertheless he was surprised. Briers was robustly teasing him, "You've seen too many murders, you have, Taffy."

Morgan took another sizable whiskey, but not Briers. It was now getting on into the afternoon. None of them had eaten. The older men showed no sign of the passing of time. About half past two Briers said that he had work to do. He and Morgan parted on another robust note, Morgan saying that if the police got into inextricable trouble, he would come and sort it out.

❧ 12 ❧

I n the local police station half a mile away from Lady Ashbrook's
house, which Briers had not yet been inside that day, or as far
as that went at any other time, he did have work to do. One of his
aides, Detective Inspector Flamson, was setting up what he chose
to call the Incident Room. Flamson was homely but handpicked.
Filing cabinets were already installed, files waiting for Briers on a
long table covered with green baize. A press officer from the Yard
was waiting. He had drafted a statement, noncommittal, bare.
Briers said that that would serve for today. Press conference tomorrow afternoon. Nothing much to say, Flamson reported. "Never
mind," said Briers, "we're used to that." Flamson had organized
the first squad, who were out on inquiries house to house. Personnel? Yard officers, local ones, division crime squads, local crime
squads. "Well done," Briers said. "How many?" About thirty that
afternoon. "We shall want a hell of a lot more," said Briers. "Still,
we're in business."

Briers said that he would talk to them all first thing next morning. "You've got everything going, George. I'm glad I wasn't here
to get in your way. Thank you." He added, "Now I'd better get
down to the papers."

There were typescripts about Lady Ashbrook, on her two hus-
bands, her son, her grandson. Much of this information came from
her lawyers, who had been identified from documents in her drawing room. That had been good quick work, Briers thought. He
went through statements, two signed that afternoon, by the per-

94

sons who first saw the body. Maria Fereira, Humphrey Leigh. Humphrey Leigh, if this was the same man, was an acquaintance, more than an acquaintance. Briers remembered that he had heard that Leigh lived in this neighborhood. They had first met when Briers was a detective sergeant seconded to a job in Cyprus. There had been a security man, described as Colonel Leigh, who had been friendly and had, unobtrusively, given him bits of advice. Those were old days, but they had been in contact since. Not so long ago, Briers had confided about his wife's illness to the other man.

Briers sent out for biscuits, coffee, and two more packets of cigarettes. He worked on in that room—which, when he had praised Flamson enough, would have to be renamed the Murder Room, since Briers liked plain words, curiously enough a legacy from the same Humphrey Leigh—until nine o'clock and was back there by eight the following morning.

At 8:30 the big room was half full of officers, men and women. Briers had become practiced in these briefings: he was cheerful, encouraging, tart. They were short staffed for the present, he said; they would be working till they dropped. That didn't matter. The first days were important, they all knew, in this kind of case. It wasn't a good idea to give anyone they were after time to think. He'd have enough time to think when he was inside. For the moment, they had to set to work on all possible lines. There were plenty of villains in the Victoria region. And all over the district. And you couldn't rule out anybody, and anybody is the operative word, yet awhile. Chief Inspector Bale would allocate squads to their stamping grounds. Things might break tomorrow. They might be at it for weeks. Good luck.

As the detectives left, Bale held back half a dozen. Briers hadn't given much indication of what he already knew, none of what he might be thinking. These half dozen were experienced in police inquiries. They were detailed for calls on Lady Ashbrook's acquaintances, such as had been traced. It meant calls on smart houses in Belgravia, Chelsea, places where rich people lived. "You'll have to tread a bit gently," Briers said. "Don't press too much just now. We don't want the commissioner to get too many screams over the phone."

Then Briers nodded to Bale, and the two of them, followed by

Shingler and Flamson, moved through the police station to another room, quite small, their private room, containing just a polished table and a few hard chairs. This room was at the back of the station, and the single window looked over the little gardens behind the Gerald Road houses, patches of grass parched in the sun. Shingler put his head out of the door and, as automatically as in America in any office at any hour of the day, called for coffee.

Those three were Briers's innermost group. They didn't appear specially homogeneous, no more so than any three middle-ranking members in any occupation. Leonard Bale, who was acting as Briers's number two, was in charge of the inquiry squads. He was gray-haired and had a fine, ascetic, long-nosed face, looking vaguely ecclesiastical, like an unpolitical and pastoral cardinal. He had champagne-bottle shoulders, such as often went with physical strength. As a policeman on the beat, he had been decorated for acts of courage. Some years before, he and Briers had been on the same official level, detective inspectors together. He had been passed over, given the one promotion to chief inspector, and now couldn't expect more. Briers, six years his junior, had gone right past him in the hierarchy. Bale appeared to bear no rancor. He behaved as though it were a pleasure to be number two.

Briers, sitting at the table and ringing for an ashtray, asked, "You've all read the memos, I suppose? What's the state of the game?"

"Well, sir"—it was Bale who answered. He made a point in public of keeping the etiquette, though he was the only one who in private used Briers's Christian name—"The machine is working after a fashion. We shall want more bodies. That goes without saying."

"Of course, I'll get the screws on them upstairs. They can't let us down on this one. But I want to know what you are all thinking. What do we know so far?"

Flamson said, "Not all that much, guv. Not all that bloody much."

Flamson was becoming known as the office manager; he was a fleshy man in his thirties, high-colored, with jet black hair, one of the dark English, from the heart of the Midlands, accent incorrigible. Both Briers and Bale had a northern undertone, by now suppressed. None of them came from the working class, but from the social no-man's-land just above.

"No, we know one thing for sure, chief," Shingler said. "Whoever we're looking for, it isn't a thug. It isn't just a layabout."

"That stands out a mile," Briers said, but not as a snub. Shingler was pushing, intrusive, but he was bright and had been Briers's particular protégé. He was young for his present rank. That could have happened on merit, but Briers had eased his way. Without being aware of it, Briers had imitated the manner in which Humphrey Leigh had once advised him.

"Our man," said Shingler, "knew what he was doing. Let's take it that he came in via the mews, over the grass, through the garden door. No marks anywhere." Shingler, the chief Scenes of Crime officer, had issued a memorandum on all this on the previous night. "The boys are looking for traces all over the place. They haven't found a tiddler yet. The man took one piece of glass out of the garden door. With the old brown-paper trick. Not a thug's job. No prints anywhere. Not a print in the whole blasted establishment."

"You mean it was a professional?" Briers was leaning back.

Flamson said, "Trying to seem like a thug—could be, could be."

"It might have been a professional," Briers said absently. "Of course, it might have been."

"It's one line, anyway," Shingler said. "I don't say it's the only one. We haven't enough to concentrate on, have we, chief?"

"Not yet."

"But our man isn't a thug," said Shingler, not leaving well enough alone.

"Why does everyone take it for granted that we're looking for a man?" Bale asked with dignity. "It might have been a woman."

The juniors regarded him with something like astonishment. The "old duck," which was his behind-the-scenes designation, was not expected to make original suggestions. He was liked but not respected, perhaps because he didn't evoke a particle of fear. They undervalued him. Now they were cheerfully, boisterously laughing.

"Not impossible." Briers stopped the jollity with a hard voice. In spite of his unpretentiousness, his cordiality, Briers did evoke fear, sometimes more than was desirable. "Not impossible at all. Nothing rules a woman out. Nothing on earth."

Shingler was anxious to please, but sometimes impatience supervened. Now, brashly, he spoke as though women hadn't been mentioned. "If he is a professional," Shingler was saying, "he didn't get much out of it. As I said in the memo, some odds and ends and about three hundred quid in notes."

Briers said, "Those notes ought to come in useful for us." Bale added, "Yes, we ought to be able to track them down, sir. You saw Norman's memo. She kept the numbers in her little book. We've sent them round to all the lads."

"Fine," Briers said. In an aside, casual and throwaway, he went on, "If he was a professional, he wasn't a very good one."

"Agreed," Bale joined in.

"He did some of it like a very good pro. He didn't leave anything much for us. But as far as business went, he was very bad. Most professionals would make sure there was something in the house worth taking, wouldn't they? And they wouldn't go so crazy, breaking the place up, pretending to be thugs."

"What are you getting at, guv? It could be someone pretending to be a burglar, is that what you mean?"

"I'm not going so far as that." Briers was impassive. "It's more likely that it was a stupid professional who lost his head. It's a great mistake, God knows we've all made it, to let yourself get blinkered right at the beginning. Chasing an idea has sunk a lot of detectives before now."

"But anyway, guv—" Flamson began.

"Anyway what?" Briers was at his briskest.

"If I get you right, guv, you're saying it mightn't be a burglar out for what he could pick up. You're saying there's a chance it wasn't, and if so, it wasn't because she caught someone in the act that she got done in. There would have to have been some other cause. That would make it real murder for my money. Deliberate by the look of it."

"Perhaps. Perhaps not," Briers said.

Flamson was sweating and mopped his forehead. He wasn't eas- ily put off and was cherishing a small triumph of his own. "Well then, we ought to be looking at the background. Why should anyone finish the old girl? Might be money. Who would get her money if she was polished off? I was thinking about that yesterday afternoon."

"It isn't very brilliant. We should all have got there as soon as we were organized. More or less routine." Shingler spoke with a sharp smile, not pleased. He realized that Flamson had been the first to catch Briers's thinking, or as much of it as he had given any hint.

"I got there yesterday afternoon." Flamson was sweating more, looking replete, like a man after a self-indulgent feast. "I had a word with Len Bale, didn't I?"

Bale gave a gentle nod.

"We ought to find out about her will. Routine if you like, Norman. We're coppers, you know. Old Len called her solicitors. They saw the point, Len says. They'll get the will read inside a week."

Briers gave an approving cry. "Well done, George." Then agreeably to Bale, "Well done, Len." Then he said, "If it turns out there is anything in this line, it won't be so nice and easy, you know. I don't specially fancy having to deal with the old lady's kind of people. I haven't had much to do with them, but they're good at closing ranks. You get me—we shouldn't be playing on our home ground."

❧ 13 ❧

That Tuesday morning, just at the time when Briers and the other detectives were conferring, Humphrey was in his sitting room reading the day's *Times*. At first sight he had picked out the reference to the murder. That didn't require excessive vigilance. There was a headline on the front page. Other papers had had more dashing headlines, he had no doubt. In newspaper terms there was not much competition. The financial gloom; the weather, still no indication of change; people talking (difficult to believe in England) of fields burning up and the prospect of drought; the Belgravia murder. The murder had most appeal.

The Belgravia murder: the phrase caught on outside London, even outside England, with a good many who had no idea where and what sort of place Belgravia could be. The murder looked like remaining news for some time to come, as Briers and his superiors at Scotland Yard had foreseen.

The official announcement told nothing, except that the police were treating Lady Ashbrook's death as a case of murder and that Detective Chief Superintendent Briers was in charge of the investigation. When Humphrey read that, he felt pleasure, quite unqualified. Briers couldn't help reading the statements of the day before, and Humphrey, knowing how rapidly he worked, expected to be called for within hours. Humphrey looked forward to it. He had both affection and respect for Briers, perhaps the special affection that one felt for a successful protegé. Humphrey hadn't had success himself, but he enjoyed it in others. There was a touch of vanity too in the self-congratulation at having backed a winner.

The *Times* obituary was formal and factual, not long, and not given the premier place. Family, marriages, son the present marquess. Prominent in London society between the two wars. Public work. President of Conservative Women's Association (1952–63), Anglo-Norwegian Society, Cancer Research Trust.

It wasn't much of an obituary. Possibly some friend would be upset enough to add something a trifle less bleak, which, Humphrey thought, wouldn't be difficult to do.

In the middle of the morning, the telephone rang. He heard his own name being asked for in a light, modulated voice. Then, "Loseby here. Look, I need a bit of help. Can we talk?"

"What about?" Humphrey was not forthcoming.

"I'm in a bit of a fix. You're a wise man, aren't you?"

"What is all this?"

"Can we talk? It would be a help—" Tone persuasive.

"I suppose so, if you want." Humphrey, with some sense of what might be coming, was recalled to old official caution. "Not on the telephone, though. And you'd better not come here. They're probably trying to trace you."

They met in a cafe, chosen by Loseby, fading, smelly, but well occupied, toward the far end of the Kings Road. Loseby might be anxious, but he still looked blooming, the golden young man, and he was still ready to order a plate of spaghetti bolognese.

"They told me at HQ," he said equably enough, "you were asking for me on Monday."

"Not unnaturally," Humphrey replied.

"I wasn't there."

"So I discovered."

"I was in London, actually." Loseby shone with his innocent great-eyed shameless smile. "What do you think?"

"It's not what I think. You'll have to explain yourself to the police. You must realize that. What were you doing?"

Loseby was still smiling, quite easy.

"Oh come, you know what I'm like."

"Do I?"

Loseby wasn't put off. "I thought I needed a bit of relaxation. In the best possible way. So I got a few days' leave. Grandmother's health was a pretty good excuse. After all, I'd used it before, hadn't I?"

"And you didn't come near her?"

"Unfortunately not. I rang her up on Saturday afternoon. She said she was fine."

"Where were you?"

Loseby answered, "Round about the place. Not so very far away."

"Where?"

Loseby suddenly spoke in a correct formal tone. "I'd rather not say." Then the shameless smile again. "I holed up somewhere comfortable. Very suitable for relaxation."

"With a woman?"

"You've said it, I haven't."

Loseby shoveled away at his spaghetti. Humphrey in his time had conducted a good many interrogations. He stayed silent. The young man would have to speak.

In an unperturbed fashion, the young man did speak.

"I told you, I'm in rather a fix. You see why. Now what do I do?"

Humphrey took his time and then asked, "Are you telling me the truth?"

"Why ever shouldn't I?"

"There are plenty of reasons why you shouldn't. I'm not going any further unless you tell me that you are."

Loseby gave his sweetest smile. "Do you want me to swear on the Bible?"

"Not especially." Humphrey responded with a smile not so sweet. "You'd be ready to do that if you were lying in your teeth, wouldn't you?"

Loseby laughed out loud. "All right. No, I am telling the truth. I haven't said where I was exactly, or who I was with. It might surprise you. I want to keep it to myself—unless it's necessary, of course. After all, you might give me the credit for behaving like an English gentleman."

Humphrey couldn't help grinning. That must be the sort of gibe with which Loseby did his seductions. You had to know his own kind to feel how edged a gibe it was. For a few moments, Humphrey spoke more amiably. "Well, let's go on from there. Anyone halfway sensible would give you exactly the same advice.

A decent lawyer would. And it's totally useless unless you're telling the truth. You have to go to the police and say precisely what you've said to me. You have to go the minute you've finished—that." Humphrey was looking without enthusiasm at the mound of pasta. "You ought to have gone yesterday morning, of course. They'll be perfectly civil. You'll have to make a statement and sign it. Then they'll check. Remember this is serious. They're not fools. They'll be suspicious. It's their business to be suspicious. They don't take a lofty view of human nature. They'll be interested in your grandmother's will. If she happens to have left you something fairly handsome—I imagine that's very much in the cards—then they'll keep their eyes especially wide open. That's why you can forget any advice I'm giving you unless you're telling the truth."

As Shingler had said in the police station the previous afternoon, the thought about the will was obvious enough.

Humphrey broke off. "By the way, what's in her will? Do you know?"

"I haven't the slightest idea. Have you?"

"How should I? I wasn't in her confidence, ever. I'm not sure that anyone was, toward the end. Except perhaps yourself."

"No, I wasn't. She was fond of me, that's all." For the first time in these exchanges, Loseby seemed grave. He asked, his eyes not watching Humphrey, "You trust me, don't you?"

"What do you think?"

Humphrey had reproduced the light flicking tone with which Loseby had met a question of Humphrey's own. In fact, on the spot, Humphrey couldn't have given a truthful answer even to himself. Did he trust Loseby? He had conducted more than enough interrogations. He had discovered a curious thing. Insight, intuition, whatever you like to call it, got lost as the interrogation went on.

Suspicions thickened and crystallized until it was like being in a paranoid web. It was something any security officer ought to guard himself against, and a great many didn't. Everything seemed as possible as anything else, and everyone seemed as possible a danger. For instance, so far as Humphrey recalled, the only persons in the immediate neighborhood who had question marks against them on the files in his old office were Tom Thirkill, inserted long before for left-wing actions in his youth, commonplace for a politician, and, believe it or not, Paul Mason. That was because Paul, exploring international economics, had traveled widely in Eastern Europe.

In cool blood, anyone who could distinguish a man from a bull's foot would realize that Paul was as likely to betray his country as the Duke of Wellington: but in an interrogation Humphrey could imagine the paranoid suspicion getting sharper—couldn't this be a classical specimen of the trained and glacial upper-class defector? You had to learn to wash away the crystallization in any interrogation. That midday, in the sleazy cafe, Humphrey couldn't have decided whether he trusted Loseby or not, or whether, if he had been a policeman, he would have been paying him unusual attention.

Loseby himself, without hurry, scooping at a large ice cream, had moved to a quiet, businesslike discussion of funeral arrangements. Presumably he would have to take charge. When would the police let him have the body? Or was it the coroner? Humphrey shook his head. He had frequently worked with policemen on security cases, never on one like this. Presumably they could get an answer. Would her son, Loseby's father, come to the funeral? Loseby was certain that he wouldn't: he's pretty far gone, Loseby said without expression. Humphrey remembered gossip that Lord Pevensey, in his early sixties, was in an advanced state of alcoholism.

What would grandmama have wanted, Loseby asked, by way of a funeral? Again Humphrey was ignorant. Perhaps there were some instructions among her papers. Loseby had a faint recollection that she had once said that she didn't like burials. Cremation? She would certainly have wanted nothing grandiose. Used to pleasing, making a technique of it, skillful with his innocence, Loseby was—so Humphrey had realized years before—as sophisticated as most men, but the young man was as certain as the simplest that he was in contact with the wishes of the dead.

That afternoon, Loseby rang up with some more questions. Over the wire, his voice sounded less mellifluous than in the morning, less persuasive than face-to-face. He hadn't begun to say a word about his own concerns. Humphrey said, "You did clear up your own position with the police, did you?"

"Coped with."

"I hope you remembered what I told you."

Voice polite again now. "I always remember what I'm told."

❧ 14 ❧

Humphrey waited for a call from the police station, but Tuesday, Wednesday, Thursday passed without one. He began to notice that there was plenty of commotion in the neighborhood, as yet subdued. Not only in the Square. Several elderly residents stopped Humphrey on his strolls, as though he ought to be able to reassure them. They were anxious. The heat, the burnished sky, had sharpened tempers. Monty Lefroy seemed to speak for them all. "If this can happen in Belgravia," he said in a stern, threatening tone, "it can happen anywhere."

The press was beginning to issue ominous comments. Following America, they were using law and order as a slogan, and the *Times* had a judicious editorial entitled just that. A very old lady, who had done service to the state, had been brutally murdered. In many ways, said the leader, it would be generally admitted that this intolerable event reflected a condition of contemporary society. Nevertheless, the event remained intolerable, and we had to search our hearts and ask essential questions.

After the official obituary there was one gently protesting addition in the *Times*, signed simply C. T.

> May a friend add a word of personal knowledge about Lady Ashbrook? Strangers or casual acquaintances were sometimes put off by Lady Ashbrook's insistence on maintaining rigid standards, often standards of courtesy that seem too rigid for the later generation. This recalls the well-known story of her rebuke to Lady Astor at Cliveden. Lady Ashbrook was the last person to

put up with rudeness from anyone on earth. But her friends knew that she had far more important qualities: absolute integrity, extreme generosity of spirit, extraordinary kindness and humility which to those who knew her were never disguised by her sometimes sharpish tongue; a profound Christian faith, which manifested itself in constant care for others.

As he read that portrait of a character, Humphrey gave a sour, regretful smile. Would she have been amused by that remarkable praise? Possibly not. For most people, even for those sardonic about others (most of all for them?), any praise was better than none.

Then there was silence about Lady Ashbrook, not about the case. By Friday, Humphrey was becoming disappointed at having no invitation from Briers, and to his own amusement, a shamefaced amusement, hurt as well as disappointed. It was absurdly like being very young again and having a friend, suddenly prominent, not ask one to a party.

In the middle of Friday morning, though, a call came through. "Mr. Leigh? Chief Superintendent Briers would like to speak to you."

Briers's voice, usually subdued, was by nature rich and resonant, a baritone so strong that it didn't fit his quiet appearance. "Hullo, Humphrey. Good to talk to you. I happen to be down here on duty, I don't know whether you've heard."

"Of course I've heard."

"Good enough. You knew the old lady, didn't you? I wonder if you could spare me half an hour?"

"Naturally."

"This afternoon? Three o'clock? Look forward to seeing you."

Humphrey was still puzzled, as he had been by the delay in making contact. It wasn't so long, no more than a couple of years, since Briers had asked him out to lunch and told him harsh news of his own. Over the telephone his voice had been cheerful and cordial enough, but no more than businesslike. However, he had seen Briers in action before, as concentrated as this.

Humphrey duly walked the half mile from his house that afternoon. The police station was pretty in the shimmering sunlight, flower boxes in front of the ground-floor windows. It might have been a picture of an idealized police station in a sleepy market town sometime before 1914, all peaceful and unsuspecting. One had to ignore the motorcycles parked beside the pavement and the cars on the other side, yet it was oddly nostalgic, as in one of those period stories, so tranquil that one could smell the flowers. Gerald Road itself was a neat and comely side street, the original developers, wasting no space, having built a row of handsome houses with wider frontages than any in Aylestone Square. A few years before, one of those houses had been a staging post for the theater's smartest stars.

When Humphrey went in, he was greeted with disconcerting promptness. "He's in the Murder Room, sir," said a constable. "I'll take you straight in."

There in the long room, Briers was sitting at the top table. He sprang to his feet, outgoing and vigorous. "Good to see you, Humphrey." He went on, "Sorry this place is so untidy. My office manager—a lad called Flamson, you'll have to meet him some-time—he's getting it straight. It's always a bit of a problem." Actually, the room wasn't untidy, except by Briers's obsessive standards, beside which Humphrey, more orderly than most, had often felt ashamed. There must have been precise instructions as to how Humphrey was to be picked out by sight, welcomed, and brought in.

Briers explained some practical details. He was friendly but—Humphrey couldn't be certain whether he was being over-suspicious—perhaps not intimate. He was certainly not taciturn, but that was nothing new. Nor were most men, in Humphrey's experience, who spent their lives in something like action, as did soldiers, businessmen, barristers. The stereotype was the opposite of the truth. For silent persons you would do better to seek out creative intellectuals.

Frank Briers began to talk about the case. There would be big trouble if he didn't get the whole thing cut and dried within weeks, if not days.

"Shall you?" Humphrey asked.

"I wouldn't bet on it if I were you." Briers wasn't given to pretending. "It may be one of the messy ones."

He broke off. "You got in on the ground floor, of course. I saw your statement—it's in the dossier; there'd be something wrong if it wasn't. I wanted to see you before, but I had to get things organized. You might like to know how far we've gone. Perhaps it's about half an inch. Anyway, we can talk. You're a pretty good security risk, aren't you? No one's been able to put you inside yet, at any rate."

Humphrey had realized, early in their acquaintance, that Briers was imaginative, subtle, sensitive. When he had first had to cooperate with Humphrey, he had seen documents with Humphrey's rank and name spelled out in full: Lt. Col. Humphrey Leigh. He had begun by calling Humphrey, colonel. He discovered in minutes that that frayed Humphrey's nerves and never did it again.

Along with his excessive energy, he had what a week or two before the murder had been called the manners of the heart. But he also had a simpler taste for a kind of gallows or penal humor. That could be disconcerting, but one got acclimatized, Humphrey thought. After all, Briers wouldn't have become a top-class policeman if he were benign all the way through.

Humphrey tried to get back to their personal relationship.

"It's some time since we last met, isn't it?" he said. "How is Betty now?"

"It's going very much as I told you. We have to live with it, that's all." Briers's wife, quite young, had been physically stricken. It wasn't a marriage breakup, but a clinical fatality. He didn't wish to talk more about it, but Humphrey felt that that wasn't the reason for constraint between them, if there was some. With a man so professionally affable, it was hard to judge.

"How far have we gone?" Briers reverted to his own question and proceeded to answer it. Though the words streamed out, there was, as Humphrey took for granted, an orderly mind behind them. There was also an admirable memory—which again Humphrey took for granted, since he had one of the same sort himself. It was a deflating reflection that you couldn't do any kind of intelligence work, police work, without it. There was no substitute. Files, dossiers, computers, were all dead unless there was a human memory near. Which was why intelligence operations got less penetrating, or sillier, once they grew outside the range of a single mind.

Frank Briers, with his memory as exact as Paul Mason's, was tabulating his answers. To begin with, he went over them exactly as he had done with his colleagues. Time of murder, cause of death, head battering after death. There Briers, without Humphrey's being aware of it, cut off. He didn't give any hint of the speculations he had let fall to the inner trio on the Monday afternoon.

"One thing is certain," he did say firmly, in good spirits. "Whoever did it wasn't just scum off the streets. The papers got it all wrong. Everyone gets everything wrong in a mess like this. It stands to sense he wasn't just a hooligan. He could have been a professional. He'd studied the geography. He was working in gloves, or else he wiped off all the prints. We haven't found one yet anywhere in the house. Of course, he seems to have gone bonkers after he killed her. He didn't need to beat her head in. That's not professional. But it's been known to happen."

"What was he after?"

Briers asked sharply, "What do you think?"

"I haven't the remotest idea."

"Nor have we yet."

They hadn't yet identified what objets d'art Lady Ashbrook had possessed and what had been taken. Maria was the only source of information so far. Some silver had gone. The pictures had been left. "He was sensible enough for that. Impossible to get rid of. By the by, how valuable are they?"

"I'm only guessing. You'd have to get someone to do an expertise." Humphrey was betraying his tinge of linguistic pedantry. That was what *expertise* meant. He was irked by the English knack of appropriating a French word and using it blandly wrong. "I guess ten or twenty thousand pounds the two, maybe more."

"Pointless," said Briers. "He couldn't sell them."

At that time, Humphrey wasn't certain that his friend was concealing some of his thoughts, nor what they were. Briers had a gift for talking at some distance off the point with complete openness. He did tell Humphrey the discovery that there had been £300 worth of notes in Lady Ashbrook's drawing room and that she was said to pay her bills in currency.

Humphrey interrupted. "I think she was close about money. Morbidly close, maybe."

Briers stored the remark in his computer memory and then went on, "If the haul he got was three hundred pounds in cash and a bit of silver—it wasn't much to finish her off for. Or put her out of her misery, if you like."

"No," said Humphrey. "In her way, it wasn't anyone else's way, I'd say she enjoyed her life."

The apparatus was already in action, Briers told Humphrey and didn't have to explain. Professional criminals the police knew all about. It meant listening to their sources all over the London underworld, checking on prison gossip, being certain who was in, who was out. It was like a peculiar and laborious piece of scholarship. It was also very much like a lot of security work in Humphrey's old office. Only the practitioners in a profession knew how much grind had to be done, hour following hour, just as part of the day's work.

A few tips had been collected in the last four days. None of the private tips sounded any good, Briers said. One was just a fake, a hanger-on trying to do himself a bit of good with the police. Another was a silly youngster trying to be helpful. Briers had no faith in public-house informers. The only informers who had been much use to him were quiet old things who used the telephone, asked him along to a decent little house in Clapham, and gave him a cup of tea.

Files, some in stiff cardboard covers, lay open on the table in front of Briers. He had not referred to them, and now he slapped one shut.

"Well, Humphrey, that's about the state of the game today, July thirtieth, as ever is. I'd still like to have it tied up in a couple of weeks."

"Shall you?"

Briers repeated, "I wouldn't bet on it, if I were you."

As Humphrey got ready to go, there was an exchange of invitations. Briers said that he would be in this office each afternoon until further notice. Humphrey was always welcome. On his side, Humphrey said that he lived nearby. (Briers: "Don't you think we've got you on the record?") And they could have a drink any evening, if Briers ever finished work.

Then Briers, naturally, casually, said, "Oh, one little point. What do you know about Lord Loseby?"

It might be as natural as it sounded, but it wasn't as casual. On the job—or off it, so far as Humphrey had observed—Briers didn't leave interesting questions to chance.

This was a man Humphrey had a liking for and something like regard: so he wasn't, as he had been with Tom Thirkill, prepared to fence at the mention of that name.

"I've seen a certain amount of him since he was a boy. That's about all."

"Have you any idea where he was last Saturday?"

"He happened to tell me." Humphrey smiled across the table, one ex-interrogator to another far from ex. "And I happened to send him around here to tell your people."

"Oh yes, we know. You sent him here on Tuesday. We knew."

"Did you now?" Even to Humphrey, who had once had others watched, it seemed improper to be watched himself.

"I didn't see him myself. I might have to. Mark you, I don't take this too seriously. Of course, I've read Loseby's statement. I expect you heard the story."

"If it's the same one he told me—"

"You know, finding an excuse to get on the loose. Coming over to see grandma, while he played around on his own. That's what he said. Is it true?"

"However should I know? It's just what he told me."

"The lads here have checked what they can. So far it all holds up. But that doesn't mean much. He had plenty of time to arrange some confirmation."

"Who was he with?"

Briers, after the remark that he didn't take the episode seriously, was apologetic. "I'm sorry, Humphrey, but I don't think I ought to tell you. There are some peculiar circumstances. Including where he was that night and all that weekend. Or so he says."

Humphrey said, "It sounds pretty plausible."

"Yes, it does." Then Briers asked brusquely, "What's he really like?"

Humphrey gave another smile of recognition. It was an old technique, the sudden switch, from easygoing to probing.

"You were talking about professional criminals. You might say that Loseby is a professional charmer."

"I don't care much for that."

"You're not asked to, are you?"

"Would you trust him?"

"That's too simple for you, Frank. You know it is. Trust him, what for? I think I'd trust him alongside me in a war. I don't think I'd trust him an especially long way with money, that is, I wouldn't like to lend him much if I wanted it back. I wouldn't trust him with a girl I was fond of. I wouldn't trust him in various other ways."

Briers's expression had become not only tough, but open and friendly. "Fair enough," he said.

"And you haven't asked me, have you, whether I believe he could have killed his grandmother?"

"I might have asked you whether I had to waste time thinking about him."

"Come clean," said Humphrey. "I'll answer what you haven't asked, if it's any use to you. No, I don't believe he could. He could do a good many things, not that." Humphrey seemed to be reflecting. He went on, "I take it, it must be rather rare for men to kill their grandmothers?"

Briers laughed out loud. The question sounded curiously academic and curiously atypical of the other man.

"I don't recall running across a case myself. There must be a few. I doubt if there is any family relationship where there hasn't been a murder."

Humphrey, ceasing to be immersed in any reflections, said, "I don't believe that Loseby could have done it. The trouble is, in this sort of shambles, anything seems possible. And that's true the more one happens to have seen."

"The trouble is, we've both seen too much. I agree with you. It's harder to say, full stop, it's just not on."

Briers opened a cupboard, brought out a bottle, and they each had a drink. They didn't return to the subject. What they had said might have been unexpected, even to themselves. They were two stable, experienced men, confiding how at times, against all sense and reason, it was hard to disbelieve.

❧ 15 ❧

On the following Tuesday, Humphrey was again asked to call
at the police station. This time it was not Briers's voice but
a deferential one, punctuated by glottal stops, that spoke on the
telephone. "Inspector Shingler here. The name won't mean anything, but I'm one of the chief's team. I don't want to trouble you,
sir, but there's a little point you might be able to clear up. It's
nothing to do with your statement, of course, just a little point we
have to shift out of the way—someone has been helping us with
our inquiries."

At that phrase, Shingler's voice had a faint inflection, one knowledgeable man to another. The phrase had already appeared several
times in the press, the smooth talk of official handouts. The papers
had nothing to go on, in spite of those references. There were already signs of criticism. One popular Sunday had run a three-inch
headline: **WHAT HAS HAPPENED TO OUR POLICE?** The article wasn't specifically concerned with the Belgravia murder and
might have been written before. Nevertheless, the chance was too
good to miss, and there were several hundred indignant words, appealing for the safety of the old and infirm, all the other Lady
Ashbrooks of the country.

As for Lady Ashbrook herself, Humphrey had seen only one
more personal notice. With nothing to do, he had gone into his
club, which didn't often happen, and, as also didn't often happen,
he had skimmed through the weekend journals. It was curious how

habits dropped away. Not so long ago he would have bought such journals as a matter of course; not now.

To his surprise, he found in the *New Statesman* a longish article entitled "Establishment Incarnate." Down the page, the name of Madge Ashbrook kept glaring out. Humphrey began to read with twisted amusement, but then his emotions became more mixed. The piece was signed with a woman's name, and soon he guessed that this was a daughter, or more likely a granddaughter, of an old acquaintance.

To anyone who knew some private language, it was a certainty that the writer was upper class, detesting her origins, determined to believe what all good progressives believed. In too many ways for Humphrey's comfort, she might have been his own daughter. The writer commented that she—Madge Ashbrook—was the establishment at its most typical. She had married into the top of the old aristocracy, so far as there was one. Then, in circumstances carefully concealed by an establishment cover-up (fair comment, Humphrey thought), she married again into the new political-commercial aristocracy. She had always lived among the rich. She had always known, without thinking, what right-thinking people should and would decide.

That was the strength of the establishment. They didn't need to cogitate; they knew by instinct. Madge Ashbrook had known that it was right to appease Hitler, right to get rid of Edward VIII, right to regard Chamberlain as a savior, and then right to deify Winston Churchill. She had never had an original idea in her life, and yet she and her kind had great influence. She was an entirely ordinary woman. If she had been born in a different environment, it was easy to imagine her as a housewife in Manchester, bringing up her children in a strict old-fashioned way, devoted to a loving, overpossessive family life. (Was this girl, Humphrey thought, working off a grudge of her own?) Nevertheless, privileged as she was, Madge Ashbrook had once been glamorous. Very glamorous, so all the memoirs reported.

She had been one of the beautiful young women who might have known—probably did know—Rupert Brooke, Julian Grenfell, Patrick Shaw-Stewart, Raymond Asquith, in that idyllic time before the 1914–18 war, a war of which Madge, of course, must have unquestioningly approved. She had survived and the young men hadn't, and she passed on to shine as one of the beautiful young women of the twenties, the last stars of a decaying civilization. It was a worthless civilization, but still she and the other beautiful women had shone in it and seemed to have enjoyed it. Now she and nearly all the rest of them had gone. *Où sont les neiges d'antan?*

Humphrey was, despite himself, a trifle touched. The girl had a romantic heart. But he wished that she had been able to resist that last flourish.

On his second visit to the police station, Humphrey was once more conducted to the Murder Room, but Frank Briers wasn't there. The invitation hadn't come from him. More likely, Humphrey thought, it was the young man Shingler making a new acquaintance, conceivably a useful one. He would certainly have known that Humphrey had been talking privately with Briers for hours on the previous Friday. He could have heard murmurs about their earlier connection.

Though Briers was absent, a dozen of his officers had been collected in the Murder Room. There were several Scenes of Crime men, detective sergeants Humphrey hadn't heard of. He was finding it hard to identify faces and remember names. There were two women whose rank he didn't catch, pretty in an active, hearty fashion, rather like less peach-fed versions of the county girls with whom Humphrey had gone hunting in his youth.

The matter that had been Shingler's reason or pretext for invoking Humphrey turned out to be puzzling but insignificant. The person who had been helping them with their inquiries was a youth who had offered himself. This was the "silly young man" Briers had mentioned. The boy was trying to help, Briers said. "The chief's got that wrong," Shingler remarked knowingly, not long after they had told Humphrey the facts. "All that guy wants is to feel important. It's his chance to get into the public eye."

The youth delivered newspapers around the Square and in the neighborhood. His story was that on the Sunday morning after the murder, at the usual time, about eight o'clock, he pushed Lady Ashbrook's paper—she took only one—through her letter box. As he did so, he had a vague memory that he heard sounds of a thumping nature from within the house. He thought nothing of it until he learned that the old lady had been killed. He did know that Maria, the daily woman, didn't work in the house on Sundays.

He thought that it was right to pass his information to the police. "It might be useful."

"So it would be," said Shingler, "if he ever heard it. Bloody little show-off."

The boy didn't know, and hadn't been told, that the police were certain that Lady Ashbrook had been murdered the night before. The chief of the Scenes of Crime squad, Shingler, was more than usually assertive. They were sure that no one had been in the house that Sunday morning. It was too much to imagine that someone else, taking all precautions known to man, leaving no prints, traces, relics of occupation, had been lurking in the house hours after the murderer had left. Not only lurking, but amusing himself by making violent noises.

"It's a bit of tomfoolery. It stands to sense it is."

"It might have been a poltergeist," Bale said sedately. He had scarcely spoken, but Humphrey had recognized that he was the senior officer there. Humphrey couldn't decide whether that was a serious suggestion. Policemen could be as addicted to the supernatural as anyone else, he thought.

They were asking Humphrey if he had anything to suggest. Did he know the lad? Humphrey said no, but he would recognize him by sight. He was efficient. Papers came regularly, on time, on the rare occasions when there were no strikes in Fleet Street. Loud police laughter: strikers of any kind, anywhere, were not their favorite characters. Could the lad have mixed up that Sunday with a day when he might have heard some noise? Humphrey inquired. Even the Monday, when at that time in the morning there would have already been several people in the house, Maria, himself, the local sergeant.

That had been thought of, they said. The lad stood on his dignity. The day was Sunday. He remembered the thick load of Sunday papers.

"Forget it," Shingler said. "It's not worth any more buggering trouble. Get rid of him."

Bale gave a judicious nod.

"He must have made a mistake," he said in a kind, paternal fashion. "There isn't any other explanation." That sounded distinctly prosaic, but no one at any time in the future did any better, though the question came up again.

For Humphrey, it was being an unprofitable morning. The room cleared, and he was left with the three who worked most intimately with Briers. Humphrey did not find them a source of insensate excitement. They were polite, respectfully matey. He was given cups of the inescapable police tea.

Shingler was much the cleverest of the three, he thought. He was also on the make. It didn't need much practice in professional assessment to tell one that. At sight, Humphrey rather liked Bale. He might be stiff, sober, overcorrect, a pillar of society. But then you needed pillars here and there, and this one wasn't an empty man. Humphrey wouldn't have been surprised to find that he had some private expertness, right outside the force.

Flamson didn't make any impression. Coarse featured, coarse fibered, why had Frank Briers picked him out? There must have been dozens of detectives as good or better. Perhaps Briers had to take what he could get. In any organization, one couldn't be too finicky: people were more interchangeable than it was agreeable to think.

As a general reflection, that could have applied. In the particular case, it wouldn't. For the past twenty-four hours, Flamson had been more useful to Briers than any of the others. Humphrey didn't know, and had no means of knowing, that the inner squad, Briers included, had suddenly become both puzzled and disappointed. This had showed when Briers and his inner group had talked together, all others barred. In secret, under the careful words, they had assumed that the will would give them some pointers. The day before, they had been informed about its contents. It told them nothing at all.

The will had no picturesque features. According to Lady Ashbrook's solicitor, it was almost a replica of a previous will, except that a bequest to an American acquaintance had been deleted, the man having recently died. All the bequests were small, £200 to Maria, £300 to Dr. Perryman, £200 to Lady Ashbrook's hairdresser. There was nothing to Loseby, except a note that she had made some provision for him during her lifetime. Possessions had been carefully bestowed, none of much value, candlesticks to Celia, other silver to acquaintances, a couple of decanters and runners to Humphrey himself. The pictures were not listed. The residue of the estate was left to the Imperial Cancer Research Fund.

The residue of the estate, since nothing substantial had been left anywhere else, meant in effect the whole of it, the tail end of the leasehold, pictures, bits of jewelry, all thrown in. There was, however, a surprise that upset the police and that, when the news spread, astonished Lady Ashbrook's acquaintances. The solicitors judged it right to drop a hint to Briers. The estate was proved to be quite small. There would be none of the money that had been expected. All assets added up, there wasn't likely to be £50,000. To Briers's squad, the will, the disappearance of wealth, came as a setback. "No bloody motive there," said Shingler. He added, "Except for the Cancer Research Fund. Perhaps they did it." Brash humor was not well received. He recovered himself. "It's just as well we haven't ruled out the professionals."

"We never have done," Briers said. Spontaneous as he seemed, he was impenetrable after a reverse.

"I don't know." It was Flamson, expression clouded, who couldn't shape his thoughts. "It doesn't fit in. Too many loose ends."

"Right, George." Briers didn't reveal his own thoughts, but he was following Flamson's. He was encouraging them, exuding energy. The thing to do in a time like this was to go on exactly as they were. The others didn't know whether he was just soldiering on or whether he really had some foresight. Probably not, he was to say later. But he also blamed himself for being dense. This latest news, which appeared as a setback, should have told him more. It was Flamson, a simple soul, who mutely suspected that some matters seemed too simple to be true.

✤ 16 ✤

Frank Briers, in Humphrey's sitting room, was comfortable, though not restful, in the mode of action. It would have been hard to read his expression, or from it guess what progress his operation was making. Like others who were designed for action, he was immersed in the operation itself. You could have said that he was too busy to think, or alternatively too busy thinking. It was obsessive, yes: but he had learned to pace himself. This was some days after Humphrey's second visit to the police station. Briers had not previously accepted Humphrey's standing invitation. Now Humphrey had asked him for a specific evening because Alec Luria wanted to meet him.

Luria had a collector's interest in able men, especially if they were doing jobs where he was ignorant. Briers, neither forward nor shrinking, had been willing to oblige—and hadn't needed to be briefed about Luria, saying that he had picked up the name already.

Briers had arrived a quarter of an hour early, which was not by chance. He could talk to Humphrey as he wouldn't be able to talk to a stranger: and in the mode of action Briers liked to talk. And yet, Humphrey accepted, though the talk was fluent, it was under control. Briers wasn't telling Humphrey, to use the old security phrase, any more than he needed to know, or rather any more than it was useful for him to know. Useful to Briers, that is. If Humphrey had heard the detectives discussing the will, he would have wondered if people he knew were feeling menaced. As it was, to Humphrey, a spectator, it was a vague heaviness, like thunder far away.

Briers was sitting in an armchair, with a whiskey on the coffee table beside him. Humphrey would have bet that, hearty but disciplined, Briers would take one more drink that evening, no less, no more. He said, "The lads are doing their stuff. They are coping with all the houses in the region. Down to Pimlico. They are checking any villain we know about—there are a fair number in the streets at the back of Victoria. Then they'll go again and countercheck. Masses of paper on my desk already. I must say, Humphrey, if I was a sociologist, I should be gathering quite a lot about the manners and customs of the citizens round about. Particularly what they were doing over a period of three or four hours on a Saturday night."

"Any luck?" Humphrey asked. He had a feeling that he was being underestimated. This was conversation not intended to inform.

"It's early days yet." He gazed straight at Humphrey. This might be a time when he was deciding whether to withhold or talk. He went on, "We have found one of the old lady's ten-pound notes. Paid into a shop."

Concentrated, active, Briers gazed again at the older man. "The first time we talked, did I give you an idea that there are one or two odd things that we don't understand? Did I do that?"

"You might have done," said Humphrey, "if you had been talking to someone as bright as you are."

"You've done some thinking in your time." Briers added lightly, "There were one or two unusual features about that room. I wonder if you noticed them?"

Then, switching off, he said, "Well, the boys will be busy around the neighborhood. They'll be coming nearer home soon. Actually, they've been in Eaton Square already."

"Why ever there?"

Briers broke into a broad monkey smile. "Purely political. If we're going to turn Pimlico upside down, it's just as well to make a nuisance of ourselves—"

To the rich, Briers implied. He wasn't being candid, Humphrey was certain—though he couldn't understand why not, any more than he had in the police station understood the echoes of constraint. But Humphrey was forming his suspicion of what Briers in reality thought.

Briers continued, "They'll be beginning round here before long. You'll have to account for yourself that Saturday night, of course."

"They won't get very far with that." Humphrey had been distracted but now was amused. "Remarkably unexciting, even to a sociologist, my dear Frank. I was either reading or watching TV. Probably both."

Policeman's grin from Briers. "Quite impossible to prove."

Soon, punctual, punctilious, Alec Luria came into the room. There was a beautiful exchange of courtesies, as if each were trying to trump the other. "I am happy to have the chance of meeting you, chief superintendent." "Not so happy as I am, professor." "I've heard so much about your career—" "That's nothing, that's nothing, compared with those books of yours."

Briers was not the man to be outplayed in any game of etiquette, but Humphrey also noticed that he could jerk himself out of the mode of duty, obsessive duty, and devote himself to a stranger. Any talent spotter would have marked that down as a good pointer for his future.

On his side, Luria was not the man, ceremonies decently concluded, to lose his sense of sardonic farce. A drink accepted, settled down in another armchair, his length extended, suitable preliminaries about the temperature, the value of the pound, and the primaries to the American election, he then said, melancholy eyes not so melancholy, "Of course, you have rather the advantage of me, chief superintendent. Your men must have given you data about me on paper. Not too suspicious, I hope."

Police interviews in Eaton Square, Humphrey had now realized—that was how Briers had already been briefed when Luria's name was mentioned. Not put off, businesslike, Briers said, "Not in the way of business, professor. You needn't take out any extra insurance. I hope they didn't waste too much of your time."

"I thought they made a very good job of it, if I may say so. They were very nice with it—do pass that on, if it's any use to them."

Luria was being paternal, suddenly ceasing to be unobtrusive. Then, unobtrusive again, he asked, "Stop me if I'm being too inquisitive. But am I right in thinking that all your men on this case are survivors from the purge that we've heard about?"

The "purge" was public knowledge. The commissioner of metropolitan police had over the past three years eliminated something like a fifth of the entire C.I.D. (that is, the detective branch, Scotland Yard), on the grounds of most varieties of corruption, criminal connivance, and conspiracy. There had been prosecutions, and people who followed the trials had followed something of what lay behind them: but it required a man as practiced with information as Luria to understand the sheer scale of the scandal.

It was an occasion when Briers felt it best to be spontaneous, though, Humphrey was thinking, perhaps not as spontaneous as he seemed.

"They wouldn't be at work if they hadn't survived, you know." He sounded bluff and cheerful.

"Can you tell me—it must have made an effect on morale, mustn't it? Everyone must have lost men they knew very well, casualties all over the force."

"There were heavy casualties, of course there were. It had to be done. You can take my oath on that. Some of us would have been glad if he could have finished off a few more."

"I don't believe it could have happened in any other police force in the world." Luria was solemn. "I don't mean yours is worse than any of the others. On the contrary. But I don't believe any other force would have stood that purge."

"Professor, I want to get this a bit clearer. Policemen are very much like anyone else. Uniformed police, in this country anyway, are comparatively honest. You have to remember that they don't have many temptations. Tiny bits of money offered, sometimes taken. Not a real problem, though. Detectives are a different kettle of fish. You try to imagine the way they are living their whole lives. It's a hazard of the job. They have to spend a great slice of their time with professional crooks. And crooked lawyers. That's their world. It isn't a very pretty world. A good many of the professional crooks and the crooked lawyers are doing very well for themselves. They make it easy for detectives to have a share in the loot. It really isn't all that surprising that a fair number of detectives decided it was pleasant to play in the kitchen. Once that started, it became part of the setup. Pleasant to receive a share of the dibs. Pleasant to be one of the lads. But even more, unpleasant not to be one of the lads. Anyone who got into the C.I.D. soon discovered what he had to conform to."

Luria nodded. "That I can imagine."

"Look here. Let me speak for myself. I don't think that I'm specially corrupt. But men are easy to corrupt, granted the right conditions. You'd accept that?"

Luria nodded again. "Surely."

"I don't think I'm specially uncorrupt, either. I'm not going to pretend that I didn't feel the temptation. The bosses would have liked to take me in. I was on the way up. I was the kind of character they wanted. And I could have made a killing."

"Why didn't you, Frank?" Humphrey's question was affectionate, sarcastic.

"Why wouldn't *you?*" Briers replied in kind.

"No, tell us." Luria was paternal again.

"Well, maybe two reasons. One respectable, one not so respectable. Long lines of decent, honest chapel people behind me." Humphrey intervened—nonconformist Protestants, that means. "It would have gone against that grain," Briers continued. "But more, not to be too kind to myself, because I'm a prudent sort of animal. I decided that they would be caught in the long run. Everyone knew. Someone, someday, would be tough enough to act. And I didn't think any money in the world was worth that risk. And also I happened to be ambitious. Money might be fun, but if I had to choose, I'd a damn sight rather try for the top jobs."

"You're underestimating yourself, you know," Luria said.

"Have it your way," Briers replied. "Anyway, here I am. I'm a survivor. A good many of them aren't. They made a killing. But quite a lot of the offices on the best floors are empty now. Former occupants don't need them anymore."

"Why don't they need those offices?"

"Because they're in jail."

There was a pause. Luria said that most of this sounded too true to be comforting. If this was what happened in a disciplined force, how was one going to keep societies even tolerably straight? Briers, younger than the other two, more hopeful then they were, more active, more robust, replied that he was a rough-and-ready liberal. You couldn't be a policeman and think too well of human beings—

123

but we weren't utterly lost. You couldn't change them inside, but you might be able to change their behavior. (Luria for an instant was taken aback to hear this kind of talk from a police officer.) We had to get on with our jobs within the social limits. Clean things up, preserve what we could, prevent things getting worse. The law wasn't everything, but it was something.

"There," said Luria, "I am absolutely with you. Heart and soul."

"So I feel pretty content working on this case, and if you ask most of my lads, you'd find they would say the same. If you forget about intellectuals—" Briers was breaking out into a matey gibe— "people with practical jobs generally feel more or less at home in this world. It's something of a saving grace."

Luria nodded but said pensively, "So long as other people believe the jobs are useful. So long as they believe in what you are doing."

"They'd damn well better. As I was saying, the law isn't everything, but it's about all we've got."

Turning to Humphrey, Luria remarked with a gentle, comradely, sardonic smile, that he felt better, listening to their friend. As a gesture of solidarity, he asked for another drink. He looked seriously at Briers and said, "I tell you what. I'd be happier if anyone around here was angrier about this murder of yours. To be sure, some of them are sad. But they're not fighting angry. They don't want any revenge. They just take it as something that happens, like the weather. They're letting what happens get on top of them. Society has just become too much for them."

"Believe me," said Briers, "I want that man as much as I want anything."

"Yes, you make me feel better." Again Luria looked at the policeman as though they were intimates.

"I am sure you wish you had capital punishment back."

There was a short hiatus. Briers, calm and positive as before, said, "Professor, today I have fifty-six detectives working on this case. Tomorrow I expect some more. I am just referring to detective sergeants and above. So far as I know, and I fancy I do know, every one of them would agree with you, and two or three of my party are going to have real influence in the force."

"I'm very glad to hear it," Luria said.

"But I ought to tell you, unfortunately I'm the odd man out. I'm against having capital punishment back."

Luria didn't often look astonished, but now he did. The great prophetic face had gone blank, and his mouth opened and shut before he went on again.

"Why ever not?"

"I don't believe in it. I don't believe it works."

"You mean, it doesn't stop murders? It wouldn't have stopped this one?"

"I'm being pragmatic. The evidence is on that side."

"I take leave to doubt it. But I'm not going to argue with you there. The real point is quite different."

"So you do believe in hanging?"

"Not hanging." Luria was recovering his poise. "Too many sexual connotations. But I certainly believe in getting rid of some criminals. Shooting if you like. The least messy method we can find."

It was Briers's turn to be astonished. He wasn't as fluent as usual. "Haven't you thought it would be a throwback? It would make the place a bit less civilized."

"That's a reason why I believe in it. I gave up accepting liberal optimism a long time ago. I'm not in the least interested in deterrents, pro or contra. I'm not interested in false hopes. I am interested in society preserving its force and virtue. I used the word revenge a little while ago. That wasn't loose or absentminded. It's a profound need of society to take its revenge on people who offend its deepest instincts. I'm sure that society can't be healthy if we pretend that that need doesn't exist. You may say I'm being too practical, but were you being practical at all when you gave yourself away. You said it would make the place a bit less civilized. You ought to ask yourself, what is your real motive? The difference between us is, you believe human beings are more civilized than they are, or perhaps can ever be."

Briers had had practice in various aspects of the argument, but not this one. He said, in a less buoyant tone: "I shouldn't say I was all that civilized. We've had some child murders in this country. Beyond description. If I'd caught the people who did them, and had had a gun handy and thought I could get away with it, I'd have shot them without thinking twice. I might have done the same to the man who killed this old lady. That wouldn't have done any-one any harm." He added tersely, "Except the ones I got rid of. But I still think it would do harm to go through the whole appara-tus of the law and string them up or go through any other ritual ex-ecution we could invent. Have you ever heard the noise in a prison when someone was being hanged? I did once, when I was just starting in the force. It might change your mind."

"No," said Luria. "I'm not moved by that. You're trying to make life hygienic. It can't be, and we have to face it."

"Well then," Briers said, not outfaced. "We had better agree to differ, hadn't we?"

The conversation changed. Often they were at one and there was an understanding between them. In time, Briers said that he had to break away. There would be reports waiting for him in his office, another couple of hours before he could leave for home. There would be supper ready for him when he reached home around ten o'clock. Policemen's wives were well trained, he said with a smile that might have been dismissive or salacious. But Humphrey, who knew about his wife's health, also knew that it was neither.

Humphrey thought later, not that night, that the meeting hadn't gone exactly as one might have expected. A high priest of Western civilization, father figure among Jewish intellectuals, illustrious aca-demic; on the other hand, a tough, striving professional policeman. They got talking on crime and punishment, and what did you an-ticipate? Not quite what had happened. Well, in those days, for Humphrey to witness that couple surprising each other didn't come amiss. It was a glimpse of the human comedy, of which he wasn't having enough, and he had enjoyed it.

❧ 17 ❧

One August Saturday Humphrey saw Kate on the other side of the Square and went across. He said he had heard nothing. Then he looked around at the houses, shining blandly in the sun, and added, "Life goes on."

"It couldn't do anything else, could it? Not one of your more original remarks, you know—"

She was wearing her ugly, disrespectful, alluring grin, and Humphrey, spirits lightened, tried to justify himself. "Would anyone guess that the country's going broke?" He didn't tell her—she was quick enough to discern it—that he wasn't thinking of that trouble but of others coming nearer. No one had yet been charged with the murder. He had his own doubts, hazy, not yet crystallized. He had no doubt at all that Frank Briers was telling him, with an appearance of absolute spontaneity, things that meant nothing and keeping back what he was really doing. Humphrey had learned that Loseby and Susan had been questioned several times. Briers told Humphrey nothing of this. Humphrey would have liked to know more of other personal inquiries. Briers was a master of the double finesse. It was the first time he had exercised that talent at Humphrey's expense. Of course, he told Humphrey, they were interested in a great many people's movements on the evening and night of July 24-25. Only an imbecile, Humphrey thought with both irritation and anxiety, would have been surprised by that piece of information.

He was irked that Briers went on treating him as an old friend but without trust. Still, it didn't prevent Humphrey from believing that he knew where the police were looking. If that was so, then there were acquaintances of his living in suspense. Nevertheless, as he had said with solemnity that morning, life went on. Not long afterward, at a dinner party, he saw an eyeflash of Kate's showing that she had remembered. He had judged it safer not to tell her his suspicions. There might be some at this table under strain.

Actually, the dinner, though not notable for well-being, proceeded without incident. It was given by Tom Thirkill in the apartment in Eaton Square. Thirkill had been obliged to cancel the luncheon where Lady Ashbrook was to have been the prize guest, the last acceptance in her engagement book. Nevertheless, hospitality unreturned continued to nag at him. It meant presenting others with a moral superiority. Hence this dinner, a large one, such as not many in the neighborhood would have given in a private house—the Lefroys, Paul and Celia, the Perrymans, Alec Luria, Humphrey, Thirkill's own daughter. That would pay off those who had entertained Tom Thirkill before Lady Ashbrook's death, and one or two more just worth collecting. More worth collecting, since Thirkill didn't propose to squander an evening, was a Cabinet minister and his wife. His political aide, Stella Armstrong, big and handsome, the most sumptuous of gray eminences, acted without fuss as the hostess.

Thirkill's dining room led out of the drawing room, was identical in size and furnished with the same confident taste. More pictures around the walls, quieter than those in the other room, and restful. A couple of Cromes, a Chinnery, a set of Bonnington watercolors. Somebody had taken trouble, Humphrey thought, as on his previous visit.

A chandelier presided over the long table. Under it, napery, silver, glass were shining. The women were wearing long dresses. It occurred to Humphrey that in his youth, for a dinner on this scale, in this place, the men would also have dressed in black ties or, at some of his first dinner parties, white ones. None was wearing a black tie now. On the other hand, the food, though less lavish, was better than Humphrey recalled and the wine at least as good. Thirkill might not drink himself, but he must take excellent advice.

It all looked so safe. Humphrey remembered dinners just before the war that had looked just as safe as this. Most people felt safe until it was too late. So many times Humphrey had seen people apparently thoughtless about danger. There must have been plenty of dinners as privileged as this before a revolution. Perhaps in personal danger too.

And yet, from the beginning, the evening wasn't smooth. At the start, Thirkill was in a persecuted mood. Staring down the table, he asked if anyone realized what was happening to him. It was a kind of pity-seeking question to which there wasn't an answer. He might be talking of the libel suits, but word was coming down from lawyers, Paul Mason's father among them, that he was certain to win. Something new in the press? Nothing of the sort, Thirkill said indignantly. He was inclined to suggest that they were now on his side.

"Do you know what's happened to me?" He took a sip from his half glass of white wine, as though to clear the grit and gravel from his voice. He answered himself, "The police." He went on. "They've been around here taking up a couple of hours of valuable time. Do they think I've got time to waste? Asking me to account for my movements that night."

"It's only a matter of routine, you know." That was from Humphrey. As in private with Thirkill, it was difficult to resist trying to soothe him.

"I must say, I wonder if they would have treated a Tory member as they did me. I wonder how many of our chaps have black marks against their names. I wonder how many Tories are on the M15 files and how many of ours."

Thirkill seemed to have regressed to his radical youth. He was looking hard at Humphrey, who he suspected would know the exact answer. Humphrey looked innocently back, as he had become practiced in doing from all the years in the old job.

Luria put in like a calm referee, "If it's any comfort to you, Mr. Thirkill, they treated me just the same."

"Did they, by God, and you're an American visitor—"

"Oh, I've been on the spot too. For what it's worth, I've talked to some of your senior policemen. And I got a very favorable impression. They are having a difficult assignment around here."

Luria had his knack of bestowing benevolence and authority at the same time.

Then Celia spoke. Humphrey had noticed that in the drawing

room before dinner she had been talking more freely than he had heard her, while Paul had been silent. It was to be the last time they accepted an invitation together: they had decided to part back in July.

Celia said, tone light but clear and curiously insistent: "Don't you think it's good to know what everyone else is going through? Mr. Thirkill, have you ever had a policeman ask you questions before? I haven't. Policemen look different when they ask you questions. It made me think."

"There's something in that, Mrs. Hawthorne." Thirkill's smile had a sudden, open, exposed charm. "There's something in that."

"It's what I've been telling the middle classes since I was a girl," said Stella Armstrong, who was as impeccably middle class as Celia herself but who suddenly spoke out of her duty to Transport House.

And yet, though Thirkill could control his paranoia, or alternately have it for moments wiped away as a fit of sexual jealousy might have been, the evening was still not smooth. To those with nerves alert, and there were several around the table, disquiet was hanging in the air. Throughout the conversation about Thirkill's ill-treatment, Humphrey had watched Kate listening to Dr. Perryman, who was sitting beside her. She was listening with rapt attention, with the mixture of affectionate mischief and concern that she had often shown to Humphrey himself. That, more than he cared for, produced a disquiet of his own.

At the end of dinner, it had ceased to be the fashion in circles like this for the men to be left over their port. Now all stayed in their places; port and brandy circulated; and Luria, who didn't easily get tired of his favorite themes, asked them all their views on capital punishment. He wasn't reassured. Most of them said they were against him.

He seemed to be conducting a somber research, Humphrey thought, surveying how far liberal opinions had carried. Paul Mason, who had been so silent, put in an independent cross-bench voice: he would eliminate terrorists and wouldn't lose a minute's sleep.

"Make martyrs of them, would you?" Tom Thirkill protested.

"They'd be less nuisance as martyrs than if they were alive. You can't try to rescue martyrs," Paul said coolly.

Kate was the first and only person to say that she was on Alec Luria's side. She said it with warmth and her whole heart. From across the table, Monty Lefroy, with the air of one delivering the final judgment, said that he was not at one with his dear wife. "I believe in the direction of time's arrow," he said, letting his voice roll around. "And it's gone in the direction of preserving individual life."

"Has it now?" Luria, not protracting that exchange, turned his gaze, quizzical, eyes shining in their brown depths, onto Kate's neighbor, Dr. Perryman. But before Perryman could give his answer, his wife intervened.

"I'm against you, professor," she said, bright, compassionate, composed. "My reason, though, would be different from what I've heard just now. It's religious. I do believe, you see, that everyone has a chance of redemption. Crimes are horrible, of course. But anyone can repent and be granted grace. If you execute them, you may be taking away that chance. Whatever anyone has done, they ought to have the opportunity to make their soul."

That was the longest speech, from an unexpected quarter. Luria was prepared for most kinds of argument, but not for that special kind of Christian idiom. Dr. Perryman helped him out, though he was speaking, as he had once done to Humphrey, as though he was off on an absent-minded fugue.

"I think, I think that I come down with Alice. But I can't pretend I believe as she does. It might be a comfort to believe, but it's no use pretending unless you're right there. I can't help coming down to earth. Are we always certain that we're executing the right man? I don't know about you, but I don't like the faintest possibility of a mistake. I can't face that—"

Shortly afterward, guests began to get up from the table. Disquiet might have been sharpened by that conversation. There hadn't been much drunk after dinner, though Humphrey noticed that Kate, who had a healthy appetite for spirits, had taken a second glass of brandy. They didn't return to the drawing room, and the party was breaking up early.

Humphrey wanted to speak to Kate, but as he approached she was once more listening raptly to Dr. Perryman who, when they got into Eaton Square, walked beside her toward her home.

Next morning, quite early, Humphrey heard Kate's voice,

strong, affectionate, over the telephone. Perryman needed some advice, she said. That's why he had been talking to her last night. He was hoping that Kate and Humphrey could go around to his house some evening that week. She was doing what Humphrey had done himself in a precarious love affair—was this a love affair? Or just a skirmishing, not yet committed? She was using a card of reentry, just a mundane excuse, to get them back into whatever relation they had, in which neither of them dared to disturb the peace of the moment.

❧ 18 ❧

In the morning, Kate had told Humphrey that Dr. Perryman was asking for advice. It took only a few hours before Humphrey had an intimation of what might be the trouble. Frank Briers rang up, friendly, energetic, surgent. "Come around some time. If you're not too busy. Quite a small matter, nothing to speak of, but you might be more in the picture than I am. Anyway, I'd like you to see our setup now we've got things organized."

Was it such a treat to see someone else's office simmering with activity? Inside the Murder Room, for the first moments Humphrey felt alien, curiously shy, as though he, not used to self-consciousness, had suddenly become afflicted. Briers had his jacket off, shirt-sleeves neatly rolled up, strong forearm muscles catching the eye, thick wrists. There was now a battery of telephones standing on his desk. One was scrambled, and he was listening to a call. Around the walls were maps of southwest London, circles and arrows marked out in red.

Chief Inspector Bale came in, decorous and sensible as before.

"He seems a good chap," Humphrey said as Bale took care to leave them alone.

"So he is." Briers was smiling cheerfully.

He leaned back in his chair and swept a hand around, displaying the room. "Well, this is a bit more like it, isn't it? We really are in business now." Then he gave a hard debunking grin.

"Not that we've got much change out of it."

"Haven't you?"

133

"Did you expect us to?" Briers's question was light, casual, as if it were social, but his glance was sharp, as though he wasn't being as casual as he sounded. Humphrey said, "It's your game, not mine. I imagined it would take some time."

"It might be taking too much time." He grinned again. "Look here, I'll tell you what we've done." Humphrey thought Briers was behaving exactly like a business tycoon in a negotiation. Presumably he would come to the point some time—if there was a point, which as before Humphrey didn't doubt. But still, ceremonies must be properly performed.

From time to time more policemen entered: questions, brisk friendly instructions, those of a man on terms with his subordinates—then back to the exposition. His lads (that was a generic term that included women) had, within fifteen days, been inside 757 houses. That was the score up to the previous night. There were perhaps as many more visits to be made. Some houses they had called on more than once. They had foraged in the local dives and pubs. They had talked to all the villains they had information about and had identified a number more. "We're picking out more of the criminal population of S.W. 1 and S.W. 3 than we have done for years. It may be useful sometime. It may not be so useful to them. But it's small stuff; it's chicken feed."

Humphrey didn't believe for an instant that Briers was showing his chief concern. Still, it was part of the job.

Briers was neither tired nor deflated. Another interruption from Bale. Humphrey had ceased to feel an alien. If you had lived any kind of active life, there was a satisfaction in watching people immersed in their job, whatever it was. It was one of the comforts, minor but a comfort, against chaos, absurdity, the cold. Humphrey had kept his curiosity. It would have been interesting to go along with some of those policemen and see how the inquiries went. Questionnaires, so far as he could make out: accounts of movements hour by hour; testimonies by relatives, wives, women; checks on what the testimony was worth. No corners turned, a mass scrutiny, anonymous, a collective action. Individuals didn't prevail against the apparatus. There were too many people. The crowd was too large. Society was nameless—and yet, out of those molecular inquiries, sometimes there could emerge one singular name.

"I must say," Humphrey remarked, "you're being pretty thorough."

"What do you take us for?"

Humphrey was smiling. "My old firm never had your resources. We couldn't have mounted a search like this."

With Briers, professional pride was strong, but so was realism. "Sometimes we get nowhere," he said. "The routine doesn't always cope."

"I'd like to follow just one day's work with some of your lads."

Briers's answer came straight but decisive.

"Too dangerous, Humphrey. If they were chasing anything like a competent villain, and we took him in some time, and he had one of those damned bent lawyers, also competent, then they'd be on to you. A regular outsider. They'd find out what you used to do. They'd call you a spy. We couldn't face it."

Humphrey nodded.

"But you're welcome to see some specimens from the file," Briers offered. "Questions, answers. It'd teach you something. It's what surprised me most when I went into the force. How inarticulate ninety percent of our fellow citizens are. Not just when they're frightened—that's understandable. But when they're prattling away." Then Briers said, "By the by, that doctor, Dr. Perryman, he's not inarticulate, is he? Do you know much about him?"

At last: this was the lead-in for which Humphrey had been waiting, but less ominous. This was a neutral topic.

Humphrey gave a neutral opinion. Perryman's patients praised him, he said. He kept up to date, was conscientious, and had good judgment. As far as Humphrey's own feeling went, he thought the man was intelligent but didn't find him sympathetic. As he spoke, Humphrey was aware that a resentment of his own was filtering in—Humphrey had often felt that Kate gave the doctor too much attention.

Briers looked acquiescent. He said there was some information from Perryman's old hospital. One of their brightest students. They couldn't understand why he had gone into general practice.

Humphrey said, "What's all this in aid of?"

"Nothing important. It doesn't signify. It's a bit of an oddity, that's all. But it's not sensible to pass over the oddities in our trade. You know the old lady kept wads of banknotes in the house. Paid her bills with them, almost every penny she spent, which weren't very many. You were right about that. She was as close as they come. She also kept the number of every note she had. Neat and tidy in her notebook. The notes in the house when she was killed—we have all the numbers. Coutts, that was her bank. We picked up that earlier note, but not one of those in the house that night has turned up. We've dug into every shop in the metropolitan area. No go. But two tenners that she drew out a year ago have turned up. I told you that before, didn't I? The numbers were in her little notebook for 1975, with a tick, which meant she'd paid a bill with them. Then they've been used to pay another bill. Perfectly naturally, in the normal way of business. By Dr. Perryman. To a newspaper shop in the Pimlico Road. He's bought his papers there for years. They know him well. He often pays in notes."

"He's not the only professional character who does."

"That fits. I didn't want to leave a loose end, so I had him in. Rather lost he was, but quite candid. Yes, she always paid him in notes. It didn't go through his books. He was escaping tax, naturally. He said what you've just said—he wasn't the only private doctor to like being paid in notes. He gave the old lady a thirty percent discount on his normal fees. They seem to have thought that it was very nice and convenient for them both, doing each other a good turn." Briers went on, "It was a good interview. He's not a nobody. He came clean. Do you think it makes sense?"

Briers seemed to think it did make sense. Otherwise he wouldn't have been so forthcoming. About some of Humphrey's acquaintances he would have kept more back.

Humphrey's smile was sarcastic, not amused. He said, "I used to think the majority of people were fairly honest about money. Now I sometimes think that no one is. To talk to, Perryman is a high-minded man. Yes, I expect he genuinely is. And one would have thought old Lady Ashbrook might be as hard as nails, but she was an honorable soul. Yes, I expect she genuinely was. And it wouldn't worry those two to get cheerfully together on a ridiculous wangle like that. Everyone's gone mad about money. Oh yes, I agree with you. It makes sense."

Briers was gratified and, with one of his bursts of ceremony, thanked Humphrey for sparing so much time. Then, a good deal less ceremonious, he began talking with much internal amusement about the sexual predicament of one of his officers. Policemen were not saints: women officers were available, young, and some of them willing. One of the chaps was in a mess, said Briers: he had walked into an affair, and the girl was hearty and wouldn't let go. There were plenty of hazards waiting for a detective. This was the latest one.

This was more like Briers's conversation when he was younger. He wouldn't tell Humphrey who the policeman was, nor why Briers himself was excessively amused.

❧ 19 ❧

Two days later, Kate having looked after her husband's dinner, she and Humphrey walked to the Perrymans' house. This was in Bloomfield Terrace, technically in Pimlico. Pimlico was the district immediately south of Belgravia and the biggest of the nineteenth-century developments, but the one that had never enticed enough of the well-to-do. Young women about to be married were sternly advised by Victorian dowagers: never let him take you south of Eccleston Square. In cool fact, the houses in Bloomfield Terrace were indistinguishable from those next door to Humphrey's.

Humphrey and Kate were walking slowly, enjoying having no one around them. The evening was sultry, and, though they had had those weeks of such weather, they were enjoying that too. Kate said, "I haven't been out at night for months. This is nice."

That wasn't accurate in strictly factual terms. She had been out to Tom Thirkill's less than a week before. In other terms, it might have had a different accuracy, and Humphrey took it so. They were walking arm in arm through a dark street, past St. Barnabas's Church.

"So it is. Shall I take you out to dinner soon?"

"Just ask me."

She inquired, what was he going to say to Perryman? What kind of advice did Perryman want? Humphrey said. Perhaps about how to deal with the police? He had already told Kate what he had learned from Briers.

"Quite trivial for serious purposes," said Humphrey. "But unless you're used to police methods, it's likely to worry you."

She frowned. "He's been stupid, hasn't he? Ralph Perryman."

"Fairly stupid."

"You know, I should have thought he was above all that."

"It's not so rare."

"It ought to be."

Humphrey smiled at her affectionately. "You wouldn't do it yourself?"

"Nor would you."

Was he as honest as she was? Humphrey was wondering. About money, probably. About anything else? He would have trusted her word when anything depended upon it. There had been times when he wouldn't have trusted his own.

Upstairs in the Perryman drawing room, the doctor's wife was more at ease than he was. She sat, face unclouded, beside the standard lamp, mouth comfortably upturned in a calm smile, giving out complete self-confidence that she was able to understand and soothe—while Dr. Perryman, authority deserting him, was fussing around a table on which stood an array of bottles. What would Kate and Humphrey care to drink? No whiskey, no gin, no brandy, the standard London spirits, Humphrey was observing. There was strega, slivova, rum. More bottles. Campari, cordials, juices, vermouths. Perryman would be glad to make them an old-fashioned cocktail that was a little unusual. Humphrey had no taste for fancy drinks, and, while the others weren't watching, Kate gave him a mocking wink.

Discouraged, Humphrey asked the doctor what he was drinking himself.

"Vodka." A trace of authority returned. "There's always the off chance that one has to see a patient."

Kate was working this out. "Less smell? It's bad if they know you've had a drink?"

"No." Perryman was firm. "It's just the smell of alcohol itself that is bad for them. I've found it makes them nervous."

It seemed as though he was driven to the limit by professionalism, or conscience, or both. Kate and Humphrey each settled for vodka. They waited for the purpose of the evening to break through. Alice Perryman made chatty conversation about the heat.

No, she didn't mind it, she just relaxed. She was too young to have much memory of the summer of 1947; that had been as blazing, so she was told. She gave a smile remarkably like the Cheshire cat's, as though her not remembering that year would give comfort to the others.

Humphrey said that he did remember, very well. He had reason to, his son had been born that summer.

Dr. Perryman shifted in his chair, eyes wide open, but the muscles of his cheeks immobile as though he were a sufferer from Parkinson's disease. That was an odd feature, not always present and not clinical, of the striking face.

"I'm much obliged to you for coming, Leigh." This was the first time he had called Humphrey by his bare surname.

"So good to be here." With clandestine pleasure, Humphrey added, "Very pleasant of you to ask us." Sometimes the simple pronouns *we* and *us* had meaning.

Perryman said, "I'm in a little trouble, Leigh. You see, I did a very small personal service for old Lady Ashbrook."

"Oh, did you?"

"I let her pay me in currency. She liked doing that."

"Why was that, do you know?"

"Oh, I took a fraction off the bill. She liked that. It was a service to her." Then the doctor broke into a confessional laugh. "To tell you the honest truth, it was a bit of a service to me too. You see, I didn't have to declare anything in my tax return." He went on, earnest, confessional again: "This does happen to some of us now and then. No harm done. No hard feelings."

Humphrey inclined his head.

"Well, you know the police have been making their inquiries. Looking for God knows what." He was speaking in a monotonous, unemphatic tone. "They found some of the notes the old lady had paid me with. Months ago. She never let a bill run on more than a few days. I think she'd have been happiest if she'd slipped me the money after each visit. Like in the old days. Anyway, the police wanted an explanation. So I told them, of course."

"That was sensible," Humphrey said. He added, out of time-worn prudence, "As a matter of fact, I did hear a little about this."

"Who from, who from?"

"Oh, rumors float around in this kind of business. You can imagine that." That was said out of old practice too. It became first nature not to mention a name. "Anyway, doctor, I'm sure what you did was perfectly sensible. You haven't anything to worry about."

"That's not the point." Perryman spoke loudly, fiercely.

Humphrey was puzzled, genuinely puzzled. "I don't follow—"

"That's not the point. That's nothing like the point. I'm not worried about the police. There's nothing in it for them. But I wanted to ask you, that's why I told Kate I should like some advice, is there a chance that they'll pass the word on to the Inland Revenue?"

Surprise, matter-of-fact surprise. Humphrey couldn't help suppress a smile. Dr. Perryman was not smiling.

"I shouldn't think so. They'll have slightly more important things on their plate."

"Do they pass this kind of information on to the Inland Revenue?"

"I haven't the slightest idea. They've got to clear up a murder."

"If they do."

"If they do," Humphrey repeated, "I shouldn't think they'd be interested in someone getting away with a little income tax. And it must be fairly little, mustn't it?"

"Not much," the doctor said.

"Well then. You know, you're getting things out of proportion. I doubt if you'll hear anything more about it. I'm prepared to bet they don't. But if the worst comes to the worst, and they do make a signal to your tax inspector, it's not specially serious after all."

"That's what I keep telling him." Alice Perryman gazed at her husband with maternal, beneficent love. "It's not so serious; we shall forget it in a week."

"And I keep telling you, the news will go around." When he spoke to her, his tone was trusting, but he became indignant and harsh. "Would you like to get into the news for anything as piffling as this? Just *silly*." He spat out the word. "There's the man who cadged his takings on the side. And thought he could get it tax-free." He spoke with as much outrage as though someone else had committed the offense. Then he quietened and became anxious, concentrated. "What's more, these taxes aren't a joke, you know." He was speaking to his wife. "They might get me for three times what I owe them. Just to teach people a lesson. *Three times*, you know."

He said to Kate, who had been listening with furrowed, acute attention. "Just you think. Three times. It's not a flea bite. I've never made the money I could have done. That's one of the problems."

Humphrey said, "People do tell me you could have done."

Dr. Perryman replied, "Yes, I could have done."

"Why didn't you?"

Perryman's expression had become transformed. Rage, indignation, had disappeared. He shone with a kind of radiance, subdued but elated, and his tone became thoughtful, temperate. "I wanted to do something different. After all, one only has one life. Any competent man can get success as a consultant. And any man a class better can get success in what they call research. Without false modesty, it would have been easy. I wanted something better. I wanted to satisfy myself. That's all that matters. In the long run, that's all that matters. It may sound ridiculous to you,"—he gazed out into the room—"but I didn't want to make medicine just a shade more scientific. Hundreds of men are doing that every day. If you understand me right, if I wanted to make it anything, I wanted to make it a good deal less. That is, until I had made a new start."

He began to talk as he had done to Humphrey in the Square garden, the morning after Lady Ashbrook had returned from the hospital. He was eloquent, fervent, borne up on his own speech. The mind-body relation (he was repeating himself). What did we mean when we talked about the *will*? (Or spirit, or even mind?) His wife gently intervened just once: that wasn't so difficult if one had faith. She was sorry he hadn't got there yet. They looked at each other without conflict. He went on. We know so little. How did the mind affect the body and the other way around? Until we know that, we know nothing. It was worth spending one's life to get just a little way.

"Have you got anywhere?" Humphrey's question wasn't just a polite throwaway, but curious, sceptical, interested.

The doctor's answer was flatly sensible, not exalted, not cast down. "I'm not sure that I'll ever know. One's only got one life. As I said before, it may not be long enough."

"Of course," Humphrey said, "there are some questions that haven't any answers. And never will have."

"Of course there are. But we're no good if we don't ask them."

Possessively, Alice Perryman said, "He's thought about these things all his life. He told me so when I first met him."

Perryman hadn't asked for any more advice or referred again to the matter of the banknotes. When Humphrey and Kate had said good-bye and were walking in the street, it was that matter, however, about which she began to talk.

"Curious, he's so keen about money. He is, you know."

She said it with cheerful realism. "He and old Lady Ashbrook must have made a very good pair. Like French peasants. Trying to chisel each other, I shouldn't wonder."

"That's a trifle hard, isn't it?"

"You can't teach me anything about penny-pinching. I've had some practice. I know the signs." She glanced at him with her ugly, endearing grin. When she was alone with him, she liked being impudent.

She had another thought. "But it does seem odd, doesn't it? I can understand Lady Ashbrook. She was a born skinflint. The more they are run after, the meaner they get. But it does seem strange in him."

They exchanged views—it was one of their pleasures—about acquaintances: who were generous, who were stingy, why? Yes, expansive people, broad-natured people, could be remarkably stingy. They both had affection for Alec Luria: he was rich, but no one could call him generous. Paul Mason, one of the better young men, was, apart from occasional times when he took out a dozen friends, distinctly careful.

"But it's not right for Ralph Perryman," Kate returned to her first thought and spoke with feeling.

"Perhaps he thinks it is." Humphrey's tone was flippant, sarcastic, dismissing the subject.

"No." Kate persisted. "He's much better than that."

"I dare say."

"He's an idealist, isn't he?"

"Very likely. I don't know him well enough." They were taking their time down Ebury Street, lights in the hotel windows and the top-floor flats. Humphrey had answered indulgently but with a trace of impatience.

"Have you noticed his eyes? He may have made a mess of things, but he is an idealist, you know. You heard what he said about his career. It sounds like nonsense, but still—"

"My girl," Humphrey said, "you're not a pushover for many people, but you are rather a pushover for—the inflated, aren't you? Call them idealists if you like."

Her arm had been resting closely in touch with him. He felt it stiffen.

"You shouldn't have said that." Her voice was hard and strained.

"Why ever not?"

"You know why not."

So far as he could trust his mind, he had spoken without intention. He could have assured her, and been honest, that he hadn't meant to refer to her marriage or her husband. Perhaps his tongue was more truthful than his mind.

"If you talk like this, we shall hurt each other," Kate said. They walked on in dense silence. It might have been a minute before she broke out. A minute was a long time.

"What's said can't be unsaid. We mustn't say too much." Her arm was not stiff now, but she was looking at the pavement as they walked. "You needn't have rubbed it in. I'm in a trap. Do you think I don't know that? I'm not too bad at not making little mistakes. I only make a big one."

He felt her shaking, but it wasn't with tears, for, taking him by surprise, she was laughing out loud, not bitterly, but as someone who had seen a joke against herself. She said, "I can't tell you much. When I can, I will. I promise you."

"Yes."

"I can't see my way clear. We mustn't say too much until I do. Because that really will bind us. But I can say something you know already. I want you. I don't think it's altogether one-sided."

"Now that's a triumph of perception, isn't it?" It sounded like a gibe, or a denial of gravity, but it was said with love.

She smiled, but it was she who spoke with the gravity he had held down.

"I'm pretty sure," she said, "we could make something good." In a hurry, she corrected herself. "That's being vain of me. I know it is. But anyway, I believe I could be giving you a better time than you're having now. That wouldn't be too much of a feat, would it? Perhaps that's not being too vain."

Humphrey was touched, as he had been often before, by that singular mixture of realism and diffidence. Was it that that had first captivated him? No, it went deeper than that from the beginning.

"I wish I could guarantee that much for you," he said with simplicity.

Then silence again, the hot thick silence of love not yet complete, as they turned down Eccleston Street. "I ought to tell you something else. Something perhaps you don't know. All I've just said is true. You'll hold on to that, won't you? So will I. This is true too. It shows you the trap I've got into. You've understood a bit about my marriage—I've realized that all along. Another triumph of perception." She gave a smile, but it was wan. "But you don't know it all. I'll tell you as soon as I can. Though when one's made a mistake, perhaps one never knows it all oneself. Anyway, anything there ever was has gone. It's all empty, flat and empty. But yesterday he had a letter from a philosopher in Poland, saying how marvelous his work was. He hasn't had a letter like that for years. He was so overjoyed that I could have cried. And I was happy too. That's part of the trap. It's all that's left. I had to tell you."

Once more they weren't talking. As they came nearer home, Kate said, "Have I depressed you?"

"Yes. But it's probably better that I understand."

In the side street, he took her by the shoulders and kissed her, like a lover. She kissed him back, violently.

"In that way," she muttered, "any time."

He hesitated, kissed her again. He wanted her. He said, "I'm afraid this has to be all or nothing. Don't you see?"

"You're thinking of yourself."

"We both have to, don't we? Look, I want you to see your way clear."

She muttered his name. "Then you'll have to wait."

"Don't make me wait too long."

She said, "I shall be waiting too."

Then, with a tense good night, she walked quickly off alone toward the Square.

❧ 20 ❧

After that evening with the Perrymans, Humphrey did not invite Kate to go out with him. For a while, she wanted to withdraw without either of them mentioning it. When he met her—by chance, not intention—on an errand in the street, she was lively and loving and didn't let him forget that resounding platitude of his: life goes on.

They couldn't help noticing that life was going on for the police as well as for others. Often Humphrey came across detectives he now knew by sight, in their shirt-sleeves and slacks, some of them looking boyish with long, untrimmed hair. One Saturday night a pair of them walked into the local pub, and he asked them to have a drink with him and Alec Luria. They were ready to gossip about their interviews. They liked talking shop. They weren't so tight-lipped as his security underlings had been, Humphrey thought, but they didn't give much away.

Luria started one of his courteous, unflurried professional inquiries. He was as discreet as they were. A question about the case was impermissible, but he had his vocational curiosity. He wanted to learn about a detective's life, what led them to it, what kept them going. They were complaining, with hearty rancor, about being needed to stay on duty on a Saturday night. They both lived in the distant suburbs, miles away. It would be late before they got home at night. They would get back tired. It interfered with your married life, they said. Policeman's malady, they said. Worse for the boys in uniform. They complained about their pay. But they relished talking about the job. Luria persevered in searching for what the rewards really were.

After they had departed, he told Humphrey that there must be human rewards somewhere. Those men were more content, or at least more alive, than most. Humphrey said that a good many people, probing into others' affairs, got some satisfaction. Luria nodded his massive prophetic head and said, with more weight or sententiousness than was strictly necessary, yes, as the French used to say, people liked living in the odor of man.

Then Luria said, "You notice they didn't talk about their chief? They all know you see something of him." He went on, "They don't know about me. I've heard some of them talking about him once or twice. Most of them are in favor of him. He's a slave driver, but they like having a leader."

"Most of them?"

"I did hear one stab in the back. From someone who must be a bit higher up the ladder. Youngish. Too well-fed and glossy for a policeman. I didn't catch his name."

For a moment Humphrey was thinking of Flamson and described him. Luria shook his head. "No, that doesn't sound right." This man might have been a cockney.

It must be Shingler, Humphrey broke out. Shingler was Briers's bright particular star, the coming man in the Murder Squad.

"That bright particular star doesn't think much of his boss. And is mean and snide about him. Briers wasn't a copper's copper, he said. He was a showman. He got there on the work of the real coppers and then took the credit."

Humphrey was cursing. "Do you realize that that bastard has been made by Frank Briers? Briers has taken care of his whole career," Humphrey went on angrily. Briers really did like talent, talent in his subordinates anywhere. He had been a hungry flyer knocking at the door himself—he was good at giving other hungry flyers a hand.

"If I were he, I should keep an eye on that young man. He could do some damage."

"Bastard."

Luria was giving his melancholy sardonic smile. "You don't often get upset by human frailty, do you? Why now? Don't you remember the old wail—*why does he hate me so much? I've never done him any good.*" Luria was brooding. "That sounded madly cynical when I first heard it. Life couldn't be as beastly as that. But folk sayings sometimes have their point. I fancy this one comes from the old Russian Pale. It must have come from my people, mustn't it? It can't be Russian."

As he grew older, Luria had come to refer to "his people" as though he were responsible for them all.

There might be a time, Humphrey thought, when he could ask Briers whether Shingler was the model of loyalty. It would be a delicate operation, and he couldn't attempt it now. The candor between them was still qualified. It hadn't been a surprise to Humphrey to hear that questionings were going on methodically among people he knew. The police teams hadn't stopped their visits to the purlieus of Pimlico, but there were others, more repetitive, to more privileged persons. Paul Mason had been questioned again; Kate had been asked to explain some of her answers about Susan and Loseby. It seemed bizarre, but Monty Lefroy had been visited, which he seemed to regard as entirely fitting. Mrs. Burbridge had been taken over a timetable of Humphrey's own movements. So had Stella Armstrong over Tom Thirkill's. Susan Thirkill, so Kate reported over the telephone, had been interrogated with an appearance of informality in her own apartment, not once but twice, for something like five hours each time by Chief Inspector Bale. Briers himself was said to have spent long periods with Loseby and some brother officers of his.

The process was grinding on, but Briers had called at Humphrey's house on several evenings, talked with affectionate openness, given bulletins about his wife's illness, gazed at Humphrey with those splendid candid eyes, and given no hint of such inquiries. It didn't even seem like professional caution. He should have known for certain that Humphrey must have already heard. Then at last, Briers did give a hint, in a singular fashion. He invited Humphrey along to the police station for a morning briefing.

It bore a family resemblance to others that Humphrey had once attended back in the army and then at the old office. It was not noticeably more exciting. From the window boxes there was a smell of watered soil. A very young detective sergeant was waiting in the hall, more than ever fitting into the mould of the accomplished aide-de-camp, like so many that Humphrey had had to negotiate with: private secretaries of ministers and civil service eminences, captains at headquarters, unobtrusively more confident than generals sitting around because they were in the commander's confidence and the generals weren't. This young man, educated at an expensive school, was acquiring like other aides-de-camp some of his master's mannerisms, which didn't entirely suit him. He led the way into the Murder Room, sweet with early morning freshness, though there were still more filing cabinets, blackboards, sheaves of notices.

Humphrey was hoping that Briers would have something to say. He did have something to say, but it didn't enliven Humphrey. Briers was a good public performer, experienced at keeping up the spirits of his team, which by this time crammed the room. There were jocular exchanges. Briers was experienced in those also. They were not in his style, but he could adapt himself to most kinds of camaraderie, particularly if it protected him from what he didn't want to say. That didn't tell Humphrey anything new about Briers. Right at the end, he made a short harangue that sounded as though it were one of his regular exhortations. Briers didn't have to raise his usual voice to fill that room.

He was saying, "I want another blitz on who was walking about that Saturday night. Oh yes, I know we've done that till we're tired. But there must have been someone walking about. We haven't tracked the one sighting we really want. And someone else must have seen that young woman. We haven't got anywhere. I want sightings of anyone between eight P.M. and one A.M., specially anywhere around the mews and in Eccleston Street, as well as the Square. There haven't been anything like enough sightings so far. You'd think this was the middle of a prairie. I want some more. Most of them will be nonsense. I've told you before, I'll tell you again, I want them. I don't care if it's the local parson, or Humphrey Leigh who's just down there [jocund laughter] or the lord chancellor, or three old prime ministers, or—[he ripped off the names of two star actors, an American diplomat, an ecclesiastical dignitary, all of whom lived in Eaton Square]—or the fire brigade. I want them. We've got a couple of miserable sightings, and those may be a bit of a break. Now I want another blitz. Detective Inspector Shingler is in charge. We go for everyone, everyone in the Square and round about. Some of them just must have seen someone. Oh, I know, you've bothered them before. A lot of these people are old. You be polite if you can manage it [dutiful laughter]. If you can't be polite, I'll look after you if you can bring me one good authentic piece of observation."

Something like that, Humphrey was still convinced, was one of his regular exhortations. The detectives must have heard it all before, for weeks past. The young woman he spoke of—they knew who she was. It hadn't been necessary to say those words to the detectives. It was strangely oblique, but he was saying them to Humphrey.

Briers dismissed the meeting. When he was left alone with Humphrey, except for the sergeant still in attendance, Briers said, "There you are. What did you think of that?"

"Interesting. Very interesting," Humphrey replied without expression.

"I must get to work myself. See you soon, Humphrey."

Smoothly, the young man took Humphrey out into the road. It had been a peculiar performance, he had been thinking, but it was one way of making a purpose plain.

In the gossip about the police interviews, there was a name that Humphrey had not heard mentioned. Paul Mason had described with some amusement how he had been pressed to answer for a discrepancy (there wasn't one—his memory was slightly better than their script, he said, for once immodest), but he hadn't spoken a word about Celia.

It would have been absurd to imagine that she was any sort of suspect. No one ever did think so, then or later on, even those so credulous that the obvious truth didn't seem believable enough. Apart from her last social appearance at the dinner at Tom Thirkill's, none of Humphrey's friends had met her for weeks. Kate remarked she seemed to have dropped out of circulation.

In fact, she was to be seen most evenings in a little garden looking over the river, across the road from St. George's Square. Around six o'clock at night, she was making a habit of walking from her house in Cheyne Row along the Embankment, her young son scampering beside her. On that Friday evening, the day of Briers's briefing, she did just that. People might have noticed a pretty young woman dressed simply, elegantly, in white, body slender and handsome, one hand holding a golf umbrella, the other a small boy's wrist, watching steadily for a chance to cross the road. The traffic was heavy, cars streaming out of the town. At last she could get the boy across. In the garden he was safe.

Sitting on a bench, with her clear clinical painter's eye, Celia regarded the statue of William Huskisson. One shoulder was bare; he was dressed like a Roman senator. Some Victorian mind, some human mind, had considered that appropriate. He had been knocked down and killed by one of the earliest railway engines traveling at ten miles an hour. Just the sort of thing he would have managed to do, she thought with detachment. She put up her umbrella to guard herself not from the heat, but the light of the declining sun. She wasn't using an umbrella in imitation of Lady Ashbrook. Lady Ashbrook might have approved of her style, but she didn't copy Lady Ashbrook's. She carried an umbrella because it was functional, and she liked it. She was her own mistress. She was capable of thinking that she was now certainly no one else's.

She was capable of thinking that, but she was sad. Not bitter, not resentful, but sad. She had lost Paul. She didn't blame him. She didn't blame herself. It was in the nature of things. Or rather, in her own nature. She was a loser. Others thought she had everything. Beauty. She dismissed that but accepted that she was good enough to look at. Fairly intelligent. She could be entertaining with the right companion. She had known since she was growing up that she attracted a reasonable number of men. She liked some of them. She could give those she liked what they wanted in the way of sex. There she was easy, not passionate, not cold, so far as she could judge herself. She had done so with her husband. She had loved him. He had left her. She had loved Paul. Now he had left her.

She gazed at her young son, who was kneeling in the grass, carefully stalking a sea gull. She loved him too, more totally, or at least with more self-forgetfulness than she loved either of her men. Would that boy leave her too? Of course. It would be wrong if he didn't. While he was a child, she would keep something of him. But afterward, sons ought not to be attached to their mothers. She couldn't wish for that. Anyway, she took it for granted that she wouldn't get it. They all found it easy, compulsory, almost friendly, to leave her.

She was thinking of herself, nothing else. All that had happened to Lady Ashbrook or acquaintances in the Square seemed insignificant, as though it were long ago. She had none of that kind of homesickness or clinging memory. It was only Paul that she remembered. Not with hatred, or violent longing, but as of someone who should be present and was not. Yes, he had bright, intent, focused eyes. When he was teasing her: nose going white when he was getting urgent about bed. In bed (it seemed out of character) never ceasing to talk, fervently, insistently, right up to the climax.

Paul had left her. She hadn't been pleased when that girl Susan had been making a play for him, but she had heard that it wasn't Susan who had got anywhere with him.

If it were not that girl, it would be another, Celia thought acceptantly. Why hadn't she held him? Why was she a loser?

When they had all been celebrating the good news for Lady Ashbrook (none of them had forgotten that night, and some of them were to go on feeling a kind of guilt), she had tried to confide in Humphrey. She knew already that Paul was slipping away. She wasn't pitying herself. She had no more pity for herself than for others. It had been a relief to talk to Humphrey, who didn't pity either and didn't blame. She tried to be honest. And yet, even the most honest, when they were losing, found reasons—to themselves as well as to anyone else—that weren't quite the reasons. Paul had wanted a bedmate, she had thought to herself in her clinical style. That was fine, that was the easy part. But, she had told Humphrey, he also wanted a hostess, and that she couldn't do, and so some time they would have to part.

She had been searching herself and found a lack that concealed a deeper lack. She could have made herself liked by anyone Paul brought in. They might have found her puzzling or far away, but they would have liked her, for she was more liked than, since her childhood, she could ever believe. She accepted that a few men loved her—but, driven into herself, she couldn't accept that she was also liked. But really it wasn't that she couldn't give others what Paul wanted her to give. The trouble was, and this was too much like a trap of fate to recognize, that she couldn't give it to Paul himself.

He was gifted, usually patient with her, confident. But, confident as he was, sometimes he needed a response, a completely ordinary response, a bit of encouragement, the feeling that the whole of her nature was with him. Occasionally, less often than most, he needed such a simple response: and she could only give him a splinter.

That had always been the trouble. With her parents: she watched them, she could be funny, but when they needed simple love, they received another of her splinters. Somehow she could not believe or seem as though she were at one. She had never been able to say, even to herself, what she wanted to do. As a girl, fortunate, courted, pursued, friends had asked her what she intended. The best she could produce—voice high, wandering away—was that she supposed that she would drift into marriage. She had done exactly that. Her husband had been a loving, conscientious man and very kind—kinder than Paul, though nothing like so perceptive. She had tried to be loving and conscientious in return. It hadn't been enough. He hadn't complained. He had left her.

She had sometimes thought that she would have been less lost at a time everyone really married for life: you made your bed and you lay in it. She wouldn't have minded if her husband had taken other women—it would have been her fault. She could have made do. She wouldn't have minded if Paul had taken other women. Again, she could have made do.

There her self-insight left her. It would have surprised even Paul—it didn't seem to fit her nature—but she was jealous. She had been more than normally jealous when young Susan had been attempting to collect Paul. All Celia had done was give one of her splintered jokes. No more. She couldn't let him see or hear what she really felt. It might have brought her better luck if she could.

Ah well. She wasn't going to begin pitying herself. Somehow one went on. Life might be a disappointing business, but there was no option. She studied her son, now raptly regarding a tug on the oil-smooth river. That was something. She looked again at the Huskisson statue. That really was a most ridiculous creation. Her face was etched into her handsome, in-drawn smile, which a good many men had found mysterious. Just now, there was nothing mysterious about it. She was smiling at the concept of the statue.

The sun was getting low. Late for the boy's bedtime. Time for her dinner. She took him out on the pavement. They walked a few yards; he was talking cheerfully. She stopped. They had to cross to the island in the middle of the road. The boy began to run across the street. A car, traveling very fast, came past a lorry parked against the curb. She shouted. The boy might not have heard, but he saw the car as it swung toward him. His reaction was quick; he checked his run; his gym shoes held fast on the tarmac. The car passed him with a foot to spare. The driver made threatening gestures and yelled.

Celia's stomach had lurched. She was pallid as, the boy's hand in hers, they stood on the mid-road landing. She waited a long time until there was no traffic at all before they crossed to the far side.

When they were walking toward home, the boy said, "Anything the matter, mummy?"

"Nothing much. You must be very careful crossing the roads. There's so much traffic. On these main roads, you must always wait for me. Please."

That was all that she said. The boy gave an intelligent, placatory smile. That was all. She said nothing more.

❧ 21 ❧

O n the Saturday evening twenty-four hours after Celia had been thinking about her mischances, sitting in the riverside garden, Humphrey and Alec Luria met for their ritual drink in the pub. By random chance, it happened that Celia's name was mentioned. Has anything been heard of her, Luria inquired? As curious, it seemed, about former acquaintances as he was about the sociology of English institutions. It was only later that Humphrey thought that there might be rather more to that inquiry. As it was, he replied simply, not by me. She had been friendly but only through her connection with Paul: now that that was broken, she had passed out of contact.

"What a pity." Luria, sipping dutifully at his pint of bitter, looked kind and thoughtful. He had had spells of silence as though he had something on his mind.

The pub was quiet with a late summer stupor. A couple of men, who knew them both by sight, had said good evening. A wasp had been whirring around, now gone. Through the window at the far end, the evening was fading gently to twilight: it was as hot as in the weeks before, but as August ended the northern nights were shortening.

Humphrey, comfortable in the quiet, said idly that newcomers didn't realize how far north London was. Luria nodded. "Like Labrador. It's lucky there's the Gulf Stream." He said it with mechanical competence but no interest, still preoccupied. He started to speak, then stopped. After a time, he spoke again. "Humphrey?"

"What's the matter?"

"There's something I want to say to you. You'll have to forgive me."

For an instant, Humphrey wondered if Luria was going to ask about the case. He was punctilious about official secrets, but maybe his curiosity was getting too active. Anyway, Humphrey had nothing to tell him except guesses, which he could have made himself.

What Luria did say was this: "I'm not in a position to intrude, forgive me, but of course you're getting very involved with Kate Lefroy? Right?"

It was a long time since Humphrey had been invaded like this. He wasn't prepared. In spite, or because of, his candor with himself, he guarded his own secrets. All he could reply, with a smile of put-on irony, was, "I think we could reasonably say that."

"Yes. This is what I have to tell you. I very much wish you would get out of it."

Again, it was a long time, many years, since Humphrey felt himself blushing. He was taken off-balance. His temper broke through; his voice was as hot as his cheeks.

"In God's name, what do you mean?"

"I'm afraid I mean, so far as I can see, there's no future in it."

Humphrey's voice had become calmer but still resentful. "She's one of the nicest women I've ever met. I think the nicest."

"That's one of the reasons why I can't see any future in it."

"I may as well tell you," Humphrey said, looking at Luria with rancor, "that if these words mean anything, I love her, and I believe that she has some love for me."

"My impression is, more than that. But if I have the situation anything like right, that could make it worse for both of you." He was looking at his friend with somber affection: under the great brow ridges his dark eyes were sunk deep, brimming with melancholy. "You don't think I specially like telling you home truths, do you? You're about the last person I should choose. But, it doesn't need me to say, at our age we haven't infinite time ahead. I don't want to see you waste too many years."

Just then, still angry, as a younger man might have been (age made no difference, though, Humphrey thought later in cooler blood), he was nevertheless touched by Alec's elaborate consideration. He had gone out of his way to speak as though he and Humphrey had the same prospect of future existence: Luria, though one often forgot it, was a dozen years the younger.

"She's right for me," Humphrey said flatly.

"If you could get her. But I'm afraid you can't."

"Why not?"

"When it comes to the crunch, I don't see her able to get away."

"You're not inside the situation." He was protesting more harshly, since Luria was voicing his own doubts. "I'm nearer than you are. There's nothing left between her and her husband."

Luria stayed gentle in spite of Humphrey's anger. "You know, sometimes an outsider sees more of the game. I'm asking you not to rely on what you think. Perhaps it's what you want to think. Listen just a minute. I'll try and explain how it looks to me. She's a real woman. She could give you life and fun, and love it. But there's something else. She has a need for someone to depend on her. She falls for phonies; we've gone over that before. Superior phonies like Monty. She could fall for that doctor who fancies himself a thinker. She seems to worship them. But this is my version. I believe that underneath she feels they're no good, and that underneath they feel that they're no good, and so they have to depend on her. She's a much stronger character than that phony husband, and I'm afraid you'll get it wrong unless you admit the thought that that is what she wants."

Humphrey had become mutinous and savage, skin dead white with temper. His voice, though, was under control. "She may want something simpler."

"You're not a phony, no one less so. You've never really depended on anyone in your life, and you never will. You would provide everything she's never had. But I wish I could think that she could tear herself away and leave a derelict behind her."

Humphrey did not utter. With a hesitation he hadn't shown before, Luria added, "I couldn't make up my mind whether to speak or not. I won't say any more." Humphrey said with civility, not with warmth, "If that is what you think, you were right to say so. Of course. Thank you." He waved to the barman, calling for another drink. There was a lull between them. Then Alec Luria

157

spoke again, deep voice rumbling away, but not so firmly, "As a matter of fact, I have a problem of my own."

"What's this?"

Luria gave a curiously sheepish smile. "Oh, my wife's getting rid of me."

"Is she, by God?" Luria's wife had been absent all summer. Humphrey had met her only twice and had no knowledge of the relationship. Luria had not been comporting himself like a man deprived. Humphrey went on, "I have to ask. How serious is this for you?"

"It's not life or death. I can't pretend that I'm heartbroken. But I do feel several varieties of a fool."

"Will it make much difference? Practically, I mean."

"Oh, I shan't see so much of the high life. Unless I marry one of her girl friends. I shall be pensioned off pretty handsomely, by the way. A couple of million dollars, the lawyers talk about."

This marriage had lasted five years. The wedding had been a social event in New York. She was part heiress to one of the older Eastern fortunes.

"That's something." Humphrey did not suppress a satirical grin. "That may help you to live modestly in the state of life to which it has pleased God to call you."

The sheepish, shamefaced smile appeared again, looking entirely inappropriate in the sculptured face.

"It's a consolation," Alec Luria acquiesced. For an instant he was satirizing himself. Then he said, "But I tell you, I do feel too many varieties of a fool." He was brooding. "Tell me, Humphrey, have you had much to do with the very rich?"

"Very little."

"Somehow I can't keep away from them. Which is an embarrassing tie for a serious scholar, haven't you noticed?" He was wanting to make confidences, finding it grittier than giving advice.

Humphrey in a mocking fashion helped him out. "Do your women really have to be all that rich?"

Alec Luria pensively considered the question. "They seem to have been, for marriage purposes. I was quite fond of Rosalind. I still am. She's very bright. But she also had an aura because of the name and the money. You know, I used to read her name in the papers when I was a boy, two rooms for the whole lot of us."

"You moved out of that with remarkable celerity, didn't you? Come on, Alec, you had your own name made before you were thirty, more than anyone I know ever will."

"Thank you," Luria said courteously, like an American woman being congratulated on a new dress. Then he gave one of his large, snorting chortles. "That was why the rich wanted to buy me, of course. The rich think they can buy anything. It's a curious experience. You ought to have had it."

"Nothing to sell. So I console myself that I shouldn't have cared for it."

"You ought to have been born in Brooklyn. I tell you, it was a curious experience. Rosalind was a bright girl. Much brighter than the first wife. But somehow she couldn't understand that if you're going to have any ideas you have to sit still sometimes. They were all restless, her family, the whole crowd. Nothing to do, so they couldn't stay put. Up and off on the spur of the moment, the Caribbean, Mexico, anywhere where they all had houses. Nice houses. Not houses to work in. And they wanted me around just to help pass the time. As a mixture of a court jester and a guru. I wasn't especially well cast as a court jester. Rather better, maybe, as a guru. You wouldn't say that I was easily bored, would you?"

Humphrey smiled. Occasionally he had wished that his friend had been more so.

Luria said, "After one or two of those vacations, the bare mention of another bored me stiff. The rich think they can buy anything."

Humphrey had a flicker of memory, quite capricious, of an old artistic acquaintance, once taken up by London magnates, who used to say the same. They think they can buy anything, so the acquaintance had pondered—they'd buy poverty too if they could get it on the cheap.

He told the story to Alec Luria, who wasn't much amused. Humphrey changed the subject. "How long did you stand it?"

Luria answered with a grimace. "I should be standing it now. It wasn't my doing, breaking up the marriage. It's hers."

Suddenly Alec Luria stripped off his authority. He had the puzzled, open, youthful appearance of one needing to confess. "I'm not a good husband," he said. "You know I'm fond of women—"

That had been clear since their first meeting.

"But I'm fond of women in a rather uncomfortable way. When I've been to bed with one, as it might be Rosalind, I almost immediately want to have another. I don't think that's uncommon. In fact I'm sure it isn't. I heard it time and time again when I was practicing—"

"Of course it isn't," Humphrey said.

"Whether it's common with women, the other way around, I've never been able to decide. The trouble with me, though, it wasn't just a thought. I wasn't just dreaming about another woman. I had to put it into action. I did so. It was a kind of aphrodisiac, if you like, though I'm not pretending I needed one. I just did it. It was another embarrassing tic for a serious scholar, like being interested in the rich. It was more embarrassing than that. Because the rich didn't like it. At least neither of my wives liked it. Especially Rosalind. She believed she had everything a man could desire. She had a good deal. But she didn't accept how odd men could be."

"Did it take long before she knew?"

"I tried to hide it. But I am fairly conspicuous." That was an understatement, Humphrey thought. "And also," Alec went on, simply, without cover, "I am a very vain man. I don't like pretending. It's a great fault, but I want people to take me as I am. I have done some harm because of that."

Luria had taken the initiative that evening, testing Humphrey, hoping that this was the time to see him uncontrolled. It hadn't happened like that. Humphrey, unobtrusive, apparently easy natured, hadn't said much. It was Alec Luria, by whom others were overawed, who had softened. Soon he was replying, again directly and simply, to questions of Humphrey's about what his plans were now. Yes, he would probably get married again before too long. He said with an apologetic smile, "I really am a born marrier. It must be another addiction of mine."

When they left the pub, Luria seemed not to want to part. Was Humphrey engaged that night? Would he drop in at Alec's apartment and have a snack? Red caviar and demi-sel, biscuits, that's about all there would be. Luria's tastes were as frugal as Humphrey's. Humphrey had to say yes. Alec Luria was in need of company, in spite of walking so loftily, taller than most though bent at the knees, grizzled hair streaming, features graven. But a man who had all the lineaments of an Old Testament prophet needn't feel like one. That was a lesson, it occurred to Humphrey, that it was surprisingly hard to learn.

Luria was making an effort to be impersonal.

"Remember that rough night in the pub?"

"Well," said Humphrey, "they're not as common as all that, are they?"

Luria was being reminiscent; the two of them had walked down Eaton Square as they were doing now.

"It seems pretty innocent. That night, I mean," Humphrey said. "After what has happened since."

"Doesn't the past itself seem innocent?" Luria asked. "One's own? Past time?"

"Does it?"

"I think the past usually does. Unless one remembers it true."

They continued to talk as they sat in Luria's flat—talked naturally, not fluently, of things they had done or not done. It was hard, maybe impossible, to remember the past as it had truly been. Yes, one could feel regret, but that was a soft feeling, an indulgence. Remorse? The past wouldn't be so innocent if one felt remorse. But wasn't the idea of remorse something of an invention? A more comforting cover for what one was really like? Remorse ought to exist, so one imagined it did. Whoever had killed the old lady should be feeling it. Wasn't that what one wished, not what really happened? Imagination could be too sentimental by half.

Luria began to regain some authority. If people were certain there were no penalties, in this world or the next, he said, if a person had only to answer to himself, he doubted whether anyone would be feeling remorse that night.

❧ 22 ❧

The next Monday morning, before Humphrey had settled down to his newspapers, there was a quick, light step outside the sitting room, and Frank Briers came in.

"Am I disturbing you?"

"There's not much to disturb."

"I want to talk," said Briers. He looked around the empty room. "Are we safe here?"

The question might have seemed demented, but they were both trained in secret conversations. For much of his career, Humphrey had found it more satisfactory to have them in the open air: there weren't many areas of the three central parks where he hadn't heard remarks that it would have been inconvenient for others to hear. Now he smiled in complicity.

"No need to worry. Unless my old colleagues have been quite excessively efficient. But I really can't believe that. Let's go over to the window seat."

Out of old habit, secrecy being as compulsive as alcoholism, Humphrey opened the window, which looked out over the garden. There it was calm and very bright. Out of old habit again, they spoke in low voices, though Briers's was urgent.

"You got the message on Friday, didn't you?"

"I fancy so," Humphrey said.

"You know what I think." Briers gave a terse smile. "And I know you know."

"Fair comment."

"And I know that you agree."

"I should think less of you if you didn't."

"When did you?"

Humphrey said, "Quite early on."

"Why?"

"Chiefly because of you." Humphrey was smiling but had also become impassive, as impassive as the professional he used to be. "I thought I could follow what you were really interested in. I happen to have respect for you, and also—"

"Also what?"

"It didn't seem right to me. All this talk about burglars."

"What didn't seem right?"

"He found his way about the house rather well, it seemed to me. These houses do take a bit of knowing. If it was a burglar, he didn't put a foot wrong. And if it was a burglar, wouldn't there have been more of a struggle? So far as I was told, there was no sign of anything at all—until right at the end. It looks to me that she didn't know what was happening. I couldn't help a rather obvious thought: she was most likely killed by someone she knew."

Briers, a yard away on the window seat, gave a hard chuckle.

"We shall make a detective of you yet. You missed one or two pointers, of course. You've not had our practice. We've seen burglars operate often enough. They almost always work in a hurry. They open chests of drawers from the bottom up. You saw the tallboy. Bits and pieces taken out, all neatly closed. That didn't look much like a burglar. My lads said that right from the beginning. Of course this man had taken sensible precautions. There wasn't a fingerprint in the whole bloody house. No trace of footprints. He may even have gone out through the garden in his stocking feet. He was doing his best to look like an intelligent burglar. Not a bad best, by and large. But the more we thought of it, the more we came round to thinking it was pretty long odds that he wasn't."

"So you're certain that it was someone she knew?"

"Certain's a big word. I've dropped bricks by being too certain. We've combed the burglars and other villains all over the place. Of course we have. We're going on with it. You never know what might turn up. It just might have been a kind of odd-job burglar. They do exist. But we've been at it for a month, and we haven't found a candidate in that fashion. I don't have to tell you, we've been looking elsewhere too. Why do you think I'm wasting your time this morning?"

Humphrey was returning the steady gaze. He said, "Anyway, all these conscientious inquiries, done with all the resources of the Yard, make a nice cover when you want to look elsewhere."

"As you said yourself a few minutes ago—fair comment."

This was something like a negotiation, the kind that Humphrey had once had to conduct with officials in the Foreign Office, men he liked but could not be totally honest with, feeling his way about one of their colleagues. There had been negotiating silences, as there was now. Then Briers said, "Yes, I think it's more likely than not that she was done in as you've just said. By someone she knew. That would mean someone you knew too, wouldn't it?"

There was a pause before Briers went on. "She didn't have many callers. We've gone into that. Somehow she'd dropped the people she must have known at one time, or they'd dropped out, or she'd become too old for them to take any trouble. We haven't found many callers coming to that house. Naturally, there may have been some we've never heard of. These things are never tidy. We do know the handful she saw pretty often. As I said, the probability seems to be, I won't put it higher than that, she was finished off by someone you all know."

"Yes."

"You're with me?"

"I think it must be likely," Humphrey said. He was admitting what he thought, but Briers knew it already.

"That's the problem. I tell you, I don't like it."

"Why not? You mean, it may be someone you've met?"

Briers gave a loud laugh, wholehearted but fierce. "Christ alive, no, no. They're your friends, not mine. One doesn't have friends in this business. A murderer is a murderer. You'd better understand me." He added, calm and professional, "I don't like it, because it makes the job more difficult."

Briers continued, half leading, half hectoring. "I told you before, when we're dealing with criminals, we know all the ropes. We know where to go for the latest news. Some of them are fairly bright; most of them aren't. By and large, criminals don't make you feel better about the human race. IQ is low. Human virtue is low. So we know how to find our way around."

"They made very bad soldiers, the few I saw," Humphrey said.

"Did they? Not surprising." Briers returned to his theme. "But when we have to deal with the upper classes, it's a different cup of tea. They're good at keeping their mouths shut. There's nowhere our lads can go for a bit of dirt. The upper classes can protect themselves. The further up they are, the more they can protect themselves. They close their ranks. God love me, Humphrey, this isn't any news to you."

Briers had had his experiences, Humphrey thought. His tone had gone stiff with resentment. It made Humphrey feel affronted and stupid. Since Briers took charge, though some of their friendship had come through, trust hadn't. Making nonsense of Humphrey's unbelief, it was class that had split them. Even now, when he had to accept it, he began thinking in terms appropriate to elderly aunts of his a generation before. They used a gentle, patronizing phrase, referring to one of his bright Cambridge friends from unelevated origins—oh, that boy could *go anywhere*—rather as though the possibility of unrestricted motion was a social privilege not granted to many. Briers could go anywhere. He would go anywhere. Why should he have made this split?

"I was wondering," Humphrey said temperately, "where these upper classes of yours begin."

"Category B," Briers replied with demolishing promptness, referring to a national income scale. "Middle-rank professionals. Middle bourgeois, if you like. Then up and up, into the really rich. And the real aristocracy. Who, by the by, are the hardest nuts to crack."

"You know," Humphrey was still speaking temperately, "I'm not sure who you are interested in, in this case—"

"I think you have a very shrewd idea." Briers was quick with the unannounced probe. Humphrey had used that technique himself and gave a smile.

"But there was no one in contact with old Lady Ashbrook who by the wildest stretch belongs to the real aristocracy. She did, of course. And I suppose we have to say her grandson. No one else."

"You are."

"No, no. The English aristocracy was always ruthless in letting its members gently decline. Primogeniture, that was the secret. That's why it stayed an aristocracy. My grandfather was an aristocrat, that I grant you. My father was a younger son. Not many pennies between them and none for me. No, Frank, I've found my proper niche in the middle class."

"You don't behave like that."

"Whatever do you mean?"

"I mean," said Briers, "that you're capable of looking after your own. That is, in certain circumstances, you would find it natural to cover up. In certain circumstances such as we're talking about."

"You know I don't much believe in that sort of loyalty. And I don't think you ought to."

"Look, if I were to tell you here and now that there are reasons to suspect Kate Lefroy of either doing the old lady in, or being a party to it, wouldn't you cover up for her in any conceivable fashion? And do it very effectively into the bargain, if I know you?"

Humphrey said, "That is rather a special case, isn't it?" For an instant, he was anxious. Then he laughed, very loud. "If you're thinking of Kate, I should feel the investigation may last a remarkably long time."

Briers gave his own healthy laugh, unresentful now. He hadn't missed Humphrey's attachment. "Kate Lefroy wouldn't have been my first choice anyway. As a matter of fact, on cast-iron police grounds, she's more in the clear than anyone around. She was in her hospital the whole of that night from early evening right through to the early morning trying to settle a porters' strike. One porter had been sacked for coming in drunk. Other porters immediately had an unofficial strike. Emergency operations stopped. Mrs. Lefroy somehow coped with those blasted porters. They seem to like her. I fancy she knows when not to be too compassionate. Christ, they bloody well are the scum of the earth." Briers, in this unlike the other senior policemen in his team, had a streak of irregular radicalism, but it didn't extend sympathy to malcontents disrupting hospitals.

"Thank you for relieving my mind about Kate Lefroy," Humphrey said, composure restored, making a pretense of relief. But his composure was soon attacked again.

"You don't always come quite clean, do you?" Briers spoke straight at him. "This is important. You don't always—"

"I thought I did."

"Not always."

"What are you thinking about?"

"You didn't tell me everything I ought to have known about young Loseby."

Humphrey was baffled.

"I'm fairly sure I did."

"Not quite."

"What is all this?"

"You didn't tell me he liked boys as well as women."

"I didn't even think of it. It was true when he was younger. There's nothing original about that. Surely it doesn't matter?"

"Actually, it might have done. It would certainly have saved us quite a bit of time. Curiously enough, it might be useful to him." Briers's eyes were bright. "You see, that night he now claims to have been in bed with a boy. It wasn't a woman, he tells us now. I've had him in three times—we've been keeping an eye on him, as you might expect—and the story has changed quite a lot. Not a girl, but a boy. Not a boy, to be accurate, but a young man."

"It might be true."

"It might be true. To begin with, it was a girl prepared to swear for him. We soon broke that down. Then it was that little bitch Susan Thirkill. She lied in her teeth for days, lied herself black and blue. Oh yes, she had been with him all weekend. She could tell us how many times they'd made it, just how they'd done it, new tricks. She has a vivid imagination, that she has. All absolutely and totally false. Which means that the young lady hasn't any backing for what she was doing herself that night. We do know that she was in her father's flat most of the early part of the day. And Loseby wasn't."

"You're sure?"

Briers nodded. "But we're not sure where he was. Of course, the boyfriend confirms his timetable minute by minute. So did Susan Thirkill. So did the other girl. A bit of overinsurance, that was, three different stories, where he was, all worked out in detail. The boyfriend's may be as false as the other two. I rather liked him by the way. He's another officer. Nothing like keeping it in the regiment. A couple of years younger than Loseby. Wasn't like the Susan girl, didn't spread himself about what they were up to. Admitted that they were consenting adults. Otherwise slightly prudish. He does seem fond of Loseby."

"That doesn't distinguish him from others. As you've no doubt discovered."

"We haven't discovered any other boys. Several women. All prepared to perjure themselves for him. One of them a dazzler, out of this earth. I did ask him—letting him think that I bought the story of the boyfriend—why he picked up a young man when he had women galore. Women he'd slept with. Most men would give their eyes for a couple of them. Do you know what he said?"

"Not quite my world."

"He said, 'Oh, chief superintendent, you can imagine, can't you now? I just thought I should like a change.' "

Briers had given a creditable imitation of Lancelot Loseby's unaffected voice, his sweet and ingratiating manner.

"He's a cool customer, that one is," said Briers.

Humphrey was not physically coordinated as Briers was, but both were disciplined. They were still sitting on the window seat, neither of them constrained, but neither shifting, men who had been trained to conduct interviews and, except deliberately, give nothing away. Briers said, "But I can't for the life of me see why he should want to murder the old lady. Or why anyone else should want to. Have you any ideas?"

Humphrey shook his head.

"I don't mind telling you," Briers went on, "I'm getting lost. We can't track anyone's movements down that give a lead, and we can't put a finger on anyone going into the house that night. Someone must be holding back. Or more than one is holding back. It's like seeing someone playing the old three-card trick, having to spot the lady."

"Three cards? You're only thinking of three, are you?"

Sharply Briers interrupted, "You believe I'm leaving someone out?"

"You haven't told me who you're leaving in."

They looked at each other, expressions hard to read. Briers spoke without inflection. "I'll tell you all right, if you can give me a motive. We might be able to start from that angle. But I'm damned if I can get one. You know as well as I do, motives are nearly always simple. Thoughts aren't; feelings aren't; excuses aren't. Motives are. It's a great mistake to make them more rarefied than they can possibly be. I've never had a murder where they're not simple when you get down to it. Sex. No sex here. We didn't rule that out. Old women have been raped before now. Not a vestige of a sign. Money. Blind alley again. None of the possibles would kill for a few hundred pounds in notes. We thought she might have a bit more stashed away, but there's no sign of that either. No one benefits under her will. We're going into her past doings. No change. Murders are sometimes done because of fear. What could anyone be afraid of here? I haven't anything to stand on. You—any ideas?"

"Nothing worthwhile."

"If you have, I trust you to let me know."

For the first time in their conversation Humphrey indulged in a sarcastic grin. He said, "Trust can't be entirely one-sided, my lad. Can I trust you to tell me what you know?"

"Come on," said Briers. "I'm a police officer. There are things I can't tell you. Or anyone else outside the force. Not so long ago there were things you didn't tell me. But I'll tell you everything I can. Which I wouldn't do to anyone else."

"This is a curious bargain," Humphrey said. "I know nothing and tell you everything, you know everything and tell me nothing."

"That's what I call a bargain." Briers's smile was wide open.

"Well," Humphrey said, "if we have to, we'll try it that way."

"Well," Briers said, "now we know where we stand. I call this a useful morning." He didn't stir. Muscular thighs remained firm on the window seat; feet didn't fidget.

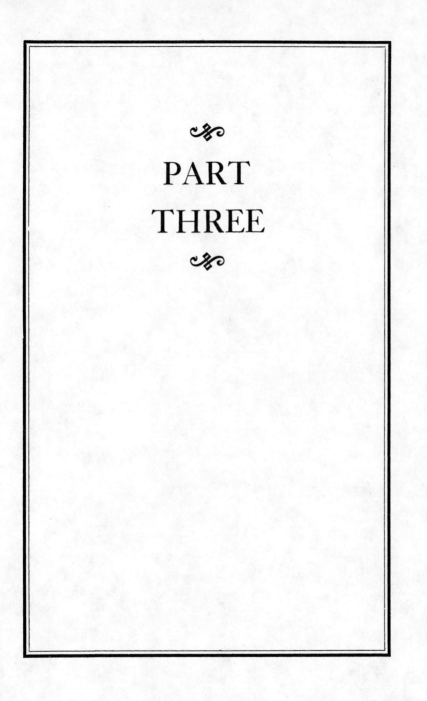

PART
THREE

❧ 23 ❧

It began to rain. This was at the end of the last week in August. The summer weather, unbroken, without so much as a drizzle, hadn't deviated for four months. Then it began to rain. It continued to rain, not with the gentle patter of a London autumn, wistful, consolatory, as a leaf or two spiraled down to the spotted pavements, but real rain, which in spite of the steady cloud cover, the town didn't often know.

People who had grumbled at the heat now, within days, began grumbling at the rain. The earth in the Square garden was still parched, but gutters were swirling. The sky was low, dark, unchanging, not the sky of ordinary Atlantic showery weather. One morning, all lights switched on in his sitting room, Humphrey had a thought intruding. During the past five weeks, since the murder, the weather had been hot and brilliant. There had been someone who must be milling about, going through the workaday routine that one takes as unthinkingly as breathing, in a state where anxiety was not far away—probably not continually present, from what Humphrey had observed of other suspects, but sometimes laden with something darker than anxiety, more like dread.

Had that person—Humphrey found that his suspicions were unstable; they flickered among three or possibly four—been taunted by the serene sunlight, benign but without pity? Alternatively, was that person, or maybe a couple of them, becoming more anxious in this pelting dark? It was depressing enough for one comparatively indifferent to climatic oddities. Humphrey was recalling the old thought about the pathetic fallacy. The external weather ought to match what was going on within. Either way, the sky outside didn't seem especially appropriate. Looking out of his window, Humphrey thought that if he had been a suspect, he would have felt deranged.

Certainly the pathetic fallacy seemed to be under attack. On a sepulchral morning, clouds at their standard thousand feet, rain steady, Kate telephoned. Humphrey had seen little of her since they had exchanged their half resolve. It would have been valueless to press her, he thought. She had said, to ease his mind, that she was occupied night and day with her hospital porters. He accepted that that was true. Yes, it was her duty, and she was obsessively dutiful. But Humphrey felt that it gave her an excuse for delaying their own decision. Perhaps he didn't accept that she was as devoted to her job as he would have been himself.

Without any doubt, he didn't accept, or like, her need to take advice from Ralph Perryman. It was sensible; Perryman was a doctor; he had contacts in the hospital, was more sympathetic to the disaffected, perhaps, than Humphrey could have made himself. He didn't often feel old, but he tried to absolve his jealous pangs by thinking that his life span was dwindling away.

However, on the telephone that morning, very early, before he had gone down to breakfast, she was elated, astonished, disquieted.

"Good news!" Her voice was very warm. "At least I hope it's good news. I can hardly believe it. Susan!"

"What about her?"

"She's getting married!"

"Whoever to?"

"You'd never guess. Loseby's marrying her."

Humphrey gave an incredulous grunt.

"Who's told you?"

Chuckle over the line. "She did. Half an hour ago. She'd been up all night, she said. No, she wasn't drunk. She sounded rational. Of course she was wild with joy. Or was she? She sounded more triumphant than anything else. But she was rational."

"I shall believe it when I see it." Humphrey's tone was bleak, reminding Kate of thoughts they hadn't so far communicated or shared.

"I'm certain she believes it."

"I dare say. They might have their reasons for getting married. Not the obvious ones."

"They might." Kate was making herself become realistic, suspicious, once more.

She knew that Susan had covered for Loseby, swearing to his movements both inside and outside her bedroom on the night of the murder: and Kate knew that the cover was a lie. She didn't know, as Humphrey was too punctilious to break a confidence, precisely where Loseby had in his present version reported himself as being, but she knew enough. Those two had been in some sort of complicity.

Kate suspected, together with Humphrey, that Briers and his colleagues might be searching for deeper complicity than that. But then suspicions were in the air, amorphous whenever she talked to Humphrey. One was reasoned away; another surfaced: it was like any kind of anxiety or jealousy. Now that Susan's cover for Loseby was broken, so was her own. Her movements that night had become unaccounted for. Humphrey had been considering Kate's feeling for the girl and had been silent, but that hadn't been enough to hide what he was thinking.

"I shall believe it when I see it," Humphrey repeated himself over the telephone. That day he was certain that this talk of marriage was an elaborate charade, though he couldn't imagine the purpose. Nevertheless, two mornings later, he did have to believe what he saw. Over his breakfast, coming to the page of official announcements in the *Times*, glancing first at the obituaries, he saw at the top of the column of "Forthcoming Marriages"—Lord Loseby and Miss S. Thirkill: "The engagement is announced, and the marriage will take place shortly, between Lancelot Perceval Livingstone Richeson, Viscount Loseby, Captain, The Rifle Brigade, son of the Marquess of Pevensey, Marrakesh, and Mrs. Grace Hoyt Reitlinger, Oyster Bay, Long Island, U.S.A., to Susan Thirkill, daughter of Mr. Thomas Thirkill, M.P., and Mrs. Thirkill, of 36 Eaton Square, London, S.W. 1."

Humphrey was still either incredulous or plain baffled. More news came from Kate, high spirited because Humphrey had been wrong. Kate's news arrived from an unexpected source. After the dinner at Tom Thirkill's, Kate had renewed acquaintance with her old classmate Stella Armstrong. To an outsider, they seemed to have nothing in common: Stella Armstrong, the left-wing party political manager, Kate as Tory as a sane woman could be; Stella influential in Westminster and more so in Transport House, Kate doing her anonymous hospital job. But there was a kind of subterranean link, such as you could find in other inexplicable alliances. Each was caught in a similar emotional, moral, sexual trap, Stella through Tom Thirkill's marriage, Kate through her own. They had recognized it at sight, across the dinner table, not having met for twenty years.

Tom Thirkill, so Stella reported, was worried, not so much about Susan's marriage, but about the wedding. It seemed to Kate ludicrously comic at a time when he had other things to worry about. He must have known that the detectives hadn't finished their inquiries about Susan, or himself—and, though Kate had not realized this, the financial crisis might give him his great political chance, make or break.

That was the nub of it. Thirkill had a man of action's capacity to concentrate on one trouble at a time. The blinkers had come on. He saw nothing but politics, that is, his own political chance. With the pound dithering on the edge, there was going to be a crisis soon, that autumn, maybe worse than a crisis. That didn't depress him. It ought to mean his chance of office. He had spent the summer making speeches about sound money. He believed what he said. It was the only way. It was also his only way to the front bench. They would have to use him if they wanted to borrow more. He was trusted in America, rich, orthodox, speaking the same financial language as the American treasury. That was why the *Tribune* group loathed him. Probably being loathed by them was more gain than loss, Stella's intelligence service was certain. He had been doing other tasks besides making speeches, Stella knowing of them but no one else outside the chancellor's confidants.

Hence the worry about the wedding. "It goes without saying, I mustn't drop a brick. Not at this point. I mustn't drop a brick." Stella performed a vigorous miming impersonation of someone actually dropping bricks, which she insisted that he had actually performed. When she was working out party intrigues, she had a professional politician's delicate antennae on top of a politician's rhinoceros hide: but off duty she made Kate forget her stately opulent presence, like an Edwardian postcard beauty, and could become as mischievously disrespectful as Kate herself.

So Tom Thirkill was worried about the wedding. If they got married quietly, he could pass that off. Loseby wasn't prepared to get married quietly. If he was to marry at all (that might have been said gently, with a gentle threat behind it), it had to be in public. He demanded what Tom Thirkill, indignantly regressing to his provincial youth, called a society wedding. That would give enemies in the party something to pick on. Tom, hag-ridden by his own phrase, talked again about dropping bricks.

To Kate, and to Humphrey hearing this at two removes, it seemed the silliest argument they had heard for a long time. In the situation in which some of them stood, it seemed gruesomely silly. It went on. Loseby wouldn't budge. Just why he had this passion for public ceremonial, Humphrey couldn't imagine. Was it, in fact, another kind of evasion, connected with the situation in which they stood? Or was it simply that, as Humphrey had observed in his own children and in Loseby's milieu, forms lasted longer than substance? Loseby didn't believe either in God or in family proprieties, but he might find it suitable or even comforting to go through the old motions.

He wouldn't budge. Tom Thirkill, not certain about the exact relation of his daughter and Loseby, but quite certain that she was avid for the marriage and wouldn't forgive him if Loseby got away, had to submit. What church? St. Peter's, Eaton Square, Loseby thought would be agreeable. No, Tom Thirkill protested, it would draw attention to the glossy neighborhood and his own fortune. The Crypt Chapel in the Palace of Westminster? Too dim, too obscure, no one about at this time of year, Loseby said. Finally, they compromised on St. Margaret's, Westminster, the Parliament church, often used for the weddings of M.P.'s and their children, but too smart for egalitarian tastes.

"There'll be criticism," Tom Thirkill said, grit and grating in his voice. "I am so very sorry," Loseby said.

One more concession, and another compromise. Tom would have liked the wedding not to take place until the New Year, which really meant when his political future would be decided. No, Loseby must have it at once. Within weeks. If so, and here Tom Thirkill prevailed, it had to be on a Saturday. That would keep it out of the evening papers and the Sundays next day.

The argument concluded. The wedding was fixed for three weeks ahead, the afternoon of the first Saturday in October.

On the Friday night immediately before that day, Humphrey was again reminded that forms lasted longer than substance. He was invited to a stag party (described as such) in White's to say good-bye to Loseby's bachelor days. That was an old custom that Humphrey thought had been dispensed with, an old and to his mind disagreeable custom. In his youth, it meant an indeterminate number of young men wanting to get drunk and duly getting para- lytically drunk. The occasions he remembered had been brutish, like an initiation ceremony in some not highly developed Papuan tribe.

Things hadn't changed much. In a room at White's—a club that Humphrey, though his own was just across the street, did not often enter—a table was laid for fourteen. Young men were stand- ing about holding glasses of whiskey or gin or vodka. Spirits before dinner were not so much a fashion when Humphrey was young, but that was a change of which he approved. Only one man, apart from Humphrey himself, looked over thirty, a major—in the hum, buzz, and clinking, Humphrey did not catch the name. Three or four of the others seemed to have been school friends of Loseby's, one of them a rising Conservative member. Paul Mason was there, which Humphrey hadn't expected; perhaps he and Loseby had been drawn closer together by the events of the summer. Humphrey noticed them having quick words together, away from the crowd around the dinner table. The rest of the party were officers in the regiment, Loseby's age or younger, captains, subal- terns. As Humphrey was being introduced, a name tapped at his memory. Douglas Gimson. That was the name—Briers had let it drop—of the man with whom Loseby was now supposed to have spent the night of July 24–25. Interest sharpened, Humphrey con- trived to have a few moments' talk. True to form, the central figure of an amorous episode did not immediately catch the eye (would Heloise, Humphrey had occasionally speculated, have looked like a squat earnest Paris student?).

This young man had a thin, pallid face and a beaky nose, noth- ing striking except an air of subdued intelligence. As they talked, Humphrey had the impression that he was much brighter than Loseby. Loseby had often attracted people more intelligent than himself, and they were unlucky, as perhaps this young man had been.

On the table, just as at Tom Thirkill's, there was the gleam and glisten of silver and glass. They sat down to dinner, one of Loseby's contemporaries, not the senior officer, at the head. It was all like the privileged messes Humphrey had once known, Christian names without distinction everywhere: though, as usual, Loseby answered to several different ones. School friends called him Lance; brother officers something like Logo, or even, as voices thickened, Yoyo. The food was good: whitebait, grouse, devils on horseback. But not many of them paid attention to the food. They had come to drink, and they drank. The wine was cheap and rough, which Humphrey thought well judged since most of them wouldn't be able to taste it before long.

All that could have happened forty years before. Humphrey recalled parties like this in the first years of the war. The randy gibes were flaring out. That was, as it had always been, the object of the exercise. These young men, however, were easier about women than their predecessors had been. They had learned, most of them, that women weren't a different species. They hadn't had to pick up tarts. It might have made them less chivalrous but a good deal more friendly, or at least understanding. Most of the bawdiness was directed at Loseby's virility and sexual powers, which, as he had tested those to his own satisfaction and that of a good many others since he was sixteen, didn't ruffle him and gave simple pleasure to most of the company.

"If you get soused, Logo, you won't be able to get it up."

"No," another intervened, "he'll get it up. But he won't be able to finish it."

"Unfinished business," came from someone else approaching cheerful incoherence. "Inconclusive."

"What a pity that would be." Loseby gave his sweetest, most innocent smile.

"What a pity for Susan."

"Poor girl."

"Still," one of the youngest said, "she knows what to expect, doesn't she?"

"Just possibly." Loseby was bland. Humphrey caught a glance between him and Paul Mason.

"Perhaps she knows what a man looks like." The boy was overcome by his own brilliance.

So it went on. To the company, sex jeers became more extraordinarily funny the more often they were repeated, as in Shakespearean backchat. Humphrey was getting bored. Among his neighbors there was a little sensible conversation. A couple of young men, either soberer or harderheaded, were talking about their future. Did one stay in the army? Would there be an army in ten years' time? They asked Loseby what he intended.

Loseby hadn't been drinking heavily. That wasn't because of the advice he had been receiving. Humphrey had never seen him do so. He enjoyed a drink, but he enjoyed sex much more. Paul Mason had been drinking considerably more steadily, but according to his habit without any discernible effect, totally against all the physical laws, as Humphrey had often thought. A scholarly, finedrawn man shouldn't be so immune: it must be a metabolic freak.

Loseby didn't answer direct questions about his future, but he was practiced in evading them. He began to talk coolly, plans well calculated, about the family estate. No, he wasn't even going to try to maintain it.

"It's a nonsense," Loseby said amiably. "My father won't come back. Anyway, he's incapable. I'm not going to scrape money together for the rest of my life, just to pretend to be a feudal magnate. It may have been nice while it lasted. The Richesons have had a fairly long run. They did better than they deserved. I'm not going to be a kind of custodian, just to have busloads of people walking through the house. It's not even a specially pretty house. That's all gone. Gone forever."

"I dare say you're right," said one of the others.

"I just saw the end of it." Loseby spoke like a man enjoying himself. "It had its points. Serfs touching their caps to the future seigneur. I expect they hated me. Never mind, when I was about twelve, I basked in it. What you've never had, you don't miss, they always say. It was rather fun to have had it, though. It still is. If I finish up as a taxi driver in New York, I'm sure it still will be."

It wasn't what was being said that surprised Humphrey—he had heard the same from others born to riches or privilege, not repining when they were torn away—but who was saying it. He hadn't heard Loseby in a speculative mood before, nor imagined that he had any.

One man's head had gradually sunk down to the table and was now resting peacefully in a plate that contained a half-eaten savory. Two others had gone out, presumably to be sick. Someone said it was time to break up. A loud cry: "Let's go and have a spot of chemmy."

That seemed a spectacularly good idea to some who had drunk enough to want to drink more. That they could do at a gambling club.

"Come on, Yoyo, finish off the night. Never mind about tomorrow. This doesn't happen every day."

"Lucky for men that it doesn't," a voice said darkly.

"No," said Loseby, sweet but firm, "I don't care for gambling, you know."

So far as Loseby had a prudish spot, they had touched it. It was pleasant to find something he was inhibited about, Humphrey thought.

Long, drunken, logistic arguments about transport: who was sober enough to drive? Many claimed, few were chosen. Paul, to all appearances cold sober, said that he couldn't risk a police test. Further, he wouldn't risk Humphrey's driving him back to Aylestone Square either. Douglas Gimson, who had drunk almost nothing, offered to drive anyone. Loseby, who was spending the night in his best man's apartment, not in Douglas's, accepted for the two of them.

That might have been callous, or the reverse. Humphrey couldn't guess. He had an inkling that Douglas loved Loseby, loved him in earnest. Perhaps Douglas was a real homosexual, who loved men who were not and so suffered a special anguish.

They went outside the club. Some of the young officers were weaving up St. James's Street toward Piccadilly as their predecessors had done before them, making that gentle incline look like the north face of the Eiger. Paul Mason insisted once more to Humphrey that they were going home in a taxi, and, in a more decorous fashion, the two of them followed the young men up the street.

❧ 24 ❧

At 2:15 the next day, people were coming into St. Margaret's, Westminster, kneeling dutifully on their hassocks, sitting up, looking around to see someone they recognized or to spot a well-known face. It was something like an occasion in the theater. In fact, someone in front of Humphrey, who was sitting in the inconspicuous dark of the back row, said in a firm, knowledgeable voice, "I must say, I don't think this is much of a house."

The church was about half full, nothing like so well attended, Humphrey thought, as it would once have been for a fashionable wedding. It was Saturday, and maybe Tom Thirkill's tactics had been successful. It was also, after a lull the day before, raining steadily again outside. Not many men that Humphrey could see had put on morning dress, though there were a number of women in smart frocks. Celia Hawthorne, whom Humphrey hadn't cast eyes on since the Thirkill dinner, was there, alone, clothes a model of how to achieve simplicity.

Nearly all of those who visited Lady Ashbrook had come, and Frank Briers, at Humphrey's side, was noticing them. It was because Briers and Humphrey had met outside the church that they were sitting in obscurity. Briers had said that he didn't want to be too obviously in attendance. He didn't resist adding, "After all, I'm not one of the family, am I?"

The bridegroom and best man, in dress uniform, walked up the aisle. Loseby's hair shone, fair, what was called golden though not accurately, burnished, under the central chandeliers. Male beauty didn't have much meaning for Humphrey, but this man seemed to have it. He looked rather like a saccharine nineteenth-century picture of Sir Galahad, or of one of the Frankish knights who fought at Roncesvalles.

As Susan and her party arrived a punctilious ten minutes late, the organ was playing the chorale, "Sheep May Safely Graze." That sounded like a nice piece of irony, Humphrey thought, but it couldn't have been. Tom Thirkill, stately, too much of an actor not to be dressed for the part, walking with an actor's command of his body, watched his daughter as a public figure should watch his daughter at her wedding. She was veiled, face so far as it could be observed solemn, demure and pretty, dress all in immaculate white, virginal white.

Briers muttered something out of the side of his mouth. Humphrey didn't catch it. It might have been "what a nerve," or "what a girl." Four tiny children were carrying her train. Either her will had turned out stronger than her father's, or else he had accepted that there was nothing for it, to hell with the enemy, they might as well do it in style.

Humphrey settled down to enjoy the service. Like other unbelievers of his period, he had a fondness for the liturgy in which he had been brought up. However, the marriage service was not one of his favorites. Cranmer was a great master of sixteenth-century English. On the other hand, he was not a great master of suspense. In Briers's company, or in Humphrey's own mind, there was enough suspense around; but still, as the reverberating words rolled on, in this marriage service the deed was done much too soon. Within ten minutes, Loseby, in a tone emollient, subdued, but audible, was saying his "I will," and Susan, in a tone meek and almost inaudible, hers. Then the vicar pronounced them man and wife. That was it. The rest was anticlimax. Not too long, for fashionable weddings were not drawn out. Nevertheless, another half-hour, spirited short address, English not so lingering as Cranmer's, hymns, prayers, Widor's "Toccata": all over, all out.

Outside the church the rain descended, not stormily, not in torrents, but with persistence. The ushers, who all seemed to be officers from Loseby's regiment, some present at White's the night before, rushed about with enormous parti-colored umbrellas, getting guests into a fleet of cars, ready to take them to Thirkill's reception in Eaton Square.

Humphrey and Briers retreated onto the porch out of the rain. Briers said, "Look here, I don't think you and I ought to be seen too much together. One or two may clam up when they talk to you, and we don't want that. So I shan't come to your house so much. Are you free tomorrow night?"

Humphrey said yes.

"Come and have supper at home. Out in the sticks. My car and driver will pick you up."

With staccato abruptness, Briers walked off through the rain up Victoria Street in the direction of New Scotland Yard.

In the drawing room at Eaton Square, guests jostling around when Humphrey arrived, waiters carrying trays with glasses of champagne, he had an impression that excluded all the rest. This was the sight of Susan. She had changed from her wedding dress, but Humphrey couldn't see anything but her face. It was transformed. It had become more than pretty, as though lit up from inside, seraphic. At first sight he responded to sheer joy. Then he was wondering. He had seen girls after their wedding night—innocent girls maybe, and certainly lucky ones, who had been transformed something like this. But Susan hadn't had her wedding night, and it wouldn't have come as a revelation if she had. How long was it since she had first been taken by the Adamic surprise? Why did one say Adamic, as though only men were totally astonished by their first knowledge of sex? Was it assumed that Adam was more innocent than Eve before either knew anything?

Here Susan was, joyous and triumphant. It was startling. Humphrey didn't understand it and soon knew that he didn't like it. Perhaps this was what Kate's ear had detected over the telephone. This wasn't the girl he had once thought easy to understand. He would have been more at ease if he hadn't come to the reception, seeing people whom he had heard talked about with suspicion and of whom he would hear again next day. Less easy mannered than usual, he said no to champagne. He didn't like it, but at any other time he would have drunk out of politeness. He felt, as he had scarcely felt since he was a boy, like an intruder, an outsider, or even more like someone with agoraphobia.

Humphrey moved among the crowd. There was no chance of

talking to Kate, who was with a group of young officers such as she might have met in her girlhood. He did encounter Loseby in the throng, who said, open-faced, as though appealing for reassurance that he didn't need: "All going according to protocol, isn't it, Humphrey?"

Just afterward, Celia touched Humphrey's sleeve. No trouble showed in her expression. She looked beautiful and tranquil. She asked, "Have you heard anything of Alec Luria recently?"

Humphrey said no; he assumed Luria was back at New Haven. "Why do you ask?"

"Oh, nothing. He called me a week or two ago. I was just curious."

Humphrey allowed himself a surreptitious twitch of the mouth. Alec was prospecting for another wife. Celia was responding to his flicker of amusement.

"Paul used to say that with Alec one had to forget the verbiage. Underneath he was one of the wiser men."

"Paul is a good judge," Humphrey said. On his own, he imagined what Celia and Alec Luria would be like together.

It was Tom Thirkill who dominated the reception. He was preyed on by many kinds of anxiety: not only Humphrey but others there must have known. His political future was on the quiver. The chance, if it was a chance, might not come again. Police inquiries, even tentative ones, were not calculated to help. Prime ministers had their own channels of information, with which Humphrey was much more familiar than anyone in that drawing room. Nevertheless, Thirkill, driven in private by worries, phantoms, hopes, dreads less articulated than those, in public could behave like a film star coming down the aircraft steps, greeted by admiring faces, radiating his own energy and goodwill. Some temperaments one could enter into just a little—one had an element of them oneself—Humphrey thought again, but he couldn't enter into this.

The best man proposed the health of bride and husband, making a limp little speech. Loseby made another little speech, not so limp but for once self-conscious, not fluent on his feet. Thirkill made a speaker's speech, easy, sometimes funny, not afraid to be sentimental.

"I'm losing a daughter, of course. If Lancelot Loseby is what I believe him to be, of course I am. And I wouldn't have it otherwise. But it is a loss to lose an only daughter. Any marriage is a loss to someone. Never mind. It is a marvelous loss. And they will make up for it for the rest of my life by their own happiness."

Kate was touched. Humphrey, who didn't like wedding cake any more than champagne, patiently ate a scrap of almond paste. Then he could, unnoticed, get out of the crowd, down onto the pavement, on his way home. The rain didn't clear his head. He was nothing but confused.

❧ 25 ❧

After their first acquaintance, when Frank Briers had returned to duty at the Yard, Humphrey had once or twice enjoyed an evening at his house—professional talks with him might be acerb, but they were usually refreshing. And, much more, it was good to see a couple as happy as Briers and his wife. On the way out to Sheen in the police car, Humphrey was now getting ready for a sight that wouldn't be so happy.

True, he had been told that Betty was going through a remission, and a long one. It might go on for months, or even years. But those two, happy, zestful, guiltless, had been hit by a fatality. Humphrey had something like total recall of the night when Briers had told him. Briers had had to find someone to confide in. He was deadened; he didn't sound angry or raging with protest; he couldn't get his energies free. All he could say, in a tired tone, was, I never thought this could happen to us.

That had been two years before, when Betty was thirty. They had been married six years. They were satisfied with each other beyond the normal run, except that she hadn't yet had a child. Humphrey remembered her as quick witted, fine featured, looking much younger than her age, anxious to make others around her as happy as she was. He had sometimes thought that she was unusually given to tears, rather like a sensitive Victorian girl. He had seen her cry at a sad story in one of Frank's inquiries and, distinctly out of her century, at a magnificent cloud-strewn sunset. She was active, and in those years she and Frank went off moun-

187

tain climbing. She believed she was utterly healthy, and so did he. She was the opposite of hypochondria. Maybe there might have been vestigial warnings, but not to her.

Suddenly, she noticed that she was seeing double. She looked across the room, and Frank was smoking two cigarettes, not one. Soon she was walking like a spastic. The diagnosis didn't take long. Frank was told that she had multiple sclerosis. It was then that he had needed to tell someone and went to Humphrey. It had been left to his own judgment to break the news to her.

There was no known cure. She might have long remissions, or she might become paralyzed quite soon. Frank was cowardly enough, he confessed, to think that it might be better not to tell her himself but leave it to the doctor.

At last Frank did tell her and found that she had known for weeks. He also found, what Humphrey found on the visit after he heard the news, that the most unnerving aspect of the situation was that she was existing in an extravagant degree of euphoria. Frank was a man of stoical and vigorous spirits, but hers had always been higher. Now they mounted to something near joy. When a friend such as Humphrey arrived, trying lamely to cheer her up, that was the last thing she needed. Unaffectedly, with love, it was she who did the cheering up.

As the car drew up outside the Briers's house, semidetached in a neat chestnut-lined avenue, Humphrey was prepared for something similar that night.

He didn't get it. So far as Betty's condition went, the evening was soothing, like a remembrance of the past, but not a perfect remembrance since the future was never quite asleep. It was Betty herself who opened the door, kissed him, and, in the light of the hall, said it was a long time since she had seen him. Her cheekbones looked a little higher. When he had last visited her, her legs had been thinning. Now she was wearing a long dress, maybe as a cover. Otherwise, apart from a just perceptible limp as she led him into the sitting room, there was little change from what Humphrey first remembered: but great change from what he had witnessed when she was in one of the worst, and also most euphoric, phases.

"She's looking after you, is she?" Frank greeted him, already pouring a whiskey. Was Frank a shade overhearty, as though all was smooth and wouldn't alter? Yet it was peaceful to be with them in that sitting room. The Brierses were living on an official salary, about £8,000 a year, much less than the income of most of the inhabitants of Aylestone Square, but they managed to live at least as comfortably. The pictures were timid watercolors: Betty was educated—she had taught in a grammar school before her marriage—but she hadn't much visual taste. But then, most of Humphrey's acquaintances in Aylestone Square hadn't much visual taste either.

There was one difference between this house and most of those in Aylestone Square. It was that Betty was an admirable cook. She hadn't forgotten meals that Humphrey seemed to like. It occurred to him as odd that he, to whom food didn't matter much, take it or leave it, should be presented with meals he enjoyed twice in the last few nights, at White's and here. There wasn't much to be said for the English cuisine, but a few dishes were good, and he seemed to be having them all. Betty had made a steak-and-kidney pudding and a lavish trifle, too much trouble for anyone in her state. But when she had been half-paralyzed, she had gotten around on her knees to make meals for Frank.

Over the meal, Betty asked about Humphrey's children, calling them by their names affectionately, though she knew them only slightly. She was made to be a mother, Humphrey thought, and as a result his reply was unaccountably brusque.

"Nothing much to report. I'm not much in contact with them. They're still trying to do good."

She smiled at him, still affectionate. "You oughtn't to say that now, oughtn't you?"

"Why shouldn't I?" he replied.

"Why do you pretend to be harder than you are. You wouldn't really prefer it if they were trying to do bad, would you?"

"Sometimes I'm not so sure," Humphrey said, with a throwaway sarcastic smile.

"Now, now. You're a good man; we all know you are."

"My dear girl, I wish you knew—"

"Good people are very wrong to be superior about do-gooders. We need all the do-gooders we can get."

Frank was wearing a tough husbandly grin. Maybe he had met some such outburst himself. At the moment, he was smiling because, though he was used to hearing younger women get spirited with Humphrey, he had never noticed one of them lecture him so naturally.

When the steak pudding was finished, Frank remarked, "It's time we did some talking. You have to sing for your supper, of course. Fill your glass up. First of all, you can say anything you want, anything about anyone on earth, in front of Betty. You know that. She's much more discreet than I am. To tell you the honest truth, I had to learn to be discreet. When I started, my tongue was ready to run away with me. I wanted to impress. I had to learn the hard way."

"I think that was the case with me."

"It wasn't with Betty." Frank gazed at his wife with an expression protective, admiring, desiring, teasing, anxious. "She's never given away a secret in her life. I sometimes think intelligent women are much better at keeping their mouths shut than intelligent men. Perhaps they don't seem to have so many temptations."

Humphrey nodded. He had made the same discovery.

"Well, you can say anything you like. I'm going to ask you something. You'll have to come clean. Not that I can talk. We've been trying to be too bloody clever with each other. To hell with that. I want to ask you what your old office can tell us about Tom Thirkill. I know they keep tabs on him and more politicians than one would like to mention—"

"They have to look as though they're earning their money, don't they?"

Humphrey knew that out of the in-grown habit, now almost an instinct, he was being evasive. Frank knew it. Soon he began to speak.

"Not good enough. Come clean. They've been watching Thirkill, as you might expect. Then I found they'd taken the job away from our Special Branch people in favor of your old lot. You tell me why. I don't need telling that Tom Thirkill is about as likely to defect as the chairman of the Midland Bank. I do need telling what they have on Tom Thirkill's movements. Nothing fancy. I very strongly suspect that they can tell us where Tom Thirkill was that Saturday night. We haven't picked up any sightings. I believe your people could tell us. What do you think?"

Humphrey regarded him without expression, still in the old mode of duty, and then a smile twitched.

"I should think that is distinctly likely."

"Well then. Can you find out?"

"I don't much like to. I suppose I could."

"What the hell's the use of having all the contacts in London unless you come to the rescue now and then?"

Betty said, "That's the trouble, isn't it? He hates pulling rank, don't you, Humphrey?"

Humphrey said: "I must say, I don't see the point. Why in God's name are you thinking of Thirkill? Yes, I've given him some thought myself, but it doesn't make sense."

"No, it doesn't make sense." Frank was in his most active mood. "Nothing makes much sense. I've told you before, this is a policeman's nightmare. Noncooperative upper classes. No motive that anyone can see. If you want to get away with murder, Humphrey, kill someone amongst your smartest friends, and just to be on the safe side, kill someone you don't know. And don't have any motive at all. Then I promise you that we shan't catch you."

Betty smiled. Humphrey wondered how long it had taken her to get acclimatized to those gallows jokes.

"Well," Frank said, "we can tot up our own score. Getting down to cases. Burglars, minor villains, professionals—drawn blank. But that was never really on, you know that as well as I do. Odd stranger, madman, hooligan—*impossible* is a big word, but as near impossible as makes no matter. So we're left with the old three-card trick—pick someone among those who knew the old lady. You said more than three to pick from. We're still casting around. But that's just for the sake of thoroughness. Unless I've gone off my head, it must be someone I've thought of already. And the same with you. I can't dream up a conceivable motive for Tom Thirkill. But when one's really up against it, it's an old tip: don't forget the oddest man around. Even if you can't see the faintest reasons. Tom Thirkill is odd enough for anyone's money. So I want to know about him. By the way, he keeps some of his movements remarkably dark."

That night, both he and Humphrey were missing an explanation that later appeared obvious enough. Humphrey asked, "Is he worth all this trouble, as far as you're concerned?"

Briers said, "As a matter of fact, there's a different reason for being interested. You can guess—it's a better one. He must know something about his daughter. She's been on the list all along—you took that for granted too. Wild as they come. Not exactly nice. The old lady was pretty effectively stopping her grabbing our friend Loseby. I don't believe anyone halfway sane is going to kill for that reason. But still, I'm not going to rule her out. There may be something simpler that we haven't latched on to. With her and Loseby. Why in Christ's name did he marry her? I want to know anything her father knows."

Humphrey nodded and said, "I don't think you're surprising me."

"Of course I'm not. It's all commonplace. Loseby's in the picture, but I still can't see why. Anyway, the boys are on the job. They're working on how he lived, moneywise. And that night, was he shacked up with the young man Douglas Gimson, or was he not? Give and take, Humphrey. You're going to come clean about your sources, aren't you? I'll do the same about ours." He looked at his wife with consideration, or respect, or a kind of apology. "You've been through it before, dear, haven't you? You know in this game you don't trust your best friend. Humphrey's one of our best friends, isn't he?"

"I'd trust him with your life," she said. She loved Frank, and she meant it.

"So would I," Frank said and then added with a professional grin, "That doesn't mean I always find it easy to trust him with some of our little ways. We don't like giving them away. Any more than he did, I hope you noticed. More often than not, our sources are nothing to be proud of. I doubt if his are either. That's how the job has to be done. Well, we've been driving on in the old groove. It hasn't paid off so far. But we have plenty of feeds in the homosexual world. Not as many as we used to have, now the law is changed."

"That was something, anyway," Betty put in with gentle but surprising firmness.

"Not so much for us," Frank said. "Of course, our boys are digging into it now. Not on young Loseby much. He wouldn't pick up working-class boys or layabouts. We haven't heard a whisper of that, it's not his line. But Douglas Gimson might. We're getting a few scraps of hard information."

"Three names on the list," said Humphrey. "Others? Perhaps

that doctor, Perryman. I haven't any idea why, but he was with her often enough."

"Not forgotten. There was that little lead. About those money deals. That got us nowhere, but we haven't forgotten. By the way, he's the only one of them who hasn't put up any cover for that night. Just dinner with his wife and a patient to see. He was only there twenty minutes. He told us before we checked. He doesn't pretend that he has any cover at all."

Humphrey said, "That sounds more sensible than most of them."

"That was our feeling too."

"Anyone else?"

"Do you know anything about Paul Mason? His girl friend, or ex–girl friend, so they say, had more access to the old lady than anyone else. She's got perfect cover, though, like your Kate."

Humphrey said, "I just can't take that seriously."

"In this state of things you can take anything seriously." Humphrey understood.

The introduction of Paul Mason's name was soon dismissed. It had been half facetious. It wasn't what Betty expected, though she had heard this kind of somber conversation before, but the two of them became more facetious. Lefroy? Because Lady Ashbrook failed to recognize his genius? Alec Luria? The local parson? Betty hadn't had any previous sign that Humphrey's psychological taste could break down, and she was not only put off but shocked. She couldn't bear to hear them fool like this. She broke out in an invalid's freedom for the first time that night, "Don't you wish sometimes you had done something different?" She was speaking to Humphrey, but against her own will to her husband too.

"Who hasn't?"

"I mean, wouldn't you have liked to have done something positive sometimes?"

"Some real concrete good, you mean?" Humphrey turned the question with an affectionate gaze. "Most of us are lucky if we manage not to do real concrete harm."

"Oh, really, I told you before tonight that's not good enough for you."

At the mention of Luria, Frank had been reminded of his phrase about varnish, which he had heard from Humphrey, and spoke to his wife with a kind of pleading, with watchfulness about her nervous movements, and perhaps in an attempt to avert the disapproval of love.

"Don't be too finicky, my dearest. Everything you want is very fine, and anyone who's worth anything wants it. But it's very fragile, and it could break up very quickly. I wish to God you'd open your eyes to that. You've heard of old Luria's coat of varnish, haven't you? You know, that varnish is bloody thin. Humphrey and I have spent a lot of our time trying to make it an inch or two thicker in places. That's all. Whether it's worth anyone's doing or not is anyone's guess. If I didn't think it worth doing, I shouldn't do it. You know that."

"Of course I know that," she said. She said it with a radiant smile on the fine-drawn face. She went on, "But I do wish you two thought better of what people could become."

The two men smiled at her and glanced at each other.

❧ 26 ❧

Although Humphrey and Frank Briers hadn't appeared to clinch a bargain, they had done so, as Betty had also understood, that evening in her house. As the first sign of it Humphrey was to explain what his old office had been doing about Tom Thirkill.

He found the need for this mysterious. As Frank had said, it was the Special Branch, the small section of the police detailed for security work, who normally were used for a job of surveillance on politicians. Himself, he had worked with them often enough. But it seemed they had been warned off. He could see no meaning there. Further, he didn't like the inquiry that Frank Briers had pressed upon him.

It wasn't going to be congenial. Few people were more extinct than an extinct official, and that was especially true when one had been in the top stratum of a security service. An extinct official knew too much: what was worse, he knew the questions to ask as well as, sometimes better than, the present officials did. They would know the way to avoid answering them as well as, though not better than, he did himself. He went to his old familiar office, still mysteriously smelling of sawdust. He made visits to his old colleagues. He had to call on his former chief, still in post but just about to retire, before he could get a straight answer to a single question.

His old boss's name was Higgs. He was a plump, cautious, bright-eyed man, once a classical don, who had retained a hobby for non–Indo-European languages, Finnish, Estonian. He looked less like a security officer than Humphrey himself. But he had a total addiction to his work. Unlike Humphrey and most of the other senior operators, he hadn't started as a member of the impoverished upper classes. His father had been a small shopkeeper, and he had made his way through his academic skills. Between him and Humphrey there had long existed a feeling not uncommon among colleagues at their level in a hierarchy, perhaps even stronger in this closed system—not exactly liking, not exactly dislike, but something of the nature of guarded, intimate, knowledgeable suspiciousness, such as you can sometimes meet in secretive families.

Humphrey didn't spend much time on preambles. Had they been tapping Thirkill's calls?

"What do you think?" said Humphrey's old chief.

"I think you have been."

"It's not for me to say you're not right."

"Am I right?"

"Of course you are."

"The only thing I can't understand," Humphrey said, "is what in the name of reason you think you're playing at."

This was an old quarrel. Higgs was a very clever man; he did his duty; he kept his opinions to himself. Yet Humphrey knew that he had the political instincts of some of the last tsar's less liberal counselors. Anyone who was not demonstrably on the right was on the left. Anyone on the left was automatically suspect. Thirkill was potentially a man of power, and so he was the more suspect.

Humphrey shook his head. There was no use talking about it; there never had been any use. And yet Higgs was smiling with obscure satisfaction, as though he was allowing Humphrey to waste his energy.

"What have you got out of it?" he said.

"Do you mind telling me why you are interested, Humph?"

Sir Eric Higgs was the only person alive who used that diminutive.

"You've heard of the Belgravia murder? Old Lady Ashbrook?"

Sir Eric had heard, though not in his professional job, of most murders. He was an amateur of crime. He was very quick to pick up references, forgot nothing, knew of Humphrey's former connection with the police. Maybe he could even have recaptured Briers's name. No further explanations were necessary after Humphrey said he would like any data they had on Thirkill's whereabouts on July 24–25. Higgs gave a plump, cunning grin.

"Oh, you're on the wrong track there, you know. We've had some curious instructions from on high. I'm not permitted to tell you the reason. It's nothing to do with what you were thinking a moment ago. Thirkill's by way of being valuable just now in high quarters."

"Well then, what were you really playing at? What was the man doing?"

"I'm inclined to think," Sir Eric said, "we ought to do what we can to help. But I don't think it will be much use for your purposes."

Those would have been something like the correct preliminaries, even if Humphrey had still been one of the inner circle.

"What have you got out of the telephone calls?" Humphrey repeated.

"Very little. Precious little." Immediately, Sir Eric became precise, businesslike, exhibiting a memory as automatic as Frank Briers's, better than Humphrey's, which was good enough. Humphrey didn't doubt that in detail he would tell the truth.

The truth was, however, not sensational. On the tapes, Tom Thirkill was recorded as talking to three or four Moscow Marxists in the Parliamentary party—just general bonhomie, asking them not to stab him in the back more than necessary. Interesting that he didn't talk in the same terms to the much larger group of the militant left, irregular Trotskyites. Not disciplined, Humphrey commented. Thirkill wouldn't trust them; no experienced politician would. Humphrey added, "Of course, the man's fighting for his political life."

Sir Eric was not concerned about party factions. There was nothing that disturbed him on those tapes. Anyway, Thirkill was in favor in the top places, for reasons that Higgs still couldn't tell Humphrey. The curious thing was, he was not dissembling, Humphrey had to realize. If high authority had a use for Thirkill, so automatically had Higgs.

"Of course," Higgs said with avuncular caution, "we're dealing with a remarkably cagey man."

Humphrey was impelled to remark, "I'm glad you've stopped worrying about him—"

"We've said that before, haven't we? And it turned out rather uncomfortably different."

Bland, obstinate as ever, but Humphrey had to accept that this was the mirror image of himself and Frank Briers. Brilliant suspiciousness through living at the center of a spider's web, feeling the twitches, losing one's sense of the impossible.

Sir Eric remarked with subdued pleasure, "He really is remarkably cagey, you know. We have some evidence that he won't talk about anything serious in his own drawing room."

"He thinks you've bugged it?"

"So it would appear."

"As a matter of fact, have you?"

Sir Eric gave a chairmanlike smile. "No, we haven't gone as far as that."

He knew nothing of Thirkill's daughter, and there was nothing about her on the file. But he did as he promised. Yes, there had been a check on Thirkill's movements, which had continued up to the present day on those same unproducible instructions. He would let Humphrey read the record of the night of July 24. It was several steps down the hierarchy, in a small, gloomy, windowless room, taken there by Sir Eric, that Humphrey saw the papers. Sir Eric had performed polite introductions, given polite instructions so that they were requests, and said good-bye.

The incumbent was called Kirby, once in the Colonial Service, sad, indrawn, at the same time requiring sympathy and giving none. He was not anxious to help, but he had to obey orders. Yes, they had been keeping tabs on Mr. Thirkill (as Kirby called him throughout).

"Have you any idea why?"

"Matter of form," said Kirby mulishly.

"Anything on July 24?"

"Usual pro forma."

Thirkill had left 36 Eaton Square at 5:39 on July 24, 1976. Got into his own car, WSK589N, and drove off via Belgrave Square, Hobart Place, Grosvenor Gardens, Park Lane. Agents' reports, except to those endowed with romantic reverence, had the devastating prosiness of fact.

Who was tracking him? Humphrey asked. One of our men, said Kirby. Humphrey asked for the name. Kirby shook his head, for once looking faintly triumphant because he was not allowed to say.

Route northward. Stop at public house, Lion, Henley. Two cars (numbers given) appeared to be following Thirkill. Occupants went in public bars. At 6:52 Mr. Thirkill resumed journey. Stopped at private house (address given), occupant Herbert Grierson, nothing known. Left house at 7:47. Continued journey to Hatfield. Stayed in car. Left Hatfield at 8:29 and drove, speed 70 m.p.h., back to London. Returned to residence, 36 Eaton Square.

"It seems a long way to get back to your own house," said Humphrey. It was a standard dodge. Humphrey himself had more than once driven around capital cities and arrived, with a certain sense of anticlimax, where he started.

Then there was a hiatus. The record faithfully reported that neither Mr. Thirkill nor anyone else had left No. 36 until 11:35. At that time a party had come down, apparently from two floors above Mr. Thirkill's apartment, got into three cars, all with German or Swiss number plates, and driven away. Not followed: destination, by sources, Hyde Park Hotel. Eighteen-minute gap. Mr. Thirkill himself left 11:53 on foot. Movements followed. Through side streets to St. George's Hospital. Entered by front portal, exit by side door. Walked along Knightsbridge, southern side. Crossed to Hyde Park Hotel. Left Hyde Park Hotel 4:32 A.M., July 25. Taxi to 36 Eaton Square.

When Humphrey thanked him, Kirby looked as though he didn't require thanks. When Humphrey added, "But this chap has left out the interesting part, hasn't he?" Kirby looked ill done by. He said, "He covered all he was asked to. That was the interesting part for him—"

Humphrey said, "If I'd been he, the interesting part would have been those miscellaneous visitors. Who were they? Why were they playing these games?"

"Majority Americans. All vouched for by their embassies. Highest credentials. Names suppressed for official reasons."

"Did you get the names?"

"We've done what we've been told to do. Then we left well alone."

Kirby became less melancholy when Humphrey took him to the habitual pub close by. Before they left, Humphrey asked a question about Susan but again elicited nothing at all. There was no mention of her in the report. Until Thirkill returned, getting on for five on the Sunday morning, there had been no lighting visible in his apartment all that night.

No more official interchanges on the way to the pub or inside it. Over his third double, Kirby said that he would have been content to finish his time in the Pacific. He couldn't get used to the dark London sky. Not that it had been dark that summer, he said with his one spicule of humor.

Humphrey had done what Frank Briers asked, with nothing sharp edged emerging, he thought. True, it was clear—since Morgan and his forensic staff were now certain that the latest time for the murder was 10:30 P.M. and this an outer limit—that Tom Thirkill hadn't done it: but Humphrey had never believed that he had and was sure that Briers had never believed it either. There was the small interval of time later, the eighteen unexplained minutes, which others got interested in, but Humphrey disregarded that too.

Still Tom Thirkill's movements that night had a certain grotesque fascination of their own. What had he been up to? Humphrey had no doubt by now that old Higgs knew. Humphrey speculated on a familiar problem of former days: how could conspicuous persons meet inconspicuously? Once, in his official life, he had been asked to find a solution and had dismally failed. There wasn't a solution. Persons who had never tried it often had great faith in disguises. That was brilliant if, as in Elizabethan plays, you could rely on putting on a wig and not being recognized by your own wife.

It would be impossible—Humphrey found the prospect diverting—for a man like Thirkill to hide for a couple of weeks in any sizable town in the Western world. On the other hand, his clandestine maneuvers did appear, at least for one night, to have succeeded. They didn't deserve to have succeeded. Any decent agent would have been ashamed of them. And yet, Humphrey had seen nothing in the press, and it seemed certain that Thirkill had been evading journalists. As to why, Humphrey had a vague idea or guess. It had all the flavor of some negotiation, with Thirkill being used as a front man. Probably the negotiations had been initiated on this side. It was deceptive that the Americans had sent a big team; the Americans always negotiated in big teams. Whether this negotiation was political or not, creditable or discreditable, semiofficial, paraofficial, or simply a deal, Humphrey couldn't know. He had guessed a lot; he thought he knew a little—but he didn't know anything like all.

So he was surprised as much as others when a few days after he had made his inquiries about Tom Thirkill, he saw the name on the front page of the *Times*. He had passed on his results, such as they were, to Frank Briers. After that, Thirkill had gone out of mind. Now he came back.

> Promotion for Mr. T. Thirkill. It is announced from 10 Downing Street that Mr. T. Thirkill, Labour M.P. for Leicester East, has been appointed an additional Financial Secretary to the Treasury. He will not at present have a seat in the Cabinet, but will have direct access to the Prime Minister and Chancellor of the Exchequer. He will have special responsibility for international financial exchanges.

That was the end of the announcement. The newspaper added its own gloss.

> Mr. Thirkill is an acknowledged expert on the international money market and has added to his reputation by his recent series of speeches in the Commons and outside.
>
> Mr. Thirkill is known to be a leading figure on the right wing of the Labour Party, and first indications are that the appointment will not be popular on the left. Reactions of major spokesmen of the *Tribune* group were—"this is a sign that the Government are selling out" and "Thirkill will see that they break all the promises they haven't already broken in the manifesto."

Official statements had a cryptic eloquence of their own. This one, saying that Tom Thirkill wouldn't have a seat in the Cabinet, meant that he would have one soon. He had almost certainly bargained and exacted the price. His bargaining position must be strong, Humphrey thought. He must have been used as an emissary in the summer's dealings with the world financial institutions, not only the IMF—used as an emissary but, it now appeared, as something more.

The gossip about Tom Thirkill had for months been subsiding.

His lawyers had done their job. Senior ministers must be well assured.

Nevertheless, they were taking a risk. Humphrey didn't like being nagged by the meaner emotions, but he was feeling them. This was too unfair to be borne, he was thinking, just as Kate had cried on hearing of Lady Ashbrook's death. Only a fool expected life not to be unfair, said the detached side of Humphrey. That was a feeble comfort. Humphrey was thinking, of all the people he knew, most were more tolerable than Tom Thirkill, most were more honest with themselves, and nearly all were more balanced. Thirkill's kind of derangement, one would have thought, ought to have been a handicap, but it seemed to have proved a strength. Quite a few of Humphrey's acquaintances were cleverer than Thirkill, and some much abler. None, he had to admit, had his flair for money.

Unfair, unfair. Thirkill issued a statement that afternoon saying that he would not have accepted the position unless he had felt it was his duty to the country and to his party. He had no ambitions but to help the country out of a dangerous patch. The pound should not be allowed to sink further. It had just reached its lowest level. It would take a long haul to restore confidence, but it could be done. We had to reestablish sound money. But we all had to form ranks and pull together, that was all. We had to build a springboard for prosperity.

He might be something of a film star, he might have a flair for money, thought Humphrey resentfully, but he wrote with his feet. Others cared less about that deficiency. On the exchanges that same afternoon there was a movement. Against the dollar, the pound rose twenty cents.

❧ 27 ❧

By this time, Briers had told Humphrey all that the police had discovered about Lady Ashbrook's finances. They had gone on false trails; they had made mistakes; they couldn't find any connection with what they had suspected of Loseby and Susan. When they had convinced themselves that Loseby's account of that night was unbreakable, they concentrated on her. It could have been a collaboration, though no one had yet imagined any reason why.

From the beginning, certainly after the disclosure of the will, they had been sifting out how Lady Ashbrook contrived to live. The will had set them back, but then Flamson, followed by young detectives more vocal than he was, had insisted that it was altogether too tidy. That was no credit to Briers himself. With Humphrey, now that Briers was telling all, he took a leader's pleasure in pointing out where his lads had been clever. He also took a sardonic pleasure in pointing out where he himself had been dense. It was George Flamson, chiefly, though not alone, who had stuck to it. George Flamson looked like a simple puce-cheeked country boy. Actually, he wasn't a country boy; his father was a minor pit-head official in one of the Midland coal fields. George Flamson to many might appear simple; certainly he wasn't overrefined, but he had a sense of fact.

As Humphrey listened, he thought that he also had been obtuse: how dim-witted could one be? On the facts known, Lady Ashbrook couldn't have lived as she did. Nor could her grandson. He was a little in debt, but very little. Brother officers like Douglas

203

Gimson were well off, and Loseby lived up to their standards. He couldn't have done that on his pay.

The explanation was not complete and was still emerging in bits and pieces. Humphrey heard it in a more ordered fashion than the detectives collected it and so might have found it less bewildering, or more obvious, than at first sight. As to Lady Ashbrook's sources of income, they were now established. She had a trifle from her investments. She had an annuity of £1,500. She had her old-age pension. Some of the grand and rich were too lofty to take their pension, but not many. Lady Ashbrook was not among them. There was no other income on which she had paid tax. From what Flamson and colleagues at the Yard could identify, she had about enough to pay her rates, heating, and lighting, and perhaps the £15 a week she paid to Maria, the cleaner. The bills for rates and the rest, and her minute income tax, she paid by checks on Coutts Bank.

Then what? She existed parsimoniously in food and drink, but it cost something. She still bought good clothes, and frequently, for a woman of her age. A smart hairdresser came to her house once a week. She might be mean, but it seemed that she didn't stint herself of what she had thought appropriate in her days of fashion. All those accounts, and Maria's wages, were paid in notes.

Where did the money come from? Occasionally she drew sums from her bank, but only small ones. The expenditure on herself year after year was hard to compute but couldn't have been less than £2,000 a year, and probably much more. Further, there were indications—not yet definite—that she passed quite large tips to her grandson.

For weeks, the police could find no answer. They searched among her old acquaintances. A good many were rich and could have helped her. Could even have helped her in some convoluted fashion devised to avoid taxation—for that some experts at Scotland Yard, used to fiscal dodges, were already looking. No sign anywhere. Then what might have seemed like a fluke or an inspired guess broke through. It was neither. It was the apparatus grinding on. The detectives pored over names of her contacts. In the will that had been superseded by her final one, there was a bequest and a message of thanks to Desmond O'Brien at a Wall Street address. Who was he? The information was easy to gather.

He was a well-known New York lawyer, head of a reputable firm, the only oddity of which was that all the partners were Catholics. He had died, nearly eighty, in 1974.

More than being a successful lawyer, he was better known as an influence behind the scenes in the Democratic party. For many years he had been one of the powers in the New Jersey Democratic machine and confidant of presidents. He was said to be one of the toughest of operators in politics. In private, on the other hand, he had a reputation for benevolence and propriety. He was a bachelor, pious, believing, and practicing. He had a famous collection of pottery. As an Irish Catholic who was on good terms with English politicians, during the last war the White House had used him as a high-powered messenger between Washington, London, Dublin.

At the same time, the Ashbrooks had been in Washington, as they were again during the second Churchill government. It was common knowledge there that they had been close friends of Desmond O'Brien. He lived an ascetic life, apart from whiskey, but he liked escorting beautiful women. It was also possible that he had an amiable weakness for the highborn. When Lord Ashbrook died, the attachment between the other two went on without a break— innocent, so the worldly said, which must have been a change for Lady Ashbrook, while the less worldly were gossiping about the chances of a marriage. O'Brien wrote her letters, telephoned her across the ocean, and while he was still able-bodied enough to travel, visited her in London.

Those bits of information had been extracted from his office by the FBI, who had been invoked by Scotland Yard officers in New York. The FBI couldn't extract much more. O'Brien's office was drilled to secrecy. But it was discovered, though through other sources, that quite early in their friendship she had transferred her holdings in American securities into O'Brien's name. Very nice of her, said a time-worn FBI executive, trying to keep the wolf from the door of a very rich man. Further, the O'Brien office volunteered that among the private funds handled by his firm there was one that he dealt with strictly by himself. It wasn't a large one, perhaps $200,000, though that was nothing but a guess.

In September, that was the extent of the hard evidence. There was not a word on paper. When, a little later, Briers told Humphrey the history as the detectives knew it, Humphrey said that old O'Brien must have known all the rules of security. With his career in machine politics, it would have been strange if he hadn't. On what they now knew, the police were able to construct various kinds of scenario. The one that survived was the simplest. They had to assume that O'Brien and Lady Ashbrook were acting with unqualified trust in each other. (The very best security, said Humphrey, if you had chosen the right person.) She had made over the major part of her capital to him—a tiny amount by O'Brien's standards, no doubt, one Yard estimate being £50,000 to £60,000. In England, it was still less than wiseacres would have expected, but it was not totally unbelievable, as after death her estate had seemed.

It was then arranged that O'Brien should get money to her in England at appropriate intervals. O'Brien was doing nothing illegal, or even improper. An American citizen could acquire any amount of English currency and give it away in England. It was conceivable that the dividends on the securities were allowed to accumulate and not declared on either side of the Atlantic. That was not resolved. Those who knew O'Brien thought it more likely that he paid the tax himself and even supplemented the fund. He could well have afforded to, and he liked doing good turns in secret.

Lady Ashbrook was, of course, evading income tax. Not on a big scale, but as much as she could arrange. What may have given her more satisfaction, she was also evading death duties. It seemed unrealistic that people should care so bitterly about what happened to their money after they died. Perhaps it was another defiance of mortality.

In the scenario, all was as simple as arrangements could be. O'Brien brought packets of notes in person or else sent them in a small parcel. The simpler, the safer. That was another rule for secret operations. Lady Ashbrook duly received about £3,000 a year—this was the police guess, but it might have been out by a sizable factor. This was partly from the income on capital, partly through slices of the capital itself, which was to be allowed to decline.

No one but the two of them could know, but transactions seemed to have worked smoothly enough—so long as they were both healthy and mobile.

Briers, who hadn't been involved at firsthand, nothing like so closely as with Loseby and Susan, made one intervention himself. It was a curious one. He asked for an interview with Tom Thirkill just after the ministerial post had been announced. Briers wanted another opinion, from someone who was supposed to know everything about financial sharp practice, but his real reason was that he might pick up a scrap of news about Susan, where he was still searching.

There he drew a complete blank. Thirkill received him with the overwhelming heartiness of a politician on the rise. Boisterous jokes, one suspicious professional to another, Thirkill suggested that the police might not be planning to run him in this time. The Ashbrook murder: the police would get into trouble if they didn't charge someone soon. "The press are after you, Frank. We all know what that is like. They'll be cutting my throat if I don't pull something out of the bag. Don't you worry, this Government is going to stagger on." Actually, Thirkill, among the blague and the bluffness, Christian names and all, sounded less persecuted than he had been, and this was the bugle call of his own kind of defiant confidence. But he had nothing to say about the murder, or about his daughter and her marriage.

That might have been his animal caution on the watch, but about Lady Ashbrook's money dealings, where he had no need to be cautious, he was almost as dismissive, and contemptuous in the process. He had listened to Briers's description—some of it wasn't proved, just a sketch plan, said Briers, who knew when to be candid—carefully enough.

"I don't call those money dealings." Thirkill gave a raucous laugh. "Fiddles in Petticoat Lane. Peasant stuff. Look here, Frank. People who have anything to do with money don't go about with pound notes. Since I made some myself, and that's getting on for thirty years, I've never carried as much as five pounds in my pocket."

"There are advantages in that, aren't there, minister?"

Thirkill was exhibiting his harsh, attractive grin, seeing that the other man wasn't being outfaced.

"Point taken." The grin developed into a laugh. "Have it your own way. It does mean that the other chap finds it necessary to pick up the tabs."

Briers joined in the laugh, as though they had both agreed that

that was the summit of all humor. Briers asked, "I want to know what you think, though. This operation seems to have worked. Or something like it. Do you think it could?"

Thirkill became suddenly competent. He reflected, not for long. "I suppose it could. Given absolute discretion on both sides. And a minimum of information to anyone around."

"You really think so?"

"If they didn't do it on any kind of scale—yes, I suppose it could work."

Briers thanked him and said that was what he had come for. Which was not true. While Thirkill spent a few minutes in ministerial obbligato, saying that of course old Desmond O'Brien was a dear old friend of his, meaning perhaps that he had met him more than once.

Not long after that meeting, Briers got clearance from Scotland Yard to send a mission to America. This was at the end of October, and Humphrey, by now fully informed, heard of the results the day after they had reached Briers himself. The mission was not a pretentious one, just Bale and Flamson. Why those two, Humphrey had asked? Well—Briers was in his briskest form—the Yard already had its officers in New York; they knew what was required. Flamson—well, he might appear too yokel-like to cut much ice with smart boys of the FBI. Old Len Bale, he had some presence; he would give a decent image. Also, Frank was able to use the visit as an excuse to get him promoted, which couldn't have happened otherwise. He needed suitable rank over there. Frank Briers displayed boyish satisfaction, as though this were the main object of the exercise.

As it turned out, whoever was responsible, the mission brought back new facts. Bale reported that O'Brien's office either had nothing to tell or would tell nothing. His women secretaries were devoted to the old man and guarded his memory. They did know that he had made up parcels himself and dispatched them to someone in London each Christmas, just as he gave each of the three women secretaries a handsome present. They knew a little more, Bale was sure. Certainly they knew that he regularly bought largish quantities of sterling notes. But they would never talk—all unmarried women, all Catholics, all used to secretive maneuvers. Bale had spent some days in the office and talked to the partners.

Only one seemed to know more than the secretaries, and then, in the sacramental security phrase, no more than he needed to know.

That was the opinion of Bale, now Superintendent Bale, and Briers accepted it. So did Humphrey when Briers told him. Although Bale was viewed with condescension by almost everyone, especially the young officers, rather as though he were a good-natured old Airedale, Humphrey had come to have respect for his judgment in dealing with human beings. In that matter, Humphrey didn't have respect for many.

As Bale had reported, just one of O'Brien's partners had been told something, but a bare minimum. This was a young man called Prchlik, not a specially Irish name, but one belonging to as devout a Catholic family as O'Brien's own. He was one of the youngest partners and selected as O'Brien's helper and vestigial confidant for that reason. When O'Brien and Lady Ashbrook were both able bodied, the transactions went according to plan. That continued until they were in their mid-seventies. Then O'Brien had a stroke. In part he recovered, but travel was over for him. His thoughts were clear, but speech not easy. This was the time that he turned to young Prchlik. Stoically, O'Brien decided that it was necessary to prepare for death, and with lucidity he prepared for Lady Ashbrook's as well as his own. He gave Prchlik a hint about an unnamed person who was his own age. There were obligations that had to be left in order.

Although Prchlik could have paid visits to London and transferred money as O'Brien had done, the old man decided that that would be nothing but a temporary solution. There would remain obligations to be discharged when she came to die. They would have to call in aid one other person whom she could trust as she did O'Brien. He wrote to her, laboriously, in his sclerotic hand. They had to find a third person, stationed in England. Could she nominate someone? He would like to know her choice without delay. After their long understanding he thought it reasonable for him to request a right of veto. That was a lawyer's stipulation of which he told Prchlik and of which he seemed very proud. However, it was not exercised. Once again there was nothing on paper, except for O'Brien's letter, and that she must have destroyed. Lady Ashbrook gave a name over the transatlantic phone. It was presumably the name of someone known to O'Brien, and there was agreement.

Prchlik was not told the identity of this third person, though in due course he learned Lady Ashbrook's. Between him and O'Brien—and secretly among the secretaries—the London agent was referred to as the comptroller. The fund, which had previously been called simply Mr. O'Brien's, became known as the comptroller fund. The comptroller was to join O'Brien and Lady Ashbrook in possession of all the details—the three of them, no more.

During the last year of O'Brien's life, a timetable was laid down. Prchlik said that, like others in old age, O'Brien had become obsessed with secrecy, obscure and sometimes meaningless secrecy. It would have saved some complications if Prchlik, as well as the comptroller, had been told everything. As it was, O'Brien insisted on a program. A messenger from the firm had to travel to London each September. This messenger would take a small parcel, innocuous, contents unknown to him, stay in a hotel, and deposit the parcel at the desk. It had to bear the name of O'Brien's firm. The comptroller would ring up the American embassy, learn where the representative of the firm was staying, and arrange for the parcel to be collected.

It was, like all O'Brien's procedures, relatively simple: but, Humphrey commented as he listened to Frank Briers, it would have been even simpler if he had given them £100,000, which he wouldn't have missed, and to hell with it.

The final item in the arrangement was that, after Lady Ashbrook's death, which O'Brien seemed to anticipate as not much later than his own, the remaining money in the fund should be transferred to London, in larger installments than before, so as to wipe the account clear within three years.

That was the story as they reconstructed it. Briers and the detectives accepted that something like it had actually happened. There was no factual evidence as to where the money had gone, except to Lady Ashbrook herself. They assumed that Loseby had some of it. They couldn't find any trace of the money being collected, and so they still didn't know who the comptroller was. There were already guesses, several of them. There were also new guesses as to motives for the killing, but to Briers it remained like a word on the tip of the tongue.

Briers continued to tell Humphrey everything he knew, or suspected, about the case. But he hadn't told Humphrey of another reason for sending old Bale to New York. It was to give him some respite from his domestic tangle. Briers was totally loyal to his own men and so said nothing—even though he would have trusted Humphrey with any such secret of his own. He had made indulgent hints about certain imbroglios caused by the appearance of lively young women police officers. He had left Humphrey to imagine that a young inspector, someone as sly and glossy as Shingler, perhaps, had set up house with one of the girls.

The truth was more unexpected. It was Bale, so priestlike, so respectable, so much a pillar of society, who had done just that. The young detectives took it for granted that Bale was a dull old thing. They had noticed nothing of this. He had considerable skill in covering his movements. But Briers had cause to know that Bale, after presiding with subdued dignity over conferences of the background squad, went back to conduct telephone conversations, not so subdued, with his wife. The trouble was, he seemed to be enjoying himself hugely.

There were times when Briers, going back to the sick room at home, could not suppress a spasm of envy. However, he had tried to help. A trip to America might bring Bale to his senses, Briers thought. He admitted to himself that on Bale's return it showed no sign of doing so. It seemed to have made him more enthusiastic. Briers gave a sour grin to himself: that would teach him to play God, he thought. If anything, Bale was in more of a tangle than ever. Enjoying himself more, though no one would have guessed it. There was only one result of Briers's good intention: if Bale retired before his time, he would now receive a somewhat larger pension.

❧ 28 ❧

After the murky rain-thick morning in the street outside, the mortuary was hallucinatorily bright. Still, for Humphrey, that was scarcely cheering. The smell (was it the clinical smell alone?) didn't make for ease. He had not been in a mortuary before. It seemed a singular rendezvous. But it was a genuine one. When Frank Briers made a contract, he kept to it. From the outset, he was speaking to Owen Morgan, the pathologist, as though Humphrey were one of them.

Humphrey had heard Briers talk of Morgan but hadn't met him. He hadn't expected anyone so strenuous. He certainly hadn't expected the joshing those two exchanged, as much a part of etiquette as saying good morning.

Briers had an official reason for calling on the pathologist. It was a piece of forensic business not connected with the Ashbrook case. Questions were masterfully disposed of within ten minutes. "Good," said Briers. "That's dealt with, then." He went on to another matter.

"Oh, something else. Taffy, do you know anything about a doc called Perryman?"

"What about him?"

"He was Lady Ashbrook's doctor."

"I thought the name rang a bell. I must have seen it in the files." Morgan was quick on the take. "Is he involved?"

"We're eliminating people who aren't." Briers was including Humphrey in his confidence. "He's still left in."

"Can't you do better than the process of elimination?"

"If you believe in your own God-given wits, you'd better get out of this job. We'll find a sensible pathologist."

Matey abuse duly conducted, Morgan said, "I don't know anything about the man. I might be able to find something out."

"Do that. If you get the chance. But don't waste your time. It's a very long shot."

Humphrey was sure that Briers expected nothing in the way of information. That inquiry had been for Humphrey's benefit, not Briers's own. It was to show that he was concealing nothing.

Jocular, affable insults as Morgan said good-bye. In the street, rain persisting, Frank Briers pointed to a cafe opposite. "I've been in there before. That'll do."

If he hadn't been at work, that cafe would not have done. The only lighting was a strip of neon lamp behind the counter, reflected, not encouragingly, on the streaming pavement. It was a minimal cafe. They carried cups of milky coffee to a bare, zinc-topped table. Frank, who when on duty went without food and just as absently took any chance of a snack, managed to buy two plastic-wrapped ham sandwiches.

It was about ten thirty in the morning, and he ate them both. He asked Humphrey what he thought of Morgan and went in for paeans of praise himself, no false mateyness, just praise.

Humphrey was waiting for news. The morning so far had been one of Frank's curious preliminaries. Preliminaries over, the news came.

"I have something to tell you," Frank said, voice quiet, though there was no one else in the cafe.

"Well?"

"Loseby wasn't in Lady Ashbrook's house that night."

"Definite?"

"As definite as we can be without having sat in with him and Master Gimson right through that blasted night. Their story is true enough. If it hadn't been, they might have invented something better."

Briers was half irritable, as though he oughtn't to have been bothered. He might have been irritable, but he was one of nature's expositors. He was describing a minor triumph for the method, and warmed by collective pride. The lads had been slogging away.

Leaving nothing out. He had told Humphrey before, he said, they were tapping all the homosexual contacts they had—and there were plenty. He broke out into his occupational grin.

They had burrowed away. Massage parlors. Dance clubs. Date fixers. Tedious work for the lads—again the occupational grin—unless it put ideas into their heads. Most policemen were straight in that respect, not all. One lad, who was a 100-percent straight man, had been greeted with the invigorating welcome—you're my sweetie pie. He wanted to take a dog along the next time. No luck for a long time. Then someone began to run across tracks of Douglas Gimson. Three or four years before, Gimson had been around. He was a cruiser, some of the informants said. He seemed to have dropped out. He might have stopped being a cruiser. There was a boy who shot off his mouth about him.

The boy was identified. Actually not a boy, about thirty. Name of Darblay, which might have been faked. Stagehand, did some modeling. Frenzied. The lads had put the pressure on him. He had sponged on Douglas Gimson for money (in the clubs, he had yelled about that). The captain made him take it, Darblay screamed at the policemen. Douglas Gimson was generous. Darblay liked money. Sooner or later Gimson got tired of being sponged on. Threats. Might have been blackmail once upon a time. Not dangerous now. Anyway, Frank doubted whether Douglas Gimson would have been a pushover for blackmail. So Darblay had become a telephone pest. The police knew all about telephone pests. There were thousands. Darblay took to ringing Gimson's clubs—the respectable ones—and asking, in a histrionic voice, is Captain Hōmosexual Gimson in? Once or twice he came to Gimson's apartment block, discovered that he had gone out to dinner, found his host's address, and on the phone elocuted the same question. He seemed to think that if he promised to stop the campaign, Douglas Gimson would pay him off.

He also seemed to have developed an obsession for spying on Gimson. Most evenings before the theater, he took to watching the entrance to the apartment. It wasn't just a coincidence that on that Saturday in July he was there as usual. Once that was established, the lads really got to work, said Briers. He was an hysteric; they didn't like him. They put the pressure on. Senior officers joined in, once Frank himself. "But I wasn't needed. The team was on the job." Fairly soon they extracted one fact. Darblay had seen Loseby (whom he had met during his peaceful period with Douglas Gimson) enter the apartment that evening. The time he gave was about 5:00 P.M., near enough to what Loseby and Gimson had themselves told the police. Darblay had hung about until getting on for theater time. Loseby hadn't left by then.

So far this statement was in line with the Loseby story, that he had been with Gimson all evening, all night, until the following morning. Though it wasn't relevant, he and Gimson both claimed that he had been there the whole of the Sunday.

It might have been a fluke, Frank remarked, but one of the lads asked Darblay what he had done during the rest of that night. Darblay said that they couldn't be interested in anything else he had done. They became pressingly interested. What had he been doing that night? He blustered and began to shriek. "What do you think a bleeding stagehand does? Would any of you fancy the bleeding job?" What else did you do? What else? They went on.

Both Frank and Humphrey knew the technique of this kind of questioning by heart. One officer kept saying, "Phone calls. How many did you make?" Darblay became enraged. How many? How many calls about Captain Gimson? It took an hour or two before Darblay admitted that he had phoned Gimson's flat five times from the theater during the performance. He hadn't liked the look of that Lord Loseby going there. He had asked whether Captain Gimson was in. What words had he used? "What the hell does it matter? They knew who I was," Darblay screamed. "Yes, yes, yes."

Who had answered? "Yes, yes." Sometimes one, sometimes the other. It must have made a row, so the policemen said. There were telephones on both sides of that bed.

After the theater? Had he rung again? Yes, yes, yes. More than once? Yes, yes, yes. Until what time? He couldn't remember. Midnight? He expected so. After midnight? Yes, yes, yes. Until they took the receiver off.

"If it had been me," Humphrey said, "I can't help feeling that I would have done that quite a long time before. It must have got in the way of an evening's gentle entertainment." Briers said that he had asked them why they hadn't. Apparently Gimson was waiting for a call from his mother.

"I must say, it's an odd way for anyone to get out of trouble." Humphrey went on, "But it does seem pretty convincing, doesn't it?"

"It does. It stands up all the way round. By the by, I asked them why they hadn't told me. It might have saved us plenty of man hours. They said they had mentioned phone calls. But they certainly hadn't mentioned the subject. That would have got us going."

"Why ever didn't they?"

"You tell me. You know these people."

Humphrey reflected later, it might be that Loseby wasn't ashamed of much under heaven, but perhaps he was ashamed of looking ridiculous. Neither he nor Gimson could have guessed at Darblay's timetable, or thought that it was any use to them. What was certain, they would have had to try hard to appear more ridiculous.

"I hope you told them that they had been insufferable fools. Trying to suppress things."

"I did." Briers gave his toughest smile. "I also told him, Douglas Gimson, that if he's obliged to pick up young men, he'd do better to stick to his own class. He wouldn't be so likely to get into this kind of mess."

Then Frank Briers turned irritable again.

"That's something we've tidied up, anyhow. But there's one spot where we haven't been so clever. I blame myself, Humphrey, I blame myself."

This had been on his mind all morning, Humphrey thought. Briers enjoyed success, but failure touched him more, which might make for efficacy, but not for animal comfort.

"It's the girl Susan. We may have missed a trick."

Then Briers went into an angry description, angry but still lucid. Susan had come off her bogus story—she had no option—Briers told Humphrey. Now she said that she must have been thinking of some other night. Briers broke off, temper no better, into words about Susan's behavior. Now she had Loseby safely in her clutches, he said, she didn't give a tinker's curse for his night out with Douglas Gimson. She took homos and their doings like a cup of tea.

Then Briers got back to business. He thought they knew, he

said, when Susan met Loseby after that weekend and agreed to cover him with the bogus story. It was sometime on the Monday afternoon. That story covered her too. Now it was all blown. It didn't enter, Briers said. He went on, voice sharpened: "What does enter is where the young lady really was on the Saturday evening. The worry is, we could have missed something. It's a great mistake to sit back and think you've got all you want. It's one of the oldest mistakes in the book. We went plugging on about Loseby, but somehow we swallowed the girl's story. We took it for granted she'd been with him part of that night, anyway. Until we really get the Gimson thing tied up. It's my own fault and no one else's."

"What about her, then?"

"The trouble is, it doesn't make much sense either. We may have missed a sighting. Or else it seemed so farfetched we didn't follow it up." Frank Briers was talking roughly, as though, in spite of his protestations of self-blame, it was really Humphrey, totally innocent, who deserved to take it.

"Come on." Humphrey had had long experience of bosses when they had slipped.

"There may have been a sighting. It didn't seem likely enough to take seriously. Those mews flats at the bottom of the old lady's garden—someone told us there had been a girl hanging about when they went out to dinner. About eight on the Saturday night. They came back later, couldn't be sure of the time, somewhere between half-past ten and eleven. The girl, they thought it was the same girl, was still walking about between the mews and the street. They didn't pay much attention to her. Medium height, smartish clothes, slacks, might have fitted anyone. They didn't know Susan from Adam—why in God's name does no one know anyone else in London? Photographs—yes, it could have been her, but it could have been hundreds of other girls. The lads asked her about it as a matter of course. But she laughed it off. That was the time when she was sticking to her old story, with Loseby left out. She couldn't be in bed in a flat she and Loseby sometimes borrowed—which happens to be true, she always gets her backup stories right—she couldn't be in bed and walking about the mews at the same time, could she? So it didn't seem worth going on. And it's getting too late now. If they didn't see much then, they're not going to after a couple of months."

"It's not very plausible, is it?"

"You're telling me."

"If she were there, waiting about for hours, she couldn't have been in the house—"

"We managed to work that out for ourselves."

Humphrey received that snub with a faint smile.

"So in a direct sense she would be more or less let out. No one would do a murder and dawdle about forever. Unless they were quite mad."

"She's as sane as you are. We managed to work that out too."

"It doesn't seem plausible. Surely it's long odds it was a girl waiting for a man to come back to one of those flats."

"That's what we thought."

"If by any miracle it was Susan," Humphrey was brooding, "I suppose she might have known who was in the house—or who she imagined might be."

"Teach your grandmother to suck eggs."

That was said with something like a return to good nature.

After a while, Frank said, "Do you believe she was there?"

Humphrey said, "If she was there, she ought to have seen someone or something."

It was Frank, quicker than Humphrey, who had seen another possibility, which was still obscure that morning. Frank went on, "If she did see someone, we can make up for lost time. God knows we've lost enough time. We'll have to get to work on her, of course."

"Will she talk?"

"She'll talk all right. Whether she'll talk anything like the truth, that's quite another matter."

❧ 29 ❧

A couple of days after the visit to the mortuary, still in that dank October, Humphrey heard quick steps on his stairs. They were steps he knew by heart. Kate hadn't given any warning that she was coming. It was early evening; she must have just returned from work. When she came into the room, she kissed him and said, fast, as though she had been rehearsing the speech and didn't want to be interrupted, "I still can't give you everything you want. I don't want to come under false pretenses. But it's a mistake to wait forever. Let's get what we can."

She wasn't pretending, excusing herself, finessing with a false story. Humphrey was startled. His composure left him. Neither of them spoke. They went, arms around each other, into his bedroom. Clothes came off. It was all as though they had been married for a long time. The flesh was kind.

Then as she lay in his arms, face lines smoothed away, she muttered, "Good. Any time. Any time you want."

Rain was slashing against the window. The night was closing in. It was a night to be safe in bed. She gave a comfortable sigh. A little later, she kissed his cheek and turned on him her disrespectful grin. She said, "I always wondered when you'd get on with it."

He freed an arm and slapped her. The flesh was as disrespectful as she was. The flesh was kind.

Comfortable minutes in the half dark, rain chuntering on the glass. Bed chatter. She said, "I want to talk to you soon."

He stirred, but she said, "No, we had better get dressed. I don't want us to be distracted. Perhaps we ought to have a drink."

There wasn't much said until they were back in the sitting room, Kate in her neat office dress, Humphrey in his workaday suit, both with whiskies in their hands. They were not sitting together on the sofa but, as it were by understanding, opposite each other in the big armchairs.

"I am trying to be honest," she said. "It's not as easy as it ought to be."

"I trust you, you know," he replied.

"I know you do. And I trust you. Absolutely. But still it isn't easy." She burst out, "I want you altogether. We're right for each other, aren't we?" That was said with an edge of diffidence, and she had to hear him say, "I knew that a long time ago."

"I think I did too. But I thought I might be fooling myself. You see, I'm not much of a prospect, am I?"

"Don't be so modest—"

"I'm not. I haven't exactly been competed for by men."

"More fools they." Humphrey understood her diffidence and thought he mustn't pamper it.

"Bless you." Her expression was unusually soft. "Anyway, I know we fit each other. It's a bit of a marvel, but I can't help accepting it. Some of the time. So it would be wonderful beyond anything I've dreamt of to give you all you want. I'm trying to tell you I can't, not yet awhile. You have to be patient. I love you very much, but I'm not quite free."

Humphrey said with a kind of stiff gentleness, "Do you still love him?"

"No. Not as I love you. But when you've lived with someone for fifteen years, there are ties you can't snap all at one go. Somehow I'm still obliged to care for him. My love, you're a self-sufficient man. Somehow you've always been able to look after yourself, haven't you?" Very close, discomfortingly close to what Luria had said in the pub that night, Humphrey thought. She was repeating herself. "You're not helpless. You really aren't."

She met his smile, but her own was mechanical.

"No, he really is helpless," she said.

"You must see, that could go on forever."

"No," she said in a resonant voice, "that's not on. Somehow I'll find a way. I can't endure it for much longer. I can't endure it if you want me just for yourself."

"I've made that clear enough," said Humphrey. "But you know it as well as I do. You're not so clear. You can't tell me when you're even hoping to be free. Even tonight you can't. Can you?"

"You'll have to bear with me a bit longer. I promise you. I love you and I'll do it."

Watching her, Humphrey believed her. Even more, he wished to believe her. This was one of the reassurances of love, more unqualified than any future could be.

"For the time being," she began, sounding firmer than she was.

"For the time being what?"

"For the time being you'll have to be satisfied with what we have."

He gazed at her without responding.

"You're good at making the most of things," she said, as though it were an appeal. "You do know, don't you, you have plenty of capacity for happiness."

"If so," this time Humphrey did respond, with a familiar smile, "I must say, I've managed to conceal it very well."

He added, "My girl, I should say that it was you who had the capacity for happiness. I've never known anyone with more. That's one of the things I liked at the beginning."

"Let's hope," she said, decision, boldness, realism, all returning, "it'll turn out useful for us both." She added, "While I can't do everything—"

"While is a long word," he said.

"We can have plenty to hold on to. I can get away quite a bit. Like this. More than this."

"Does he know anything about it?"

"I haven't the faintest idea."

"Is that true?"

"I wouldn't lie to you. I haven't the faintest idea. He'd never ask me. I can see you very often."

"Better than nothing." Said with sarcastic affection.

"Yes, yes. Bed, any time. I told you." She gave her monkeylike grin. "Good for us both."

"Good for us both."

"Don't think that I don't know that I'm not giving you all you want. You've never had too much of what you want, have you? For God's sake, I can't understand why not. If anyone was made to have a decent life, you were."

"It wasn't God's fault," Humphrey said. "It must have been my own. Something wrong with my character or nature. Or whatever you like."

"Nonsense, love. Sheer nonsense. Just luck." She was silent for an instant, then said, struggling out with a confession, "I've never had much of what I want either."

"I think I'd guessed that."

She hesitated again. "I don't like being disloyal to him. Even now," she said. "But you have to understand, that's the first thing. I never really got on with him, ever. Even in ways I ought to have coped with. You'd have thought I was practical, wouldn't you? I wasn't really. When I was a girl, I had all sorts of dreams."

Humphrey was thinking again of Alec Luria's reflections and advice. Humphrey was also thinking that Alec Luria ought to be listening.

Kate continued, "You know he's always taking care of his health?"

Humphrey laughed out loud.

"Well," said Kate, "four or five years ago, I was thirty-five or so, he talked to me very seriously. He was concerned about his blood pressure. He had seen his doctor. His blood pressure had to be kept down. Otherwise he wouldn't be able to do his thinking. Otherwise his life might be shortened. So he had to ask me, did I mind if we gave up intercourse?"

Humphrey was sure that that was the actual word Monty had used.

"Not that there had ever been much of it."

"What did you say?" Humphrey asked, offhand, gentle.

"Oh, I agreed. I took it. I thought I had to take anything. It wasn't altogether easy. I'm not cold. As you may just possibly have discovered."

She chortled, so did he, with satisfaction, maybe desire.

Soon they could return to bed. They had had no real clarification. She had tried to explain, but what did she mean? There were promises away in the future. But they had confidence in each other, much more than that, a kind of unanxious delight, as though, just for once, the present was good enough.

They were tired of explanations, as a couple could be after a quarrel, though there had been none. It was then, absently, as though for casual relief, that Humphrey brought in Susan's name. He had for a long time trusted Kate as an ally, and now that trust was absolute. He was telling everything that was known, or suspected, of Susan's doings on the Saturday night.

"This is rather a facer, isn't it?" she said, eyes acute, head nodding.

"What do you mean?"

"Do you really believe it was Susan? Knocking about outside?"

"You know her miles better than I do. What do you think?"

She pressed him about the Loseby story. There was no getting away from it, he said. Loseby had spent all that evening and the small hours and probably the next day with the unfortunate Gimson. Loseby wasn't innocent of much on this earth, but he was certainly innocent of being with his grandmother that night.

"I wasn't brought up to these goings-on," Kate said, remembering her father, a steady, conventional soldier. What would he have thought of Loseby?

"Loseby's a free soul. You and I are mildly constrained. You don't often meet a free soul, even now."

"If that's a free soul, Lord deliver me from them."

With Loseby disposed of, where had Susan been? On the Monday, she had been with Loseby concocting an account of the Saturday night, the two of them together, later described to the police, as Humphrey had been told, with uninhibited thoroughness. Humphrey, not especially given to sexual outspokenness, nevertheless gave a few details. Kate guffawed. "What a girl," she said. But where had Susan really been on the Saturday? And why after all this had Loseby married her? Neither he nor Kate could understand how she had finally landed him.

"She's a resourceful creature," said Kate. "She's not her father's daughter for nothing."

"That doesn't get us any distance, does it?"

She asked sharply, intimately, half accusingly, "Why are you so interested in her?"

He answered, also straightforward, "You know Frank Briers is a friend of mine? I wouldn't mind saving him some trouble if I can."

"Do you really like him?"

"Very much."

"Why?"

"He's as honorable as you are, which is saying something. He's doing a job. On the whole, I prefer people who are doing a job."

"He struck me as pretty hard."

"No harder than the rest of us have to be in order to get along."

She didn't often run against Humphrey's dark stoicism, but she was glad that he wasn't uniformly gentle, all the way down.

"Well, have it your own way," she said, though not conceding about Frank Briers. After a moment she said, "Look, you can talk to Paul Mason, can't you?" He acquiesced.

"He might be able to give you some light on Susan. If that's what you want."

Humphrey explained the practical point, whether she could be eliminated as a suspect. Loseby now was; her father was.

"Whether Paul could have anything useful to tell you, I can't say."

"Why ever should he?"

"Come on, you're supposed to be perceptive, aren't you? Haven't you noticed that she was running after Paul when Loseby seemed to be cooling off. On the rebound. Or she may have fancied Paul. He'd be a better bet than Loseby for my money. Anyway, he could have picked up something."

She smiled and began to stretch herself.

"But whether you ought to be doing this at all, I'm not too sure. If you must, you must. But I am sure that we have had enough of it for just now, haven't we?"

This wasn't tenderhearted, as Frank's wife might have been. Kate was thinking only of him. She didn't want him to regress to anything like his old underground existence. He was so different when he was breaking free. That night, looking at him with expectancy, she was wishing that she could have known him when he was young.

❧ 30 ❧

It was pleasant, Humphrey was thinking, to take the advice of a woman one was fond of, particularly if the advice was likely to be sensible. Thus Humphrey invited Paul Mason to have dinner with him. Humphrey said that they might as well go to Brooks's, the one club he kept up. Though young men hadn't much use for clubs by this time, Paul in his job had to coexist with a more old-fashioned life, and Brooks's seemed an appropriate background for him. It was a mild November night, windless and misty, soothing to the senses. Humphrey decided that he would walk across the park.

Not that his senses needed soothing. Exactly as though he were a younger man, he was high spirited because a love affair had begun, really begun. It was absurd for one who so distrusted his own fortune, but he found himself looking passersby in the face and thinking that they were dumb beasts and didn't get much fun. He was looking forward to his evening. In his rational fashion, Paul was the most intelligent of company. He might provide a piece of information. It had been a good idea.

That was the tone, cheerful, interested, uninvolved, in which they began. They were sitting in the bar downstairs. There were only a few men around, and they were comfortably private in a corner seat. Paul was satisfying his curiosity about Humphrey's family. How many generations had been members of this club? Humphrey said, his father certainly, his grandfather certainly, his great-grandfather certainly—maybe one more, but that wasn't sure. Humphrey expatiated, sounding sarcastic to conceal his secretive pride. They were really modest country gentlemen. They never did much. The grandfather did get a job in Gladstone's last Government. They never made much money. The curious thing was, they were Whigs. Their kind were almost always Tories and, if they had a London club, went across the road. (He meant White's.) Why the Leighs were Whigs no one ever knew. Just perversity. The real Whig grandees were immense landowners. They lost fortunes at the tables upstairs. The Leighs were very small beer. None of them would have ever been asked to Devonshire House, nothing like grand enough, or Holland House, nothing like clever enough. "It isn't a very creditable record," said Humphrey, "considering that they started with certain advantages. As you see with me."

Paul was entirely capable of playing this game. "I guess," he said, "that the poor old Masons might have been slightly superior servants in some of the poor old Leigh houses. They came from the Norfolk land. The first to emerge from outer darkness seems to have been my grandfather. Somehow, God knows how, he managed to make himself into a country lawyer. It may not have been so difficult, if you had a knack for passing examinations, which the Masons haven't been so bad at. He built up a practice as a provincial attorney in Norwich. He made a surprising amount of money. Then came my father. Process repeated on a more lavish scale. He made a much more surprising amount of money. The rest you know."

Being English, they took a pleasure in these exchanges, which might have mystified others. They both liked hard liquor, and Humphrey fetched their third drink. There was nothing much in the news that day, said Paul, who by profession and by private preoccupation studied the European and American press each morning. Things were going roughly according to expectations. It didn't mean that they were going well, he added.

Humphrey said, "A bit more criticism of the police, I noticed. About that murder of ours."

"Yes?" Paul's voice was uninflected.

"I bet they're being pretty thorough."

"I suppose you know."

"I fancy they're getting some of the answers."

"Should you say so?"

Paul's voice had now gone brittle-hard, more so than Humphrey realized until some moments later.

"Paul," Humphrey went on, "I wonder if you can tell me one or two things about Susan. You know Susan?"

"Yes, I know Susan."

"You might be able to tell me one or two things."

"Why do you think I can?"

"You said you knew her."

"Why in Christ's name do you think I should?" Paul said that in dead quiet, but with violence.

"She's produced some stories that contradict each other, and it's bad for her if they're not cleared up."

For minutes past, Humphrey had been mishandling the talk. He had been slow to detect the young man's tone. Now that it was too late, he was suddenly attacked by a wave of bitter temper.

"When I accepted your hospitality," Paul said with frigid formality, "I didn't think I was being invited for the sake of evidence. I have none to give you. As I take it that exhausts my value. I can see that I have outstayed my welcome."

It was curiously elaborate, almost like bad theater, for someone who was such an easy talker. Humphrey said, "I'm sorry. I wouldn't have had this happen—" and went on, using any sort of speech to keep the young man from walking out. Humphrey was thinking of something silly, a relic from the days when he played games. It was a piece of games-players' folk wisdom that men in crises divided into two classes, those who went red and those who went white. It was the latter you relied on when things were tight. In the last moments, Paul's face, which never had much color, had gone corpse-pale.

It was a foolish thought, but also Humphrey was thinking that this was a strange kind of anger. It didn't need saying—a trigger had been touched, but as to why, Humphrey was at a loss. Yet Paul, as a rule abnormally controlled, had thrown civility or even common good nature right away.

Humphrey took him into dinner. By a principle of natural injustice, it was Humphrey who didn't feel like eating, while Paul, with all the signs of good appetite, ordered a standard club dinner, smoked salmon and steak, and began methodically to eat. Humphrey consoled himself by starting on the bottle of claret.

Neutrally, without any introduction, Paul said, "What precisely are you interested in about Susan?"

"No one knows where she was on the Saturday night. I mean, the night Lady Ashbrook was killed."

"I don't know either." Paul's voice was distant but civil enough. "I simply don't know. You must have been told, I have been gone over two or three times myself, and I can't prove a single thing. Actually, I was in my own house. By myself. Doing nothing more remarkable than reading. Quite impossible to prove for anyone under suspicion. But I have a faint idea that I'm not."

"No, I don't believe you ever have been."

"No doubt you'd know." That was said distantly again but with a faint ironic edge. "The only thing I can remember about that whole damned night is that I rang Celia Hawthorne. That was after we split up, you know."

He mentioned Celia with complete equanimity. Whatever or whoever was a forbidden subject, she wasn't.

Plates cleared, Paul was gazing down at the table, brow furrowed. Then he stared across at Humphrey.

"I am prepared to tell you one simple fact about Susan. I did see her the following day, the Sunday." He was talking with the care and accuracy of a high official. "I am prepared to tell you that, to the best of my judgment, she hadn't any knowledge that Lady Ashbrook had been murdered. Again to the best of my judgment, she didn't know anything of it until I did, on the Monday morning."

"It is pretty well established that she met Lancelot Loseby that Monday afternoon."

"Perhaps that was when she would have heard of the murder."

"That was when she concocted one of her stories about the Saturday night. Entirely fabricated. Maybe you've noticed, but the young woman doesn't suffer from certain bourgeois frailties, such as a slavish addiction to the truth."

That was a deliberate attempt to touch the trigger, but Paul gave merely the impersonation of a smile. Humphrey tried another flick: "Where did you see her on the Sunday?"

"Nowhere particular. It's not material."

Paul repeated that he had nothing more to say about Susan. Some while later, however, as he was eating some Stilton, he did remark, as though back to his normal gibing poise, "Since you're so interested in the Thirkill family, you might like to know that I am working close to father Tom. Had you heard?"

No, Humphrey couldn't have heard. It was one of the quasi-secret financial maneuvers of that autumn. A treasury team, reporting to Tom Thirkill, was negotiating in Washington, and Paul had been seconded to it from his bank. "The deal will happen all right," he said with his natural calm authority, transformed from the blinding rage of not so long before. "It'll keep us afloat for a while. Reasonable, as far as it goes. But it won't go very far."

Paul delivered some more comments on the national and Western situation in his own style: realistic, not bland, but not apocalyptic. Then he said, as though nothing had for an instant disturbed his impeccable manners, that he really must go; he had a paper to write for the said Tom Thirkill. He thanked Humphrey for an admirable meal. As he thanked Humphrey again, on his way into St. James's Street, he added, "What a pleasant club this is. If you could bear it, perhaps you would put me up for it some time."

Passing on to Frank Briers those fragments of news about Susan, Humphrey remarked that they didn't add up to much. Frank, restive, thought that that was overstating the case. They added up to nothing at all—unless they believed Paul's assertion that, on the Sunday, Susan was still in ignorance about the murder. Was Paul trying to help her out? Even if he wasn't, it was nothing but a subjective judgment: worth putting on the files, no more.

❧ 31 ❧

When Humphrey gave another report about his meeting with Paul Mason, this time to Kate in the bedroom, he evoked more interest. It had been a disastrous evening, he said, like Briers dissatisfied with himself. Kate soothed him. For Paul's behavior there must be some explanation they didn't know. He must be more complicated than either of them had guessed. It didn't have any bearing on the practical problem, Humphrey said, telling her, self-mocking, how he had had his "head bitten off" by Frank Briers. "To hell with the practical problem," said Kate. "To hell with Frank Briers. I want to know what was driving Paul mad."

"Easier said than done," he replied. She didn't cross him anymore. She wasn't capable of splitting love into compartments. For her it was all or nothing. So she wanted to help. She had to feel that what he thought worth doing was just that. She couldn't help much, but she thought that she might be able to squeeze some fragments of the truth out of Susan. After all, she had had some experience with that girl. At the worst, it would do no harm. And Kate had some internal amusement at her own expense; she was also inquisitive.

It happened that the governor of her hospital had given her two tickets for Covent Garden and an invitation to a party. Opera remained the most lavish entertainment in London. The fact that it was state subsidized didn't mean it was a popular entertainment. The governor of Kate's hospital also doubled as a trustee of the opera and had a private box there, in which he was running true to the form of other well-cushioned men. Kate knew that Susan was totally unmusical, but she suspected that an invitation wouldn't be rejected. The opera house was a suitable place to be seen. The suspicion proved to be justified.

Susan arrived at Kate's house in a limousine provided, so Kate assumed, by her father. She arrived also brilliant with diamond necklace and earrings, provided, Kate further assumed, by her father. Kate, to whom music was the one aesthetic joy, was looking forward to a night at the opera. At this glittering sight, she felt more than a little dowdy. She was skillful at making do with her clothes, but she felt she had better keep out of sight if this was going to be the evening's competition. Still, she thought, self-taunting, it served her right. She had brought it on herself.

She might have brought it on herself, self-taunting she might be, but when they arrived at Covent Garden, she couldn't suppress a sharper lurch of envy. Their host was receiving them in the corridor outside his box. He greeted Susan with manifest enthusiasm, holding her hand as she stood calmly still, diamonds glittering under the chandeliers, dress elegant and quiet, expression at the same time self-possessed and demure. "How very good of you to come, Lady Loseby! How very good of you!" Lady Loseby was being introduced to members of the party, who were, so far as such elevation still persisted, considerably more lofty than anything Aylestone Square could have risen to. Lady Loseby smiled unself-consciously, unassertively, as others made the rounds. She was looking like the model of a young married woman, or alternatively—Kate recalled with satisfaction an old phrase of her nurse— as though butter wouldn't melt in her mouth.

Another old phrase drifted through Kate's mind as she listened to the singing. It was Tristan, and Wagner was too oppressively romantic—though it was tempting to think of the real thing, with Humphrey, not this noise whirling around her. The box was a large one, but the party was a dozen strong and they were jammed together. She was placed in the back row. Susan was beside her host.

The wicked flourishing, the old phrase teased Kate, like a green bay tree. Why a green bay? Did green bay trees flourish? Tom Thirkill was one of her least favorite men. He was certainly flourishing, more than anyone she knew. Certain to be a member of the Cabinet in the new year. Not an agreeable thought. She wasn't fond of him. She couldn't help being fond of his daughter, sitting a few feet away. Not that the girl deserved it. She was flourishing as much as her father. Kate liked her own sex. Liked Susan more, perhaps, because she was no feminist and saw women with no more illusion than she did men. Susan was flourishing. No one in his senses could think she was a more estimable character than most men. No justice in this world. What did Humphrey say? Anyone who expected justice in this world was a born fool. That night was being a triumph for Susan. Never mind. Kate had a job to do.

She found her opportunity after supper. Leading out of the box was another room, considerably larger, tables set for a meal. The meal was as sumptuous as any cold supper Kate had seen. There was a slice of pâté de foie gras for each (someone didn't like it, and Kate, comforting herself, got two), a spoonful of caviar, game pie, pheasant, champagne, burgundy. The host was being handsome. He was also flirting, not unskillfully, with Susan.

Intermission over, the party filtered back to their box. Kate contrived to hold Susan back.

"No reason to hurry. Let's have another drink. You needn't tell me. I know you're bored out there."

With Kate, Susan didn't pretend to musical tastes. She had a trait, which Kate found endearing, of being honest when there was no reason not to be.

They had the supper room to themselves. It could have occurred to one of them, or each of them, that there would have been a certain mild luxury in sitting in the box with a lover, just the two of you, and knowing that there was this good safe place to enjoy yourself just a few steps away.

Susan, abstemious about alcohol, wouldn't have another drink. Kate poured herself a whiskey and said, "How's Loseby?"

"Oh, he's all right. Mister's usually all right, you know." Susan spoke with casual acceptance. Kate had ceased being surprised about her. When she had been desperate about that man—had Kate been wrong? Or could the girl throw it off like a jacket, once she had won?

Kate came straight to it. She had dealt with Susan before and knew that there was no merit in being delicate. She had to be taken head-on.

"I suppose you know he's safe, about that murder? They do believe what he's told them."

"Nice of them." Susan smiled.

"Anyway, he's safe enough. Unless someone did it for him. He can't have been there himself."

Clearly, this was no news to Susan. "How did you know?" she asked. She had a shrewd idea and gazed at the older woman with sisterly interest. In fact, she had assumed that Kate and Humphrey were sleeping together long before they were. Susan went on, "I expect you know the whole story."

"Some of it, anyway."

"All boys together." Susan spoke without rancor. "Damn fools. Mister doesn't really go for men. He hasn't got the necessary taste." Suddenly Susan specified what the necessary taste was. She still looked like a demure young wife, but she had the vestige of a prurient grin. What she said was simple and brutish. Kate had not heard genuine homosexuals defined like that before. It might be right. Women such as Susan had a knack of taking the covers off.

"He couldn't get the real taste if he tried." It was Loseby's wife speaking. "Of course he tried. He's tried most things. He never knows what he wants. But with luck, I ought to be able to put up with him."

"Anyway, he's out of trouble." Kate hadn't the time to listen to this curious prognosis of a marriage. "What about you?"

"What about me?"

"They still want to find out what you were doing that night."

"I've told them, Kate dear. I really have." Susan's expression had become simple, sincere, and faintly injured.

"You've told them too many things. You never have grasped that one excuse is better than three. How many times have I tried to get that into your head?"

Susan now looked repentant. "Oh, but you can understand, can't you? I was trying to protect Mister. You'd have done the same. Any girl would have done."

"You didn't do it very well." Kate wasn't moved by Susan transforming herself into a guilty child. "You never could make a lie stand up for long. What were you doing that night?"

"Just hanging about. I was at a loose end, you see."

"Tell that to some nice old man." Kate was amused, contemptuous, cross. "What were you doing that night?"

With a candid face, half sullen with innocence, Susan gave several different accounts supported by realistic detail. It had been a very hot night. She had no one to take her out. There was no one in the apartment in Eaton Square. She had gone for a long walk. No, she had tried to see whether any of her acquaintances were at home. No, she was searching for someone to take her to a film. Or to one of the gambling clubs. Sometimes she did like a flutter, she said with confessional honesty.

Kate said that she didn't believe a word of it, the less so the more confessional it was. At last she forced out a version that might have been somewhere near the truth. Susan had been attempting to run Loseby down. "He's several kinds of a rat, you know. I thought it was time to have a showdown." Just as Humphrey had done the following Monday, she telephoned his headquarters in Germany. Just as Humphrey was told, so was she. She heard that Loseby was in London on compassionate leave. Staying where? Seventy-two Aylestone Square. If he was staying with his grandmother and Susan hadn't been told, he had another date for that night. He had left the house often enough, after his grandmother had gone to bed, to join Susan in one of their hideouts. Now she was going to catch him at it. Vigil. No sign of him.

At last she decided that she had got it wrong. Next morning she rang Loseby's friends in London. Where was he? She had previously had an eye on Douglas Gimson. Douglas said that she was not to worry. He admitted that he had found Loseby a bed for the last couple of nights.

"Found him a bed. Good way of putting it." Ripples of laughter, as shameless as Loseby's own. Then about midday on Monday, Loseby had called her at home, told her that Lady Ashbrook had been killed, said that he was obviously in a fix, and that afternoon they invented their story.

What Susan had at last admitted seemed to Kate to be plausible. Some things had been left out, no doubt. And some tastefully decorated. It wasn't clear how she had proposed to use her will on Loseby. What resources did she have? Yet he had married her. It would be foolish to think that Loseby was above mundane considerations, such as Tom Thirkill's money. But it could also be, Kate thought, that he had discovered Susan was not only a randy little liar, but also had a strong and ruthless character. Maybe that, lacking it himself, he was searching for. It could have been a sign that he had turned to her at once when he was in a crisis. Unlike Briers, and intermittently Humphrey, Kate paid no attention to the idea that Loseby and Susan had been acting in complicity.

Susan had almost persuaded the police with her bedroom story, Kate was thinking. Maybe that had been the most realistic of her romances, or had she overdone it? The police heard enough bedroom stories, though one from this good-looking girl might have given them a certain amount of pleasure.

By now Kate was indulging her curiosity. "Why ever did you spread yourself like that?"

"Oh, it didn't do any harm, did it?" The concept of nonmelting butter was difficult for Kate to drive away.

"Did it ever happen like that? Not that night, I know."

"Perhaps it did."

"When?" Kate's antennae were suddenly all alert.

"The Sunday night. The day after."

"But you didn't see Loseby that Sunday night. Not till the Monday, so you said."

"No, I didn't. As a matter of fact, it wasn't Loseby I was with that Sunday night."

Kate exploded into a laugh, a little astonished, even shocked, much more amused. "You little bitch. What you want—" Curiosity was too pressing. "Who was it?"

"Can't you guess?" Susan asked gently.

"It might have been any male within miles." Kate wasn't so gentle.

"No, it was Paul. Paul Mason." Susan justified herself. "I always rather liked him. You may have noticed that."

"I've noticed that with quite a lot of men." Kate's language was tarter than her grin.

Meekly, Susan replied, "That's not very kind, is it? You see, I was rather upset about Loseby. He is one hell of a rat, you know. So I wanted some comfort somewhere. So I thought I could push Paul into it. He doesn't sleep around much, actually. But he was on his own. That girl Celia had let him go. What an idiot she must be. Paul doesn't much like me," she added, with factual composure. "Except for a spot of you know what. Still, it worked that night."

She went on with secret satisfaction. "He wasn't pleased at being used as a consolation prize. He's too proud altogether. And he's furious if anyone gets inside his goings-on. He's cagier than any man I've ever had." Then she let show an impudent, defiant pout. "Still, I may have another go at him sometime. He's very satisfactory when it comes to action. He can go wild. Rather exciting. He's very satisfactory when he gets to the point."

Kate was pleased with herself when surreptitiously they tiptoed back into the box. Susan's actions might not be significant (she didn't know what Humphrey would think when she told him), but it couldn't do harm to clear them up. Kate thought she had done well. So did Humphrey when, before leaving for her hospital, she broke in on him at breakfast the following morning. "That's good work, my girl. I don't like unfinished business." He chuckled. He could still regress to the official life he had once lived. He gave her a hearty, and more than hearty, kiss. "No time," she said. She had done a little for him. Now she wanted him to do a little for them both. She would like to give a dinner for him in that house. She was feeling her way toward a pattern for the future. It would be pleasant to have people in and explain nothing.

"Very pleasant." Humphrey was touched. She had been making plans for his sake; as usual he was infected by her spirits.

"Any night you like. Mrs. Burbridge loves you anyhow."

"Who shall we have?"

"Alec Luria's flying in next week. What about Celia? It's a pity she's dropped out of things."

Humphrey thought it would be diverting to see Luria in search of another wife.

"And really," Kate went on, happy with her project, "what put it into my head, I ran into Ralph Perryman in the street the other day. We ought to have those two. We owe them a meal, remember?"

"Oh." To her astonishment, she had seen Humphrey's face go, not so much cloudy, as washed blank of any expression.

She jumped to a conclusion. Lively, scolding, affectionate, she said, "Come on, my love. You're not still worried because I enjoy talking to him now and then, are you? You don't think I give a rap for anyone else? I don't know what else I can do to prove it."

She forced him into the habit of a smile.

"Well then?" she challenged him.

He was at a loss. He said, "You'd better have them if you want. I'll try to cope." He said it without inflection and without his normal tenderness. She was upset. They hadn't had a quarrel before. Even when they disagreed, he was more articulate than she was and more considerate. Once or twice she had seen him in a dark mood, but she had been able to read it, and then she had liked letting him have his way. But now she was so much upset that this time she was going to insist on her own.

❧ 32 ❧

Humphrey and Frank Briers were sitting by themselves in the Murder Room. Humphrey repeated not only the substance of the opera house conversation but also as much of Kate's detail as he could recall. Briers listened with his acute attention.

"This may be more likely," he said. He added, once more back in active policeman's form, "Your Kate is a hell of a sight better interrogator than you are, my lad. You're too much of a gentleman, that's the trouble with you."

For once Humphrey defended himself. He had done more interrogations than Briers, some of them secret for the next thirty years. Briers gave his mateyest smile.

"Oh, I dare say you were okay with the delicate stuff. But you didn't get far with the young man Mason, now did you? Kate would have gone right through him. I bet she's got the truth about that Sunday night. Whether she's got the truth about anything else—"

He paused. "If she has," he said, "we're getting close. You know what I mean?"

"I suppose I know what you mean."

"No alternative," said Briers. Humphrey did not respond.

"Of course," Briers said, "that wretched girl may be tying us up again. Anyway, it will be worthwhile having her in. Nothing like holding a few surprises up your sleeve."

Susan was called (invited, they said) to the police station. Not just for one spell of questioning but two. Briers took on the work himself, Leonard Bale sitting in with him. It might help, they had decided, to impress her with seniority. Kate would have told them that Susan regarded men as much the same, regardless of age or any other discriminant.

At the first session, the questioning went on for many hours. This was mainly because Susan talked so fluently. Briers hadn't questioned anyone to whom the words came with less hesitation or, so it seemed, with less thought. She was nice and helpful, Briers said tersely to Humphrey afterward. She didn't complain at being kept; she didn't want a lawyer.

She didn't want a lawyer, Frank said, because she could always invent a new story. She admitted cheerfully that earlier stories must have applied to different dates. No, she hadn't spent that night with Lord Loseby, her present husband. She might very well have been wandering round the mews, however. As a matter of fact, she rather thought she had been. Reason: there was an apartment there occupied by an ex-boyfriend, who often lent it to her for weekends. She had even spent an occasional weekend there with Loseby. Of course, it wasn't convenient to take a man back home to Eaton Square. She had to think of her father's official position. There were too many journalists around. So the friend's apartment had sometimes been a great help. Oh yes, she had borrowed it since, that is, before she got married. Why was she waiting about outside? There was a chance that the ex-boyfriend would be returning there himself. She hadn't seen him for quite a while. She had suddenly had a fancy to meet him again. Asked whether she often took up again with former boyfriends, she had said, with innocent surprise, of course she did. She was nearly always friendly with them. She liked love to be a friendly business. When it was over, it was cozy to have a nice time together again.

Before the second questioning, detectives made inquiries. It turned out that her story of the mews flat was entirely true. In the midst of her lying, that wasn't the first time she had deviated into the truth. Briers had said before, it didn't make things easier. The occupant of the flat had been traced, a rich, casual young man who sometimes played in a band. Yes, he had often lent the place to Susan. Yes, she had been a girlfriend two or three years before. Yes, he sometimes saw her, and they had a good time. No, he hadn't been in London that weekend, but now and then Susan came round on the off chance.

They let a week go by before the second session. Then Briers without any preliminary took the offensive straightaway.

"We don't believe that you were looking for Angus that night. We know that you were expecting to meet Lord Loseby."

"I couldn't have been, you know. We'd had a little misunderstanding, if you want to know the honest truth."

She used the prim word demurely. Kate, who was familiar with Susan's real language, would have jeered.

"We know that you were looking out for him. You'd rung up his regiment, and you thought he might be in his grandmother's house. Now then. You've told us enough stories."

She gazed at him with innocent eyes.

"Oh, I suppose I had a vague idea I might run into him, just a vague idea that I might. It would have been nice to make it up. You know how it is."

"I'm not sure that I do. We also know where you were the following night."

"Do you?" She dropped her eyes modestly. "Oh, I wanted a friend to talk to. You can understand that. I was very unhappy about Loseby. I was afraid he'd stopped loving me. I wanted to talk it out with someone kind."

"Talk it out?"

"Talk it out," she repeated firmly.

Briers considered pressing the point and then left it. He knew. She knew he knew. That was all that mattered. Both he and Bale put sharp questions: hadn't she been in Lady Ashbrook's house that night? All that time in the mews—she had been in the house, hadn't she? She could have gone inquiring for Loseby, couldn't she?

Those questions she had been asked before, time after time, in the early interrogations. The detectives got no more information now. They had produced enough concrete facts, where they really knew, to shake her. She didn't invent a story this time. She said little. She just said that she hadn't been inside the house. She was ready to go on saying it. She was quite unshaken. Briers was ready to accept—as in fact he had been after the report from Kate—that there was nothing to shake.

In any questioning, those two men could have told her—so could Humphrey—it was wise not to talk more than one needed. That applied to the most collected and experienced talker extant. In those last replies, she had given a textbook example of how to do it right. Then she began to talk fluently again.

Briers was almost ready to finish. He didn't expect to get any more out of her. It hadn't been unsatisfactory, as far as it went. Just as a formal end, not especially interested, he asked where and how she and her husband were living. He was not especially interested since the detectives had already obtained statements from Loseby in several interrogations. He had been secretly seconded to the Ministry of Defense. They had rented a comfortable house in Radnor Walk, not so far away from the police station. They couldn't have supported themselves there on his pay, and he had admitted, businesslike and candid, that there was an allowance from Tom Thirkill.

Briers said, without intention, half affably, "You're managing very nicely, aren't you? It's nice to have a rich father, isn't it?"

Susan looked all girlish devotion and was prepared to emit expressions of gratitude.

"Oh, daddy always has been generous. He's given me everything I wanted ever since I can remember." She added with reproachful seriousness, "I'm not sure that it was good for me sometimes."

"Perhaps not." Bale was a paternal man.

"He always said he would look after me when I got married. He was very anxious for me to get married. He worried about me, I think. He impressed on me that it didn't matter if the man had money or not, so long as I was going to be happy. There was plenty of money on our side. Of course, daddy didn't want someone who'd marry me for that. He hoped that I would just choose someone decent."

"Very natural."

"He came round about Loseby, all right. He knew Loseby had been rather extravagant. But he decided that Loseby would bring in another kind of dowry. That's what he said. I don't know whether he expected Loseby to collect anything on the side."

She was talking on. "As a matter of fact, he does, now and then. It isn't daddy who buys my clothes as a rule. Loseby does that. When he gets a little installment from the comptroller."

Bale had heard the word. Sharply, for him severely, he broke in, "What did you say?"

"Oh, I don't know what I was talking about. Just nonsense."

"You were talking about the comptroller."

"We're interested," Briers said, exuding force once more. "We're very interested. We've discovered quite a lot about the operation— you must tell us. Who do you mean by the comptroller?"

She was quick to recover herself. Poised, smiling placidly, she said, "Oh, that's just a family joke. It's a name for money coming out of the blue. I think it began with old Lady Ashbrook. That was what Loseby called her when she gave him a big tip."

"We don't believe a word of it."

"I'm very sorry. That's not nice to hear, is it?"

"Who do you mean by the comptroller?"

"I haven't a notion."

Briers was getting rough with temper.

"Can you ever tell the truth?"

"I'm telling the truth now."

"You're saying," Bale put in more gently, "that money some-times reaches your husband. You don't know where from. That's what you mean by the comptroller, isn't it? You'd like us to believe that."

"Exactly."

"Of course you know," Briers said, "or you can make a very good guess."

"I wonder about it, that's all," she said, gazing at him with lim-pid eyes.

"You mean to say your husband doesn't know?"

"He's wondered too. Of course it must have come somehow from the old lady. That's all he knows for sure."

"If you can believe that, you can believe anything. You're not a fool. Your husband receives large sums of money."

"Not very large," Susan softly intervened.

"He receives sums of money, and you haven't any idea under heaven where they come from?"

She looked injured. "I don't think a wife ought to be too inquisi-tive about her husband's finances. I don't think that is a wife's place."

That was too much for both men. It made Briers more angry,

Bale colder. It protracted the questioning. Unmoved, with resources of stamina, she produced more arabesques of explanation.
She didn't shift from her central position. She didn't know for certain who the comptroller was, nor precisely where the money came
from, nor did Loseby. Yes, they had theories. They had discussed
it often enough. It was a family puzzle, rather a pleasant one so far
as they were concerned. At last Briers said that that would have to
do for the present.

When a woman detective led Susan out—Briers's courtesy had
failed him—the two men stared at each other. Briers broke into
another packet of cigarettes.

"Christ," he said, "it's worse than having half a dozen teeth out."

"She's a bit of a handful," Bale said temperately.

"She doesn't think it's a wife's place to inquire into her husband's
finances. God love us. That girl just thinks a wife's place is in
another man's bed."

Bale, who had known more women than his chief, was more indulgent. "It'll be interesting to see how she turns out," he said.

"Have you ever in your born days come across such a liar? She
doesn't even do it for any purpose so far as I can see. Just for the
sheer bloody beauty of it."

Soon Briers was cooling down.

"The curious thing is," he reflected, "if she hadn't gilded the lily
so often—if she'd stuck to the core of what she was saying without
the trimmings—should you have believed any of it?"

"I don't know."

"Nor do I," Briers said.

Bale reflected, "But if those two are just a bit uncertain about the
comptroller, then that lets them both out, doesn't it? Unless our
present thinking is right off line. Right?"

"Right. That little tart was too clever by half. If they don't
know—can you credit that?—if they don't know, she could have
told us the unvarnished truth, and we'd have given them both a pat
on the head. I can't think of any two who deserve it less."

Then, with maximum briskness, he asked Bale to send a couple
of men around to question Loseby once more. Immediately, before
those two had had time to confer. If they were in real complicity,
they wouldn't have talked over the telephone. Very sensibly, said
Briers with a hard grimace.

Rapidly briefed, Flamson and a detective in the Fraud Squad were sent around to meet Loseby outside his office in Whitehall. It was all discreet and composed, a casual gathering of three acquaintances on a raw November evening. Hospitably, Loseby took them to one of his clubs, which was in Pall Mall.

Back in the police station, Briers and Bale waited, Shingler now in attendance. The others weren't used to seeing Briers appear as tired as he did that night. He dropped out of the conversation. Bale sent for sandwiches and another bottle of whiskey. The others ate. Briers smoked more cigarettes, took stiff drinks. It was two and a half hours before Flamson and the Fraud Squad detective returned. As soon as they got into the room, Briers said, "Well?"

The fraud man, whose name was Steen, was senior to Flamson and, what counted more, considerably more articulate. He did most of the talking.

"I think it's okay. It looks as though you got it right."

Susan's story had in substance been confirmed. Loseby had been as easy-mannered as ever. He hadn't concealed that he received presents of money, yes, presents, in banknotes. No one had asked simple questions about them, or he would have given simple answers. While Lady Ashbrook was alive, similar presents came from her. He thought he remembered mentioning that she gave him a little help. He was inclined to think that this posthumous present was another arrangement of hers, instead of making him a bequest in her will.

"I'll bet my bottom dollar he knew," said Steen. "But it would take third degree to make him tell us."

It was true that the money arrived in pounds from an anonymous source. That was when they began to talk of a comptroller. Was there such a person? Loseby was inclined to think there was.

"Inclined to think, my blasted arse," said Flamson. "He bloody well knew."

"I'm inclined to think," Steen mimicked, cheerful, a man with a job polished off, "that he knows who it is. He wasn't in the scheme himself. That wouldn't work. But he knows who's been handling the business this side. Likely as not, he wouldn't be able to prove it in a law court. And anyway, that's the last thing he'd ever want to do."

Steen swigged at his glass of whiskey.

"He did indicate that he'd had a tipoff from someone whom he wouldn't mention by name or else couldn't remember. Who knew that some money would arrive in due course. Someone whom Lady Ashbrook trusted with money. That's the most that we got out of Captain Loseby. But it sounded like your man."

"It fits the bill," Shingler said.

"I don't see that it can be anyone else," Bale said. Briers stirred himself, vigor pouring back, as though he had had a blood transfusion.

"God love me," he cried, "we were all fools. We ought to have seen it the minute we got a whisper about the money. We haven't been clever, have we?"

"You can't be clever all the time." That was from Shingler, possibly trying to please.

"I don't know about you lads, but I still don't know the reason why. Why did he do it? I don't need an answer on a postcard." He loomed over the table, though physically he was one of the smaller men there. He broke off. "Forget that. We've got it. We don't deserve to, but we've got it."

Steen said from outside their charmed circle, "I don't mind telling you, you're going to find it hellish difficult to clinch."

"I agree that," said Bale.

"Could be," said Flamson.

Reserves fell away. The bottle went around. Briers didn't drink more, but he was filling the others with energy.

"We'll do it," he said. "We're over the hump. Of course we'll do it."

❧ 33 ❧

The next morning, Briers came into Humphrey's sitting room and, with a curious formality, inquired about the other's health. Humphrey, smiling because he couldn't remember this happening before, said that it was much as usual. Briers smiled back, like one who had been caught in a bit of solemn silliness. He said, "I've something to tell you."

"Important?"

"It depends who to. I think you'd like to hear. It won't come as a surprise."

"You're certain, are you?"

"I'd better tell you."

Drilled by old habit, Humphrey suggested that they should take a walk. He was more comfortable listening to secrets in the open air. It was a blowy autumn morning, Atlantic weather, a strong west wind, and in the gusts, as they walked toward Pimlico, words were getting lost. In a more undisciplined mood, Humphrey might have reflected that excessive security had a knack of being neither comfortable nor efficient.

"It all adds up," Briers was saying.

Humphrey shouted back, "What adds up?"

"Everything I've told you and a bit more."

In a patch of calm, he said quietly, flatly, "It's the doctor, of course." Then, "You'd got there yourself, hadn't you?"

Humphrey replied, "I knew you were getting there."

"Don't you buy it?"

246

"It's very hard to take."

"Why?"

"Why should he?"

"We may find out sometime."

Just as one could believe anything in a suspicious state, so one could disbelieve. Judgment didn't hold one steady. Frank Briers was arguing them back to the plane of reason. With one of his lucid expositions, he recapitulated all they now knew of the O'Brien arrangements.

"Mind you," Briers, who had been bred with dark Protestant prejudices, said, "that mick lawyer didn't make a penny out of it. But he was a cunning old bastard. It's a beautiful thought, those establishment characters trusting each other. Just to save a dollop of tax over here."

He went on equably, reasonably. "Doing it on a basis of trust was the only way. O'Brien had shown foresight. As they grew old, he and Lady Ashbrook had to let one other person into the operation. She wouldn't have accepted Loseby. She might have been too anxious to protect him, maybe, or else she thought him too unreliable. There was someone else whom she had trusted with other fiddles. Her doctor. Perryman.

"He'd touted around her pound notes already. You know. You remember. She knew he didn't like paying his taxes either. She knew he was as silent as the grave. He was the only person around whom she had talked to about money."

"That's the strongest point you have."

"It ought to have given us a lead weeks ago. But when we got on to O'Brien and the comptroller, then it all made sense." Briers went on, "We happen to know that he met O'Brien once before at least. When the old man could still come to London. And the doctor had done a little commission for him."

They walked along Belgrave Road, down to the river. For a while they didn't try to talk, the gale flapping, whistling, thumping, tree boughs bending and straining, the last leaves seething. Briers was organizing his argument. Humphrey was attempting to be fair.

"Yes," Briers said, "we don't know why he did it. But all the rest of it makes sense. He had access, freer than any of them. He's an unusual man. You've said so yourself. It's a good old maxim—don't you remember we agreed on this before?—in this sort of business keep your eye open for an unusual man. He's kept astonishingly cool. You're not so used to villains. When we've talked to him, he's been cooler than any villain I've seen."

Along the embankment they walked, the wind pressing and pushing behind them, toward Millbank. Briers said, friendly, cajoling, "Come on, Humphrey. You'll have to admit it. We've got it right."

"Have it your own way." That was also friendly, but it wasn't quite an admission.

Shortly afterward Humphrey said, as though they were officials again working together, "The evidence is going to be thin, isn't it?"

"Unless we can break him down."

"Can you?"

To that, Briers replied that there the other's judgment was as good as his or better.

❧ 34 ❧

Within minutes of getting home from that walk along the embankment, Humphrey received a telephone call. It was from Briers. The words were cautious, codelike, the meaning clear. All that he had said was to go no further. The position was critical. Nothing must be said to anyone else, not to anyone else at all.

For a time Humphrey was irritated. Did Briers think one had lived one's life for nothing? Humphrey was the more irritated, hurt rather than irritated, because he knew that he was being told to say nothing to Kate. As Briers had made apparent when Humphrey visited him, he had no secrets from his wife. Was this warning nothing but professional mistrust? Humphrey was half angry, half in conflict. He was being put in a false position for no cause. Kate was as safe a security risk as he was. She was one of his loyalties. He didn't like two loyalties contradicting each other.

Meanwhile, when Kate had invited her guests to that dinner, she worried about Humphrey. In the midst of her buoyant spirits, she was both suspicious and acute. She wasn't ready to pity herself, but alone on those evenings she found herself thinking, with tart realism, that she hadn't a lucky life. Now that she had had a piece of luck in Humphrey, she couldn't trust it. What had gone wrong?

She thought she understood him, but she had scarcely seen him since he had been so reluctant about letting her entertain for him. She searched for explanations and found none. Was he getting tired of her already? Once or twice she got near the right explanation but dismissed it. She remembered a time only a few weeks before when, happy in bed, she had said, relaxed and confident, "There's no love without trust, is there?"

Humphrey, also happy, gave a sarcastic, loving smile. "Oh yes there is. I've had it. I don't recommend it. It wouldn't do for us, thank the Lord. We've been lucky. We've been lucky, bless you."

Then somehow she had spoiled it. She cursed her idea of this dinner party, but it had been well meant. She was wanting to show, without making a fuss about it, that she was his or that they were in some fashion together. She couldn't and didn't blame herself. In fact, having—as well as love—a streak of fighting temperament, she blamed him. Not all the time, not when she was most worried, but often she thought that he was behaving like a child. It was his fault.

Nevertheless, as the day of the dinner party came around, she was dreading it. She forced herself to go early across to Humphrey's house. There, to her relief, she found him in the dining room, affectionate and to all appearances composed. He was methodically sniffing at a couple of bottles of wine. "None of them has any idea of what they're drinking, of course, except us," he said, as if this were the most ordinary of parties, "but we may as well consider ourselves."

After they had gone upstairs to the drawing room, Luria arrived first, then the Perrymans, then Celia. To Kate's further relief, Humphrey became impeccably welcoming, his manner easy and outgoing. Whatever was the matter, none of them would have detected any sign. If she hadn't known, she wasn't sure—though she responded to each flicker of his nerves—that she would have done so herself. Perhaps she shouldn't have been so surprised or so relieved. She hadn't seen him when he was leading a disciplined existence. There the objective mattered, not how one felt. Expressions of feeling couldn't enter. You couldn't be concerned with your own ego if you were occupied with others. Humphrey had become practiced at that kind of self-neglect.

At the dinner table, Kate, not free from her anxieties, still enjoyed sitting at one end of the table, Humphrey at the other. It was the first time they had given a dinner, and quite as much as the simplest of women she didn't deny the simple pleasure. She had seen to the food. With protective attention, she watched

Humphrey drinking more than usual, but she trusted him to stay in control. In fact, there seemed less strain around the table than at that other dinner which she remembered, at Tom Thirkill's three months before. As she remembered it, there was a tightness in the circle of anxiety around her head.

Humphrey was alert, professionally competent, at showing interest in each of them. To Ralph Perryman there was career talk. Humphrey hadn't forgotten the conversation at the Perrymans' house. Humphrey had been wondering, he said, how many people chose not to compete, not to stretch themselves.

"More than we think, I fancy," Perryman replied with an air of comforting certainty.

"If they have any capacity for coming to terms at all," Luria put in, "then plenty of men and women can make do on very little."

"Fortunately," Kate said. She couldn't prevent herself glancing at Humphrey with a flash of happiness, which didn't pass unnoticed.

"No, I asked you before, how much effort is justified if one can't do something of the first importance?" Perryman was once more firm and certain. "Most of us can do little things, can't we? How many of us can do the great things? If we can't, what's the use of making ourselves miserable, trying and not getting there? Any of us round this table could have done something if we'd spent our lives at it. And we should have been forgotten in ten years."

"Every human being who has ever lived will be forgotten in finite time," Luria said.

"No, look, Professor Luria. You're famous in your line. We all know that. No one else is. But you're not Freud, are you? You're not Marx, are you? When you look back, will it really seem worthwhile?"

None of them had heard Alec Luria treated quite like that. He took it with magisterial calm.

"No man in his senses thinks he has done much," he said. "You just have to do what you can in your own place and time. In that sense, I agree with you, doctor. But I don't think it's much excuse for relaxing into quietism, you know."

After a time, Humphrey diverted these exchanges. Alec Luria wished to devote himself across the table to Celia. She was so quiet, it was impossible to feel how she was responding—except that she was pleased to be in company and, Kate thought with good-natured malice, not disinclined to be courted.

To the unperturbed, the evening continued in peace. They might have observed that once, deliberately but without exhibition, Humphrey made it clear that his and Kate's was a serious affair and that he loved her. This wasn't news to most of them. A few hours before, Luria had told Humphrey cheerfully, with a snorting, volcanic laugh, that among the many occasions when he had been wrong, this was the one he was the most glad of. It did seem to be news to Alice Perryman. It also seemed to be news to which she reacted with disapproval and regret. Otherwise, nothing in the way of incident or argument.

They stayed a long time at the dinner table, Humphrey finding another bottle of claret. They moved upstairs and, in the English fashion, went on drinking. At about half-past eleven, Alec Luria was asking Celia if he could take her home, and at the same time the Perrymans said good night.

Humphrey had seen them all downstairs. Kate could hear the front door shutting. He rejoined her in the drawing room, took another drink, sat on the sofa beside her. After a pause: "Now I suppose you know."

"I'm not sure."

"I mean, what I haven't been able to tell you."

"You should have done. Whatever it is."

He was gripping her hand. "I had to promise secrecy. Even to you."

"I think you should have trusted me." She was frowning with anger as well as hurt.

"Of course I trusted you. But I'd made an undertaking. You know I trust you. Look here. You know as well that I'm not much of a one for moral dilemmas. But I couldn't see the way out."

"You ought to have done. You were wrong. You'd better tell me now."

"I think you know." He was still finding it hard.

"I said before that I'm not sure."

"I'd better tell you." His voice was hard. "They are fairly certain now who did it."

"Who?"

"Perryman, of course," he said with a trace of impatience. "Why

252

do you think I wasn't specially enthusiastic about having him here tonight? I was pretty sure about what they were thinking when you wanted to ask him. I hadn't been told."

"I can't believe it," Kate burst out. "I can't believe it."

"I'm afraid you may have to. You must take it from me that they are certain." Humphrey began to speak more easily, more lovingly. Yes, he had found it hard to believe himself. Of course he had been jealous of Perryman, in spasms, when he hadn't had any security with Kate. Yes, that made him doubt whether he did suspect or didn't suspect. But anyway, any suspicion of his wouldn't have counted. It was the police who had settled it by themselves.

"How?"

"It must be him. They've settled it—if it's not someone absolutely unknown."

"That's a big if."

"They don't think so."

"Do you. Do you?"

He hesitated a long time, as though he were stammering. "Intellectually, I can't get away from it. Somehow I'm not absolutely convinced."

"Oh, for God's sake," Kate flared up again, "why ever should he?"

"It looks as though for a certain amount of money. For a relatively small amount." He told her some objective facts about Lady Ashbrook's arrangements and the fund.

"Do you think it makes sense?"

"I don't know whether it makes sense," said Humphrey, "but I told you, intellectually I can't see any way out."

"What do they think Ralph Perryman got out of it?" She said *they*, not *you*, projecting her bitterness, or her disbelief, away from Humphrey.

"He can't have had much yet. It would have come slowly. And not very much in all." He told her some more of the objective facts. The Ashbrooks hadn't been well off. "Heaven knows," he said dryly, "they can't be said to have been careless with what they had. Up to the present, the police believe that Perryman had taken no more than he was entitled to, just for his services. If all had gone according to plan, he might have picked up another few thousand pounds."

253

"You mean to tell me—" their hands were touching, but she confronted him—"he's supposed to have done all this for a petty little sum like that?"

"I've seen people do all manner of things for less."

"Oh, drop your reminiscences." Then she said she was sorry. Her skin was flushed, eyes brilliant, temper lost. She could be a spitfire with others, not with him, except to provoke, which she wasn't doing now.

"Do you honestly believe that this man—you know him, so do I—did all this just for that?"

"Perhaps neither of us know him."

"You do believe he did all this?"

"I'd prefer not to."

She was brooding. In a practical fashion, she suddenly said that the evidence sounded weak, wouldn't the case be difficult to prove? Humphrey said that he had said as much to Briers, almost in the same words. Perhaps that would make them wait until something more had broken. Perhaps that was why he had been sworn to secrecy.

They were hankering to go to bed. They then thought again. It might have left a chagrin or the sadness of the flesh, which neither of them was used to feeling or wanted to risk that night.

❧ 35 ❧

Humphrey was sitting in Frank Briers's office in Scotland Yard, waiting for him to return. This was the latest Scotland Yard, the office block in Victoria Street—indistinguishable from other office blocks, nothing like so picturesque, Humphrey thought (who was old enough to be disaffected by change) as the good old building down by the embankment, also and confusingly still called, in the English style, New Scotland Yard. Humphrey walked over to the window. This room was on the top floor, what in an apartment block would have been the penthouse. Down below was the lighted snake of Victoria Street. Humphrey, disaffected again, thought that was indistinguishable from other streets in any big city anywhere. He could get a glimpse of Big Ben, which was rather more appealing. It was nearly nine o'clock at night, since Briers and his colleagues worked late hours. Under the clouds, beyond the river, there swirled the russet-lurid glow of London. All towns had their nightly luminescence, but to Humphrey, London's seemed further to the red end of the spectrum than any other.

Quick steps outside. As Briers came in, he was saying, "Sorry to keep you."

"Gone all right?"

Briers had been explaining to his superiors what he intended to do. He had a good tactical sense. It was as well to be insured if things went wrong, and if they went right, superiors felt they had earned a share of the credit.

"Quite all right." Briers was terse, cheerful, intense with action.

Humphrey didn't take the initiative. Briers had asked for him presumably to tell him the program. That, however, Humphrey already as good as knew, after the talk of the previous week. Now that it was all worked out, Humphrey couldn't be any further use, not that he had been much effective use before.

Humphrey observed like a friendly visitor, "Grand office you've got here, haven't you?"

This was the first time Humphrey had seen it. Yes, it was a sumptuous office by London official standards, something like what would have been prescribed for a high civil servant: carpet, sofa surrounded by easy chairs, suitable for informal meetings; long table surrounded by hard chairs, suitable for formal meetings; drinks cupboard, private lavatory.

"A bit above my rank." Briers thrust out his underlip. "As I told you—didn't I?—the previous occupant is being entertained by Her Majesty." Gallows gibe, meaning prison. "Still, I might get a step up before too long. So I gather. Unless I blot my copybook."

Briers was being calmly realistic about his career. Shortly afterward, he proceeded to be calmly realistic about the case. He had been conferring with the lads. It was a time to get morale steady, expectations not too high, not too low. Public grumbles were needling away. Some newspapers didn't leave them alone for long. Nor did some M.P.'s. A handful of Tories talking of law and order, a couple of left-wingers who proclaimed that upper-class persons (pointing toward Loseby but not naming him) were being protected.

"God help us," Briers remarked, as he thought of those politicians, with the only stab of venom he showed that night. He stabilized himself. "That's neither here nor there," he said. "But other things being equal, it might be just as well to show a bit of our hand."

"Are other things equal?" Humphrey was thinking that his old job had almost all conceivable disadvantages, but, since no one knew what they were doing, there had been one advantage. His name hadn't been mentioned in the press or the Commons once in his official life.

Briers said that with the evidence now in hand, they couldn't bring a charge against the doctor. All his team agreed. So did the high-ups downstairs. He pointed at the floor, but as though he had the direction wrong and was speaking of elevated beings. Further, they all agreed that there was no serious chance of decisive evidence coming nearer. They might extract more details of the fund from New York: that would prove nothing. They could have a streak of random luck. It sometimes happened, but it was no use reckoning on that. There was only one thing for it. They had to make a direct attack on Perryman himself.

They couldn't charge him, but he could help them with their inquiries. Briers used the sanctimonious phrase with a grin. When he was a young man, he had often heard Humphrey say that modern English consisted of taking the meaning out of words.

He maintained his mordant grin. "Sometimes they help us quite a lot, you know." Then he said, "You see, it's the only way, isn't it?"

"So it seems."

"We know a lot now that he doesn't realize we know. We can give him a thorough going-over. It may take some time. It's the only way."

"I dare say."

Briers was talking like a detective immersed in the job and nothing else, but he was also being considerate to his friend. He believed that Humphrey still had his reserves. Briers wouldn't press him to agree or even to disagree. It was better to leave it. Humphrey understood. But he was also beginning to understand why Briers had wished for his company that night.

"There's one question left," said Briers. "When? When do we do it?"

"I need hardly tell you," Briers went on, smile truculent, combative, "that there have been differences of opinion. Among the lads, I mean. Now or later. That's the alternative. Some of them want to wait for something to turn up. It's only a chance in hell, they say, but it's worth waiting for. Old Len Bale has been sitting on his hands on that side. He's a bit of an old auntie in some respects. Not all." Briers seemed to be feeling surreptitious amusement, for reasons not disclosed to Humphrey. "But some of them want to jump in straightaway. The argument is, we'll get him by surprise. He might be thinking he's home and dry and we're not giving him a thought. He can't have any idea what we've worked out. He doesn't even know we've been busy with Loseby and that girl. Loseby hasn't been in touch. We know that. We don't think he ever was. Anyway, nowadays Loseby and his wife are thinking of their own precious skins. She doesn't think of much else, that one."

Briers made some observations about Susan. Then, back to order, he said, "The argument against, against going in now, that's straightforward. If it goes off half-cocked, then he'd be prepared next time. Now that we're in the driver's seat, we ought to know enough to break him down. If we muck it up, then we've thrown the advantage away."

There was no tension in the room. This was a witness of friendship, of the old friendship quite restored. Humphrey knew, though, with detached amusement, that it was something more. He was serving a purpose. Briers needed someone outside the machine who had nothing to gain, on whom he could try out the arguments and the doubts. Humphrey had seen something of men of action in his time. When they were making a decision, they needed someone who would listen, not persuade them, not disturb them. It was the reason for the mysterious cronies whom prime ministers relied on. As a rule, they were anonymous figures. The civil service used to have a name for them—the top man's sounding board.

"Well," Humphrey said without expression, "which side are you coming down on?"

"Do you have to ask?"

Humphrey gave the twitch of a smile. "I think not."

"No, we go straight in. It's a bit of a risk, of course. But the pros are stronger than the cons. That settles it."

Briers spoke like one weighing his judgment, but he had made the decision days before.

He asked another question. "By the by, what do you think the chances are? I mean, will the man give?"

Humphrey was certain that his answer would affect nothing. He could indulge in some detached reflection. They both knew, he said, if you had seen something of people, that some responses you could foresee. But two you couldn't; at least Humphrey had never met anyone who could. One was physical courage. No one had been able to predict that. The other, and it wasn't the same, was resistance to breaking strain. He wouldn't have put a penny on his own guesses. Perhaps he might have said that anyone like the young woman Susan, soft and unresisting on the surface, viscous-tough underneath, would survive most interrogations. Perhaps harder and more brittle natures were more likely to crack. That might be true with the doctor. "I wouldn't like to bet on it, I'm telling you. But I should have thought there was a chance."

"Fair enough." Briers had listened with friendly attention, nothing more.

He returned to his calm, realistic assessment. "I've told the lads, of course, that they must be ready for a disappointment. We haven't too much going for us. We may be left flat on our faces. I have reminded them of the times when we were just as positive and the man went away laughing at us and is still scot free."

Briers continued about his warnings against excessive hope. He had issued them, Humphrey had no doubt. Briers had a realistic mind. He had suffered his failures. And yet, he was warning himself more than anyone else. Humphrey, who had thought earlier of the habits of prime ministers, was reminded of another one. He thought of Churchill before the desert campaigns, solemnly warning the nation that nothing was certain in war and that no one could promise victory. The trouble was, no one believed it because he didn't himself. The message was sober, the tone was not. Briers could have given his colleagues all the professional cautions in existence, and they would have felt that he was confident: and they would have been right.

PART
FOUR

❧ 36 ❧

It was all scrupulously polite in the back room of the police station. This was where Briers's inner squad had conferred on their first afternoon and often since. Now it was being used for questioning, or what a less delicate observer might have called interrogation. On one side of the table there were Briers himself and Inspector Flamson; on the other, Dr. Perryman.

It would have been difficult for an outsider to be certain which way the initiative was going. It might not be easy for the insiders. Perryman had been brought into the station just after 5:30 in the evening, and the process had started at 6:00 P.M. It had not been an arrest, for, as Briers had told Humphrey, they had nothing like enough to make a charge. A couple of the team had been sent around to the doctor's house with a quiet request—there were some things to clear up. Yes, perhaps he had better bring a suitcase; it might take a little time. The sergeant in charge reported that Perryman seemed prepared. He was careful and slow in his movements, as though conscious of his own breathing. He made some sort of joke. He had plenty of patients in Belgravia, he said, but this would be the first time he had ever slept there. The policemen didn't see any distinction between Bloomfield Terrace and Belgravia and didn't respond.

Briers listened. That manner of Perryman's told him nothing he didn't already know: the man was cool, assertive, in command of himself. So were many men in trouble. It was no guide either to guilt or innocence, just to temperament. Briers had interviewed a good many men, completely innocent, who at the first prick of suspicion went in for bravado. He had done so himself when once he had been the subject of a police inquiry. If he had ever believed the conventional wisdom about human behavior, he didn't now.

There weren't any shorthand answers. It wasn't in his mind that night, but he was apt to tell his young men about the silliness of shorthand answers. Bullies were not always cowards: rather more often than not, the reverse was true.

Perryman had not asked to speak to his solicitor. Both he and Briers knew that the detective had a card to play. If Perryman didn't want to help the police, he might prefer to help the income-tax authorities. Those simple transactions about Lady Ashbrook's medical payments were docketed in the files. That would be enough for the present.

Days before deciding to fetch Perryman in, Briers had concluded that Perryman would be thinking much as he did himself. Just to make sure, he began the evening with some thoughtful questions about Lady Ashbrook's standard of living.

"We are rather interested, you know," said Briers.

"What is the problem, chief superintendent?" said Perryman in a similar, thoughtful, unexcited tone.

"Well, it is a bit of a puzzle, how she managed to live on her income. That is, on the income she returned to the Revenue."

"I'm afraid I don't know enough of the details. I wish I could help."

"It would be very valuable if you could help, of course."

"I'm sure you realize"—Perryman's lustrous eyes were gazing straight into Briers's fine, acute ones—"that she did live very economically. As her medical adviser, I often told her that it was time at her age to have someone permanently in the house."

"That was very sensible advice, you know. But we still don't quite understand how she managed. It was an expensive house to keep up, wasn't it? You must have thought so yourself."

There followed a knowledgeable discussion of the minimum outgoings on Lady Ashbrook's house. It might have sounded like an exercise in domestic science, all of them earnest seekers after a balanced budget. It was something like a parody of other discussions in that room, when the detectives first tried to make sense of Lady Ashbrook's finances.

Flamson, who had been taking notes and who continued to do

so, began to have a speaking part. Briers asked him questions, inviting Perryman to do the same, saying, what was true, that Flamson would have made a good businessman. To himself, looking at his junior, Briers thought he would have made a better businessman than detective. He sat there, solid, fleshy, with heavy eyelids and underlids, shrewd and self-indulgent. He was shrewd enough but not committed enough, maybe. But he hadn't been a bad pick of Briers's. After all, it was he who had first disbelieved in Lady Ashbrook's will. He might be slow, but somehow he had lumbered on to the right track.

Now he was testing Perryman about Lady Ashbrook's expenses. "They didn't fit," he said with a slumbrous accountant's pleasure. "They can't have fitted." This again was a recapitulation of what the police had long since seen. Flamson brought out the facts as, weeks before, he had done to his colleagues.

Briers intervened. "You were familiar, weren't you, with her habit of paying bills in ordinary notes? Not checks. She even paid some of her major bills that way. That was a curious habit, shouldn't you say?"

Perryman gave a companionable, superior smile, the smile that Kate had once found attractive.

"You must live in a very sheltered world, chief superintendent."

They were all three speaking in even tones, more like a conversation than a detective inquiry. This was Briers's style. He wouldn't change if he didn't get his results that night. He didn't believe, any more than he did in other conventional wisdom cherished by outsiders, in a soft–hard series of sessions with his suspects. That wasn't for professionals. The professional method for an interrogation was simpler than the conventional wisdom thought. It was just to be oneself. Interrogators weren't clever enough, nor was anyone else, to put on an act for long. If the man on the other side tried it, so much the worse for him.

There were, of course, one or two techniques. One was to hold a fact in reserve and spring it as a surprise. That was something you could teach. Another, much harder to teach, was to know when to change one's pace. A good interrogator did that as it were by nature, and only another interrogator would recognize the art: just as only a good interrogator would recognize the quiver of the nerve ends that another showed.

They had been at it for an hour. Repetitively, Flamson had been

265

going over the puzzles of Lady Ashbrook's income. There was much repetition in any process like theirs, which was why tapings of interrogations were among the most tedious records ever made. A young woman constable—who, though it wasn't Flamson who was the happy adulterer in Briers's squad, made his eyes light up underneath the padded flesh—entered with three cups of tea. The tea was very weak and very milky. Briers, who had smoked half a dozen cigarettes in the first hour, lit another.

"You might care to know," he said casually, offhand, as though he were mentioning that the BBC television news that night would be twenty minutes later than usual, "that we have information which you could be interested in. About a source of money for Lady Ashbrook. You know. The American fund."

"The American fund?" Perryman said without expression or concern.

"You know. Money came over at intervals. Reached someone here in English currency. Went to pay those bills."

"That's interesting," said Perryman, as though nothing could be less so.

"And this has been going on after her death."

"Has it now?"

"Yes, it has. The fund has gone on operating. A sizable sum—we don't know the exact amount, let's say a thousand pounds—has been passed to Lord Loseby." Briers didn't change his tone. "Our information is, passed by you, doctor."

Perryman's face had gone smooth, youthful, for a moment transformed by shock. For a moment he didn't utter. Then he began to sound harsh and haughty.

"I think I ought to congratulate you or whoever else it is on their imagination."

"You'd better think before you go any further." For once Briers let authority emerge. "Our information is solid. You were also responsible for passing money from the fund to Lady Ashbrook in her lifetime."

Just then, Briers made his single mistake of the night. Up to now he had been a shade more positive than the information would have supported. It wasn't a bluff, but perhaps half a bluff. Perryman hadn't challenged him. So far it had gone easier than Briers expected, as easy as he could have hoped. He went on with what he thought was certain knowledge: "You were the comptroller, weren't you?"

"The what?"

"The comptroller."

"I haven't the faintest idea what you mean."

"Shall I spell it? C o m p t r o l l e r."

"No one's ever called me that in my life. It seems to me a very silly word."

Briers knew, had known for instants past, that he had made a mistake. This wasn't like Perryman's other protest. The incredulity, the ignorance, were total. It was only later that Briers understood the origins of the mistake. It was oddly mechanical. In O'Brien's office, before and after the old lawyer's death, there had been talk about the control of funds. There was someone in London to whom money was transferred. They weren't allowed to know his name. He had better be called the comptroller. So, by a piece of inadvertence, had Susan and Loseby come to call him. There was a tag of paper with a typewritten inscription inserted in one of Loseby's payments, and they adopted the title. The American and English detectives had picked up the term. Perryman had never heard of it.

It was a piece of carelessness. Briers was blaming himself. As a rule he checked his references. It gave Perryman confidence back and a share of the initiative. He had enough assertion, affected as it might be, or even disdainful, to break into the questioning. Briers was just lighting another cigarette.

"Forgive me, chief superintendent," said Perryman, "but aren't you smoking too much?"

Briers looked blank-faced, at a loss.

When he replied, he said, "I dare say I am."

"If I were your medical adviser, I should want to have your lungs examined. Regularly."

Briers said, "Well, you're not, are you?"

Perryman went on, "That might be unfortunate for you."

Briers said, "We'll wait and see, shall we? We all have to die sometime."

That was accompanied by the grim policeman's smile that Humphrey would have recognized. It would have been grimmer if the end of this interrogation could have been the gallows. In retrospect, Briers felt some respect for Perryman's nerve. It might have been the kind of nerve that some patients showed—as by a perverse irony Perryman himself had seen them—when mortally anxious in a medical examination: to get on terms of moral equality, they would inquire with concern about some symptom in the doctor's own health.

"We'd better get on," said Briers with a shade of roughness that he hadn't let enter before. "There's a lot to do." He went on, "Yes, we know that you passed money after the old lady's death and before. You can't hide that business any longer. We're going to know it all."

They weren't able to know it all, but, as the night went on, they came to know more. Much of what they pieced together came to be near the truth. Not everything. Perryman was prepared, apparently even gratified, to explain. It had been a harmless, friendly, benevolent service.

"We can leave that to the tax boys," Briers remarked, but without emphasis. It was possible, perhaps probable, he was deciding, that Perryman didn't know the whole story. Certainly he wouldn't have known it from the beginning. That went back thirty years, to the end of the war, long before he had heard of Lady Ashbrook. However, he had met O'Brien and he admitted it.

"Lady Ashbrook didn't trust many people, did she?" Briers said.

"I should say not."

"She did trust him?"

"And she was right. She was right." Perryman went on with unusual emotion. "He was a good man."

It was a curious tribute, spoken as though by an authority.

At eight o'clock, more cups of tea. Toward nine, a plate heaped with sandwiches. Perryman ate more than his share, either through strain or appetite.

For the present, Briers was not letting Perryman loose from the financial dealings. Who had thought out the method? Perryman didn't know. That was probably genuine. Nothing had ever been put on paper. There the detectives had guessed right. Silence. Simplicity. That was the way to do any secret job, Briers was thinking. Humphrey would have agreed. It was the experienced who knew better than to try anything complex.

The method was working years before Perryman became Lady Ashbrook's doctor, he said.

On the whole, the detectives' reconstruction had again not been far from the truth. When O'Brien had his stroke, the difficulties were sharpened. He was immobile. There was no inquiry-proof method of getting money, messages, instructions, to Lady Ashbrook. This had not been foreseen as clearly, or as far back, as the police had imagined. That was an old story, Briers thought; one often overestimated the other side. Lady Ashbrook and O'Brien didn't seem able to think of another recourse—there was no help for it: they had to find a third party. She might not like it, but she had to find someone she could trust in England. That was how Perryman had been invoked.

"When was that?" Perryman gave the exact date, June 1968. "Why did she turn to you?"

"She had been my patient for several years. She trusted me."

"That was lucky for you, wasn't it?" Suddenly Briers shot out the question.

Perryman didn't show a flicker of surprise, resentment, worry, didn't alter his tone of voice. Instead he spoke with an aura of satisfaction.

"Also she liked me," he said.

It didn't need that expression to tell Briers that the man was vain, more than normally vain. But there was an effect that Briers, for the moment, couldn't place or understand.

He said, "Sexually, you mean?"

Perryman replied, still with satisfaction, "Oh, between any man and woman, when there's genuine liking, there's bound to be some kind of sexual attraction. Of course she was in her seventies, but as a doctor, let me tell you, sexual feeling doesn't disappear with age."

Briers broke out, control for an instant snapping, "Christ, man, you needn't tell a policeman that."

Unperturbed, Perryman continued. "Yes, there could have been a sexual element. We all realize that elderly women often make a cult of their doctors. But not with her. This was different. Nothing came of it, naturally. If one had been in a different capacity, it would have been possible—"

"I dare say, I dare say." Briers got back to business. How did the money reach Perryman? How was it picked up? As Humphrey had said, that was one of the oldest problems in security jobs. Briers wasn't certain that he was getting the full answers, but it wasn't material, and he let it go.

"You didn't do any picking up yourself?" Briers asked.

"Certainly not. That would have defeated the object of the exercise."

"Why?" But Briers knew; this was the obvious truth.

"I happen to be reasonably recognizable, I should have thought."

Briers gave a side glance to his colleagues. They had foreseen questions about how Lady Ashbrook got her money. It might seem primitive, but it had worked.

Perryman had been Lady Ashbrook's agent, he said. That was what in a satisfied tone he called himself. He said with scorn that neither he nor she would have imagined calling him a comptroller. She left the distribution of the money to him, both before and after her death.

"She told me what she wished. As I said, she trusted me."

"Yes, we heard that. And after her death, did she tell you about that too?"

"She did."

"Who was to get anything?"

"Loseby, that goes without saying. The main share. One or two others. None of them knew there was anything coming. This has to be kept dead secret, of course. In fact, I haven't worked out a way to get it round—"

"Anyway, you needn't trouble yourself about that now," said Briers with emollient politeness.

Perryman wasn't outfaced. With equal emollience, with mocking politeness, he said, "And you needn't trouble yourselves about those people. They weren't given the slightest expectations. All the sums would have been very small, at the most a few hundred pounds."

"This was all arranged in conversation?" By now, Briers took that for granted.

"That was the whole point."

"Completely uncheckable?"

"Completely." Then Perryman added, as though willing to help,

"There was one person who had further expectations. That was Lord Loseby."

"I think I should tell you straight away," Briers remarked without stress or inflection, "that for our purposes we are not interested in Lord Loseby."

Poised and unaffected, voice slightly more haughty, Perryman replied, "I suppose that I have to assume you know your job, chief superintendent?"

"Perhaps it might be easier if you do."

With the same civility, Briers went on, "Well, I think that's as far as we need go about the financial question. I don't know whether you agree, George—" he turned to Flamson.

"We've got quite a lot, chief. We know where to get some more."

"You see, doctor, that's all going to be a present for the tax boys, as I said. My guess is that they won't worry about Lady Ashbrook's income. That wouldn't be worth time and trouble. But they will have to worry about the estate duties."

There was a spell of silence, not long, a kind of deliberate doldrums.

Then Briers said across the table, "How much money is there left of that American fund?"

"I just don't know."

"I can't take that."

"It happens to be the hard truth." As though imitating Briers, Perryman also was deliberately quiet for an interval. He went on, as though pleased to be prosaic, "The other two were good at keeping their mouths shut."

"You must have a very good idea." Briers was showing an edge of temper.

"I have told you, no."

"We can clear that up in our own time." Briers went on, "Perhaps you can tell me something else. How much did you stand to get out of the business yourself?"

Perryman stared past him, eyes distended.

"How much?" Briers repeated.

"I was trying to think. The old lady discussed that with me, of course. She didn't want me to be out of pocket. It took a certain amount of time, and it was a responsibility, naturally. So she suggested that I was entitled to a small commission. Lady Ashbrook used to mention sums of two or three thousand. That's what an agent might reasonably expect."

"Not much," Flamson interjected.

"She was careful with her money. O'Brien was careful with it too. I was just doing a friendly service, after all."

"There's no proof of any of this, of course?" Briers said.

"There can't be."

"Then when she died? What did she tell you to keep for yourself?"

"Oh, nothing very grand. Loseby was to get twenty thousand pounds in dribs and drabs. The other gifts didn't matter. And I might have another agent's fee from what was left."

"And you've told us that you've no idea what that might come to."

"None at all. I didn't imagine it would make much difference to me."

"Of course you didn't." Without changing his tone, Briers went on, "Now if you don't mind, I'd like to drop all that. We shouldn't be wasting our time here on a piece of tax fiddling, you know."

"What should we be wasting our time on, then?" Deliberately Perryman looked at his watch. It was after ten. The interview had been going for four hours.

Briers said, "There is a matter of murder." Voices told little, faces less. A tape recording, a photograph, would have shown no more open emotion than if they had been talking about the National Theater.

❧ 37 ❧

I needn't tell you what all this is in aid of, need I?" Briers was speaking carefully and slowly. "It's the murder we want to ask you about. I don't have to tell you that."

"I can't pretend to be absolutely astonished." Perryman said it with superior, condescending, as it were benevolent, sarcasm.

"I don't have to tell you why we've been paying all this attention to the money. I can leave that thought with you just for now."

Briers pressed out a cigarette end. The ashtray was littered with stubs. He relaxed into silence. Then, as though at ease, not insistently, he said, "What about yourself? You could have killed her, couldn't you?"

"I'm not sure what that means." Perryman's calm hadn't broken.

"Perhaps you will be sure. Sooner or later. You can't give us any account of your movements that night. I know, that could happen to anyone. But for all you have told us, you could have been in that house. Agreed?"

"I can't prove that I wasn't. Agreed. In theory I could have been."

"I said before, that could apply to others. But you had access to her, didn't you? You had your own front door key."

"I thought I'd made it plain"—Perryman threw back his head—"that I was a close friend."

"You were also her doctor. That puts you in a special position? That could give you certain advantages, couldn't it?"

"I don't know what that means."

"I think you do. It ought to be clear. You're an intelligent man. If it's a question of killing an old lady, a doctor has certain advantages. Particularly if she happens to be his patient. She's used to him, isn't she? She's used to his hands."

"In theory that would be true."

"You have good hands, doctor." They were tented in front of Perryman's chest, long-fingered with filbert nails, firm, strong thumbs.

"So I've been told."

"And you'd have another advantage. You'd know exactly where to put those hands, without fuss. Of course, you'd have to explain beforehand why you were wearing gloves. But that would be no trouble to a smooth talker. You could have been treating another patient with an infection earlier on that night."

Perryman smiled. "Yes, a doctor could have done all that. I really do congratulate you on your imagination. Yes, it could have happened, in theory. The only trouble is that it didn't."

To that last flick Briers paid no notice. He went on. "There's one thing about that murder that we still don't quite understand. A doctor would have known that he'd killed her, of course. Then why would he smash her skull in? Unnecessary. Risky. He was lucky not to collect some blood. Unless he did and took precautions we haven't traced so far. Anyway, if he'd thought twice, he wouldn't have done it. He wouldn't have picked up that hammer. Naturally, we know better than anyone that a man often goes mad after he's killed someone. There are more nasty reminders of that than we reckon to talk about. But we didn't find any this time. Never mind, it mightn't have been a fit of madness. Maybe an attempt to make it look like a killing by a brute, just a dumb thief. The same with the way the room was left. That was a bit of make-believe. We saw that as soon as we walked in."

"Another effort of your imagination, I take it," Perryman commented.

Briers switched away. Abruptly he said, "In the summer you must have thought that the old lady was going to die soon?"

"Not so positively as that." Perryman's reply was sharp, competent, less measured than when he was under direct attack. "My clinical judgment was that it was rather more likely than not. My clinical judgment turned out wrong."

"If it had been right, she would have been dead by now. And you would have been coping with the dispositions just as you are at present."

"That must be true."

"And as there had been no murder, no one would have thought twice about it. The money would have come in according to plan?"

"Naturally."

"But since your judgment didn't prove right, she might have lived for years?"

"She could have done."

"And that was a reason for impatience?" Without stress, Briers was switching back.

"It could have been. It could have been," said Perryman. "On someone's part."

"It must have been a shock to hear that she was going to survive."

"If someone was impatient, it might have been." Perryman didn't change his tone. "I saw no sign of it. I suppose I didn't have the right acquaintances."

Briers said, as though brooding, "If you had been able to do anything to help her survive—you being her doctor of course—you'd have done it, wouldn't you?"

"Naturally."

"Whatever else you were thinking about?"

"I don't know what you mean."

"Professional duty is a very strange thing. You'd agree with that, wouldn't you?"

That exchange had for an instant brought a touch of sympathy between them, which on and off had been latent much of the night. Not liking, for there was none; on Briers's side, something like revulsion. But there was also a feeling more surreptitious and closer than liking. He knew that he would get no further that night. They passed into long passages of repetition, the money dealings, the way the murder could have been done. Briers wasn't dissatisfied. He had to subdue optimism, the optimism he warned others against. This man wouldn't break, but was going to give. Briers suddenly remarked across the table that they had had enough for one day—some of his colleagues would be ready to ask more questions in the morning—and said a polite good night.

275

A little later, the background squad assembled like a team wishing to have an inquest on the day's play. They could see that Briers was forgetting the tiredness of one who had been exuding energy for hours. They were counting on the time when they had the case to their credit, another job cleaned up. They had a bottle of whiskey on the table in the Murder Room, and someone said, "It's going to be all right, isn't it, guv." That wasn't a question. There was collective well-being in the air. Briers, who had sometimes suffered from his own hopes, said, "I'll believe that when I see it. I'll believe that when I see the jury coming down for us."

"You're touching wood."

"It doesn't do any harm to touch wood," Briers said.

❧ 38 ❧

The following evening, while the second pair of detectives were at work questioning Perryman half a mile away, Kate and Humphrey were sitting on the sofa in his drawing room. She had recently come up from the kitchen, having cooked him a savory now on the little table by his side. It was a comfortable domestic picture, sardonic observers might have said. With changes of menu, it happened most nights of the week.

Yet in form, their relation was unaltered. Kate hadn't made the break. She worked at her hospital, provided for Monty, then gave Humphrey the attention of the most vigilant of lovers. She wanted to give him pleasure and got pleasure from doing so. Otherwise she didn't want anything for herself—except, as Humphrey told her with the liberty of his kind of love, her own way. For they were living on her terms, not his.

She couldn't bring herself to leave Monty—to leave him to his helpless self. She thought she was realistic, more than most. She wasn't sentimental. But she couldn't bring herself to make the clean and clinical break. Habit was too strong maybe. Or the comfort— not so noble as it might have seemed to one who flattered herself more—of having someone who needed to cling.

It didn't sound realistic. Yet perhaps it was. Kate had announced to Humphrey that it wasn't time for the final move. They settled down to go on as they were. She was half living with him. It was a singular kind of happiness. After all, there were more kinds of happiness than complacent or self-important persons thought. As for

Kate, she positively enjoyed the activity and the effort, though sometimes she had daydreams as to where she and Humphrey would live when they were free.

Did Monty know? He could scarcely have helped knowing, both Kate and Humphrey thought. She didn't conceal her movements. She didn't volunteer confessions or explanations, but she wouldn't lie. Probably, Humphrey suggested to her, Monty both knew and didn't know, that state in which many existed when living with a suspicion they didn't want to accept. Knowing and not knowing: he was being treated just as he had always been, everything in order, kindness, cheerfulness, money coming into the house, all paid for—while he continued with his thoughts. In spite of his superbity, he might possess a kind of self-protective cunning. If he had confronted her, it would mean a chance for her to break for good. So Humphrey thought to himself, but he believed that that view of Monty would still bring her pain.

That evening, sitting in peace on the sofa, Kate was following another thought of his. She knew that, like the detectives themselves, he was excited about the interrogation. This excitement wasn't a special compliment to human nature. It was like that which had spread around Lady Ashbrook's acquaintances when they were waiting for news as to whether she was mortally ill. People— it didn't matter whether they were good-natured within the human limits—felt their pulses beating stronger at the prospect of someone else's calamity. Yes, Humphrey was as good-natured as most men, Kate thought—she had the best of reasons for realizing that. But, loving him, she knew that he was carried away, half absentminded, by the thought of those interrogations. She knew too that he had spoken to Frank Briers that afternoon. She was sure that Humphrey wished he were taking part, and was envious.

If he had known about the talk of the background squad late that night, he might have been more envious. That was the inquest after the second session. Morale was high. It was like being at election headquarters when the swing was beginning to look certain. The well-being was almost palpable: or at least odd pats on shoulders really were so. Briers, lifted with the rest, making up his mind about tactics, had intervals when he could forget other cares.

The next day, interrogations went according to Briers's standard routine, using a second couple, in this case Bale and Norman

Shingler. By now most of the financial operations were clear enough, or as clear as they were likely to be. They had got no nearer, though, to any admissions about the murder, or even a single fact about the doctor's whereabouts that night, except the visit to a patient, short, just to keep up a woman's spirits, corroborated on her side, proving or disproving nothing. The doctor had been superior, sarcastic, difficult to trouble, the second pair reported. He had answered just as he had answered Briers the night before. Yes, of course, he could have let himself into Lady Ashbrook's house that night. Or any other night. It merely happened that he hadn't. Yes, of course, he could have taken hold of her. Patients were used to their doctor's attention. It merely happened that he hadn't. Yes, of course, strangling an old woman would present no problems. Any doctor knew that. A doctor might do it more quickly than the average layman. He himself was a competent doctor. It happened that he hadn't tried.

It was Norman Shingler, sharp as well as pertinacious, who contrived for a few minutes to make him appear less lofty. Shingler had been pressing questions about the sums transferred in Lady Ashbrook's lifetime. They were not more than a couple of thousand pounds or so at a time? Piddling sums, considering the precautions and the amount of planning. Yes, you could say that if you wanted, Perryman had replied in his indifferent fashion. Piddling sums like that were a reason for killing her? Shingler was probing. Then suddenly Perryman had lost his temper. Lost it for the first time in the two interrogations. Was that the best they could dig up by way of a reason? Money, money, all they could understand was money.

"What else? You tell us." Shingler wasn't letting go.

"Money, money, you can't see anything else."

"Well then, you tell us what the motive was. You know, do you?"

Perryman was getting back his control. "You don't know it. I don't know it. Why should I? But it can't have been money. That's all you seem to think of."

Shingler couldn't shake him any more. He had thrown his head back—both Bale and Shingler had been irritated by that mannerism—and regained his contemptuous poise. None of the detectives had been used to interrogating anyone so articulate and so much in command. All four had come to find him not only irritating but repellent, quite out of the common. They also felt a kind of forced respect. Later, some of them said that he was a brave man.

Shingler's notes on the day's interrogation were before them on the table. Briers turned again to the record of Perryman's outburst. "Well done, Norman. I want to hear you tell me all about it again." He was soaking in what he heard. He asked Bale for anything he had noticed. He confirmed that Shingler had touched a nerve. "Well done," Briers said. "I'll take that up next time I talk to him."

Next time, however, was not next day as the others took for granted. The others knew that there was a purpose when Briers did the unexpected. Even so, they were astonished when the following morning, without any explanation, Briers let the doctor go home.

❧ 39 ❧

It might work, Frank Briers told Humphrey, letting Perryman have time to think. By now he must have realized that the police knew a good deal. Even control as armored as his might wear thinner in solitude. He might think that the police were holding back something that counted—

"I wish we were," said Briers. "That's our weak spot. We'll have to get it out of him."

He hadn't talked in confidence to Humphrey for a couple of weeks past, since he and the squad had been formulating their tactics. Now, restless, he wanted to talk. He was forcing himself to be patient. He was starved of action.

He had telephoned Humphrey at his house, asking him if he were alone. It was a dark November night, not cold, the smell of wood smoke in the air. When Briers arrived in Humphrey's drawing room, he gulped down a drink.

He began, as though in the middle of a conversation that had just been interrupted, why he had broken off the interrogations. "I had a hunch that he was getting stuck in, ready to let everything bounce off him. The blame's on me if I've got it wrong."

Then after a pause he said, "Let him puzzle it out. He thinks he's cleverer than we are. Let him. Then we get him in again in a couple of weeks. Cat and mouse if you like. It's not nice, but I've done it before. It's make or break."

He told Humphrey about the results of the first two sessions. Fair enough, he said.

"Your chaps have done a good job over the money business, I should have thought," Humphrey said. Enthusiasm wasn't called for. It was a time for detachment.

"Of course they have."

"On the murder they haven't had much in the way of luck, have they? You'd have expected something to come loose, wouldn't you? And it hasn't."

"He's a bastard, but he's not an ordinary bastard."

"If you're right about him, that's rather an understatement."

"I'm right about him. You know that, don't you?"

At that moment, Humphrey didn't reply at once. Briers said, "He's not given an inch, except when he had no option."

Humphrey hadn't often seen the younger man unwilling to keep still, but now Frank Briers got up, stretched, walked down the long room toward the window. From where Humphrey was sitting, the panes looked glossy black, opaque. Then Briers said, "Plenty of people about. Why the hell weren't there a few that night? Someone ought to have caught a glimpse of the man."

When he got back to his chair, they talked as they had done often enough—Briers obsessive, repeating what they had gone over until they were tired, the missing facts, the facts that would have stopped what Briers called any more chuntering. What clothes had Perryman worn that night? Where were they now? Untraceable. Not a chirp from anyone, not a whisper.

Other factors didn't signify so much, but still one ought to know the answers. Who had Perryman used as his courier, collecting the pounds at those hotels? No information, not a sighting.

Humphrey commented, "I suppose you've thought about his wife?"

Briers gave an impatient curse. "You're a hell of a lot of help, aren't you? You've said that before. We've squeezed nothing out of her. We've gone on at her till we're sick. I've had another go at her myself."

"Any results?"

"Not a sausage. She's as cool as he is."

"Do you think she knows?"

"She might know everything. She might know nothing. She just smiles like a Cheshire cat. Then I suppose she goes off to the R.C. church around the corner."

"You'd like to hear the confession, would you?"

Briers cursed again. Just then he forgot that he was an enlightened man and remembered his old grandfather denouncing confession and similar debased papist practices.

Humphrey was wondering what kind of marriage the Perrymans' was. Were they close? Was it a deep marriage, so that the two of them couldn't help accepting all, aiding in everything?

He had met Alice Perryman only casually and had been put off by the complacency of such a faith. But the thought of that marriage diverted him to Briers's. He asked, offhand to disguise the caring, how Betty was.

"Not well." Briers's reply was suddenly bitter. "It looks as though that remission has finished."

"I'm sorry." The words were lame, unavailing. "I didn't know."

"No one knew." Frank added, "She's seeing double again. She's gone lame."

"She's having too much to take."

"She's never done a scrap of harm to a living soul. Now she's going to have years of this. And people believe in God's justice. The insufferable fools."

Humphrey hadn't heard him make that protest before. It was violent and then quenched as soon as uttered. Briers said in a subdued tone, "She was talking about you a day or two ago. She wished that she could get around just a little."

Then Briers got back to business. He had been doing his job with that wretchedness dragging at him, that home waiting for him, Humphrey thought. The curious thing was, his energy was so strong that no one had noticed.

Briers was recurring to observations about Perryman and what he had seen in his own interrogation. "He's very hard," Briers said, "very hard physically. I fancied we could tire him out. But he wasn't any more tired than I was."

Humphrey gave a smile of recognition. He had had to put up with Briers's feats of endurance.

"He's very vain," Briers went on. Humphrey nodded.

"Some of our regular villains are very vain," Briers said, "but I think he's the vainest man I've ever met. Anyway, the vainest man I've ever had the other side of the table."

Humphrey said, "I think I'd go a bit further. There's an old quality people used to talk about—they called it arrogance of soul. I should think he'd get high marks for that." He gave a faint smile. "It's a curious quality. I knew a couple of war heroes, genuine heroes who had it, pressed down and running over. I fancy some of the most spectacular martyrs had it too. It's what puzzled me most about Perryman when I used to meet him—"

"I don't want to run across it again, for God's sake. I'll sacrifice the war heroes and the martyrs if we can get rid of the Perrymans."

"It takes some people above themselves. It gives them the guts to die in torture. It takes other people below themselves; then they can kill in torture."

As Humphrey finished, he regarded the other man. Between the two of them, they had seen a fair amount of what human beings could do. It wasn't so long ago, in this same room, that Briers had wondered how much of it ought to be public knowledge. He took it less objectively than Humphrey did himself. "Anyway," Humphrey went on, "it gives you an opening. Anyone as arrogant as that isn't going to guard every spot. You've got somewhere near, haven't you? That young man of yours—what's his name—"

"Shingler."

"Shingler—he got nearer. Perhaps he was lucky. You'll work on that again, of course."

"Of course."

As they had once done, they were talking like fellow professionals.

"Money," Briers was saying. "They say he was furious at the bare suggestion. Shingler didn't even tell him that he had killed for money. But the faintest idea of it was outrageous. Too lofty for such things, this one is. I'll try it out all the ways I can think of. I'll have Shingler with me just to remind him of the last occasion. There's a hope that he'll come out with another motive. If we upset him enough." Briers went on. "You know, I can just imagine a man like him, wanting to do something on the grand scale. Anything goes. What's to stop a man who knows he's ten times brighter than the rest of us? And cooler. Surrounded by dull brutes, cattle. Anything goes. That would be something to do."

Briers paused and then broke out, "Can you imagine that?"

"Not as well as you can."

"I rather doubt whether I could feel like that myself," Briers said, as though braving the other's sarcasm, "but I can imagine this man feeling something like it."

"Yes, I know you can." Humphrey's previous remark might have sounded like a gibe, but this was meant. He was referring to Briers's great gift as an interrogator. He immersed himself in the human being opposite. He wasn't just questioning; he was feeling with him. It was a curious gift. If you didn't possess it, you could never learn it. Humphrey didn't possess it, or to anything like the same degree. Once or twice he had reproached himself for not being able to enter Tom Thirkill's paranoia. Briers could have done. He had what they now called empathy. When they had worked together, Humphrey, if he wanted to cheer himself up among pompous persons, reflected that though he hadn't Frank Briers's empathy, he himself might have a clearer insight. Know-alls, meeting the two of them, would have confidently assumed the precise opposite in both respects.

"Another gambit you might try," Humphrey said. "Remember the old lady thought she might be dying of cancer. This was her doctor. It's long odds there was an understanding." Humphrey was recalling a conversation in the Square garden. "It would be surprising if she didn't trust him to put her out quietly—if she couldn't bear it any longer. She would be in his power. It must have been a dislocation when you heard she was healthy, no cancer, no need of trusted doctor. No more power."

"Noted." Briers was as ready to listen as when he was much younger. He wanted to stay there, so it seemed, talking to Humphrey. He blamed himself for taking so long to see that Perryman was different from the others. He ought to have identified him from the start.

It's no use jobbing back, though, Briers said, and went on doing so. When once he had picked out Perryman, then they hadn't gone far wrong. It's not been an easy one, he said. He took another drink, breaking his own discipline. He had nothing to occupy him that night. He would have been glad of any sort of action, Humphrey felt: it would shut out imaginings about his wife. It was ungrateful, Humphrey also felt, that he himself, happy with Kate, nothing to be anxious about in her health, would still have been glad of some sort of action too.

Briers was saying that some of the detective work had been "bright enough." He was proud of his lads. The pride was genuine—but this was something else to talk about. He returned to what Humphrey had said about the financial fiddling—yes, it had taken digging into. That was what they were paid for. It wasn't earthshaking, but it was good work.

Suddenly, without connection, Humphrey broke in. He had his deprecating smile. He said, "I think I'd better tell you."

"What's that?"

"I was wrong to have any doubts. You were right about Perryman."

Briers's eyes lit up, but he replied in a matter-of-fact tone, without triumph or conceit, "Oh yes, I was. Mind you, I've been wrong two or three times already in this business. The score sheet isn't all that pretty."

Humphrey's smile sharpened. "I agree with you; he did it," he said in another matter-of-fact tone. "I'll tell you something else. He may say more wonderful things. He may believe them. But he did it for the money."

Briers, expression washed clean, mouth set, didn't reply for a time. "Perhaps not entirely," he said.

"He wouldn't have done it without."

"You don't believe in giving people the benefit of the doubt, do you?"

"I don't believe in flattering ourselves. Look, Frank, you've seen a lot of crime. It's easy to invent motives. You've said so yourself. It's much too easy to make them more complicated than they are."

Briers answered affectionately, obstinately, "You've seen a lot of other things as well as crime. You don't think any of us are much good, do you? So you like to see everything bleak and simple, don't you? That's because you don't think much of yourself."

❧ 40 ❧

Within a few hours of that conversation, information arrived from the Scotland Yard team in New York. Their American colleagues had done some more gentle talking with the O'Brien firm. The old partner's wishes had to be respected, but in the circumstances his colleagues felt justified in giving them confidential information. They had made an estimate of the amount in the comptroller fund. It was disconcertingly small. So small that the detective studying the brief had to ask the lawyers to search the documents again. They found no more traces. There was less than fifteen thousand pounds to be paid out. Briers told Humphrey this without comment but not without satisfaction. If Perryman had killed for money, it would have been for a few thousand pounds. He left it for Humphrey to think about.

Humphrey didn't comment either. Instead, there was a task that he didn't look forward to but couldn't shirk. Just as he had felt cowardly on that visit to Lady Ashbrook back in the summer, when she didn't know the result of the hospital examination, so he felt cowardly driving to the Briers's house.

He might have hardened himself with age, but he wasn't hard enough for the sight of this young woman. He had to force himself to call on her that afternoon. Frank would be at work in the Murder Room. Humphrey had to face the sick girl alone. He was fond of her. She was good. He could still hear Frank's bitter outburst.

After he had parked the car, he glanced at the houses opposite, secure behind their gardens, standard roses still in November blooming on the lawns. It was a fine afternoon, and the low sun made brilliant shields of the downstairs windows. It all looked so tranquil, so trouble-free. He walked up the strip of gravel to the Briers's door as reluctantly as he had walked to Lady Ashbrook's in July.

He pushed the bell gently. Then he had to push again. There was a drawn-out pause. Then, from inside—something moving along the passage, the tessellated floor, a curious scraping noise.

The door opened. Betty was propped up inside a walking frame. She smiled, a beautiful welcoming smile.

"Oh, Humphrey, what a nice surprise." She smiled again. "You go on. Down to the back room. I'm not all that quick."

She got herself to the back room and managed to settle in a chair. "I live here most of the time," she said. "It used to be Frank's den. I had to turn him out. I don't have to move about so much. Ridiculous, walking like an infant."

She had the high spirits Humphrey had witnessed before and couldn't take. Her face looked little changed, perhaps a shade thinner. Eyes sunken and perhaps a shade overbright. She wanted to make him tea—that was easy; the kitchen was just the other side of the passage. Humphrey wouldn't let her. He wasn't fond of tea, he said. For an instant, he held her hand. It felt hot, not quite steady.

"Oh, it's good to see you," she said.

"Frank hinted that you might like a visitor or two."

She gave another of her brilliant smiles, but this time open, impatient, candid. "No, no." Her voice was quite unaffected, full and clear. "I want to talk to you. Can I talk?"

"Anything you like."

"It's what I've done to poor old Frank. I'm afraid for him."

"Yes, you're bound to be." Humphrey had to meet her with the same openness. She wasn't the woman to deny the moment in which she stood. Nor should he.

"No, no. I didn't mean anything that doesn't need saying. Of course I'm a drag on him. And I shall be for a long time. Did you realize that this isn't a killing disease? They tell me not, positively. I'm pretty likely to live as long as he does. All right for me. You'd be surprised how much I get out of life on these terms. Difficult for him. He's very good. But that's not the point. I meant something quite different."

Humphrey, having once misinterpreted, waited for her. She said, eyes brilliant, concentrated, hectic, "Do you remember the last time you were here?"

"Very well."

"Do you remember certain things I said?"

"What things?"

"No, you have to remember. I said that I wished he could do something positive. You too. He must have felt that I wasn't happy with how he was spending his life."

Humphrey had scarcely noticed those remarks. He had to pretend to bring them back to mind.

"I suppose you did suggest something like that," he said, "but no one cared."

"I cared." Her cheeks, skin still fresh and delicate, had flushed. "But I never ought to have said it. It may have done him harm."

"Oh, come on." He was speaking sincerely because she was so intense. "We all know most decent men would like to help make the world just a trifle better. But there aren't many jobs that can possibly tell them they're doing so. What Frank is doing may help the world from getting rather worse. That's enough justification for most decent men."

"It's negative."

"How many people do you think have ever found a genuine moral solvent? Among those I've known I could number them on the fingers of one hand."

"I'm not arguing with you. That isn't the point. Once again that isn't the point. I'm afraid that I may have done him harm. It doesn't matter whether I was right. I oughtn't to have said it. I wish you could remember—I was sure you would. I've been wishing ever since that I could take it all back."

She couldn't take it back, but she could live it again with total recall. Tears were dripping down her cheeks, not wiped away, ignored as though they were as commonplace as her loving smile.

Perhaps this frenetic concentration on words dropped months ago, by others unnoticed or forgotten, might like the tears themselves be a sign of her condition. But also she was so sensitive to any inflection between her and anyone she loved, or even anyone she was fond of, that she had made Humphrey feel that he had three skins too many—while she had three too few.

"Betty, dear," he said, "what are you really afraid of? For him?"

"Oh, it's very simple, don't you see? His work is what he's got left. Except for looking after me. I'm afraid that when he thinks I'm not happy about his work, he'll get unhappy about it too. We've been very near together always. It's that sort of love. And it sounds horrible, but he respects me. That's the trouble. I'm afraid I may have weakened his will. He wants all his will for work like his, doesn't he? I should be very guilty if I weakened it."

Benevolent she was, Humphrey thought, as he watched the fine-drawn face, kind, high-minded, unself-pitying, tender with loving kindness: but she too had her share of vanity. Moral vanity in her case. Frank might feel that she was a better person than he was. But Humphrey didn't think that he was so open to influence as she imagined, even hers. In her state, though, Humphrey couldn't tell her so.

"I rather fancy," he said, unusually circuitous, "that you're worrying too much. I'm almost certain you are. You see, I'm not sure he caught the full meaning of what you said that night any more than I did. I've not seen any sign that he heard anything that upset him. He hasn't made any reference to me. Not the slightest."

"I hope you're right. You don't sound convinced."

Humphrey weaved on. "My one fear about Frank would be rather different. Because of what's happened to you, he hasn't anything else to lose himself in. That's what you just said. He's absolutely immersed in his present case. He may get even more involved in his job than he is now. That's good as far as it goes. At present he's probably the best professional at his game in the country. He'll get all the success he wants. But he may have to pay a bit of a price. Part of his skill depends on the fact that he's not as brutalized as most of us become. He's kept his imagination. Perhaps you'll find he gets more brutalized. Not with you. But because of you. That would be a pity. You'll have to watch him and help him. You're the only one who can."

She was crying again, but comfortably. "I know," she said.

"Most things have gone right for him up to now, haven't they?" Humphrey needed to keep her comfortable. "This is the first real suffering he's ever had. With characters like his, suffering can make one stronger. But one loses a good deal. I had a certain amount once or twice. I don't think I was an especially nice young man, but I do know that I emerged a great deal less nice than I had been. But considerably tougher. That might happen to Frank. Be careful with him."

"I'd like to talk to your friend Kate," Betty said. She wasn't able to make new acquaintances and had never seen Kate, but her interest in those she heard about seemed to have become more intense. "I'd like to ask her if you've lost all your illusions as much as you pretend." She looked at Humphrey, eyes brilliant. "There's something else I should like to ask her. She knows about—married love, doesn't she?"

"A certain amount, you might say."

"Well. Until I get the next remission—of course we don't know when, we hope it won't be long—I'm likely to have no feeling below the waist. That happened the last time. It's very hard on Frank." She was fumbling for words; Humphrey was thinking that Kate wouldn't have been. "He's not the sort of man who likes having—relations with a woman who can't respond. I don't mind. But he hates it. He stays away. What would Kate do—if you two were in our position?"

"She couldn't do much, could she?"

"She lives in the world, doesn't she? Would she tell you to console yourself somewhere?"

"Possibly she might," Humphrey said. "She's not a saint. She wouldn't like it much."

"But she would do that?"

"I think it's more likely that she'd leave it to me to look after myself. And not tell her anything about it. She's not a bit naive, and she's pretty wise. She's seen more damage done by enthusiastic candor than by keeping quiet. There are times when it's best to keep quiet."

"You think that's what Frank ought to do?"

Humphrey said, "No one who isn't inside the situation can say that."

"I'm not sure he could."

When Humphrey told her that he must go, she said, with a smile naked, tender, without a skin of politeness or pretense, "It hasn't been restful for either of us, has it? But you've been a help. I don't think you know."

Humphrey felt relief to be out in the street, in the calming autumn air. Relieved as he had once been leaving Lady Ashbrook's. But his spirits hadn't sunk so low by the side of this young woman as they had beside the other. Maybe because this one was lovable and made lovableness seem natural; or maybe it was just that, afflicted as she was, the shadow of death wasn't so near.

❧ 41 ❧

In the Murder Room those last days of November, the detectives talked. It was known that within days Briers was going to have the doctor brought in for another session. There was excitement in the air that some tried to damp down. In climatic terms the air was damp enough, for the street outside the station was glumly dark, the cloud cover hung below the jets' flight paths, rain didn't fall much but didn't cease to look like falling. Around the corner in Elizabeth Street, umbrellas streamed by in the mournful drizzle. The shops—game, fish, groceries, wine—were already brilliant for Christmas. On the way to the pub across the street, the policemen could catch the smell of cheese and fruit, as though they were back in a market town.

Briers spent his time listening to anyone who wished to talk. Now they were near the end, he aroused a kind of faith. The squad believed that he would find a way through. When they noticed that Morgan, the pathologist, spent a long time with him, the faith got stronger. Some of them knew that Morgan was one of the best of foul-weather allies: but they didn't know that he had been forced to tell Briers that there was no more to expect from forensic evidence within foreseeable time. He had said that Perryman as a student had a reputation for consummate perfectionism—to which Briers had replied, "Tell me something I don't know."

Members of the squad came and left as Briers sat there for long hours. He asked for others—though the three who had been sitting in at the questioning—Bale, Flamson, Shingler—were usually present. Briers was making up his mind about the final attack. "I don't like set plans," he announced more than once. "In anything like this, we have to play it by ear. Set plans are always wrong." But he didn't mean quite what he said. He had plans, contingency plans, some not yet put into words. He listened just as he had listened to Humphrey and Morgan. He told his colleagues what he was thinking. He was open and at times secretive. Even to Bale, whom he could confide in, who was short on ideas, long on action, he didn't tell all.

It wasn't much like a streamlined operation, such as when a top civil servant had consulted his officials about how to prevail over another department. It was much more like a producer in the entertainment industry, creative, used to an existence where nothing was certain and words meant nothing, or alternatively everything, casting around for openings before going to meet a backer, powerful, obdurate, and whom he didn't trust.

It was Bale who on the morning of December 2 was deputed to ask Dr. Perryman to come along again to the police station. The invitation was considerate. Bale delivered the message—they all knew it would be inconvenient for him to leave his practice. It might have seemed considerate also that the invitation was conveyed by this senior and grave-looking superintendent.

When, having brought the doctor, Bale arrived back at the station, he reported that there had been a show of temperament. On the previous occasion, Perryman, asking police officers into his own drawing room, had been lofty, indulgent, patronizing.

Now he had broken out in protest, asking who compensated a citizen for his time and expenses. Yet, after telephoning another doctor (only that one call, none to a solicitor, Bale noted), Perryman came along. On the way, he hadn't spoken much, just a sarcastic grumble about the weather. It was a foul morning, the lights of shops and upstairs windows beaming through the murk.

Perryman was led to the room where he had been questioned before, brought a cup of tea, left to himself. In the Murder Room, the detectives were hearing Bale's impressions. There was a stir of approval. "It sounds as though he's cracking up," said someone. One of the youngest there added, "He won't give you too much trouble today, chief." They were all standing, and the young man spoke across the group to Briers, "I'll bet you he's ready to come out." Briers gave a truculent smile, but his voice was quiet. "We'll see, we'll see." The young detective went on, "He'll come out today."

That was a curious idiom. It meant come clean, confess. A generation before, it had become a protest phrase among students of English when they wanted to proclaim an opinion; then it got caught up by homosexuals when they wanted to proclaim their faith. Just at that period, smart young policemen couldn't resist borrowing it for their own purposes. Now Briers let it pass. He was in no hurry, though that was studied. It was nearly eleven before he nodded to Shingler and walked through to the back room.

"Good morning, doctor," he said, back in his punctilious vein.

"Good morning, chief superintendent." Perryman didn't rise, just inclined his head.

"I think you know Inspector Shingler."

Perryman again inclined his head.

The little room was comfortable. Outside the window, it was as dark as the preamble to an eclipse. Lances of rain were flashing by. In the room, it was bright and warm, not too warm, judiciously so. The tray of teacups had followed behind Briers and Shingler. An ashtray, burnished, was waiting in front of Briers's place, and two packets of cigarettes stood ready.

It was physically snug in there. Perryman threw back his head, in the mannerism that had fretted Briers's nerves before, and said, "Before we begin proceedings, I should like to make a statement."

"I'll take it down," Shingler said eagerly.

"No, no. Not your kind of statement. I want to tell you, chief superintendent, naturally I'm anxious to help you in any reasonable way I can—"

"I'm sure you are." Briers's tone was utterly unstressed.

"But I think I ought to remind you that I have work of my own. This is a serious interference, and it might be more than a serious interference to some of my patients if I am called away again without proper notice. There are limits to what I can accept in fairness to other people and myself. That should be clear enough. I am at your disposal today, but if you wish to repeat your invitation, I should feel obliged to take official advice."

"That's your privilege, doctor."

"You understand, I was more helpful than you could have expected last time I was here—"

"That might be a matter of opinion, perhaps?"

Perryman had shown one way of recovering himself, Briers thought. Not many men would have had that degree of control, he thought later. It made it harder to keep his own.

It wasn't a time to begin with emollience. He said, "I want to get back to old Lady Ashbrook's illness. That is, when it was believed she might have cancer."

"I've said all I can about that."

"I want to be certain. You did tell me that you thought the hospital tests would be positive?"

"I did tell you I thought it was possible."

"You thought it was more than possible, didn't you?" That was from Shingler. Perryman didn't glance at him but replied, "I've already told the chief superintendent—"

"That you regarded it as more likely than not? Well, then." Briers pressed on. "You had your patient who might be terminally ill. Right?"

"Certainly."

"And she was more than a patient? She was someone you knew intimately. Who let you handle her financial affairs—"

"We've been over all this. Tediously, if I may say so. It isn't a profitable topic, you ought to realize by now."

"We'll be patient."

"I'm having to be patient myself."

Briers looked blank, as though he hadn't heard.

"We all agree, don't we, that you had your friend and patient there under your eyes. And you had good grounds to expect that she'd soon be told the worst. She expected it. She must have talked about her death—to you, doctor. You must have been the first person she talked to."

"Certainly she talked about it. She didn't pretend."

"She had to rely on you, didn't she, if the worst came to the worst? You could ease her out? Did she talk about that too?"

Perryman answered with a condescending smile, "You seem hypnotized by this topic. The answer would be a confidence between patient and doctor. I'm not prepared to reveal it."

"You're nothing if not correct, are you?" For once there was bite in Briers's voice.

"If you mean that I don't break solemn confidences, that is so." Perryman was relaxing into superiority. Briers, quickly, wanted to jangle it.

"The point is, she was in your hands. For day after day. She thought death could be getting nearer. She had no one to rely on but you. Right?"

"It's not the first time that I've been in that situation."

"It must have been strange for you both when you knew that it had been a false alarm. So she needn't rely on you anymore. For release if it came to that."

"You can go on making assumptions, chief superintendent. As I have tried to impress on you, any conversations with my patient were in confidence. And there they will stay. It was obvious that she was in an extreme situation. Then she heard the news. The extreme situation ceased to exist. That is all."

"So she also ceased to rely on you?"

"I didn't have to see her every day. But you might remember, I was still her doctor."

This line, which Briers had followed after the hint from Humphrey, wasn't getting far. He and Shingler had agreed on another. Up to now, Shingler had been quiet, taking notes like a decorous secretary. Suddenly his sharp voice broke in, "You were a whole lot more than that, weren't you?"

Perryman, who had been ignoring him throughout, had to regard him now. Then Perryman, head tilted back, was staring up at the ceiling, as if bored by a subordinate taking too much on himself. "You think so, do you?" Perryman said dismissively.

Perryman might not be taking notice of Shingler, but that didn't apply in reverse. The young man's face, at the same time good looking and vulpine, was concentrated. Glossy brown hair shone under the table lights. So did the big brown eyes shine. The staccato accent, lips not using their muscles, sounded out.

"You were a whole lot more. It isn't every doctor manages his patient's money, is it?"

"Haven't we finished with that business?" Perryman addressed himself to Briers.

Shingler was not deterred.

"You said this was not the first time you had been in such a situation. Have you been in another situation when, if your patient died, you'd be in control of a secret fund? You don't mean to tell us that you didn't think of that. If she died, you would have been in control of the fund. Just as you were when she died by different means." Shingler added, "When you heard she wasn't under threat of death, what did you think then? Did you make another plan? About the fund? How to get hold of it?"

Briers saw that Perryman didn't flush with anger, but his nostrils were both blanched and pinched. He said, voice rising higher pitched, "This is intolerable. Intolerable."

Then, as though going through a drill, he folded his arms on his chest, tautened his neck and shoulders, and slowly said to Briers, "I do not propose to answer questions from this officer of yours."

Briers said, matter of fact, unyielding, "You are here to help, doctor. You aren't obliged to reply, but we shall draw our own conclusions if you don't."

In the same slow and stately manner, head and body quite still, Perryman said, "I shall decide precisely which questions are worth answering."

"Did you think how to get hold of the fund?" Shingler repeated, sharp, unsoftened.

"Not worth answering."

More questions about the fund, after Lady Ashbrook's reprieve. The same slow and routine answer. Briers was realizing, and Shingler not long after, that Perryman had rehearsed himself. He wasn't to lose control if provoked about money. It wasn't only the police who worked out openings in advance. It seemed that Perryman didn't trust his own temper, except with this statuesque self-discipline.

The fund in New York—Shingler was needling him. "Are you aware that we know the whole setup now?"

"Really."

"We know the balance you would have had at your disposal, of course."

"You must be better informed than I am."

"You knew all right, didn't you?"

Arms together on chest. Routine answer.

"You knew how very small it was, didn't you? Pathetically small for all your trouble."

"Not worth comment."

"It does seem extraordinary. A few thousand pounds. So little for a hell of a lot of trouble. Killing the old lady. Wondering when we should catch up. Seems fantastic to us. What about you?"

Perryman was kept rigid by his discipline. He didn't speak. He gave the slightest indication of an indifferent smile.

Against such attacks by Shingler—so Briers was judging—he had prepared himself too well. To change the tactics, Briers tried a line of his own, expecting nothing of it, except to make Perryman less careful. Was it possible—this in a ruminating manner—to forget things one had actually done? Significant things. Did a doctor forget when he had given wrong, maybe mortally wrong, treatment? Perryman didn't think so. He had made fatal mistakes himself, once for sure, possibly twice. He still shut his eyes stock still when he remembered them.

Everyone did that, said Briers, and went on to agree that he didn't believe much in forgetfulness. People didn't forget crimes, though sometimes they pretended to. What was genuine was to do something—write a criminal statement, forge a check, drive in a knife—remember the act with absolute clarity, and yet as though it didn't matter. With innocence, if you like. Hadn't Perryman run across that kind of innocence? Yes, he had. He could still remember when he was very young writing a letter. Someone had treated him badly. The letter was intended to do harm. He could still remember the words on the paper. They still seemed like the words on any other letter.

Could that apply—Briers asked as though it had just occurred to him—to the night of the murder?

Perryman stiffened himself and gave another indifferent smile.

"I've told you what I did that night, haven't I?"

"Have you?" Briers said, as though the matter were of no special interest. But he had gone far enough just then. Perryman was good at preparing himself. Instead, as a distraction, Briers glanced at Shingler, signaling that he was to play on about the money, money motive, all that Perryman had armored himself against. Questions, police facts repeated, insinuations, sneers at petty proceedings, all the resources of a knowing young man. The same responses, rehearsed, routine, frozen dignity, no sign of temper or any emotion. Trays were brought in. Unsurprising cups of tea. Rather more surprising, Cornish pasties instead of sandwiches. As at the first interrogation, Perryman ate methodically; Briers nibbled at half a pasty. Shingler was still asking questions about the money when Briers interposed. "I suggest we drop that for the present, Norman," he said with an affable, offhand grin. "I fancy Dr. Perryman is getting rather tired of it."

Perryman appeared taken by surprise. His routine smile faded away. Briers said to him, across the table, "You are a rather remarkable man, aren't you?"

✌ 42 ✌

Briers had said to Perryman across the table, "You are a rather remarkable man, aren't you?"

But Perryman replied, with magniloquent composure, large eyes gazing past the other man, "Is that for me to say?"

"Come on, you've said it to yourself, haven't you?"

"How many people say such things to themselves?"

"A fair number, as far as I've seen. But not many with as much claim as you have. Of course you're an unusual man." Briers's strong face showed no assertion. He spoke as though in a reflective mood. "Do you know, though, I've wondered about you? Several people have told me you don't seem to have done much. With everything going for you, I would have thought. I've wondered about that myself. You've got brains; no doubt about it. You're impressive. You must have been impressive as a young man. You've got more than your share of courage and nerve—in my job one gets to be a bit of a judge of those qualities. What's happened to it all? Why have you been satisfied to be one more nice safe middle-class doctor?"

"That's a question one need only answer to oneself," Perryman said, again magniloquently.

"Is it, though? Perhaps you haven't been satisfied?"

"You'd better make up your own mind." Perryman said it with good-humored patronage, indulgent, almost friendly.

"No, I guess that you had a sense you were above the rest of us. Poor little things, scrapping and scrabbling to make some sort of life, all messing about in the ruck. You never did feel you were part of the ruck, did you? Commonplace people living commonplace lives. Like your patients. Like those respectable characters round about. Like me."

"You don't strike me so commonplace, if I may say so."

"Oh, I am. I haven't done things thousands wouldn't have done, not many things anyway. I've been faithful to my wife. I've been honest about my debts. I've paid my taxes. I'm part of the ruck, all right; I've behaved like one of the respectable characters. Never mind about that. The curious thing is, doctor, you've behaved very much like the rest of us. Until recently. Of course there were those financial maneuvers. They showed what a good planner you are, but let's forget about that. They didn't test you enough; they didn't pull you right out of the ruck. Otherwise you were no different from anyone else. There were no women that we've been able to trace. Not for want of looking, believe me. You had plenty of opportunity. But so far as we know, and by now we should know, you've lived a blameless life. Maybe you weren't tempted, though. But I'm sure you were tempted to break out somewhere. You've always wanted to show you're not like ordinary men. You haven't much use for the ordinary human rules, have you?"

"What are the ordinary human rules?"

"If you don't know them, that would be interesting. But of course you do. The real point, for a man like you, is what makes people keep them."

"I think I know that. Do you? You may as well tell me."

Briers replied, "Some sort of good feeling or good instinct, I should like to say. But I'm not so certain of that as I used to be when I was a starry-eyed young policeman. I'm afraid the crude answer is sanctions. We're losing those. We've lost religious sanctions, most of us. That really meant fear of judgment and the afterlife, didn't it? You're not a believer, are you? Yes, we've explored that too. Not many of us fear judgment now. But there are other kinds of fear. Fear of what other people think. In the long run, though, it's mostly fear of the law. Without the law, there wouldn't be much left in the way of moral rules. I wish I believed something else, but nowadays I can't. The trouble is, doctor, you're an astonishingly fearless man."

"That's an unexpected testimonial, isn't it?"

"Do you accept it?"

"I've told you before, you have a powerful imagination. Too powerful for your job, I'm inclined to think. But I do accept that it's fear that makes most people conform. If there weren't fear, how would everyone behave?"

"Horribly." Then, steadily, Briers corrected himself. "No, not everyone, of course not. But enough to make the world a shambles."

"You'd rather they conformed like good tame beasts?"

"Of course."

Perryman broke into a smile, as though they were intimate. "I thought we had something in common. But I rather think that I have more hopes for human beings than you have."

"Are you in a strong moral position to say that?"

"You've spent quite a long time suggesting that I'm not in any moral position at all."

"I shall become more practical very soon."

Whether he had reached close enough Briers couldn't tell, but he couldn't delay his hidden card much longer.

However, he didn't back away at once from their codelike exchange.

"Tell me," Briers was saying, "do you put much value on human life? As the rest of us do?"

"I'm a doctor."

"You are also not an ordinary man. We've agreed on that, haven't we? Do you feel above the way ordinary people regard life and death, or do you think that's a piece of nonsense?"

For a time Perryman's answer didn't come so smoothly. Then he said, "I'm a doctor. Doctors live very near to death."

"Not as near as we do. In the Murder Squad. When you're on a job, you see live bodies. When we're on the job, we only see them dead. Like old Lady Ashbrook. That's why we're here." That was one of Briers's spasms in which force and authority showed through. Then he relapsed into the manner he had used right through that interrogation. More than casual, not judging, not kind, but understanding.

"You know as well as we do," he said. "You saw that dead body before we did. I should like to be certain why you killed her. Did you really want to do something no one else could do? Not many will believe that, you know. Too fancy. But that's not what I want to clear up. I want to find out—from you—some facts about that night. I ought to tell you, we have worked some of them out for ourselves."

Perryman's face turned youthful, as it had just once before. Lines were wiped away, as with sculptured faces at startling news, good or bad. To Perryman, this move of Briers, quiet, so long delayed, seemed to be entirely unexpected. He made a kind of reply, half inaudible, something like how interesting, as though he had been hearing some remarks at a party on which he hadn't thought it necessary to concentrate.

His gaze, not staring into the distance now, became fixed on Briers. He must be collecting himself, the policemen both thought, wondering if this was a bluff or how much they knew.

"Yes," Briers said, like one continuing a conversation, "we do know now how you spent that night. That had us guessing, I don't mind telling you. For much too long. There ought to have been sightings all through the early evening, if that was when you called in at the house. There were plenty of people about, and you're a very noticeable figure. Then afterwards, later that night, Susan Thirkill, Loseby's wife as she now is—"

"That girl's a whore." That was a flash of protest, of moral indignation, curiously spontaneous.

Briers blinked, twisted his lips, went on, "Well, she was prowling in the mews around the house, on the watch for someone else, for hours."

"What did she tell you?"

"It was very interesting. She knows you very well, of course."

"Whatever she told you, she made it up. What did she say?"

"She didn't see a glimpse of you. She didn't see the slightest sign of you anywhere."

Perryman's face was impassive, but he inhaled, as though he had been having trouble with his breathing.

"I must say, chief superintendent," he said with his shadow of a smile, "this isn't the most sensational bit of reporting anyone's ever made."

"It helped us decide where you were that night."

"I told you."

"Certainly you've told us. But the truth is rather different, isn't it?"

"I shan't go on repeating myself."

"You needn't. You were in Lady Ashbrook's house. You were there from the middle of the afternoon till the small hours. You killed her round about nine, not later than half-past, and then stayed for a longish time afterwards. Several hours. Not many men could have done that. We think, without being quite certain, that you spent nearly all that time, after you had killed her, sitting quietly upstairs in her bedroom."

"I was in her bedroom in the morning. Examining her. The usual routine examination."

"Yes. You've told us. You'd thought of most things. You're a perfectionist—you always have been, so we're told. You did know that it's very difficult to pass any time in a room without leaving some sort of trace behind. Yes, you left a bit of fluff from your tweed suit in the morning—all explicable, all in order with your own account. But you went back to that room again that night, after you had killed her, and presumably settled down. If you left traces then, it didn't matter. They could be put down to the morning. You settled down nice and peacefully, didn't you? You must have known that not many men would have been capable of that."

It was here, for the first time, that Briers was overstating his case. They had no discernible evidence that could have distinguished the morning traces from any in the evening. In fact, the bit of tweed fluff was all they had picked up. There had been exhaustive studies by Owen Morgan, but nothing more had come. Briers was letting Perryman think that they had another find.

Perryman didn't protest or deny. He didn't speak at all. In the past few minutes, he had been sitting slackly, half slumped. He was looking, not at Briers, but at the table, and anyone entering the room, not aware of what had been happening, might have thought that he appeared, not distressed, but something like amused and confidential. That was the moment, Briers said later, when he was sure that Perryman had resigned. Perhaps with the kind of surrender that Briers had seen often enough in other suspects, but this time there was another aura too, as though the man hadn't been beaten down but persuaded, even wooed, arrogance untouched, perhaps enhanced.

Shingler afterward gave a different account from Briers's. He hadn't Briers's candor. He said that, on the spot, he didn't believe that this was the breaking point. He did admit that he had been certain that something decisive would happen soon.

Briers went on. "There's just one other matter. I've not been able to make up my mind. Perhaps you can't either. After you had killed her, and that wasn't much trouble naturally, you went upstairs for a good long stay. Very bright. You must have worked out that we should wear ourselves into the ground trying to pick up sightings just after the murder. You were quite right. That is exactly what we did. We must have located every human being who was in the locality between nine P.M. and midnight. Meanwhile, you were sitting in her bedroom. But before you went up there, after she was quite dead, but very soon after, you smashed her skull in. I've asked you before. Why?"

Perryman's body was still slack, mouth still half smiling.

"I suppose," said Briers, "you might have thought it would lead us up the garden path. Looking for villains or any sort of scum. I told you, in that case you underestimated us. We had to go through the motions because anything can happen in this business, but it didn't take us in for half an hour. But I've never been convinced that was really why you had to belt in her head. I think you lost your own. I think you were just the same as all those others. You're not as unique as you'd like to be. You might have reckoned on that, doctor. Of course you recovered yourself very quickly. Then you left the body and you went upstairs." Briers went on. "You'd been very lucky. I expect you know that. Blood. Whether you had made preparations—we haven't found anything on your clothes yet. We don't know whether you changed or where. We don't know exactly how long you stayed upstairs. Our guess is that you left when it was still dark, but not long before dawn. Perhaps about four o'clock at that time of year. It must have been a nice fresh morning."

Briers looked across the table and said, "You're ready to talk to me, aren't you?"

There was a time of silence. How long it lasted none of them could have told. Perryman was stirring, straightening his back, sit-

306

ting upright in his chair, neck like a pillar. Very slowly he once again folded his arms over his chest.

"Oh yes, chief superintendent, I'm ready to talk to you."

Shingler smoothed out his notebook, though this couldn't be a formal statement.

"Yes"—Perryman was speaking with a curious expansiveness—"I fancy this will be the last time I'm ready to speak to you in these particular circumstances. We've come to the end of the road, haven't we? You can't accuse me of not letting you take your time. I've listened carefully to your various profiles of my character. Interesting, sometimes quite flattering, if one accepted your view of my moral position. I have also followed your reconstructions of certain actions of mine. I'm going to take a leaf out of your book, chief superintendent, and tell you that you are an unusual man. But we have to settle our bit of business, don't we? And I'm bound to tell you that I'm getting distinctly tired of it. It's high time we wound it up. In my profession I sometimes tell an intelligent patient that I'll treat him like a specimen on the table being examined by the two of us. I've been doing a certain amount of thinking about this case of yours, if you can call it a case. I am completely disregarding whether there is any justification for any of your reconstructions. For any serious purposes of yours, they really aren't any more relevant than your thoughts about good and evil. I can't take these thoughts of yours all that seriously. And I can't take your case seriously. According to my calculations, if we put the case on the table and look at it like that, there's really singularly little left."

Briers had realized almost before Perryman began to talk that this was going to be an exhibition of control. Even so, he was astonished. Perryman had been shaken at the early interrogation—more than shaken, assaulted—by questions about his money motive. That had made him look as though he were crumbling. But he had come up that morning, front as impenetrable as ever. He had a kind of inner resource. Briers now accepted it, which not only gave him assurance against enemies but to himself. When Briers had told Perryman where he had been on the murder night, once more he had seemed to be giving up—not so outraged as about the money, but with less fight. And yet, within minutes, perhaps a quarter of an hour, he had recovered himself again.

"There's no need for excessive palaver, you'll agree as a reasonable person," Perryman said, immobile, lofty, and in a tone both unresentful and contemptuous. "Just consider your case like a body on the table. You should forget about me and your efforts at psychological creation. You have to keep things straightforward. I'm surprised that I have to tell you that. Just look at your case with clear eyes—you haven't much there. Yes, I was connected with Lady Ashbrook. That's been open since the beginning. Yes, I did some business for her. Yes, some of the business evaded some minor tax regulations. What does that signify? Yes, I was something like an executor after her death. Yes, I was in a position to make a little money. As this young man of yours took it on himself to point out, a very little money. And that's all you have in straightforward fact."

Shingler had flushed at the sneer in his direction, uttered as though he weren't present or were a waiter at a dinner party.

"The chief superintendent has told you, we know about your movements that night—"

"Yes, he's told me. He has a powerful imagination. He's also interested in facts. I congratulate him on both qualities. It happens that I'm interested in facts myself. I've been thinking quite carefully about his history of my movements that night. It was an impressive exercise."

"Well then?" Shingler was both mystified and angry.

Briers sat still, face set, eyes luminous.

"Impressive but useless." Perryman loosened an arm and made a gesture, sweeping, wide, and grand. "It might have taken in some innocent creatures. In fact, you have nothing. Nothing solid. You know it. I know it. So that there is no point in going on with this dialogue, chief superintendent. If you'll forgive me, I had better begin to get back to my patients."

Laboriously he was getting to his feet, clutching the edge of the table as he stood up.

"Oh, two minor things," he said. "I consider that I've helped you as much as I reasonably can. As I said this morning, I don't feel like affording any more time for this kind of performance. If you are calling on me again, I shall need to bring in professional advice. I haven't the time or the leisure. I'm sure you understand."

Briers gave no indication.

"Oh, the second thing, chief superintendent. I'm suffering from a touch of fibrositis. It makes walking distinctly painful. Have you ever had it? I'd be obliged if you could lay on transport."

Without a word, Briers glanced at Shingler, who accompanied Perryman out of the room.

When Shingler returned, Briers was sitting as though no muscle had moved.

"You had to let him go, of course." That was Shingler's remark.

"Of course." Briers's tone was firm and normal.

"Well, sir?"

"It's a failure." Briers spoke in the same unmodulated tone. "It's my failure, no one else's. I'm sorry I've let everyone down."

❦ 43 ❦

No one outside the background squad knew precisely what had happened to Perryman. One official statement had been issued to the press: Dr. Ralph Perryman, Lady Ashbrook's medical attendant, had spent some time helping the police with their inquiries and had now returned to his professional duties. Most people, even those who had been questioned themselves, found those items baffling. It looked as though there had been one of the police gaffes. Among Perryman's patients, there was talk of making a protest to the commissioner of the metropolitan police.

As Humphrey read those words in the newspaper, he made more sense of them. Something had gone wrong; that was glaring enough. It was a pity for Frank Briers, Humphrey had a passing thought, but he must have kept his judgment cool. If he hadn't been able to break the man down, there would have been no choice but to let him go. Humphrey felt disappointment and a nagging regret. The man was getting away. It was wrong, it was taunting, it left one with the excitement still lingering, no sort of consummation after which one could sit back. There was no rightness, none of the bliss of justice being achieved and paid for. Humphrey didn't cover up his own feelings. Nor did Kate. She had her own biblical sense of justice, but also she felt, like Humphrey at the news of Lady Ashbrook's reprieve, a kind of visceral relief.

Now Humphrey could understand another thing. He had been told the date of the last interrogation. He had expected a call from Briers. It hadn't come. The days passed, and Humphrey had heard nothing nor caught a glimpse of Briers. It was as though he had gone into hiding. Humphrey knew. He had behaved like that himself. One went on in the mode of duty, soldiered on with the job, official, competent. But one wished to avoid the notice of those who knew one was in trouble, particularly those who knew one best.

A week after those first press statements, there was one more. This merely said that papers relating to the late Lady Ashbrook's estate had been sent to the director of public prosecutions and the Inland Revenue.

As soon as Kate came into Humphrey's drawing room that evening, blinking after the opaque dark outside, he showed her the newsprint.

"Well," he said, "this business began in money. It looks as though it's finishing in money." He added, "It looks as though Frank is trying to rescue something from the wreck."

He had kept nothing from her. She was less forgiving about financial fiddling than about most sins. Now she grimaced. "It really is pretty cheap, isn't it?"

And yet, even with her, tenacious and loyal, memory was proving short. She felt guilty about it, but it sometimes seemed that Lady Ashbrook had been killed years in the past. Others had told her that they felt the same. That was what she had confessed to Alec Luria one night when he was back in London for an end-of-the-year vacation.

"You mustn't grumble. You look very well on it," Luria said in what—Humphrey had heard it before now—was his preliminary manner with an attractive woman: paternal, severe, but not calculated to deceive the person addressed. Kate gave a surreptitious eyeflash in Humphrey's direction. But then Alec Luria had another thought.

"You've all forgotten what you were like in the summer."

"What have we forgotten?"

"I don't mean you so much. I don't mean poor old Lady Ashbrook. But morale was very low, lower than I have ever known it here. Most people I've talked to thought you might all be sunk. Money worth nothing. The whole show going bankrupt, though no one seemed to have much idea what that might mean."

Did many people really get anxious about public affairs, affairs outside themselves, for more than a few minutes a day? Humphrey was wondering. Even in a war. Of course, Alec Luria moved among the prosperous, who might have thought they wouldn't be prosperous much longer. Yes, there had been anxious faces.

Luria was continuing. Whitehall acquaintances of his had admitted that they went through sleepless nights. "And the weather didn't help," said Luria. "You shouldn't have weather like that in London. Hot nights. Brilliant days. About as surprising over here as when the sun first broke through the primeval fog. And everyone was worried to death." Luria regarded them both. "Now you're having awful weather. Even by your standards. The darkest winter days I've ever seen. And everyone is pretty cheerful. You ought to be safe from disaster for two or three years. And two or three years is a long time in this world of ours."

Luria, with cheerful solemnity, gave a gloomy prognosis about the West in general and his own country in particular. Then he proceeded onto a less magisterial plane—gossip.

He had been in London three days. He told them the latest news of people they knew well. As usual, nearly all that he told them was later shown to be accurate. Oh yes, Tom Thirkill would get his payoff; he would be in the Cabinet in the new year. He had made his terms. Special responsibility, independent of the treasury. He had had to give something in return. That nice woman of his—

"Stella," said Kate.

"That's her. She has to get out of her political job."

"For Christ's sake," Kate broke out, "she's made him. She's sacrificed all those years for him."

"Dear Kate," Luria said, "you know what politics is like."

"I don't want any part of it, ever. I bet that skunk didn't think twice."

The story was, according to Luria, that this was a concession to the backbenchers of Thirkill's own party. They didn't mind so much about the two living together: what they hated most was a woman's having so much influence.

"So the bastard didn't protect her." Kate was violent. "Perhaps it will open her eyes. No, it won't. She'll find an excuse for him. She'll go on being used."

Neither of the men—for Alec Luria knew some of the history of Kate's marriage—felt that it was appropriate to comment. In his three days in London, Luria had not only been dining out but had been taken to bars in both the Commons and the Lords. It was just before the December recess. In the latter place, he had met Loseby sitting with some friends. Loseby would soon be there in his own right, Luria had heard. His father was in an alcoholic coma. Luria had also heard Loseby might be facing charges for tax offenses.

Humphrey shook his head. "No," he said. The Revenue might mulct him with largish fines; that was the worst he could expect. If so, those fines would be paid quickly by his father-in-law. No publicity about Loseby's finances. Thirkill would have to see to that. Someone had said that was why Loseby had married the girl—that was in the Lords' guest room, Luria remarked. He gave his honking laugh but for once not at his own expense. He said, "In any case my heart isn't going to bleed for that young man. He'll have come through without a scratch. He was saying as much to his friends. Decent intelligent characters, by the way. Loseby was telling them that he was in a spot of bother. That's what he called it. But somehow he always managed to get out of spots of bother. Or someone got him out."

Kate said, "I can't stand him. I never could. He's too indestructible to be true. How was he taking it?"

"Just as much the Shining One as ever, as far as I could see. He went in for some mild self-analysis. He said that from what he could remember, he hadn't been perfectly honest at fifteen. And if you hadn't been perfectly honest at fifteen, it wasn't reasonable to think that you would be any more honest at thirty. Which he seemed to think settled the matter."

After that evening in his house, Humphrey didn't see Alec Luria again until Christmas Day. Then they went out for dinner, both loose in the great closed town as though they had been young students. It happened that Kate, apologetic, near to the tears she didn't often show, angry with fatality and with herself and Humphrey, had announced a day or two before that she couldn't come to him on Christmas Day. It was the treat of the year for her husband. She had tried to suggest that he go to friends, but he had looked like a child crying. On the day itself, Humphrey was left with nothing to do and nowhere to go. Then Luria telephoned. The bass voice inquired—by any miracle had Humphrey an hour or so free? When he heard of Humphrey's state, he offered dinner at the best Chinese restaurant in town. Chinese restaurants were suitable for Christmas, he said. If you'd been born in my family, said Luria, you wouldn't have affectionate memories of the Christian festivals.

So the two of them, like eccentric and lonely bachelors, settled down to a prolonged Chinese meal. Whether Luria was lonely or not, and whatever his memories of childhood persecutions, he was in a state of well-being as pervasive as in Humphrey's house a couple of weeks before. He had brought along a magnum of one of Humphrey's favorite clarets. He was happy, and he needed Humphrey to be happy too. Clearly something was happening in his life. It must be the prospect of another marriage, but he was cherishing the secret to himself. He might be determined to keep a secret, but he couldn't resist letting out indications. From those, it wasn't hard for Humphrey to guess that Luria, having been turned down by Celia, had then found a girl much younger than himself, in the English upper class. Not with money: Luria had had more than enough of that. Probably with antique English connections. Possibly from one of the grand houses. The heritage might sound like a stuffed exhibit in a museum, but for Alec Luria it was old, it was a world he had once dreamed of. Further, thought Humphrey, the girl might be someone Luria could love. Humphrey was fond of his friend, but a sardonic voice was telling him that Luria was not hard to please in the way of love, other requirements being met.

"I'm glad I thought of this," Luria said, manipulating chopsticks with long, dextrous fingers. "One doesn't have people to talk to at our age." That seemed a bizarre remark from someone who spent so much of his time pontificating in two continents, but he was speaking with a kind of timid intimacy. A little later he said, as though at random, "I used to detest Christmas. But it wasn't the worst. Good Friday was the worst. When you were young, you never had people in the next block who hounded you for no reason you could understand—"

Humphrey said no.

Luria was eating vigorously, happy and benign. He said, "Christianity looks different, my boy, when you see it from that angle."

Suddenly Luria switched away from Semitic experience and said, "Things are going well with Kate? I needn't ask. I could see the other night."

314

"Wonderfully well."

Just for that moment, Humphrey had dropped his irony. In return, Luria dropped his pundithood. Acquaintances would have been astonished to find them talking, and even looking, like young men.

"I remember I tried, with the very best intentions, to warn you off. I'd never thought she'd be able to cut away from that phony." Alec Luria broke into the extraordinary mirth reserved for the times when he had made a mistake. "I was a hundred percent wrong."

"Not a hundred percent." Humphrey gave a simple confessional smile. "She still looks after him, you know. Otherwise I shouldn't be here with you tonight."

"Never mind. Count your blessings. You're very lucky."

"Don't you think I know it?"

Casually Luria said, "I didn't get anywhere with Celia, as you probably guessed. I thought I might have been right for her. I fancy she thought so too for a little while. Then she sheered off. Probably it's just as well for both of us. She seems to have found what she really wants. I've nothing to complain about myself."

For an instant it seemed that he was ready to confide, then smiled—shamefaced? guilty? triumphant?—and went back to talking of Celia. "Yes, she's found a schoolteacher. They're going to live a commonplace life, she told me. Not even trying to do good in community relations or anything like that. No, they're going to live in Woking. That's as petit bourgeois as they come, isn't it?"

Humphrey grinned. "Well, it wouldn't do for you."

"It's very odd. She has everything. She's beautiful. Clever. Sweet. Strong character. Born and bred in the establishment, if that means anything. But all she wants is not to draw attention to herself. Just to look after her little boy and perhaps have another one. And do her best for the people around her. It's all very kind and humble—but when characters like that just give up any kind of struggle, then I have an awful feeling that it's a bad lookout for the world she comes from. It does seem like a sign that they will lose out too."

"I'm very fond of Celia, though," Humphrey said. "If that's what she wants for herself, she'd better have it."

"She's a good girl," said Luria gravely, like an old-fashioned hostess receiving congratulations on her daughter's looks. "She did say something that might interest you." Luria switched off again, his conversation losing its structure either because he was jubilant or because he had drunk more than usual, or maybe both. Soon he was saying, "The police have decided that that doctor got rid of the old lady, haven't they? That seems to be common knowledge. They can't tie it up, but they know. You're close to that bright detective. Do you agree?"

"Entirely."

"Celia doesn't."

"She can't possibly know the score."

"Nor does Paul. I had a drink with him in Washington. He and Celia have a theory of their own. They think it was a couple—"

"What couple?"

"Susan and her father. Susan doing the job and Tom Thirkill cleaning up afterward."

Humphrey asked a question. Yes, Paul did volunteer that he had changed his mind.

He recalled the timetable of Tom Thirkill's movements that night. For an instant, Humphrey was seeing the kaleidoscope of suspicion. Yes, there would have just been time for him to make the killing look like a burglar's, lam out with the hammer, a simple kind of clearing up. Then Humphrey's mind cleared.

"There's nothing in that," he said. "I'm surprised at Paul, but intelligent people can believe anything."

"That's exactly what I thought." Luria gave a mischievous, lurching grin incongruous among those marmoreal features. "I even told Celia so. Probably the last masculine words I shall impress upon that lovely young woman."

They relaxed into their long and restful evening. That report about Celia had brought back the gnaw of frustration. Humphrey hadn't been a principal in the case, but in anticipation he felt aggrieved. Afterward, by himself, he felt that niggle of disquiet growing. Those thoughts of Celia's wouldn't quite leave him. The murder would join those that outsiders thought mysterious and on which they speculated with pleasure. They would believe that they were cleverer than the persons actually involved. It would be a nice topic for the ingenious to play with. All he had witnessed would become a piece of unfinished business.

❧ 44 ❧

Humphrey had no intention of passing those Christmas Day vexations on to Frank Briers. Briers would expect them. He would know, as well as any man, that plenty of persons, acquaintances and strangers, would bask in thoughts of agreeable superiority. They would be certain that they could see the truth that he had missed. There was no point in adding to displeasing realizations. Humphrey still had no contact with Briers. The days passed, and it was getting on for six weeks since they had met.

In the middle of January, Briers called on the telephone. His voice was firm as usual, more resonant than it sounded face-to-face, not overcordial.

"I want to raise a small matter with you It won't take long."

"Any time you like."

"Tomorrow morning. I'll come around. It's nothing to do with the Ashbrook thing, of course."

Briers arrived early, just after half-past nine. Though he looked smart, hair freshly cut, face freshly shaved, he didn't look bright. There was, from the first moment, another constraint between them. Humphrey didn't need any searching to recognize it for what it was. He had seen it often enough in the official life. It was the constraint of allies in defeat. Defeat could bite into alliances, or into friendships, as deeply as enmity could. He would have liked to cheer Briers up; he was as constrained himself.

"Do you mind walking up to the house?" Briers said in his briskest tone.

317

Humphrey was blank, then caught the reference. The house was Lady Ashbrook's house.

"You'll need your overcoat," said Briers, as though hygienic comfort was the only concern. "It's a bit raw outside."

They walked up the Square. On the wind, there was a faint, sharp winter smell from the garden. Neither of them had spoken till Humphrey asked, "How is Betty now?"

"Like last time. It's gaining on her."

Humphrey cursed and said, "How long do these phases go on?"

"No one knows. She can't move as well as when you saw her." Briers added, "She's very good."

"More than that."

Briers said, "She sends you her love. She knew I was going to see you today."

Humphrey had a sense that it was she who had made Frank do it.

Humphrey returned the greeting, sending his love back. Then they were quiet until they were outside the house.

"You don't mind coming in?" Frank said. "We can talk here as well as anywhere."

Humphrey saw a young man in a mackintosh standing on the pavement. Briers, watchful, detected the glance.

"Yes, he's one of my lads," he said. "I'm taking him off that job this week. The executors want to sell the place. We've no call to hang on. There's nothing to get out of it now."

Briers brought out a key ring and turned two locks. These had been installed the day after the murder. Humphrey remembered when Briers told him that Perryman had had his own key. That must have been a convenience, Briers had said.

"You'd better keep your coat on," Briers said as they went into the hall, showing the preoccupation with Humphrey's physical state that seemed like a substitute for good nature. "It'll strike cold in here."

It did strike cold, and damp. It also smelled musty. Flakes of paint were coming off the walls, and there were patches at the end of the hall that looked as though they would be moist to the touch. They went upstairs, and Briers with another key opened the door of Lady Ashbrook's drawing room.

The last time Humphrey had been in the room, which he had

once known so well, was the morning when he was taken to see the body. Briers had kept each piece of furniture as it was that day. The only difference: the body was no longer propped up against her habitual chair and the carpet beneath had been taken away. The pieces of debris, pottery, bric-a-brac, lay scattered. All had been photographed and rephotographed, but still the scene had been preserved intact. The pear drops of blood on the wall had gone black by now and to one who didn't know the history might have been taken for an eccentric piece of mural decoration.

Standing in the room, Humphrey didn't feel himself moved. That didn't come to order. This was bleak, untidy, a bit of desolation, no more. But there was one attack on the senses. In the past, there had always been the scent of potpourri bowls, which had been a pleasure to Lady Ashbrook. Now that had gone without trace. Instead there was a smell that irked the nose and the back of the throat—the smell of dust. The room was filled with dust.

Briers drew attention to it. He went over to the windows that overlooked the Square, and on one pane he drew lines with a fingertip. "It collects before you can look round."

Then, in a tone brisk and at the same time awkward, he said, "I have a proposition to make. We may as well sit down." He added, "It doesn't matter about disturbing things. I've finished with this room."

He brought two high-backed chairs close to the far window, and dusted each seat carefully with his handkerchief. When Humphrey was settled, Briers said, "I have been told to get ready for a move. Round about the summer."

At the first impact, that sounded as though he had had bad news. Humphrey was disconcerted, angry, and showed it. Frank, quick as ever, smiled as he hadn't done that morning.

"No, it's a move up. They want me to take over the antiterrorism game."

So it was a promotion. Perhaps the Yard bosses were looking after him, Humphrey thought, not allowing a highly charged man to stay discouraged. Or perhaps it had been planned before the cul-de-sac with Perryman, and they were just using a flier where he was needed. It meant a step up the hierarchy. That had its disadvantages, Briers said: he would be behind a desk most of his time; he wouldn't be so near to the real operations. But still, he had been prepared for that—it was going to be a rough assignment; any disaster would be right in the public eye. "I'd guess," Briers said, "that there will be a hell of a lot more terrorism in the next few years."

"My guess too."

"It's altogether too easy. The odds are all in their favor. We have the wrong end of the stick."

They were both thinking of modern weapons.

"I was wondering"—Briers spoke with awkwardness again, with something like assertion—"whether you'd come in and lend a hand. You'd have your uses."

"Too old."

"You're too young. Too young to fritter your time away. I know we didn't make much of a fist of it last time. But you'd have your uses in the new job. You've been around. You're not altogether a fool about people. I'd feel better if you were somewhere on call."

Humphrey knew what the other man was doing. Humphrey had been prepared to try to hearten him. It was Briers who was doing the heartening. This was an act of friendship. But it wasn't spontaneous; it was the friendship of the will. Briers still felt the resentment of an alliance gone wrong: you blamed your collaborator for your mistakes as well as his, or even for bad luck. You wanted him out of your sight. It took a strong nature to act as though those feelings didn't exist. Just as—Humphrey had a flickering reminder of young Shingler—it took a strong nature to forgive a benefactor. Humphrey was touched: not so much by a return of affection, for he too had his pride, though not so prickly as Frank's, but by respect. They mightn't be easy together for some time to come—but not many, beset as Frank was, would have forced themselves to act like this.

Humphrey said, "It's very thoughtful of you. I'm extremely grateful." Humphrey had his own kind of spontaneity, and he let it show. With a lurking grin, he went on. "It must be about twenty years since I was offered a job."

"Will you do it?"

"I think I'd like to." Humphrey went on, "But could you possibly work it with your people?"

"Simple. There are a couple of nonpolicemen already. Called consultants. Fair game for the terror squads, like the rest of us. We

320

try to keep their identities secret, but that won't last long. You're all reasonably likely to have bombs going off when you don't expect them."

It was some time since Humphrey had heard one of Briers's black-edged jokes. "As a matter of fact," Briers said, "I've mentioned your name already. Great enthusiasm. Of course, your previous experience wasn't exactly a hindrance."

"You took it for granted that I'd say yes?" Humphrey had dropped back into the former matey terms.

"I took it for granted that Kate would make you. She'd be more useful on this team than any of us."

There was a pause, and they gazed out across the derelict room, preserved as though it were a relic in a museum. Briers said, "Well, that was what we came for."

But he didn't move. There was another pause, one that became tense. He said, "I used to think it would be fun to have my own command. And have it young. But I don't mind telling you, if I'd have had the chance of getting that man Perryman clean and cold, but no new command, I wouldn't have hesitated for a single blasted instant. My God, I can't get it out of my mind. The first thing a detective has to learn is to cut his losses. This shows I'm not fit to be a detective."

"Nonsense. It shows why you're first-rate. Of course you have your obsessions. It's only the obsessive who do the first-rate things." Humphrey was speaking as when they first met, when Frank was taking advice from a man twenty years older. "You'll have to forget all this——" He made a gesture toward where Lady Ashbrook used to sit.

"That's easier said than done." Briers had now broken out with passion, sounding as though he had gravel in his mouth. "I tell you, it's maddening. I know it all. I know it all except how to nail the man. I know how he did it. I know why he did it. Or part of that—no one is ever going to be sure. But it's all no use. I've come into this room time and time again. I've been hoping something would hit me that we've missed. Now I don't believe there is anything. Owen Morgan keeps telling me that just for once we ran across a man who didn't make mistakes. We'll never get him unless we have a streak of luck right out of the blue. They may make him pay for that finagling over the money. But that's bloody poor comfort. The only thing we've had to wait for is a stroke of luck. And the luck has all gone to the wrong people."

His voice, still gritty, went quieter. "He had all the luck in the world. He thinks he worked out everything. But there were three points, at least three, where the odds ought to have been against him. They all went his way."

Another pause. Briers said, "Tell me. I ought to have had him. What did I do wrong?"

"I've thought about it. Naturally I have. With hindsight. But I still haven't had an idea. You hadn't enough to play with. Your team couldn't find much for you. It looks as though there wasn't much to find."

"Ought I to have waited longer before I showed our hand?"

"You wouldn't have picked up any more, would you?"

"Did I handle those question sessions wrong?"

"I shouldn't have thought so."

"Would you have been cleverer than I was?" Briers didn't say that as a challenge but asking for the truth.

"Not cleverer. I might have done it a bit differently."

"Tell me what you'd have done."

Humphrey said firmly, protectively, "Look, Frank, it's no good harking back. It's over and done with, and you'll have to forget it."

It was in a curiously boyish fashion that Briers nodded, stiff-necked, like a Teutonic student.

"Of course I have to. Of course. The trouble is, I can't help thinking that something else will turn up. I can't help thinking that it might come by a telephone call or any means of communication open to man. It might be in the morning post. It interferes with anything I have to do during the day. It's insane, but there are times when it's poisoning my life. I'm putting a stop to it. I'm putting it out of mind. The file is still open, but that's all that's left."

They were sitting in their stiff-backed chairs, heads high, as though they were guests on the fringe of one of Lady Ashbrook's tea parties.

"You'll get going on another case, of course."

"I'm on one now. That's all right. Tied up. But it is maddening, you understand. I know all about Perryman. I know he's guilty. I know he's as cold-hearted a brute as it's given to a man to be. But I can't do anything. Do you wonder that policemen have been known to invent convenient pieces of evidence? To fix a man like that, who if there's any justice under heaven deserves to be fixed."

"Have you ever done that?" Humphrey asked the simple question in a matter-of-fact tone.

In the same tone Briers replied, "Yes. Once." He went on. "It was a squalid case. A woman had killed her stepson. She'd covered up. We couldn't prove it. Yes, I invented a bit of evidence. She was put down all right."

"Would you do it now?"

Briers considered. He said, "No. I don't think so. I'm not so certain of where I stand as I was a dozen years ago. Now I don't feel I'm so qualified to put everything in order. But don't get me wrong. I don't feel an atom of guilt for what I did then, and I shouldn't if I'd done the same about Perryman."

Briers was expressing his resolution once more. "I keep telling you I've finished with anything to do with Perryman and the Ashbrook case. The lawyers may as well have the house. I told you that, didn't I? It's going to cost something to make it habitable, isn't it? They're welcome to it. They can have it. And they want to have the body. We've had it a long time. They may as well have it now. The old lady gave instructions that she was to be cremated, but of course that's not on. They can have the body to bury if they want."

At last Frank Briers was getting to his feet.

"Ready?" he said. He looked around him, at the wall, at the floor. "Well," he said, "you've heard of criminals returning to the scene of the crime, though to be honest I've never known one who did. Anyway, this has been a detective returning to the scene of the crime. No one has ever told us anything about that. But this detective has been doing it too much, and he isn't going to do it any more."

He went out of the room in front of Humphrey and locked the doors behind them. "There," he said.

It felt warmer, out in the Square in the January morning, than inside the house. Briers, active, competent, not so intimate as he had been for the last half hour, said that Humphrey would receive a formal letter about the new job. Humphrey asked if Betty would

323

like him to call on her again. Briers said, "As long as you give her notice. She needs someone to get the house tidy. She can't do it herself."

It was businesslike, more so than business usually was, Humphrey thought. In the same spirit, Briers refused, civilly enough, to return to Humphrey's house. With his quick athlete's step he was moving off toward his car, behaving like someone with a train to catch or, more exactly, like someone who was leaving a woman for the last time, determined to be free.

❧ 45 ❧

It was a quiet funeral. None of Lady Ashbrook's occasions while she was alive had been as quiet as this. No singing, no organ, the barest of Protestant services. That was an attempt to pay tribute to her memory. She had attended this church because it was suitably evangelical, and there the funeral was taking place.

There were eight acquaintances in the congregation, no more. There were Loseby and Susan, Celia Hawthorne, Humphrey. Her lawyer was there, and a very old woman in an elegant mourning dress, a dowager contemporary of Lady Ashbrook's. There were also Kate and her husband. He had made a fuss about coming, Kate had told Humphrey, having to apologize again. Humphrey thought it not inappropriate. Lady Ashbrook in her time must similarly have preserved the forms at other funerals.

The news of the funeral had been quieter than the service itself. There were circumstances that all of them knew, except perhaps the dowager, and some found it fretting to the nerves. It was true, as Frank Briers had told Humphrey, that the old lady had left orders to be cremated. She had also ordered that her ashes should be disposed of by the vicar of this church. But it was also true, as Briers remarked, that that was forbidden. It was forbidden because of thoughtful forensic rules. If ever someone was charged with a murder, he had a right to his own pathologist's examination. So the body was not to be disposed of.

Thus the body of Lady Ashbrook, once desired by a good many men, which had been dissected, reassembled, kept in the refrigerator, now lying in a coffin in the nave, had the chance of going through the same processes again.

Kate, who lived on such good terms with the flesh, had been saddened at the prospect. It was remote, Humphrey told her. There wouldn't be a charge. But that didn't soothe her. In her own hospital she had been invited to watch a postmortem, but it was something she couldn't take.

It was Susan, who lived on wilder terms with the flesh, who had gone out of her way to watch postmortems and reassemblies. At the latter, she decided, with a not too pure satisfaction, that the pathologist's technicians were suitably accomplished: particularly with the bodies of orthodox Jews, where the requirements were at their most rigorous.

The great words of the service were being spoken, not loudly, but in a clear voice. To everyone there, they were familiar. Celia had heard them many times in her father's churches, so many that she didn't hear them now.

"I am the Resurrection and the Life. . . ." "Sown in corruption, raised in incorruption."

Humphrey was taken back to some of Alec Luria's observations. Jesus was a good rabbi. But Paul was the founder of Christianity, Luria liked to say. Resurrection was a wonderful slogan. Yes, it was a wonderful slogan. People had believed in it, in the simplest, most concrete terms. It was the answer to the human tragedy. It was the ultimate consolation of this mortal life. How many people believed it now?

The service was soon over. They went out of the church into the sunshine, chilly but tranquil. The bearers lifted the coffin into the hearse; the undertaker assembled the flowers. There were half a dozen wreaths, the rest of them outshown by a sumptuous gleaming of orchids. The cortege moved off down Chester Row toward the south, members of the congregation driving their own cars. The dowager left; it was time for her to go home now, she said.

They were proceeding to the old Fulham cemetery. Since Lady Ashbrook, insisting on being cremated, had made no provision for a grave, this had been another trouble. It had been dealt with by an agent who, to Lady Ashbrook herself only the previous summer, would have seemed a profanation. The agent was Tom Thirkill. She would have felt sheer outrage that such a man should have controlled her own funeral. And yet he had been the master of it all. It was he who had dictated that it should be as clandestine as could be. There might still be leaks about his son-in-law's dealings. There was to be no publicity, he ordered. He wouldn't attend the funeral himself. The movements of a Cabinet minister were public property. The lordly wreath came from him, but without a card. No announcement of the funeral. Loseby was given his instructions. Thirkill paid his debts, was keeping him out of the courts. Loseby wasn't asked about arrangements; he existed to do what he was told. In this, Susan was at one with her father.

It was the two of them, father and daughter, who had picked a burying place. The Pevensey churchyard wouldn't do, what with the detested first husband and the detested home. They couldn't take her there. Susan might be ruthless, but she had too many qualms for that. But Susan was revealing some of her father's lust for detail. She had tracked down the records of another family, that of Lady Ashbrook's second husband. The name had been Jones before he emerged as a politician and in due course became Lord Ashbrook. The Joneses had been steadily successful printers in the City of London. They had acquired a family plot in the Fulham cemetery. There had been no burials in the cemetery for years, but Lady Ashbrook had a tenuous claim, and neither Thirkill nor Susan was too proud to be squeamish. Influence had its uses. So that morning the tiny party stood around the clear-cut grave.

The mourning scene was as still as a photograph. The grass didn't stir. The weather was at peace. After the howling winds, there were hours of an anticyclonic lull, sky pale and without a cloud, air without motion.

As they stood around the grave, there were glances straying as they listened, without hearing, to the words rubbed smooth with time. Down in the grave, there was a glint from the coffin plate. Another glance saw couples, elderly couples, sitting placidly on the garden benches. Away to the river, the verticals of the great new hospital were in harmony with the uninflected sky. Words went on in the calm, unassertive voice . . . "has but a short time to live and is full of misery. . . . In the midst of life we are in death. . . ."

One of the bearers had taken a handful of earth from the mound nearby and was standing ready. ". . . suffer us not, at our last hour . . . for any pains of death, to fall from thee. . . ."

Earth rattled on the coffin. That was the noise all of them had heard at other burials. It was the noise of finality or of the last contact. Sometimes it was too final to be borne. Not so that morning. The death was far away. There was nothing immediate to those standing, spectators in the static morning.

With dignity, the words went on. "Our dear sister, Alexandrina Margaret [unlike the words of the service, those struck strange] . . . sure and certain hope. . . ."

It was a quiet end. It was a quiet end, quieter than her life, and like the rest of us, Humphrey thought on his solitary way home, she would be soon forgotten.

A life, any one of our lives, was disagreeably like that day's weather, a spasm of light between the dark before and after. But was she going to be so totally forgotten? Was this truly the end? Perhaps not. Paradoxically not. Not for any reason for which she might have chosen to be remembered. No one would be interested that she had once cut a figure in a little world. No one would be interested in what, as a human being, she was like. Personalities did not have ghosts. No, she would be remembered because of the grotesque nature of her death.

For some time, there would be speculation about how it happened, who had killed her, why. Chapters would be written in accounts of famous crimes. There would be theories, ingenious and complex like that thought out by Celia and Paul, which Humphrey remembered Luria telling him about when they dined on Christmas Day. Now, he thought, if those two, who were clear minded and knew everyone concerned, got it wrong, what were the startling prospects in the future? It was a kind of immortality Lady Ashbrook would have found disappointing.

A COAT OF VARNISH

C·P·SNOW

Many great novelists have made murder the center of a serious study of life and character. Balzac, Stendhal, and Trollope, Dickens, Dostoevsky, and Tolstoy all wrote works of this kind that are now famous. For murder is a subject that can call forth a writer's deepest insights into human nature and unlock his greatest narrative powers. It does so in the case of this remarkable new novel by C. P. Snow, which claims a place in this select category of the literature of crime.

At first sight, the London neighborhood where the story takes place seems an improbable setting for a brutal, vicious killing. Quintessentially civilized, Aylestone Square is virtually the last bastion of upper-class gentleness and decorum. When a shockingly gruesome murder occurs there it catches everyone by surprise. The police themselves seem out of their depth as they investigate the Big People who were neighbors or friends of the victim. Yet policemen know at first-hand that civilization is little more than